wishes
Peter

Both Sides Now

by

Peter Morris

The Conrad Press

Both Sides Now
Published by The Conrad Press in the United Kingdom
2025
Tel: +44(0)1227 472 874
www.theconradpress.com
info@theconradpress.com
ISBN 978-1-916966-50-5

Typesetting and Cover Design by: Levellers
The Conrad Press logo was designed by Maria Priestley.
Printed and bound in Great Britain by Clays Ltd, Elcograf S.p.A.

To Suzanne, Natasha and Rory

1 FIVE YEARS

East Berlin, Friday 21st February 1975

In a Germany where overt displays of dissent were as unwise as they were rare, Ulla Wolfram, a final-year student at the Immanuel Kant Extended Upper School, knew better than to remind her history teacher of the time.

Although the school day ended officially on the stroke of one, Frau Humboldt would under no circumstances conclude her lesson on the October Revolution until she, and she alone, was ready. Ulla had little option, therefore, but to sit tight, stay calm and say nothing. Carefully maintaining the demeanour of an attentive student, the eighteen-year-old slipped her hand into her pocket and fiddled with the crumpled twenty-mark note that she would soon exchange for a bootleg copy of a prohibited David Bowie cassette.

Whilst the acquisition of unsanctioned western music was far from straightforward and was unquestionably contrary to the law, scarcity bestowed value and value attracted trade. Almost two years previously, Ulla had been introduced to her supplier by the trusted friend of a trusted friend and she now possessed a small collection of raucous English-language albums that could not be acquired in any of the state-controlled music stores. The dealer, who unconvincingly referred to himself as Mick Jaeger, generally touted for business in the busy central district of East Berlin, but insisted that money and goods should change hands in significantly quieter locations with obvious pedestrian escape routes.

Eventually, Frau Humboldt dismissed her class and Ulla left the school premises without waiting for her friends. She knew exactly where her contact would be. The young man with the overcoat, the vaguely convex nose and the easily recognisable, black goatee beard had positioned himself on a cleanly swept bench in the small, snow-covered park near the *S-Bahn* overground station at Nöldnerplatz. At a discrete distance from the surrounding streets and with the shrubs and trees deterring easy scrutiny, Mick Jaeger was as confident as he could be that the transaction would not be observed.

When Ulla arrived, he stood up, smiled and shook her hand warmly as though greeting an acquaintance.

'Better late than never,' he said, his breath condensing in the air.

As Ulla withdrew her hand from his grasp, Mick Jaeger wrapped his fingers around the twenty-mark note and the pair sat down. The bench was cold.

Following little more than thirty seconds of ostensibly genial conversation, the bootlegger stood up, nodded and left. On the slatted seat lay a copy of *Neues Deutschland*, the official mouthpiece of the Socialist Unity Party. Ulla scanned the headlines briefly, before stuffing the abandoned newspaper, and the recording it concealed, into her school bag, walking nonchalantly to the station and riding the S-Bahn to the Ostkreuz interchange. Beaming with delight at the trouble-free completion of her purchase, the final-year student found her friends Rosa and Jenny waiting for her on the platform. They knew where she had been.

To a casual observer the three girls would have betrayed few outward dissimilarities to their contemporaries in the western districts of the divided city, particularly when dressed to keep out the cold. The girls had simply cut, shoulder-length hair and came across as a tight collective of warm, hooded coats, woollen scarves and dark trousers. Ulla even sported a pair of Levis that her grandfather had persuaded his brother to bring her on one of his occasional visits from Munich. When the red and cream S-Bahn finally rattled into the station, they sought out an empty carriage.

'Did you get it?' asked Rosa.

Widening her eyes, Ulla rooted in her bag and to the delight of her friends produced a recordable music cassette. The handwriting on the insert identified the album simply as *Ziggy Stardust*, but that was all the diehard David Bowie fans needed to know.

Unable to contain their enthusiasm, the girls launched into 'Starman', the one track on the album that they already knew. Having recorded the song from a weekly rock show on the BBC World Service, they had already made a stab at transcribing the lyrics into plausible English. Though some of Bowie's wordplay had undoubtedly defeated them, they belted out the refrain with almost total accuracy. The intriguing song, as far as they could make out, seemed to herald the arrival of an otherworldly messiah whose music would liberate the inhabitants of Earth from their unfulfilled lives if only they would find a way to 'let all the children boogie'. Although unsure of the meaning of certain lines, the girls sang with unrestrained gusto until the train clattered to a halt at Rummelsburg station and two older passengers opened the doors, allowed a blast of cold air into the compartment and chose their seats.

Deprived of their privacy, the longtime friends pressed pause on the exuberant singing. Ulla returned the cassette to the safety of her schoolbag and the girls travelled the next three stops sharing little more than knowing looks. Occasionally, and to the disdain of their fellow passengers, one of them would randomly hum the refrain from 'Starman' and the others would guffaw with laughter.

Following their arrival in Karlshorst, Ulla, Jenny and Rosa covered the 500 metres from the station to the Wolframs' apartment in Loreleystrasse in little more than five minutes. The street itself was unerringly straight and was lined with snow-covered birch trees still weeks from bursting into leaf. The residents had largely cleared the pavements and white mounds now filled the spaces between the vehicles which occupied almost every available parking space.

The Wolfram family occupied a comfortable and relatively spacious flat on the top floor of a three-storey block towards the end of the quiet residential street. Like most of the buildings in Loreleystrasse, the apartment block displayed the clean lines and functional design of 1930s modernism, but in the years since the war a sooty patina had settled on the concrete facade and undermined the once powerful impression that the architecture somehow heralded the future.

As the girls passed the block housing senior Red Army officers, they broke into the joyful, wordless outro to 'Starman'. If anyone complained or fired disapproving looks, they would insist that it was a Russian folk song.

In the warmth of the Wolfram's apartment, the friends prepared lunch for themselves and for Ulla's mother, who had returned from her post in a nearby primary school. After eating, the girls washed up, withdrew to Ulla's room and began a co-ordinated assault on their maths and Russian homework. Within half an hour, the calculus was done and dusted and they were debating how to render the opening lines of Lenin's *Speech to Working Cossacks* into sensible German. No more than twenty minutes later, the three friends applied themselves to the final task of ensuring that there were enough discrepancies between their individual translations to obviate any suspicion of collusion. The job done, they turned their attention once more to *Ziggy Stardust.*

'I love this guy,' said Ulla, tucking her blonde hair behind her ears as she often did when she was excited. 'I'm going to play this every night until my brain bleeds.'

She snapped the cassette into her underpowered recorder, set the volume to maximum and pressed play. Although Ulla, Jenny and Rosa all studied English as well as Russian and they were bright, conscientious students, they knew that certain lines or combinations of words would inevitably pose problems. The home-copied cassette did not come with a lyric sheet and if they wanted to get beneath the skin of the songs, some attempt at a hand-written transcript was going to be essential.

The first track began with an almost stuttering drum beat and sparse piano chords. David Bowie sang something about mothers in a market square and the tearful news that Earth had only five years left. The music built slowly in intensity and as the narrative shifted to visions of social meltdown and lost love, the three girls scribbled down anything that seemed to make sense. Eventually, the enthralled Bowie fans gave up trying to keep pace with the lyrics and simply joined in with the repeated chant of 'five years'. Having replayed the track perhaps a dozen times, Ulla,

Jenny and Rosa were forced to agree that they had captured about as much of the song as they ever would.

Once Ulla's long-suffering mother was certain that the enthusiastic racket had at last subsided, she ventured into her daughter's bedroom carrying a wooden tray loaded with mugs, a pot of freshly brewed black tea and a plate of home-baked biscuits.

'What in heaven's name have you three been listening to in here? Don't tell me that was homework.'

'We were practising our English,' said Jenny, obfuscating with a smile.

'Well, it sounds like you need the practice.'

'That's just the way I sing,' said Jenny. 'I'm one hundred percent tone deaf.'

'But loud,' quipped Ulla.

'Oh we're all loud,' said Rosa.

Eva Wolfram shook her head and smiled. 'Well I can certainly vouch for that. Let me know if you want more biscuits.'

Although Ulla was taller than her mother, the family resemblance was unmistakable and it was clear from which parent Ulla had inherited the blue eyes and the engaging smile. The independently movable eyebrows and the prowess on the ice hockey rink were undeniably gifts from her father.

'So what exactly was that noise you were listening to?' asked Ulla's mother after Jenny and Rosa had delivered their goodbyes and set off for home.

'David Bowie. He was singing about the end of the world. We've got five years, apparently. Well, we did when he made the album.'

'Maybe we should tell that to the Party leadership before they write their next Five-Year Plan.'

'Definitely. Better make it a good one, Erich, because there won't be another.'

Mother and daughter exchanged a smile. Their mockery of Erich Honecker, the General Secretary of the Central Committee of the Socialist Unity Party of Germany, was not something they would have expressed in public. Although jokes about Honecker abounded in the GDR, it was nevertheless wise to share them only with family members or friends whose trust and discretion could be taken as absolute. Careers were too easily blighted by injudicious remarks about those whose unshakeable grip on power seemed to preclude any suggestion of a sense of humour.

Eva Wolfram was still curious about the unusual and shouty music that her daughter had been playing. 'So who is this David Bowie? Is he American?'

'He's English. Anyway, you know who he is. You've seen him on *Rockpalast* on West-TV. He's the one with the spiky hair and the jump suit you said looked like it was made out of curtains.'

'Oh, him. The weirdo. You can't tell if he's a man or a woman. He looks like he's from another planet.'

'Mum, I think that's the whole idea.'

'Does he dress like that all the time?'

'I don't know. Maybe.'

'Well, he's not normal if you ask me. Mind you, if we've only got five years until the end of the world, I don't suppose it really matters what he looks like.'

Having thanked her mother once more for supplying her friends with tea and biscuits, Ulla applied herself to the task of assimilating the three sets of incomplete notes into something approaching a coherent text. Feeling increasingly frustrated by the gaps in the lyrics, the eighteen-year-old wondered briefly if she dared approach her English teacher for help. Perhaps she might persuade Frau Bamberger to play 'Five Years' in class and invite the other students to make suggestions for the elusive words and phrases. Although the song was not a product of the socialist fraternity of states, Ulla wondered if she could plausibly assert that it was in essence a revolutionary work, a portent of the inevitable and imminent demise of capitalism. Her English teacher, however, was no fool and might well have seen David Bowie on West German TV. If Frau Bamberger valued her career, she would not relish the thought of explaining to the school's Director why she had seen fit to pollute young minds with visions of despair peddled by an androgynous degenerate from the non-socialist sphere of influence.

Furthermore, Ulla had not the slightest desire either to jeopardise her university application or to compromise her place in the GDR ice hockey squad. Had she been looking to sabotage her own future, publicising an enthusiasm for proscribed western music would have been a promising way to start.

2 PRIMARY RESEARCH

Coventry, Monday 3rd March 1975

It was shortly after eleven and Jack Gilmore, a somewhat disheveled second-year student of Spanish and German, waited somewhat impatiently outside Professor MacKenzie's office. With one of the UK's pre-eminent authorities on the Cold War still voicing her concerns about his plan to conduct primary research in the East German capital, he was not expecting an easy conversation.

Presently, the door to the office swung open and the Professor welcomed her guest with a smile.

'I'll make us some tea,' she said. 'You know where the biscuit tin is.'

Although Jack was in many ways off-beat in his appearance, he had, within two weeks of arriving at Lanchester Polytechnic, taken the fairly radical step of paying a barber to shear off his Che Guevara locks. A year and a half later, Professor Madeleine MacKenzie could no longer recall her tutee with his brown eyes and smiling face partially obscured by a curtain of unkempt hair.

The Professor's office was surprisingly compact considering her position as Director of the Modern Languages Faculty, but she had enough shelves to cope with her extensive personal library and she was eminently happy with that.

Substantially grey-haired and now presumably somewhere in her fifties, MacKenzie was wiry, bright-eyed and erudite. She exuded self-assurance and, if you caught her on a day when she was not snowed under with minor crises, she could be positively charming. Jack liked the Professor enormously and considered himself not just lucky but privileged to be her tutee. An author of several well-respected books on the divided Germany, Professor MacKenzie made no secret of the fact that she had worked as an interpreter for British Military Intelligence in the aftermath of the Second World War. Whilst the Official Secrets Act, as she readily pointed out to her students, precluded her from revealing the precise nature of many of her duties, she occasionally alluded to her presence at the interrogation of a number of senior Nazis in the run-up to the Nuremberg Trials.

Professor MacKenzie began the tutorial, as she always did, with enquiries of a distinctly pastoral nature. She quickly ascertained that Jack was physically well, that he had no personal issues he wished to discuss and that the small terraced house he rented with two friends was still as habitable as it was cheap. She also observed that her tutee seemed palpably more at ease with himself than on his arrival at Lanchester the previous year and this assessment pleased him enormously. Jack had grown up in York with his widowed father and his older brother in a semi-detached house which changed little after his mother's sudden death when he was still only nine. Abandoning his increasingly risk-averse father for college had been unexpectedly stressful for Jack and his transitional weeks at Lanchester had been marked by feelings of guilt and separation.

The Professor poured two mugs of tea, reminded her student that there was no charge for the chocolate digestives and moved swiftly to the unresolved issue of his forthcoming study year abroad. In their previous meeting, she had approved without hesitation Jack's proposal to write his Spanish thesis on the socio-cultural and historical dimensions underpinning the rivalries between the major Madrid football clubs. With regard to his semester in Berlin, however, MacKenzie continued to entertain concerns about his proposal to undertake research into environmental policy on both sides of the Berlin Wall. Although the professor was a practised listener, today she was doing most of the talking.

'Honestly, Jack. I think you may be in serious danger of romanticising the situation in Berlin. Fascinating as post-war German history may be, the city is still a political powder keg. Do you know, there are currently 12,000 allied troops stationed in West Berlin, but they are surrounded by over 100,000 Soviet and East German troops? In spite of the peace and normalisation talks in Helsinki, the Soviet Union maintains, reviews and constantly upgrades detailed plans for the seizure of West Berlin. Should they ever put that plan into action, they would overrun the allied sectors of the city in less than a day.'

'But is that really likely? Isn't the Cold War, and I quote, a state of political hostility characterised by threats, propaganda, espionage, subversion and other measures *short of overt and sustained military action*?'

MacKenzie smiled. 'Well firstly, thanks for quoting from my most recent book. You get another chocolate biscuit for that. And I'll grant you, an invasion of West Berlin is, at least as things stand, highly unlikely, but the material point here is that such a scenario is not impossible. Both sides know this and the ensuing tension never really dissipates. Never. The problem with your proposal, Jack, is not so much the imminence or otherwise of World War Three, it's the uncertainty and the unpredictability implicit in any dealings with the East German authorities.'

'I understand what you're saying, Professor, but honestly, I really want to do this. I'd be the first ever student from this Polytechnic to conduct primary research on both sides of the Wall.'

'You see, Jack, as soon as you put it like that, you make it sound like a race and I start to feel nervous.'

'But surely, thousands of people visit the Eastern side of the city every day. They get their twenty-four-hour visa, they change some currency, then they go up the TV tower or photograph the Brandenburg Gate. And at the end of the day, as long as they haven't broken the law in any way, they return back to the West without the slightest bother.'

'Indeed they do, almost always, but you know as well as I do that situations can, and do, arise. And were you to get yourself into any kind of difficulty, your Lanchester Polytechnic Student Union card would not grant you diplomatic immunity. Of that you can have no doubt.'

'Honestly, Professor, I appreciate your concern, but I don't see a problem with approaching the Ministry for the Environment and trying to arrange an interview. I don't see how there can be any harm in at least asking.'

'Well, let's hope so. But I can't sit here and promise you that interactions with the East German state would be straightforward, or even without risk. It's not something I would normally give my blessing to.'

Jack took a tentative swig from his mug.

'So, what are you saying? Are you telling me you wouldn't sanction my research proposal?'

'No, Jack. Of course I'm not saying that. At least not at this stage. But nevertheless, I'm duty bound to point out the possible ramifications of your idea and invite you to consider pathways that might be, shall we say, a little less susceptible to complication.'

The tutor and the tutee were at something of an impasse. Whilst Jack Gilmore was by nature easy-going and had a capacity to drift with the tide, he could on occasions be impulsive and almost obstinate once possessed of an idea. The Professor clearly had a soft spot for her respectfully unrelenting student and although she shied away from saying it too often, she was quietly impressed with the ambition of his proposal. Certainly, she could not fault Jack for his enthusiasm and began to wonder whether she was allowing some of her experiences in British Military Intelligence to colour her judgement. Perhaps she was seeing pitfalls where none might lie. Sliding her tea to one side, she ferreted a packet of Embassy Gold from a drawer, lit a cigarette and exhaled slowly as she thought.

'Listen, Jack, I'll tell you what I'll do. A friend of mine from Cambridge, someone who now works in the Diplomatic Service, has a very detailed knowledge of the issues relating to dealings with the GDR. I'll give her a call and see what I can do for you in terms of practical advice. She may well be able to suggest how you might approach your research in such a way that it would respect established protocols as well as East German law and would not set any alarm bells ringing.'

'Thank you, Professor,' said Jack with an appreciative smile. 'That would be enormously helpful.'

MacKenzie flicked the ash from her cigarette into an unused mug and pushed a cloud of bluish grey smoke from her nostrils. For the time being, there was no need to discuss Jack's proposal any further. She would find the time to consult her friend before arriving at a final decision.

Having agreed to meet with Professor MacKenzie in a fortnight, Jack thanked her both for the biscuits and the concern for his wellbeing and was rewarded with an appreciative smile.

Waiting in the corridor for her own tutorial with the Professor was Mirka Kimmich, a student of French and Spanish, who also planned to spend the first semester of her external study year in Madrid.

Mirka glanced at her watch and raised an eyebrow as Jack emerged from the smoky, book-lined office. The meeting had overrun.

'Sorry,' he said. 'MacKenzie had the bit between her teeth today.'

'As ever,' said Mirka, clearly familiar with the scenario. 'Watch out. One day she's going to legally adopt you. Anyhow. Your big proposal for Berlin. Did she go for it?'

Jack pinched his lips. 'Kind of. In principle, anyway. But she's got her knickers in a twist about the unpredictability of dealing with the East German authorities.'

'She's just trying to ensure you don't do anything stupid, I suppose.'

'Yeah, I get that. And that's fair enough. And obviously you can't fault her understanding of the geopolitics, but I'm hardly going to spark some kind of incident just by asking for an interview.'

3 LONG-TERM PROSPECTS

Munich, Wednesday 5th March 1975

Lacking the strength even to turn on his side, Ulla Wolfram's eighty-one-year-old grandfather lay in the Intensive Care Unit of a West German university hospital. The citizen of the German Democratic Republic had a cannula inserted into his left arm and a selection of wires and pads had been taped to various points on his torso. Medical staff in blue scrubs regularly noted his pulse, his temperature, his breathing rate and his blood pressure from the monitors to the side of his bed. Though unable to do much more than lie there, Karl could still muster something resembling a smile for the seemingly indefatigable nurses who checked his vitals, ensured that he was comfortable or sometimes sat beside him and held his hand.

Since Karl's retirement from the German Red Cross ambulance service some seventeen years previously, he had experienced little difficulty in securing visas to visit his brother in Munich. As long as individual pensioners did not have a head brimming with state secrets, the Government of the GDR harboured few concerns about allowing economically unproductive citizens to pass through the checkpoints into the capitalist West. More often than not, the East German retirees returned home with cases full of premium coffee or small electrical items, all of which, the regime quietly accepted, helped to mollify the growing demand for consumer goods in the East. Perhaps surprisingly, the Erich Honecker government viewed with equanimity the many thousands of pensioners who abused their temporary exit visas and chose never to return. Implicit in the West German government's automatic acceptance of emigrants from the GDR was an obligation to take responsibility for their pensions and the Honecker regime saved millions in the process.

Dr Seidel smiled at Herr Wolfram, before talking her patient through the confusing situation in which he found himself. Whilst she did not fight shy of the truth, the cardiologist made a conscious effort to stress the positives and concluded on something approaching a cheery note.

'If you're going to have heart failure,' she said, 'right outside the University Hospital is just about the best place in Munich to do it. You chose a good day to accompany your brother to an appointment.'

Privately, Dr Seidel harboured major concerns regarding Karl's long-term prospects of recovery. Although he had done well to survive the critical first twenty-four hours after his cardiac arrest, ECG tests had revealed the kind of severe arrhythmia that would require the surgical implantation of a pacemaker, an operation that of itself would not be without risk for a patient now in his eighty-second year. She would need permission for the procedure from her patient's next of kin.

Once back in her office, she sat at her desk and dialled the East Berlin number supplied by Karl Wolfram's brother.

In the Karlshorst apartment, Ulla and her parents were quietly mapping out her forthcoming ice hockey fixtures. It was Udo who went to the phone.

'Herr Wolfram,' said the caller, 'my name is Dr Seidel. I'm a cardiologist at the University Hospital Munich.'

The sentence immediately triggered a release of stress hormones into Udo's bloodstream and time seemed both to accelerate and to stop dead in its tracks.

'Is it my father?' he asked, fearing there could be no other reason for her call.

'Please try not to be alarmed,' continued Dr Seidel in as reassuring a tone as she could muster. 'Your father is currently here with us, but his condition is stable and he is receiving round-the-clock care.'

'Is he OK?'

'As I said, he's receiving the best possible care. Earlier today, your father suffered a cardiac arrest, virtually on the steps of our hospital. Fortunately, Herr Wolfram, one of our medical students was on hand to give him CPR and within a matter of minutes, your father was transferred to our Intensive Care Unit.'

'But he's OK?'

'Your father is conscious and our scans reveal good cognitive function and that's excellent news. But. Without intervention, the prognosis is not certain.'

'Meaning what exactly?' said Udo, his mind now racing. 'Is he going to die?'

'Meaning that, unless we implant a pacemaker, we can't rule out the possibility of his suffering a stroke or possibly another cardiac arrest. I'm therefore seeking your permission, as his next of kin, to carry out the procedure.'

'Do it,' said Udo without a moment's hesitation. 'If he needs it, do it.'

'Before you give your consent, Herr Wolfram, I need to make sure that you also understand that the implantation of a heart pacemaker, though a relatively minor procedure in many ways, is not entirely without risk, especially for someone of advancing years.'

'Do it. You have my consent.'

'Excellent. Your uncle has also given the procedure his blessing. We will keep you updated with your father's progress and you are, it goes without saying, welcome to visit.'

'Thank you,' said Udo, now struggling to process what he had been told.

'I will of course,' said the cardiologist, 'send you a letter recapping the material points of our conversation. If you're thinking of coming over, it may also add weight to your application for a travel permit. In the meantime, and I know this is easier said than done, try not to worry. Your father is in good hands. We'll be in touch if we have any news.'

Udo thanked the doctor once more, before ending the conversation and catching his wife's concerned gaze. She had heard more than enough to understand that the situation was serious.

Still reeling from the thought that he might be about to lose his father, Udo Wolfram recounted the details of the conversation as well as he could. In light of the unexpected and troubling development, the family agreed without question that they should apply for the necessary visas to visit Udo's father in Munich. Whilst day-to-day travel to West Germany was impossible for most citizens of working age, the law in the German Democratic Republic allowed for special permission to be granted in exceptional circumstances. Confident in the merits of their case, Udo and Eva resolved to begin the application process at their earliest opportunity.

Karl Wolfram had for many years lived no more than two hundred metres from the apartment in Karlshorst occupied by his son, his daughter-in-law and his beautiful granddaughter. In the early years of his retirement the widower had collected Ulla each day from her primary school, walked her home to Loreleystrasse and prepared her a wholesome lunch. On the innumerable occasions when Eva Wolfram had been unable to leave work before two or even three, the doting grandfather had kept Ulla entertained with silly games and animal stories, but more often than not with the deftly executed conjuring tricks which never ceased to delight his young grandchild. Once Ulla was older and could safely make her own way home, Karl still called by to see her and to help her with her homework if he could. When Udo returned from work, he often found his daughter preparing simple but hearty evening meals under his father's skilful direction.

The trust that already existed between grandfather and granddaughter developed further as Karl privately introduced her to the skills that underpinned his extensive repertoire of conjuring tricks. In due course he began to involve her in short performances at family gatherings, at school or trade union social events and at the birthday parties of friends and neighbours. Although Karl Wolfram artfully adopted the stage persona of a bumbling, forgetful pensioner, he was a consummate perfectionist and left no aspect of the performance to chance. Each illusion had its acutely considered and well-rehearsed moves, its misleading gestures and apparently innocent patter. Each had its own chosen moment when both Karl and Ulla knew with unshakeable certainty that the attention of their audience had been misdirected by an intriguing question, the sharp tapping of Karl's magic spoon or one of Ulla's seemingly ingenuous requests for guidance. In time Karl Wolfram trained his granddaughter to accept ever-greater responsibility until eventually they could exchange roles as illusionist and assistant from performance to performance and from trick to trick.

During Ulla's uneasy adolescence his flat had been a bolt-hole, a first port of call in times of trouble. Her grandfather had been a constant source of common sense and calming reassurance whenever she argued with her parents about the suitability of her friends or the length of her boyfriend's hair.

'Worse things,' he had often reminded Ulla in the quietly philosophical voice of someone who had seen it all before, 'happen at sea.'

As a piece of advice to any angry teenager impatient for an immediate and simple solution, Karl Wolfram's folk wisdom was as good as useless, but his granddaughter always knew that she had been listened to without judgement and she always felt better for spending time with him.

'You know what?' he once told her. 'Your father was just the same when he was a young man. Full of feelings. Angry. Unwilling to fall into line. And a bit like today, they were times when it wasn't the best idea to stand out from the crowd.'

As hard as it was for Ulla to imagine her father storming out of the apartment, yelling abuse at his parents and threatening never to return, she knew that her grandfather was not making things up. It was the truth, even if it was somehow his own truth.

Even harder to imagine than her adolescent father having a teenage strop, was a world in which her *Opa* Karl no longer played a part. Distraught at the possibility of losing her mentor, her comfort and her friend, Ulla became gripped by the anxiety that the family might not be granted permission to travel to Munich.

Though struggling with his own fears, Udo Wolfram sought to persuade himself that his father's life-threatening illness constituted exactly the kind of circumstance that the authorities would acknowledge as exceptional. Immediately after work the following day, he would make his way to the state-run travel agency and request the necessary paperwork to secure visas for a temporary visit to the Federal Republic of Germany. Reluctant to dwell on the likelihood of a refusal, Ulla's parents engaged in a conspiracy of optimism. Their case, they repeatedly assured their daughter, would be viewed with compassion and the visas would be granted without delay. There was little point in saying anything else.

4 REPUTATION

East Berlin, Monday 10th March 1975

The best part of a week after Dr Seidel's initial contact, Udo Wolfram received her official letter detailing the precarious nature of his father's condition, the proposed procedure and the risks implicit in the operation. With a heaviness of heart, Udo read the letter to his wife and his daughter, but reassured them that they would soon be in Munich, sitting at Opa Karl's bedside, taking turns to stroke his hand. Quoting Dr Seidel verbatim, Ulla's father added the relevant medical details to their visa applications and attached the letter from the Munich hospital as corroboration.

Shortly after lunchtime the following day, Eva Wolfram delivered the official visa requests and the small processing fee to the government-controlled Travel Office on Alexanderplatz. Having previously enjoyed camping holidays to approved destinations within the socialist bloc, the Wolfram family were already nominal holders of GDR passports. In line with East German protocols, however, their travel documents were retained by the authorities when not in active use. Given the urgency of the situation, Ulla's mother allowed herself to hope that their passports, complete with the necessary visas, would be available for collection by the weekend at the latest.

No-one in the Wolfram household slept well that night. Udo got up shortly after five, showered and ate a slow breakfast whilst listening to the radio. By six thirty he was sitting in a crowded S-Bahn carriage, craning his neck to read the newspaper headlines held at an unhelpful angle by the passenger directly opposite. Udo did not recognise his fellow traveller, but the navy blue overalls, the safety shoes and the frequent yawning suggested that he too was making his way to work. The two-stop trip from Karlshorst to Rummelsburg complete, Ulla's father walked the short distance to the gates of the Berlin Gas and Light Company, where he was a respected senior fitter. As he entered the site, he greeted his fellow workers with a smile that belied both his lack of sleep and the sense of impending loss.

Perhaps two hours after Udo Wolfram's arrival at work, Director Maffay, the boss of the state-owned power company, sought him out, invited him into his office and closed the door in a manner that signalled that their conversation was to be entirely private. Udo was puzzled. He had spoken with the Director before, but throughout his long career he had not once been invited into the executive's personal domain.

Director Maffay sat at his desk with a pained expression on his face and his hands clasped almost in prayer.

'Herr Wolfram,' he began somewhat formally, 'you have worked at the Berlin Gas and Light Company for over twenty-one years and have done so with enormous credit. The quality of your work, your team leadership and your contributions to output have all been outstanding. As a committed member of the Free German Federation of Trade Unions, you have consistently encouraged and inspired your co-workers to meet the targets set for the company by the Ministry for Coal and Energy. You are, without any shadow of a doubt, an exemplary member of the workforce.'

'Thank you,' said Udo with a gentle nod.

'So, I am just wondering whether you have given any thought to how it might appear to your co-workers if their senior fitter and his family were suddenly to remove themselves to the capitalist West for a week.'

Fewer than twenty-four hours had elapsed since the submission of the visa applications and already the boss of the Gas and Light Company was involved. This did not bode well.

'My father has suffered a cardiac arrest,' said Udo. 'The doctors are saying he may not have very long.'

'You see, Herr Wolfram, I'm more than a little concerned about the damage that a visit to the West might do to your reputation here at the plant. I'm wondering whether you would still command the same level of respect from your colleagues once you returned to the GDR. Assuming of course that you do indeed plan to return.'

There it was. The authorities were clearly afraid that once Udo and his family had been afforded the opportunity, they would simply stay in the West. They would be seduced by the flashy cars, the overstocked supermarkets and the lurid advertising hoardings that promised unbridled self-realisation to all who could afford it. They would turn their backs on the progressive republic that had banished poverty and unemployment, had provided them with healthcare and education and had rejected both the fascism of the 1930s and the continuous war-mongering of the NATO alliance.

With his pulse beginning to race, Udo thanked the Director for his appreciative words and reaffirmed his commitment to the company and to the German Democratic Republic. He explained the perilous state of his father's health and respectfully assured his boss that he had every intention of returning to his post. He simply wanted, as he believed anyone in his position would, the opportunity to spend some time with his father whilst he still had the chance.

The Director listened intently.

'It's a shame,' he said, sounding genuinely regretful, 'that you did not come to me personally before submitting your visa request. Perhaps with my guidance something could have been agreed. Perhaps a visa for you to travel alone.'

Udo said nothing.

'Yes, such an arrangement might, with the support of the company, have been possible. As things stand, your application for the whole family to cross to the West has aroused concerns amongst those whose responsibility it is to take an interest in these matters.'

Oblique as the Director's allusion to the Ministry for State Security had been, Udo was in absolutely no doubt that his boss was referring to the MfS, commonly known as the Stasi.

'I am sure you can see,' the Director continued, 'how your visa application might easily be construed, perhaps misconstrued, as an attempt to desert the Republic. As such, it reflects poorly not just on you and your family but on the Berlin Gas and Light Company. In all honesty, the best thing for all concerned would be for you to withdraw the application. You never know. Your father may yet recover.'

'You never know,' said the senior fitter, battling to maintain a respectful tone whilst repressing the mix of frustration and anger now flowing through his veins.

'Should your father not survive his illness, then a single visa to allow you, but not your family, to attend the funeral might still be possible, although, as I am sure you will understand, these things cannot be guaranteed.'

'Are we done?' asked Udo, more curtly than was wise.

'I'm sorry,' said the Director. 'As I said, by far the best thing would be for you to withdraw your visa request. It would be a shame if it affected your daughter's application to the University of Leipzig. Or somehow caused the selectors to question her suitability for our national ice hockey programme.'

With the working day done, the Wolfram family sat down to a comforting meal of Königsberger meatballs with salt potatoes, carrots and peas. It was a dish that Karl Wolfram had cooked for the family at least once a week and the smell of the ground pork in the creamy dill sauce inevitably evoked his presence.

'It's good,' said Eva, clearly impressed. 'What did you use instead of lemons?'

'Just a touch of vinegar,' replied Ulla.

'He taught you well, you know.'

'He really did.'

Ulla's father had not yet tried the food.

'I have some news,' he said, clearly struggling for composure.

With his hands tightly clenched and his eyes lowered, Udo slowly recounted the details of his conversation with the manager of the Berlin Gas and Light Company. Still avoiding eye contact with his wife and daughter, he announced that regrettably they would not be travelling to Munich to spend some time with Opa Karl. They would just have to hope that the doctors in the West had been unnecessarily gloomy in their assessment. As Ulla's father spoke, a tear trickled lazily down his left cheek.

'How can they do this?' asked Ulla. 'How? What's their problem, for God's sake? Do they think everyone in the whole country will just run away? God, it's so stupid. We just want to see Opa Karl before he...'

The eighteen-year-old left the sentence unfinished. Her mother stood up, slipped round to Ulla's side of the table and enveloped her daughter in her arms. Udo wiped his face with the sleeve of his shirt and sat in front of his untouched meal, stunned into silence and frozen in ambiguous grief.

Once Ulla had regained sufficient equilibrium to speak, she bitterly contested her father's capitulation to the advice from his boss. In her heart of hearts, however, she knew how these things worked. The Director of the Gas and Light Company was in all probability a Party member and had undoubtedly been contacted by the Ministry for State Security. To avoid repercussions, her father had little choice but to bow to the pressure and withdraw the visa application.

Ulla allowed her chin to drop and she wiped tears from her own cheek with the hooked index finger of a clenched fist.

'I'm sorry,' she said, eventually raising her head and sharing a look of bewilderment with her father.

'I know,' said Udo. 'We all are. You hear about these things, but it's always something that's happened to someone else, someone with more opinions than sense. You think, if you get to work on time and do your job, attend all the meetings, go to the rallies, keep your nose clean, you think, if you do that, you'll be OK. It's not like I did anything illegal. It's not like I've ever done anything illegal.'

Udo wiped his sleeve across his cheek once more. Father and daughter exchanged a sympathetic but fleeting smile.

'I want to…,' said Ulla, her voice buckling. 'I want to see Opa Karl. I want to tell him I love him.'

Ulla's mother nodded in pained agreement. 'We all do. But whatever we are feeling right now, whatever any of us might think or might want to say about this situation, those thoughts and feelings must not leave the apartment.'

Ulla and her mother finished their meal with little else to say. Udo left his plate untouched. With the table cleared and the dishes washed and stacked, the family watched the news on West German TV before retiring to bed in the unlikely hope of a comfortable night.

After work the following day, Ulla's father took the S-Bahn to Alexanderplatz, withdrew the application for the travel permits and apologised for any inconvenience or misunderstandings he may have caused.

5 LEFTIE LAYABOUTS

London, Saturday 15th March 1975

'So why Berlin?' Hannah Cheung asked her prospective boyfriend as the protest march ground once more to a halt some hundred metres short of the entrance to Trafalgar Square.

'Because the former capital of the Third Reich,' replied Jack without the slightest pause for thought, 'is the crucible of modern European history.'

The unwitting object of Hannah's affection had rattled off his answer with all the confidence of a well-prepared candidate at a job interview, but he was doing no more than quoting Professor MacKenzie.

Hannah's eyes widened. 'The crucible of the what now? Seriously, Jack, it's so pigging obvious that you're just regurgitating your lecture notes. Do you even understand what you just said?'

'OK, fair enough. That was from a lecture, but basically, if there's ever going to be a Third World War, it's probably going to kick off in Berlin.'

'What? And you want to be there when it happens?'

'Well, hardly. But honestly, Hannah, don't you think it almost beggars belief that deep within East Germany there could be this massive advert for western freedoms constantly taunting the communist government from over the Wall. And as a divided city in a divided world, what happens in Berlin really matters. And not just the politics. At a human level, the Wall separates real people from each other. It cuts its way through families and streets and neighbourhoods. I mean, where else in the world could you see something that preposterous and at the same time that important? The human faces of the Cold War, either side of a wall.'

'OK. That kind of makes sense. Why didn't you say that in the first place? Anyway, I surrender. You've won me over. You can go to Berlin.'

'Thanks. Permission accepted.'

'Come on,' she said, gently taking his arm. 'We're moving.'

Hannah liked hanging out with Jack. During the spring term the pair had been to the theatre together, had manned the Friends of the Earth stand at the entrance to the Union bar and had conducted spirited debates about ecology, music and politics over several drawn-out coffees in the refectory. The first-year applied biology student had grown up on the Wirral where both her parents were dentists and proud owners of their own practice. She had undoubtedly inherited her pencil-straight, ebony hair from her father, who had arrived in the UK from Hong Kong towards the end of the nineteen-forties.

Hannah was by far the most interesting woman that Jack had met since arriving at Lanchester. She was also, he suspected, way out of his league. In any case, she had a boyfriend currently studying maths at the University of Durham. Hannah, for her part, had become irretrievably dissatisfied with the limitations of a long-distance relationship and intended, the next time her boyfriend called, to make a clean break of things.

Although Jack was always pleased to see her, Hannah had never been able to fathom whether he might be interested in the more intimate relationship that she was quietly hoping for. The Right To Breathe march in London, she had decided, would be a chance for the two of them to spend an entire day in each other's company and would allow her to leave him in no doubt that the position of boyfriend was his if he wanted it.

The stuttering procession, marshalled from the northern edge of Hyde Park by several hundred officers from the Metropolitan Police, took the best part of two hours to trace its uncomplicated route through the streets of rainswept, central London. Beneath the leaden sky, some passers-by applauded the marchers whilst others hurled salty abuse. Many of the latter questioned the hygiene, the common sense and the employability of what was supposedly the flower of British youth.

As Jack and Hannah approached the end of Pall Mall, angered shouts of 'Stop the bloody cull!' and 'Save our seals!' indicated the immediate proximity of the Canadian High Commission. Once in Trafalgar Square itself, the chatter of maybe ten thousand voices competed with the indistinct directions from the marshals and snatches of an impassioned but poorly amplified speech by a member of the Ecology Party. Around them, an abundance of rain-soaked banners advertising the names of environmentalist groups from colleges and universities around the UK were interspersed with printed placards urging Britain to go green, save the whales and say no to nukes. Amongst the forest of official slogans, one homemade placard declared 'Down with this sort of thing!' and was as good as guaranteed to earn its creator a photo on the front page of one of the national dailies.

The demonstrators were for the most part dressed against the buffeting wind and the repeated squalls of rain and, regardless of gender, had defaulted to drab, knee-length coats with scarves and knitted bobble hats providing occasional flourishes of colour. Whilst shoulder-length hair was still commonplace amongst the male students, it was by no means the convention of the early seventies.

Beside a phone box, a small group of police officers in traditional helmets and black knee-length raincoats, traded opinions as they kept watch for potential breaches of public order.

'They're all a load of leftie layabouts, if you ask me,' said a disgruntled officer with a Cardiff accent. 'Anyone would think we've got nothing better to do than watch students traipsing about in the pissing rain, whingeing about God knows what.'

'Easy, Sarge,' said another. 'We fought two world wars for the right to do this.'

'Don't give me that,' said the sergeant. 'Churchill would turn in his bloody grave. Jesus, look at them. What a right bloody shower. Haven't they got essays to write or something?'

The rain-soaked demonstration passed off without incident and eventually clusters of protesters found their way in dribs and drabs to the lines of coaches waiting, their engines running, along the northern flank of Hyde Park.

Reassured that they recognised other Lanchester students on the coach, Hannah and Jack found a seat and settled down for the trip back to Coventry.

'Anyway, answer me this,' said Hannah, wiping at the misted window. 'If you could board a coach to anywhere in Europe right now, where would you go?'

'I dunno. Berlin?'

'No. Not good enough,' she said, poking him in the arm with her finger. 'And don't say Madrid either. Say somewhere you're not already planning to go to. Anyway, I vote for Athens. So, Jack Gilmore, have you ever fancied going somewhere like that?'

Whilst Hannah was clearly aware that any involvement with Jack would ultimately be compromised by his extended disappearance to universities abroad, the allure of the here and now was all-powerful. It would be a good six months before he departed for Madrid and in the meantime there was an entire summer to be enjoyed. As the bus eventually rumbled onto London's notoriously busy North Circular Road, Hannah gently grabbed Jack's arm and rested her head on his shoulder. If he didn't get the message now, he never would.

6 SEMBLANCE OF NORMALITY

East Berlin, Thursday 20th March 1975

After a short but nevertheless anxious period without any further news from Munich, the Wolfram family's fears were substantially eased by a letter from Uncle Thomas explaining that his brother had been successfully fitted with a pacemaker and was now recuperating in hospital. Karl remained weakened, he stressed, but the cardiologists were delighted with the outcome of the procedure and were confident that they had significantly reduced the likelihood of a second cardiac arrest. Once Ulla's grandfather had been discharged from the University Hospital, he would continue his recovery in a nursing clinic on the outskirts of Munich, before spending perhaps three months in the care of his brother.

It would therefore be some time, Thomas regretted, before Udo's father would be well enough to return to Karlshorst. The worst, however, was over and the prognosis was cautiously optimistic. Although the Wolframs were, more than anything, simply relieved to hear that Karl had survived his operation, their immediate reaction was followed by an unrelenting sense of frustration. They could not, in any meaningful way, contribute to his care.

In the weeks that followed, neither Ulla nor her parents broached the subject of their rejected visa applications. Intent on taking the first steps towards some semblance of normality, Udo and Eva attempted to go about their daily routines much as they always did. Nevertheless, whether by accident or design, whispers of the family's political indiscretions began to leak into the public domain. At work, Ulla's parents became increasingly certain that the Party diehards would be judging them for their disloyalty. Others, they knew, would be viewing their plight with unexpressed sympathy. In the apartment, Ulla became aware that her parents were at once more subdued than was usual and yet more inclined to bouts of tetchiness. Although Udo and Eva each made conscious efforts to accommodate the other's feelings, the uneasy mood hung about like a mouldy smell.

With regard to school, Ulla worked as conscientiously as ever towards the end-of-year exams which would open the door to a university degree. Keen to embrace any form of distraction from her grandfather's situation, the young star of the Dynamo Berlin U20 ice hockey squad trained with undiminished focus and continued to play an often pivotal role in weekend matches.

At least twice a week, Ulla still made time to hang out with Rosa and Jenny. On a typically quiet Thursday afternoon, the three girls had polished off their homework and were puzzling over the still incomplete lyrics to *Ziggy Stardust*. One track in particular, intriguingly entitled 'Suffragette City', seemed almost wilfully to defy interpretation. Ulla snapped the cassette into the player and, following a frustratingly fiddly process of repeatedly winding and rewinding the tape, eventually located the start of the penultimate track on the album. Over the course of three and a half minutes of partially grasped images and raw, guitar-driven riffs, the song built to a hammering climax and left the girls thrilled but largely none the wiser.

Jenny scrunched her nose as she shook her head. 'You know what? I don't even think it's a place.'

'Oh, now who's not making sense?' said Rosa. 'If it's not a place, then why is it called Suffragette City? And if it's not a city, then what is it?'

'I think it might be a woman,' said Jenny tentatively. 'Bowie's telling this guy Henry to leave him alone because he wants to be with this suffragette woman.'

'Or maybe it's a reference to drugs,' said Rosa. 'Maybe Henry could be like a reference to heroin and he's telling the drugs to leave him alone, so that he can be with someone or maybe get to somewhere.'

'Yeah, if in doubt,' said Jenny, 'assume it's about drugs. It works for the Beatles.'

'Well, whatever it is, or wherever it is,' said Ulla, her disdain for the authorities resurfacing in the presence of friends, 'I'm guessing the shit-brained sleazeballs who run this country wouldn't give you a visa if you ever needed to go there.'

7 THE SOFT SPEECH

East Berlin, Tuesday 13th May 1975

In the penultimate month of Ulla's school career a number of things began to change in ways she could not have anticipated. The Wolfram family's application for an exit visa was by this point common knowledge and divided her classmates into three clearly defined camps. The hardline members of the Free German Youth immediately and irrevocably ostracised Ulla, refused to use her name and referred to her behind her back as 'the blonde' or, in a sideswipe at her sporting successes, 'the Ice Princess'. A number of classmates who had known Ulla since primary school took the decision, or accepted the advice of others, that it would not be in their interests to associate with a student whose commitment to the Republic had been called into question. From that point on, they did little more than greet their longtime friend sheepishly at the start of each day and avoid eye contact with her for the remainder of it. A significant number of Ulla's friends refused to condemn either her or her family for wishing to visit an ailing grandparent. In spite of the creeping fog of disapproval that threatened to envelop Ulla, they stood shoulder to shoulder with their classmate and did not grieve for the lack of attention from the political hard-liners.

When Frau Berger, Ulla's physics teacher, asked her to remain behind for an informal chat after a lesson in the lab, the final-year student was uncertain of what might be coming, but sensed that it was not going to be good.

‘I was just wondering,’ began Frau Berger with uncharacteristic circumspection, ‘if studying physics in Leipzig is still the best way forward for a student such as yourself.’

‘Why wouldn’t it be?’ asked Ulla, her heart rate beginning to quicken. ‘I get the highest marks in physics of anyone in the class.’

‘But it’s not just about performance in tests, is it?’ said Frau Berger somewhat patronisingly. ‘The university must also consider your attitudes, your behaviour, and your commitment to the ideals of our Republic.’

‘I understand,’ said Ulla, feeling increasingly edgy. ‘And I am completely committed to the ideals of the Republic. No-one could question that. I get consistently high marks in Civics; I organised the Students’ Peace Initiative; and I represent the GDR at ice hockey. I honestly don’t see, Frau Berger, how the university could have any kind of problem with my application.’

Ulla knew exactly how the university could have a problem. The only question was how quickly Frau Berger would work her way round to the inevitable. The teacher decided not to waste any more time. She had a substantial quantity of ungraded exam papers that urgently required her attention.

‘For someone who is apparently so bright, Ulla, you can be uncommonly obtuse at times. So let me spell it out for you. Your family’s recent, unwise choices may have put the Immanuel Kant Extended Upper School in a position where it can no longer endorse your candidature.’

Ulla said nothing.

'Perhaps,' said Frau Berger, 'it would be better to withdraw your application than to be rejected.'

'I have no intention of withdrawing my application,' said Ulla adamantly. I've worked hard for my grades. I have a right to a place.'

'And the state has a right to expect that each and every one of its university students will repay the generous investment in their education with unswerving commitment to its social and political goals.'

If Frau Berger was not a member of the Party, she was definitely in thrall to someone who was. Ulla's pulse began to race and her neck flushed.

'I am the best physicist in the Emmanuel Kant Extended Upper School,' she said indignantly. 'And in the future, our socialist motherland will require science graduates such as myself to develop clean solar power, devise computers that outperform the machines in the West or put citizens of our Republic into space. To withdraw my application would be a betrayal of socialism.'

Frau Berger could not determine whether Ulla's assertion constituted bluster, veiled sarcasm or some heady cocktail of the two. Either way, the conversation seemed to be going nowhere. The physics teacher imagined that she would soon be sitting in the Director's office on the first floor, regretting that her efforts to steer the potentially disloyal pupil in the right direction had been anything but fruitful.

'Ulla, your enthusiasm for physics is admirable,' continued Frau Berger. 'It always has been. But, not to put too fine a point on it, you may no longer have the options you once thought you had. In the current circumstances, a university degree is, I would say, completely out of the question. I was simply trying to suggest that you might have more promising employment choices if you withdraw your application yourself than if the school felt obliged to withhold its recommendation. In fact, it would be better for all concerned.'

The silence reassured Frau Berger that the message was now being taken seriously. She allowed her pupil time to absorb the significance of what she had been told.

'So I won't be going to Leipzig,' said Ulla eventually.

The teacher shook her head as if in regret. 'I think not. In the circumstances.'

Again, Ulla did not reply.

'So,' said Frau Berger. 'That will be all, I think.'

Without either apology or valediction the teacher turned, walked out of the lab and headed in the direction of the staff room.

A knot was tightening in the pit of Ulla's stomach. This, she imagined, was how her father must have felt after being blindsided by his boss over the visa application. This was how things worked if you were judged to be out of line. Outwardly benign advice to the errant citizen; a whisper rather than a yell; the soft speech backed by a weighty stick.

On the wall to the left of the teacher's dais, the standard-issue portrait of Erich Honecker looked down on her and smiled his self-assured yet avuncular smile.

'Shut up!' she scowled, as she vented her bewildered anger by slinging her copy of *Physics 12* at the General Secretary of the Central Committee. The blow from the textbook, though considerable, nevertheless lacked the force either to break the acrylic pane protecting the image or to dislodge the photograph from its lofty position. Supremely unruffled by the outburst, the builder of the Berlin Wall did not bat an eyelid.

'Go to hell,' said Ulla.

Still seething, she retrieved her physics book, stuffed it into her brown leather school bag and switched off the lights as she left the room. From his elevated position on the laboratory wall, Honecker simply remained where he was and smiled as though nothing had happened.

8 THE BENEFIT OF HINDSIGHT

East Berlin, Saturday 17th May 1975

In the aftermath of Karl Wolfram's operation, news from Munich was sparse. The Wolframs found their telephone increasingly subject to connection problems until, from one day to the next, international calls became impossible. Although the family wrote regularly to Opa Karl, they received no acknowledgement of their communications beyond two substantially belated postcards. The first was from Uncle Thomas confirming that his brother was continuing to make slow but steady progress. The second was from Opa Karl himself. On the back of an oversaturated photo of the onion-domed towers of Munich cathedral, Ulla's grandfather declared in disturbingly spidery handwriting how much he missed them all and regretted that he was still not yet strong enough to travel.

The morning after the arrival of the second postcard, Ulla's parents accompanied her to the Werner-Seelenbinder-Arena in Prenzlauer Berg to watch her turn out for Dynamo Berlin. The physical exertions would, Ulla knew, provide her with at least some measure of respite from the suffocating situation that now dominated the life of her family. On the ice, Ulla's characteristic speed of thought and innate game aggression were immediately in evidence. Her remarkable acceleration and fleet footwork enabled her, to an extent which often flummoxed the opposition, not only to attack from deep positions but also to track back and defend resolutely when required. On this particular day, she was almost unplayable.

Following the particularly hard-fought victory over SC Karl-Marx-Stadt, Ulla thanked her parents for attending the match, before hooking up with Rosa and Jenny at the Metzer Eck, a small bar not far from the arena. Given the political cloud that hung over the Wolfram family, neither of Ulla's friends had required any real explanation as to why the most promising scientist in their year group had suddenly withdrawn her application to the University of Leipzig. Yet, until Ulla felt the need to elaborate, they could do no more than view her plight with profound but unspoken sympathy.

Over simple and inexpensively priced home-cooked food and a glass of Berliner Pilsener, the three friends lamented their lack of progress with the *Ziggy Stardust* lyrics and mocked each other's appallingly poor track records with the opposite sex.

Later, as they stood on the platform of Senefelder Platz underground station, Jenny made an honest but clumsily timed reference to the excitement she already felt at the prospect of going to university.

Neither Ulla nor Rosa replied.

'Sorry,' said Jenny, the insensitivity now exposed by the silence. 'Ulla, I'm really sorry. It's all so unfair.'

Ulla gently shook her head. 'Don't worry. None of this is your fault.'

'But neither is it yours.'

A second silence ensued. Rosa pursed her lips and tilted her head sympathetically to the side.

'Anyway,' said Ulla, hoping to move things forward. 'What are we doing tonight?'

'Your call, I think,' said Jenny, looking again at her friend. 'What do you fancy doing?'

Ulla shrugged. 'Oh, I dunno. Fly to Paris?'

'Oh come on, you two,' said Rosa, trying to strike a note of encouragement. 'Why don't we do what we always do when we need a bit of a lift?'

By seven that evening Ulla, Jenny and Rosa had each grabbed something to eat at home and made some concession in their choice of clothing to the dress code at their agreed destination, the Riviera Ballroom in Grünau. As usual, Ulla had chosen one of the exuberant 1950s blouses that her mother had cast off so disparagingly some years previously and matched it to a pair of close fitting beige slacks of similar provenance. Jenny wore a black waistcoat over a check blouse, a black A-line skirt and calf length boots. Rosa opted for a red bow-tie neck blouse and a navy blue corduroy skirt.

On the short S-Bahn journey to the once genteel Berlin suburb of Grünau, the normally abstemious Ulla produced a bottle of Berliner Kindl from her handbag, used the metallic edge of the window frame to prise off the cap and drank the sputtering beer directly from the bottle. Declining Ulla's offer of 'liquid dance skills', Rosa decided she needed to keep an eye on her friend who, regardless of the alcohol, seemed to be in an unpredictably carefree mood.

From the somewhat run-down 1930s S-Bahn station in quiet Grünau, the tram would take them most of the remaining distance to the Riviera.

'Hey, I'll show you a trick,' said Ulla, spotting the antiquated ticket machine at the tram stop. 'Look. Everyone knows what to do. You put your money in here, then you press the handle on the side and out comes the ticket. But what if we simply press the handle without putting any money in?'

Ulla smiled, depressed the metal lever and, without depositing a coin in the dispenser, availed herself of a ticket. Again, Ulla's brazenness struck Jenny and Rosa as completely out of character and the pair exchanged a concerned glance.

'So,' said Ulla, 'if you can get the ticket for free, why does everyone pay? Is it out of ignorance? Or solidarity? Or is it because we're all so shit-scared of putting a foot wrong that we don't dare do anything else?'

Jenny shrugged as she reflected. 'Probably a mixture of all three. Or maybe it's because the tickets are so cheap that it just seems a bit, I dunno, kind of pointless not to pay. Anyway, are we going to the Riviera or not?'

Located beside a meandering tributary to the River Spree, the Riviera Ballroom was an ensemble of formerly elegant nineteenth-century rooms in which those Berlin residents who could afford to do so had once wined, dined and waltzed in the most ornate and comfortable surroundings. Following a moderate and only partially sympathetic programme of refurbishment in the 1960s, the complex was now a popular disco and bar. Once inside the high-ceilinged ballroom, Ulla rapidly knocked back a beer before dragging Jenny and Rosa to the centre of the growing crowd and insisting that they dance, and dance joyously, to whatever the DJ played.

Whilst permitted western hits by Stevie Wonder and Abba were cast-iron floor fillers, popular singles by East German artists such as City and Puhdys also galvanised the young crowd to escape the everyday in an act of collective revelry. With the dancefloor awash with swaying and twisting bodies and the music growing steadily louder, the evening was shaping up to be exactly the kind of lively blow-out that the friends had agreed was long overdue. After perhaps an hour, however, the DJ called time-out from danceable hits and dutifully fulfilled his obligation to play a specific quota of GDR-produced music with a sequence of thankfully short B-sides by the Herbert Boss Combo and the Elektra Brothers Septet. Thwarted in her desire to let off steam on the dance floor, Ulla simply ordered another beer.

'Steady,' said Rosa, aware that under normal circumstances, Ulla rarely made it as far as a second drink and often did not finish her first. 'We don't want to have to carry you home.'

In due course the DJ announced the resumption of normal service by cranking up the volume and blasting out a potentially unsanctioned crowd-pleaser by Roxy Music. Before long, Ulla's vivacious moves had become so animated that they threatened to be a source of injury to those dancing anywhere near her. When eventually her reactions to the comments of the inconvenienced began to verge on the contemptuous, it was clear to both Rosa and Jenny that their friend had probably had more than enough to drink. They should, they quickly agreed, leave of their own accord whilst they still had the freedom to do so. Quickly, Rosa retrieved their coats and Jenny steered Ulla towards the door.

'You know what?' said Ulla as they walked along Regattastrasse in the direction of the tram stop. 'I'm done. I'm done with this place, this effing do-as-you're-told shit-hole of a place.'

'Oh, Grünau's not so bad,' replied Rosa, concerned that they might somehow be overheard.

'No. Not Grünau. Not the Riviera. You know what I mean. You both know exactly what I mean.'

'Well, whatever you mean, this is not the place to talk about it. We need to get you home.'

As the three walked onwards, a car with blue lights and twin bullhorns on the roof was briefly illuminated as it passed beneath the street lamp ahead of them. Just before the police vehicle was level, Ulla spat forcefully at the car, landing a glob of spittle almost directly in the centre of the windscreen.

'Run,' shouted Ulla, as the driver slammed on the brakes and brought the car to a halt. Unable to turn easily in the narrow street and unwilling to conduct a pursuit in reverse gear, the furious police officer was forced to drive the hundred metres or so to the next junction before effecting a turn and speeding back the way he had come. By the time he reached Wassersportallee, a tram was trundling across the junction and he could go no further. As soon as the line of carriages had cleared the intersection, the officer climbed out of the car and scoured the dimly lit streets for any sign of movement. To his frustration, the three delinquents had disappeared from sight and there appeared to be no potential witnesses who might possibly be of assistance. Still fuming, he turned his vehicle around once more and continued in the direction of the ballroom.

After crouching in the shadow of a low hedge for maybe twenty minutes, Ulla, Jenny and Rosa emerged as inconspicuously as they could and improvised a circuitous route back to the S-Bahn.

Once seated in an otherwise empty carriage to Karlshorst, Rosa worked hard to calm Ulla who at first wanted to celebrate as though she had single-handedly taken on the USSR Olympic ice hockey team and handed them a famous drubbing. Only when Jenny repeatedly laid bare how their evening might have panned out, had the police officer succeeded in catching them, did the alcohol-fuelled buoyancy begin to subside.

'Shit,' said Ulla, staring blankly as reality finally sank in. 'What the hell was I thinking? Listen. If I ever suggest going to the Riviera again, slap me. Slap me hard.'

'Don't worry,' said Rosa. 'We will.'

Although caught off guard by Ulla's sudden and hopefully temporary loss of inhibition, Jenny and Rosa felt only solidarity for their inebriated friend. With the benefit of hindsight, the eruption of Ulla's feelings was an entirely predictable reaction to the unjust treatment dished out by a system that so proudly and so frequently proclaimed itself to be a paragon of justice. For the foreseeable future, thought Jenny, she and Rosa would need to maintain a watchful eye on their friend, particularly when in the presence of alcohol or uniforms.

9 ADVICE

Oxford, Saturday 17th May 1975

With the help of a tourist map acquired at the station, it took Professor Madeleine MacKenzie no more than fifteen minutes to cover the best part of a mile to the Eagle and Child on St Giles Street. The respected academic had no idea how she and Kate Wildegood had allowed four years to pass without making a point of seeing one another. At Cambridge they had been almost inseparable. As she pushed at the door to the pub, she wondered if Kate would already be there, and if so, which book she would be reading.

'PG Wodehouse?' queried MacKenzie, on locating her friend ensconced in a smoke-filled corner. 'I have to say, I'm surprised.'

Wildegood smiled. 'Ah yes. His questionable activities during the war. I think the jury's still out on Wodehouse, regardless of the knighthood.'

'I just meant, isn't it a bit lightweight?'

'Oh, it's definitely lightweight. That's exactly why I'm reading it.'

Kate Wildegood balanced her cigarette on the edge of the ashtray, placed a bookmark between the pages of *Right Ho, Jeeves*, and hugged her friend of over thirty years.

Wildegood was relatively slender if somewhat taller than MacKenzie. She exuded an intelligence and a self-assurance that had been granted by nature, honed at Cambridge and solidified by extensive experience. Her dark hair now substantially infiltrated by wisps of grey, the brown eyes and the olive skin hinted at a Mediterranean heritage, but the surname offered no further clue. Although MacKenzie and Wildegood had once worked together in British Military Intelligence, the Professor did not know, and was not permitted to know, either her former colleague's exact job title or the extent and focus of her current responsibilities. Nevertheless, the MI6 officer had, on a number of occasions over the years, allowed herself to allude obliquely to the fact that her career had flourished in the Service.

'Well, Maddie,' said Wildegood, 'a ploughman's lunch and a glass of house white. You certainly know how to treat a girl. But an Oxford pub? It's like sleeping with the enemy.'

MacKenzie smiled. 'It's not exactly the Savoy, I know, but Oxford is half-way more or less for both of us. And this is where Tolkien and CS Lewis used to drink, so I thought it might appeal to you.'

'Yes. I do like that. It's quite a thought, isn't it? Two tweedy old professors, plying each other with real ale and stealing each other's ideas.'

'I suspect that says more about your line of business than it does about theirs. Anyway, how's John? How are the kids?'

The longstanding friends proceeded to compare the chaos of family life with the well-organised stresses of work. They congratulated one another on the progress they had made in their professional lives, but tempered the celebration with the shared recognition that they had needed to be head and shoulders above their male rivals even to be considered as legitimate competition. Similarly, they lamented the unstintingly determined efforts they knew their daughters would have had to make in order to compete with their sons.

'Who knows?' ventured MacKenzie. 'You may yet become Head of Service.'

'And pigs might fly,' said Wildegood without a moment's hesitation. 'The old boys' club will never break ranks on this one.'

'Well, if you'd asked me six months ago whether a woman would ever lead the Conservative Party, I'd have said exactly the same thing. Yet Margaret Thatcher might well be Prime Minister before the end of the decade.'

Wildegood drew on her cigarette. 'I'll believe it when I see it. Maybe not even then.'

As the pair chatted their way through lunch, they drifted back to their undergraduate days at Cambridge, the mayhem they had created in the Amateur Dramatic Club and the men they had been involved with. When the conversation meandered, almost inevitably, to their shared experiences in uniform, they couched their references to their work in post-war Germany in the most guarded of terms. Before they knew it, Wildegood was looking at her watch.

'Well it's been good to catch up,' she said, 'but I have the distinct feeling that you wanted to do more than reminisce about our exploits in Nuremberg, or the Drama Club for that matter.'

'Astute as ever, Kate, astute as ever. I'm glad you're not my boss. But you're right. I do have a small favour to ask of you. To put it in a nutshell, I have a student who is hellbent on conducting primary research in East Berlin, regardless of my guidance to the contrary. Fools rush in, as they say. Anyway, I was wondering what advice you might be able to offer.'

'You or him?'

'Either.'

'Well, it's perhaps not the cleverest idea. What is he hoping to look into?'

'Environmental issues. He's heavily involved with saving the whale and recycling newspapers and all of that kind of thing. He's a bright young man, but his idealism borders on naivety. He thinks he can just waltz into the Environment Ministry and ask if he might be able to conduct an interview on GDR environmental policy.'

'Well, I'd be surprised if he made it through the front door, to be honest, but you never know. The GDR is desperate for international legitimacy. They might want to make something of it. Maybe stage an interview for the press as a shining example of their openness and their world-beating commitment to combatting pollution. That sort of thing. On the other hand, he might just set alarm bells ringing if he turns up unannounced.'

'Indeed,' said MacKenzie. 'In a perfect world, I would ensure that our young friend was furnished not just with all the standard Polytechnic documentation but also with some form of bona fides provided by a credible intermediary.'

'For example?'

'Well, that's the point where I'm out of ideas. As I said, Kate, it's been a long time.'

Wildegood slowly stubbed out her cigarette. The Service did not exist to grant favours to its alumni and her immediate response should have been to remind MacKenzie of that fact. They were, however, not just former colleagues but old friends.

'Listen, Maddie,' she said finally. 'There is obviously a limit to what I can say on any matter relating to anything whatsoever, but I'll see what I can do. What's his name?'

Perhaps an hour later, the intelligence officer was sitting on the train back to London. Already beginning to tire of the *Times* crossword, thoughts of a recent and unexpected approach from a middle-ranking officer within the East German Ministry for State Security danced in the back of her mind. The wholly surprising contact had been initiated by a Stasi captain ostensibly claiming that he wished to defect to the West. Too long in the tooth to take walk-ins at face value, Wildegood questioned the veracity of the East German officer's story and had instructed her operatives in Berlin to exercise caution. Whilst the contact was potentially an asset of immense value, double agents were hardly rare. She would not, therefore, even consider approving a full-scale exit package until the MfS officer had produced incontrovertible proof of his worth.

Pushing the newspaper to one side, Wildegood looked out of the window at the rapidly changing Oxfordshire countryside. As farm tracks and hedges flashed by, she reflected on the all too brief afternoon she had spent with her friend and how they had slotted so easily into behaviours that dated back decades. They should not wait another four years, she decided, before they next made time to have lunch together. It was only a shame that it had taken Maddie's desire to call in a favour to get them to the pub in the first place. As the train was pulling into Paddington Station, the seasoned MI6 officer wondered if MacKenzie's headstrong student might represent some kind of opportunity, but dismissed the thought as fanciful at best. The Stasi walk-in, on the other hand, if managed judiciously, might conceivably turn out to be the gift that would keep on giving.

10 REUNION

East Berlin, Thursday 22nd May 1975

Trusted by his peers and respected by those he commanded, Captain Hartling was, in the eyes of his colleagues, an exemplary MfS officer. Before leaving the Stasi complex in Berlin-Lichtenberg, he checked that neither his clothing nor any item about his person would compromise the next phase of his Romeo operation in the capitalist West. The lean, fair-haired forty-year-old had purchased the shoes, the well-cut suit and the silk tie in an upmarket West Berlin department store. His wallet contained five hundred deutschmarks in cash, a credit card from a prominent West German bank and two American Express travellers cheques. The high-end rimless glasses, the grained calf-leather travel bag and the matching briefcase completed the confident look of a thriving businessman.

In due course Hartling would replace his Stasi ID card and his service-issue passport with the two immaculately counterfeited documents he routinely used for his operations in the West. The first was a West German passport in the name of Rainer Schwarzenbeck. The second was an ID card which, if push came to shove, would confirm to anyone who needed to be convinced that the holder was in fact an operative of the BND, the West German intelligence service.

Satisfied that his appearance was exactly as it needed to be and that he had the documentation he required, Hartling phoned for the MfS service vehicle in taxi livery that would take him to Friedrichstrasse station, his exit point for West Berlin.

Friedrichstrasse, the brick-and-glass interchange station which stood barely a kilometre from the Wall, was at once workaday and absurd. Whilst a cursory glance at any West Berlin transport map easily created the impression that the underground *U-Bahn* and overground *S-Bahn* lines from both sides of the city converged and connected at Friedrichstrasse, the impression was entirely illusory. Although certain platforms were directly accessible via lines emanating from the West, others were dedicated exclusively to services running in the East. The two sets of passengers, however, were permanently segregated by a formidable combination of steel fences, bricked up doorways and ever-watchful border guards. Movement between the discrete precincts was possible but only via the tightly controlled checkpoints hidden within the station's labyrinth of staircases and passageways. Although Friedrichstrasse served each day as the main point of entry for substantial numbers of visitors from the West, only East German citizens in possession of exit visas were permitted to travel in the opposite direction. To underline the dislocation of the two halves of the city, the transport maps produced in the East neither showed nor referred to West Berlin in any way and presented Friedrichstrasse not as a hub but as the end of the line.

The sharp-suited Hartling thanked his driver and walked briskly towards the entrance to the station. He ignored the sign ushering departing visitors into the modernist, glass-walled waiting hall whose nickname 'the Palace of Tears' was a clue to the emotional scenes that so often played out at its doors. Choosing instead to enter a part of the station identified as a restricted area, the MfS officer nodded curtly to the uniformed guard and headed directly to the door marked 'Service Entrance – Staff Only'. At the end of a passageway were a small curtained window and the door to the room used by the MfS to facilitate and control the flow of its operatives into West Berlin. Hartling rang the doorbell and held his Stasi ID to the window. The duty guard pulled back the curtain, noted the identity card and unlocked the door.

In the poky internal room beyond, the MfS captain greeted his colleague before presenting his GDR passport, his border pass, his Ministry for State Security ID card and his detailed order papers. Satisfied that everything was in order, the sergeant stamped Hartling's travel documents, saluted his superior and unlocked the electronic door to the warren of corridors which by-passed all other checks and controls.

Less than a minute later, the Stasi captain emerged from an anonymous service door close to the left-luggage lockers in the western precinct of the station. In the walkway, the queues of West Berliners still waiting to be processed grew longer by the minute. Calmly, Hartling deposited his GDR documents in an unmarked locker, replaced the key in his trouser pocket and boarded the first underground train to the other side of the city.

The order papers which the MfS officer had safely stowed at Friedrichstrasse detailed his assignment as a 'meeting with operative target Artemis'. The codename referred to Petra Fichtenberg, the personal assistant to Pastor Stefan Niemeyer, a Lutheran priest whose parish straddled the border between the two sides of the city.

Although Niemeyer lived in West Berlin, the church building for which he was responsible stood unused and locked, no more than thirty metres to the East of the Berlin Wall. To date, the Church of Reconciliation remained the sole structure to have been spared by the GDR demolition teams as they cleared space for the infamous death strip which deterred access to the Wall itself. The neo-gothic tower and steeple of the lonely, red-brick church stubbornly protruded into the rows of tank traps and barbed wire and obstructed the sight lines of the patrolling guards.

Unusually cautious of incurring the displeasure of the ecclesiastical authorities, the East German government had spent years attempting to negotiate with the implacable Pastor Niemeyer and had repeatedly failed to secure his assent to the demolition of his parish church. Consequently, it was now the responsibility of the Stasi's Main Directorate for Reconnaissance to find a way to change his mind. Whilst the pastor was invariably tailed when he made visits to his rump parish in the East, his well-appointed offices in West Berlin had proved impermeable to penetration. In the early spring of 1975, however, Petra Fichtenberg had been scouted by the MfS and identified as a promising target for a Romeo operation.

Hartling had received his exhaustive preparation for such missions at the Institute for Operative Psychology at the Stasi's elite training school in Potsdam. Whilst the trainees inevitably received detailed instruction in sexual technique, even greater emphasis was placed on more traditional aspects of courtship such as politeness, manners and the ability to listen. Although the manipulation of his lover's emotions had required skill and a degree of patience on Hartling's part,

Petra Fichtenberg had proved herself to be a textbook acquisition who would ultimately do exactly as was required of her. As the Stasi captain strolled from the U-Bahn station to the five-star Hotel Kurfürstendamm, he ran through a mental checklist of her hopes, fears and inclinations. Once settled into his fourth-floor room, a ten-year-old single malt nestling in his hand, he rehearsed the details of his notional business interests in South America.

Shortly before three in the afternoon, Petra Fichtenberg was sitting expectantly in the hotel lobby. By her feet, a leather shoulder bag contained everything she needed for a night away from home. Although her ever-thoughtful lover would inevitably compliment her on the stylish floral-print dress, she had invested in a shade of lipstick that she hoped would appear somewhat daring. As she waited, she ran her fingers through her freshly trimmed auburn hair.

Presently, Hartling sauntered down the stairs from his room, walked into the lobby and gave Petra a friendly wave. As their eyes met, she stood up from her armchair and flashed him the warmest of smiles. The couple had not seen each other for almost a month and Hartling knew that the lovelorn thirty-year-old would be overjoyed at their reunion.

The pair shared an intimate, celebratory drink at the bar before walking arm in arm beneath the leafy planes of the Kurfürstendamm, a wide, almost Parisian boulevard lined with jewellers, fashion houses and expensive car dealerships. Hanging on Petra's every word, the smartly turned-out businessman took care to point out interesting balconies, cute dogs and the shops selling the Bohemian glass which she so avidly collected.

'I can't even begin to describe how much I've been missing you,' said Hartling as the couple drifted in the direction of their favourite restaurant. 'I just find myself thinking about you all the time, regardless of what I'm doing. And you know what, my brown-eyed darling? I've decided that I've had enough of this crazy merry-go-round of business trips to God knows where. Being apart from you has got me thinking about what's really important in my life.'

'And?'

Hartling smiled. 'And I'd like to think that this is heading somewhere.'

'Meaning?'

'Meaning,' he said, catching her eye, 'that I hope that one day, whenever I wake up in the morning, I'll see your face beside me. And meaning also that I hope I haven't left it too late to be a father.'

The Paris Bar was quiet for a Thursday evening. As the couple dined, Hartling was confident that Petra Fichtenberg would already be visualising her future with this successful and impossibly empathetic businessman and might already be wondering how many children they would one day have.

Once back in his room, Petra slipped off her shoes and smiled.

'If you're going to make a move,' she said demurely, 'you might like to begin by standing behind me and kissing the nape of my neck.'

The exhaustively trained Stasi captain did not disappoint. He seemed to know instinctively how she liked to be touched and the stroking of his lips on her skin gave her gooseflesh.

'Take your time,' she whispered, closing her eyes and tilting her head slightly to one side.

The first time they had slept together, Petra had told him that she was sick of men who treated lovemaking as though it were some kind of a race.

'Intimacy,' he had smoothly replied, 'is a journey not a destination.'

In the morning, as they lay quietly in bed, the man Petra Fichtenberg knew as Rainer, rolled onto his stomach and kissed her softly on the lips.

'Do you trust me?' he asked.

'Of course.'

'Well, there is something I need to tell you, something about me that's going to come as a surprise, but it's something that I really need to share with you, especially if we're thinking of spending our lives together.'

The look of utter confusion on Petra's face was exactly what Hartling wanted. He knew how this would play out. The target he had been grooming would be experiencing a flat spin of anxiety. She would instantly assume that he was about to confess to being a married man, a wanted criminal or possibly even both. He would then supply an eminently more palatable lie and Petra, relieved to have been disabused of her fears and perhaps even embarrassed by her lack of faith, would readily accept his fabrication as the unshakeable truth.

When Hartling tentatively offered her his BND identity card, the sigh of relief was exactly what he wanted to hear. He allowed her a moment to let the astonishing revelation sink in.

'You work for the West German intelligence service?' said Petra, with the tone of someone whose understanding of life had just been cracked like a nut.

Hartling nodded. 'That's what it says on the card. At least, until I complete my contract. As I said, I've been thinking about our future.'

'Hell, Rainer,' she said, now holding his gaze, 'this is… well, this is…'

'A surprise?'

'Well, yes. Hell, I don't really know what to say. This is… well, it's just completely… I just didn't see this coming. But you know what, Rainer? If I'm being honest, I thought you were going to tell me something really bad. Something that I couldn't bear to hear. But the BND? I mean, the BND? Since when? And I mean, what do you actually do? Shit, Rainer, is it dangerous?'

'Petra, I know this has come as a shock, but I've already told you way too much. Please don't ask me questions about the specific work I do. All you need to know, my love, is that I help keep our country safe. As far as you're concerned, I'm still a high-flying businessman who is away from time to time. Just trust me that I won't be doing my real job for much longer.'

Petra stared at the ceiling. 'I don't know what to say. I honestly don't know what to say.'

'Don't say anything,' he said, tapping her lightly on the nose. 'In fact, you can't say anything. To anyone. You understand that, right?'

'Of course,' she replied, still manifestly astounded at the turn of events. 'I wouldn't dream of it.'

Hartling knew exactly how Petra would be feeling once she had processed his disclosure. She would know that it had taken both courage and unshakeable trust to reveal such a secret to her and, if it were at all possible, she would now feel that she loved him even more.

After breakfast, Petra dragged Rainer back to bed. She didn't care, she said, if it made her late for work. When the call of her professional duties could no longer be ignored, the putative BND agent took her in his arms and reassured her of his love. As he stroked her hair, Petra pressed her head gently to his shoulder.

'You know something,' said Rainer almost reluctantly. 'Pastor Niemeyer's name cropped up in conversation at work. It's not one of my cases, but apparently one of our sources has intimated that your boss might be visiting East Berlin a little more frequently than is strictly necessary.'

Petra furrowed her brow. 'Really? You know he has hundreds of parishioners over there? It's part of his job.'

'Yeah, you're right. It's probably nothing. Absolutely.'

Having done no more than plant a seed of doubt in Petra's mind, Hartling expressed his frustration at their looming separation and assured her that she would never be far from his thoughts. At a carefully prepared moment during their next reunion he would deftly return to the subject of her boss and wonder whether Petra might be prepared to make a mental note if ever any of Niemeyer's behaviours struck her as unusual. Once she had reported something curious, as inevitably she would, the man she knew as Rainer would compliment her on her capacity for observation. As a measure of his trust in her, he would then ask her to supply a photocopy of the pastor's appointments schedule or some easily accessible correspondence. More challenging requests would come later.

As the pair waited arm in arm on the busy pavement outside the hotel, Hartling promised his lover that they would see each other again within a fortnight. He reminded her quietly that she would endanger not just his work but also his life if she were ever to let slip that he was anything other than a successful businessman with substantial interests in South America. Before she knew it, the taxi had arrived and he was gone.

Although the tryst with operative target Artemis was the only operation listed on Captain Hartling's order papers, he had no intention of returning immediately to East Berlin. In an hour he would be sitting with his MI6 handler in a small private room in the Rive Gauche, a men-only bar that purposefully did not advertise its existence to the outside world. Away from prying eyes, they would continue to discuss the terms of his defection. Predictably wary of an approach from an unknown MfS officer, the British had thus far been circumspect in their negotiations. For his part, Hartling had little objection to their caution. What mattered was the depth of their pockets.

11 EXCLUSION ZONE

East Berlin, Wednesday 20th August 1975

The cooler days of late summer heralded the not too distant approach of the first term at university. Ulla listened with an inevitable sense of regret as Rosa and Jenny grew increasingly excited at the prospect of taking their first meaningful steps towards independence and beginning their chosen courses of study in Dresden and Magdeburg.

Although cut to the bone by the blocking of her own university application, Ulla had not the slightest desire to cast a shadow over their understandable excitement. Publicly, she stuck doggedly to the fiction that she had made an impossible choice between her desire to study physics and her dream of representing the national ice hockey team at senior level. Rosa and Jenny fully understood that this fabrication was probably the most believable of the available lies and privately corroborated her story whenever enquiries arose. Following an interview at the Employment Office, Ulla was currently awaiting news of a suitable position.

When the eighteen-year-old castaway received an invitation from Kirsten Beck, her closest friend in the GDR U20 ice hockey squad, to spend a weekend at her parents' home in Wohlenberg on the Baltic coast, she jumped at the chance of some time away from Berlin. Kirsten was a full twelve months younger than Ulla and, having only just started her final year at upper school, was guaranteed not to regale her visitor with bright-eyed accounts of preparations for college. Unfortunately, Kirsten pointed out in a separate note, the small coastal resort of Wohlenberg was situated within the five-kilometre exclusion zone that ran the length of the GDR coast and Ulla would need to apply for an entry permit from the police in Berlin. It would not, Kirsten was sure, constitute any kind of a problem. The family had received visitors on many previous occasions.

Kirsten's mother worked as a cook in the popular Hotel Baltic some two hundred metres from the beach and her father enjoyed early starts on a nearby agricultural collective. Manfred, her older brother, was currently completing three years' compulsory service in the National People's Army. Ulla, Kirsten wrote, would be able to sleep in his room and she promised to give it a thorough airing before her friend's arrival.

A quick-thinking winger on the ice, it was Kirsten who had earned the two players an unforgettable dressing down at the 1974 Friendship Games in Bratislava. During a dreary cultural visit to Devín Castle, Kirsten had impulsively yelled 'Hello, gorgeous!' from the elevated medieval ramparts to an Austrian farmer obliviously ploughing his fields on the opposite bank of the Morava river. Her 'egotistical and unseemly attempt to make contact with a representative of a capitalist power', the coach had fumed, was not just thoroughly inappropriate but a potentially major source of embarrassment for the national team. Ulla, for her part, was reminded in no uncertain terms that she had a duty to act as a role-model and should have set an infinitely better example than simply to laugh at her younger comrade's antics. The pair were solemnly warned that any further infringement would result in suspension from the squad. For the remainder of the trip, the girls' behaviour, at least in the presence of the coach, had been impeccable.

Ulla's parents agreed that a couple of days away might do her the world of good and readily stumped up the cost of the train tickets. Contrary to Ulla's expectations, the entry permit for the coastal exclusion zone was issued without fuss on production of the letter of invitation and a valid ID card. With the travel permit sitting on the desk in her bedroom and 'Suffragette City' blaring out from her cassette recorder, Ulla penned a postcard to Kirsten informing her that she had acquired the necessary documentation and would be coming to Wohlenberg for the final weekend of August. Unable to resist the temptation, she began the card with 'Hello, gorgeous!'

12 IN THE WATER

Wohlenberg, Friday 29th August 1975

As the train from Schwerin crept to a halt in Grevesmühlen, Ulla glimpsed Kirsten and her parents eagerly scanning the carriage windows for confirmation of her arrival. The unabashed delight of the teammates' reunion was followed by a formal introduction to Kirsten's parents and a somewhat bumpy drive to Wohlenberg in the Becks' pale blue Trabant. In response to the polite questions coming from the front of the vehicle, Ulla guessed at the duration of the rail journey from Berlin, confirmed that she was indeed a little hungry and reassured Kirsten's parents that she was the exact opposite of a fussy eater. When Kirsten inevitably asked her teammate to tell her what was new in her life, Ulla carefully avoided all mention of her family's political issues, but choked as she tried to explain that her grandfather had required heart surgery whilst visiting his brother in Munich. Kirsten squeezed Ulla's hand and allowed her time to regain her composure before deftly switching the topic of conversation to increasingly hilarious reminiscences of their time at the Friendship Games in Bratislava. Ulla was happy, at least in front of her friend's parents, to keep the focus on ice hockey.

Five kilometres outside Wohlenberg, the car was required by armed border guards to stop at the checkpoint marking the beginning of the coastal exclusion zone. The Becks respectfully showed their ID cards and confirmed their permanent address within the unassuming seaside resort.

With a deferential smile, Ulla handed over the official coastal travel permit issued by the police in Karlshorst.

Fifteen minutes later, Kirsten was showing Ulla around the family's modest timber-framed house, from which, with the windows open, the young Berliner could hear the sound of waves breaking on the shore and smell the salt on the air.

When, over dinner, the subject of university eventually raised its head, Ulla avoided all mention of her family's visa application, but surprised Kirsten's parents with the revelation that she had applied to join the Navy. The armed forces maintained high-level representative sports teams, Ulla explained, and she would, if accepted, probably be able to spend most of her time playing ice hockey.

'That's a ballsy decision,' said Kirsten.

'Don't let that give you ideas,' cautioned her father.

Ulla, for her part, had not the slightest intention of enlisting. During her interview at the Office of Employment in Karlshorst, her adviser had made it clear that only a limited range of career pathways were open to her. There were, for example, currently no opportunities in the armed services for women with her 'particular educational record'. Ulla's speculative application to the Ministry for National Defence had, she had known from the outset, been destined for rejection. Nevertheless it would force the shadowy people who kept files on these things to note that she had volunteered to serve her country.

'I'll wave to you,' said Ulla mischievously, 'every time I sail past Wohlenberg.'

'And I'll be waving right back at you,' said Kirsten's father, clearly not expecting any such event to happen.

'Anyway, what do you two featherbrains have planned for tomorrow?'

'Boltenhagen,' said Kirsten brightly. 'Ulla can borrow Manni's bike.'

Later, as the two girls cleared the table, Kirsten revealed more of her plan for the following day. The somewhat larger seaside resort of Boltenhagen was no more than ten kilometres along the coast and could be reached comfortably in under half an hour. Manfred's bike, Kirsten thought, was possibly slightly too large for Ulla but would nevertheless be manageable. With regard to lunch, there was a restaurant in the resort that had an excellent reputation, but as a result never had any free tables. To ensure they didn't starve, Kirsten would therefore make sandwiches and the pair could picnic on the beach or, if it was too windy, in the dunes nearby. After lunch they could bathe in the clear but chilly waters of the Baltic, get an ice cream and maybe pay a surprise visit to a schoolfriend of Kirsten's who lived in the nearby village of Klütz. It all sounded perfect.

Shortly after nine the following morning, Kirsten entered her brother's room and roused her visitor with a gentle shake of the shoulder. Through the open bedroom door, the smell of fresh coffee drifted invitingly from the kitchen below and made getting out of bed that little bit more straightforward. Kirsten's parents, who were by now already at work, had set out a breakfast of fresh rolls, butter, blackberry jam and salami. Kirsten had brewed some of their dwindling stock of West German coffee whilst Ulla was still sleeping.

Following a leisurely breakfast, more hilarity at the expense of their ice hockey coach and a brisk walk with Otto, the neighbour's energetic, wire-haired dachshund, it was almost half eleven and Kirsten and Ulla finally set out on their cycle trip to Boltenhagen.

By the time the two friends had reached roughly the midway point on the route to the resort, the narrow country lane that Kirsten had chosen was devoid of traffic and the chances of being overheard were remote.

'Have you heard the one about the Rolex watch?' asked Kirsten with a familiar glint in her eye.

'No.'

'OK. So. Margot Honecker buys a Rolex on a shopping trip to Switzerland and presents it to her beloved Erich when she gets back. The General Secretary of the Central Committee is so pleased with his expensive new watch that when the pair go to bed, Erich puts the Rolex back in its presentation box and hides it underneath a pile of underpants in his bedside cabinet. The following morning, he wakes up and he can't find the Rolex. It's certainly not next to the clock-radio where he always leaves his watch during the night. Honecker gets more and more anxious until eventually he phones Erich Mielke, the head of the Ministry for State Security, and tells the Minister that his brand-new Rolex has been stolen and that the Stasi must commit all of its personnel to the task of finding it. At lunchtime, having dealt with a number of matters of state, Honecker suddenly remembers that he had hidden the Rolex under his Y-fronts. He phones the Minister for State Security and tells him to call off the search.

"Too late," says Mielke. "We've already arrested twenty suspects and six of them have confessed."'

Ulla laughed so hard at the punchline that she jerked the handlebars of the slightly oversized bike to the left, initiating an ungainly wobble, a shriek of surprise and a second bout of shared hilarity. Once their laughter had subsided, and in spite of the certainty that they were alone, both girls instinctively looked over their shoulders to ensure that they had not been overheard. Kirsten's joke, after all, qualified under GDR law as 'slandering the state' and was punishable by a prison sentence of up to two years.

'What's the beach like?' asked Ulla as they approached the outskirts of Boltenhagen.

'The beach is brilliant,' replied Kirsten. 'White sand, maybe two kilometres end to end. But I'm warning you, it gets crowded.'

Immediately before the beach, the girls left their bikes outside the popular Restaurant Pavillon, a rotund structure whose dominant, grey-slated roof and protruding lantern gave the impression that the architect had perhaps designed the building whilst staring at a Prussian military helmet.

'So, you meant crowded like a walrus colony,' said Ulla as she caught sight of the hordes of holidaymakers.

'Yep,' said Kirsten, nodding in acknowledgement, 'pretty much.'

The beach was so overrun with tourists that it was verging on impossible to pick out a patch of sand where the latecomers could sit without becoming a feature of someone else's holiday. Separating the girls from the sea were hundreds of the boldly striped, winged and roofed upright chairs the Germans referred to as 'beach-baskets'. Some of these personal wind-shelters were occupied, others not, but as a shield against the prevailing westerlies, they all faced towards the East, which Erich and Margot Honecker, had they ever taken their holidays somewhere as busy as Boltenhagen, might have considered to be some kind of moral victory. Between the beach-baskets, children in colourful swimming costumes dug in the sand, lost their inflatable balls to the vagaries of the breeze or chased each other tirelessly. Adults, the overwhelming majority in trunks or bikinis, mooched, chatted and watched their children. Occasional, reassuring aromas of traditional German pork dishes wafted from the kitchens of the Restaurant Pavillon to the beach, almost wantonly pricking the appetites of those who had been unable to reserve a table. At intervals of perhaps a hundred metres, red, glass-windowed cabins were perched some four metres above the sand on muscular steel stanchions and provided the lifeguards with an uninterrupted view of the shore and of any swimmers who might require attention.

Looking out across the blue waters of the Baltic, something struck Ulla as inherently odd without being immediately apparent. Finally it dawned on her that it was not what she could see that had unsettled her but what she couldn't see. In spite of the blustery wind that repeatedly blew the girls' hair across their faces, not a single dinghy or sailing boat punctuated the view from the shore.

In response to Ulla's enquiry about the absence of any form of craft on the water, Kirsten drew her friend's attention to one of the several large, black and white signs installed at regular intervals along the promenade. The rusting metal notices, Kirsten explained, warned that Boltenhagen beach was part of the protected border area of the GDR and that specific rules were to be respected. Sailing and the launch of sea-going craft were not permitted at any time. Similarly, the use of rowing boats, canoes, inflatables or surf boards was strictly forbidden. Between 8 p.m. and 8 a.m. all access to the beach was prohibited. During the hours when the beach was open to the public, no access was permitted to the long wooden jetty that stretched tantalisingly out to sea. Kirsten also pointed out the small police station located directly behind the beach and the pairs of border guards, rifles slung over their shoulders, who patrolled the promenade at regular intervals. To the west, beyond a white concrete wall, a clifftop watchtower erased any last shred of doubt that the beach was under close surveillance. For the thousands of swim-suited visitors, the overt security measures were simply a fact of life and there was no reason to let them impinge on a well-deserved holiday by the sea. Nevertheless, whilst some adults splashed and played with their children in the shallows, few holidaymakers ventured more than ten metres into the water for fear of provoking a misunderstanding about their intentions.

'At night,' said Kirsten, carefully restraining her voice, 'they sweep the beach with searchlights. They have sniffer dogs to check all the beach-baskets and the guards search the dunes for people trying to sneak canoes to the shore.'

'Shit,' said Ulla. 'That's scary. Not exactly the place to make out with your boyfriend, then.'

'Come on,' said Kirsten, looking to make the best of things. 'Let's just go and get our feet wet. Then we can buy an ice cream from the kiosk.'

As the friends picked their way between the beach-baskets, the picnics and the towels, the distant but throaty growl of a motor running at high revs competed for their attention.

'Something's going on,' said Ulla, squinting out to sea.

In the middle distance, a silver-grey patrol boat, its nose forced proud of the waves and a trail of spray and foaming water in its wake, was heading rapidly in the direction of the shore. A ripple of commotion spread amongst the bathers and the holidaymakers who were stationed closest to the sea. To the girls' left, two life guards had emerged from their watchtower onto the narrow walkway directly in front of the windows. The first pressed a pair of binoculars to his eyes. The second held a walkie-talkie to his cheek and was presumably communicating with the pilot of the launch. Maybe fifteen seconds later the roar of engines eased back and the patrol boat curved around in a wide arc, perhaps some five hundred metres from the shore.

'I think there might be someone in the water,' said Ulla.

Whilst it was by no means beyond the bounds of possibility that a hapless swimmer had been caught out by an unexpected current and would be only too relieved to be rescued, both girls were aware that other, more desperate scenarios were likely and the majority would not be blessed with a happy ending.

'They shouldn't be that far out,' said Kirsten. 'It's really not a good idea.'

The deliberate circumspection was sharply interrupted by the unmistakeable clatter of machine gun fire followed by a brief roar from the boat's powerful engines. By now the events being played out on the water had captured the attention of almost every visitor to the beach. At such a distance, no-one was in any position to ascertain whether the shots had been fired directly at the swimmer or had served to signal the consequences of non-compliance. The border patrol boat lurched forwards momentarily before coming to an almost silent halt and bobbed a little as it held its position for maybe thirty seconds. The crew's task presumably complete, the launch then throttled up its engines, turned and motored back round the headland and out of sight. Ulla looked briefly to see what the lifeguards were now doing, but they had disappeared, presumably back into the shelter of their windproof cabin.

Gradually, the holidaymakers returned to their holidaymaking, though some with markedly less enthusiasm than others. It was impossible to discern whether the beachgoers clustered nearby were everyday citizens with little involvement in politics, diehard Party workers or even off-duty Stasi officers. There was no way of expressing shock or of engaging in any overt discussion of what Ulla and Kirsten had witnessed without perhaps being overheard by those who were proud of the GDR's ability to maintain the security of its borders. They would have to keep a tight lid on that conversation until the privacy of the bike ride home.

'Come on,' said Ulla. 'Let's just take a stroll along the water's edge, then we'll go and get that ice cream. My treat.'

They were by no means the first to leave the beach.

13 WITH BOTH HANDS

East Berlin, Sunday, 31st August 1975

Waiting for Ulla upon her return to Karlshorst were two official-looking letters. She ripped open the envelopes with her forefinger and read the contents to her parents. The first was from the Ministry for National Defence and the second from the Office of Employment.

The letter from the Defence Ministry thanked Ulla for her public spirit and acknowledged her desire to defend the territorial integrity of the GDR, but regretted, as Ulla had expected, that the People's Navy was not currently recruiting citizens with her particular qualifications and skills. The Ministry wished the aspiring recruit every success in her search for suitable employment.

Ulla would never know precisely to what extent the implied patriotism of her application to the Ministry for National Defence had oiled the wheels at the Office for Employment, but the second letter contained concrete news of a job which, all things considered, exceeded her expectations. The school-leaver had been assigned, she was politely informed, a clerical post at the Ministry for the Environment and would be based in their building in Hans-Beimler-Strasse, directly across the underpass from the official GDR travel office. Although Ulla knew the precise location of the high-rise state travel agency, she could not for the life of her visualise the buildings opposite. The new appointee was to report for induction on the first of October and would follow an intensive course in typing and shorthand before beginning her duties proper. The Employment Office trusted that she was satisfied with their offer of a position and wished her every success in her future career.

'I know it's not what you wanted,' said Ulla's mother sympathetically, 'but it could have been a whole lot worse, in the circumstances.'

'None of this is what we wanted,' said Ulla. 'None of it.'

Ulla's father shook his head. 'That was risky, applying to the Navy. What if they'd accepted you?'

'They were never going to accept me,' stated Ulla flatly. 'But I figured it would look good on my file. Anyway, the Environment Ministry's OK, I guess. That's doing something good. Something that benefits people. As you say, it could've been worse.'

'But keep up with the ice hockey,' said her father, steering the conversation in an entirely different direction. 'You need to focus on that now.'

Eva Wolfram handed her daughter the previous day's copy of *Neues Deutschland*. 'Take a look at this.'

The front page of the newspaper presented an image of an impeccably turned out Erich Honecker proudly congratulating the GDR senior men's ice hockey team following their unexpected defeat of France in Chamonix.

'It says at the bottom that the 1980 Winter Olympics are to be held in Lake Placid. That's in the USA. America. Ulla, you could be there. And who knows? With a bit of luck, maybe you could, you know, stay. Leave the hotel one day, find your way to a police station and ask for political asylum.'

'Well,' said Ulla, 'it's a thought, I suppose. But it's a complete long shot. You know as well as I do that women's ice hockey doesn't qualify as an Olympic sport.'

'But you never know,' countered her mother. 'You never know.'

'Exactly,' said her father.

'Anyway, if I deserted the GDR, you'd have the Stasi knocking on the door within days. They'd assume you'd put me up to it or you were in on the whole thing somehow.'

Udo Wolfram shrugged dismissively. 'But what evidence would they find? Absolutely nothing. In the end, they'd have to accept that you'd seen an opportunity and taken it.'

'What's more,' said her mother, 'by 1982 we'll both be retired. We'll both be free to emigrate to the West. So if you get the chance, Ulla, you take it. Seize it with both hands. We'll be fine.'

Ulla smiled. Her parents had clearly given the matter a lot of thought.

The young ice hockey star glanced towards the window. 'There was some kind of incident at the beach yesterday. There was someone in the water, quite a long way out, where you're not allowed to swim. This big patrol boat came and they shot at him. With machine guns, it sounded like. Then they dragged him out of the water and took him off in the boat. Everyone just sort of watched.'

14 PROSPECTS OF ADVANCEMENT

West Berlin, Wednesday 8th October 1975

Sitting in the rear of the taxi that would take Captain Hartling to the negotiation with his British handler, the Stasi officer drew on his cigarette and considered the complexity of his situation.

He was under no illusions regarding the treatment that would be meted out should his involvement with MI6 come to light. The penalty for treason was death. Yet Hartling was, he felt, far from being a traitor. If anything, it was he who had been betrayed. Ultimately, his disappearance would be a poke in the eye to the Stasi commanders who had overlooked his leadership potential in favour of comrades with personal connections to prominent Party members. It was now several years since Major General Konrad had made any kind of reference to Hartling's prospects of advancement and the MfS captain knew exactly what that meant. He no longer had any.

Yet with London still playing hardball, his defection was far from a done deal. Until such time as an agreement with MI6 had been reached, the MfS officer would need to conduct his regular duties with such dedication that no-one within the Ministry would entertain the slightest concern about his loyalties. Without doubt, his progress with the Church of Reconciliation case would be guaranteed to impress his commanders. Significantly, the MfS now had a reliable informant inside Pastor Niemeyer's office. Furthermore, Petra Fichtenberg had shown herself to be as malleable as she was naive and would without doubt commit any act of espionage that Hartling might require of her. All things considered, it was an exemplary operation.

The taxi pulled over in Motzstrasse, twenty-five metres from Hartling's destination. The MfS officer paid the driver, climbed out of the vehicle and extinguished his cigarette with the sole of his shoe.

The 'Rive Gauche' sign above the shopfront offered no real clue as to the nature of the establishment and the substantial and closely gathered net curtains precluded observation from the street. Hartling rang the bell and waited. The curtain covering the door moved slightly to one side and a man with neat black hair sized him up before opening the door.

'Table in the name of Martin,' said Hartling.

'Ah yes. He's expecting you,' said the barkeeper, before inviting the visitor into the fastidiously renovated premises of a former grocery store. The combination of white-painted walls, original artwork, and an eclectic collection of flea market chairs and tables created the impression of a fashionable salon that was at once a bar, a café and a private gallery. In one of the window corners, beneath a fiercely expressionist portrait of a Weimar Republic trapeze artist, two men stirred their coffees and quietly shared a joke.

The bartender ushered the new arrival into the now familiar side room where Hartling's contact preferred to do business. The MI6 case officer, whose real name was not Martin but Turnbull, wore a brown corduroy jacket and a plain blue tie. He was under orders to treat the Stasi captain's offer of defection with implacable suspicion.

The British spook offered a peremptory smile. 'I took the liberty of ordering cappuccinos and a small plate of Berliner doughnuts.'

'The economy must be booming,' said Hartling drily.

The Stasi officer took a seat and placed his briefcase carefully on the floor.

Turnbull sipped at his coffee. 'I trust you are well, Captain Hartling. I note that you made a point of bringing your briefcase. Presumably it contains the kind of primary intelligence that will impress my superiors and allow me to sanction your generous relocation package.'

Hartling pinched his lips momentarily. 'The briefcase is neither here nor there. I carry more classified information in my head than MI6 could collect in a decade. Your commanders will be wetting themselves with excitement at the prospect of securing my services.'

The conversation had begun exactly as its predecessor had left off. Two inscrutable operatives, each trying to appear as though they held the stronger hand, each trying to read the other's position from the tone of voice or the flicker of an eyelid.

Turnbull pushed his coffee forward. 'Well. Who knows what secrets lurk inside your head? As it stands, we have no concrete evidence of your value beyond a promise to tell all, the moment you receive a new ID, the keys to a house on Vancouver Island and a substantial deposit into your savings account.'

The MI6 officer continued to harbour massive concerns that his MfS counterpart might be a double agent. Yet, if Hartling were a Stasi diehard attempting to grub his way into British intelligence by presenting himself as a willing recruit, he would have been unwise to make such excessive demands. On the other hand, perhaps his hard-nosed requests were all part of the subterfuge and had been conceived to convince Turnbull, or his masters in London, that Hartling was the genuine article. Either way, the British MI6 officer was constrained by his orders and would require more than mere promises before making an agreement.

Hartling knew that ultimately he would have to choose between making some kind of concession or kissing goodbye to the material rewards he was seeking. It was not simply a question of which player possessed the stronger faith in his hand, but who, when it came to it, could afford to lose their entire stake and walk away without a moment's regret.

'So,' said the prospective defector, reaching for his coffee. 'What exactly do you want me to do?'

Ninety minutes after asking the question, the MfS officer stepped from the U-Bahn at Friedrichstrasse, retrieved his official Stasi documentation from a left-luggage locker and quietly allowed himself through the anonymous door that led to the discrete Stasi checkpoint. He was not in the easiest of moods. Turnbull had demanded, as a demonstration of good faith, the provision of the kind of strategic intelligence to which an officer of Hartling's rank could not reasonably be expected to have access. Furthermore, he had imposed a deadline of the end of March. It was a shrewd move. If the Stasi officer were to come up with the goods too readily, MI6 would inevitably suspect duplicity. If he acted too slowly, they would question his value. As matters stood, time was on Hartling's side. But time, he knew from experience, was not the most dependable of allies.

15 TRUST

West Berlin, Tuesday 14th October 1975

Pastor Stefan Niemeyer spent much of his morning in the offices of the Church of Reconciliation fielding calls, responding to correspondence and dictating replies. Shortly before lunch, he informed his PA that he would not be returning until the following day and left for his appointment at the Immanuel Hospital in the leafy southwestern suburb of Wannsee. Throughout the afternoon, Petra Fichtenberg cheerfully completed her administrative tasks, but took care still to be at her desk when, sometime after five in the afternoon, the last of her colleagues offered her a friendly wave and headed for home.

With the premises to herself, the PA locked the main doors from the inside. She let herself into Pastor Niemeyer's office, opened the filing cabinet and calmly removed various folders of recent correspondence. Slowly, she leafed through the collection of documents, carefully selecting letters that she might duplicate and pass on to the man who so completely professed his trust in her.

Returning to the main office, Petra Fichtenberg diligently photocopied a variety of individual letters from parishioners, journalists and fellow priests. Additionally, she reproduced sequences of correspondence from representatives of the Green Party, the Berlin Senate, the Federal Environment Agency and the Christian Democratic Union. Finally, she allowed her eyes to rest on an innocuous letter from a Professor Madeleine McKenzie who enquired in flawless German about the possibility of a five-month unpaid internship for a student with ambitious research plans.

After twenty minutes of repeatedly waiting for the photocopier light to shunt its way backwards and forwards, Frau Fichtenberg decided to call it a day and secured the illicit copies in her shoulder bag. With her task complete, she returned the original correspondence to the appropriate sections of Niemeyer's filing cabinet, closed down the office for the night and made her way to the U-Bahn.

She was not certain when she would next receive a call from the impossibly empathetic intelligence officer at whose behest she had made copies of her employer's correspondence. She was more than confident, however, that he would perceive her readiness to do his bidding as a manifestation of her love.

16 COMRADE WOLFRAM

East Berlin, Monday 17th November 1975

A forceful wind carried the chill air from the Arctic across the North European Plain and south to Berlin. On both sides of the Wall, pedestrians pulled their winter scarves tight to their necks, buried their hands in their pockets and walked as quickly as possible. Quietly, many cursed the crossing signals that seemed almost wilfully to prioritise the internal combustion engine and mock those hurrying to work on foot.

It had taken Ulla roughly twenty-five minutes to walk the two kilometres from the flat she now occupied in Fehrbelliner Strasse to the Ministry for the Environment on the corner of Karl-Marx-Allee and Hans-Beimler-Strasse. Although the post she had been assigned was scarcely the equivalent of the physics degree which she had set her heart on, Ulla was nevertheless keen to start work, particularly after the almost military intensity of the preparatory course in typing and stenography. The high-ceilinged reception area of the multi-storey tower that housed the Ministry was spacious, quiet and smelled vaguely of cleaning fluid.

'Comrade Wolfram, I presume,' said the bespectacled man who had been awaiting her arrival. 'Thomas Fischer. Welcome to the Ministry for the Environment. I don't think we met during your initial visit. Anyway, I am the Press Secretary here at the Ministry. You will be directly responsible to me.'

He shook her hand firmly and ushered her towards the stairs. In his office with its view across the busy underpass,

Fischer hung his jacket on the back of his chair, invited Ulla to take a seat and ordered coffee for two.

'So, this is my office,' he said entirely unnecessarily. 'You will be based predominantly at the desk in the reception area, but if you need me, or if I need you, this is where you will find me. When you've drunk your coffee, I'll give you a tour of the Ministry building and introduce you to the people who matter. With me so far?'

Ulla nodded and forced a smile. 'Absolutely.'

The plan for Ulla's induction was hardly complicated and she was already feeling patronised. Nevertheless, she knew that this job was probably the best that was on offer and she was determined not to make a poor impression. The Press Secretary produced a folder from a drawer in his desk, flipped it open and perused its contents. Ulla simply waited.

Fischer raised an eyebrow. 'I see that you speak English as well as Russian.'

'I also speak very passable German,' said Ulla without the slightest hint of irony. The joke fell completely flat.

'Well, of course,' replied Fischer.

'I hope my skills will prove to be of value to the Ministry,' said Ulla, still trying to sound enthusiastic. 'How often do you have visitors from the Soviet Union?'

The mention of the USSR seemed to trigger a more serious tone in Fischer's response.

'I assume, comrade Wolfram, that you read the secrecy clause in the document you signed. If you need to know something regarding the vital work of the Ministry, I assure you, you will be told. You will not need to ask.'

'And will that information always come from you, comrade Fischer? No hang on. That was another question, wasn't it?'

'Exactly.'

Fischer closed the file and breathed in slowly. 'Perhaps you might like to return to the reception area and install yourself at the desk whilst I finalise the arrangements for your tour.'

'Is there anything that I could be getting on with?' said Ulla. 'Just say the word.'

The Press Secretary looked at his new charge and was not sure what to make of her. He felt as though he'd been assigned a colleague's untrained puppy to look after for the day.

'Your enthusiasm is laudable,' he said, 'but rest assured, you will be fully briefed. In due course. Patience is, comrade Wolfram, a virtue.'

Fischer had, Ulla decided, a talent for condescension. He was, nevertheless, her boss and she would have to make a conscious effort to tolerate his unfortunate personality traits. In his favour, the Press Secretary had not made a single reference to the political cloud that still hung over the Wolfram family. Perhaps there was a beating heart behind his supercilious air.

Having found her way back to the reception area, the new appointee installed herself dutifully behind the desk and wondered what she would say to any visitor who might suddenly arrive. Presumably they would have some form of documentation explaining who they were, the purpose of their visit and who exactly they were expecting to meet. Presumably the phone number of that colleague would be on the list to the side of the phone. And presumably that colleague would tell the raw recruit precisely what she would need to do next. Pending an explanation from the Press Secretary, any incoming phone calls would have to be fielded in similar fashion. In the following twenty minutes, no-one of any description either entered or left the building and the phone on her desk steadfastly refused to ring.

To fend off boredom, Ulla examined and reorganised the contents of the drawers to the reception desk, stowed her lunch in the now empty lower drawer and, still with time to kill, turned her attention to her immediate surroundings. Behind her, portraits of Erich Honecker and the Environment Minister, Hans Reichelt, conferred their benediction on anyone who might approach the desk. Amongst the handful of photographs of visiting dignitaries, the bright eyes and unaffected smile of Valentina Tereshkova, the first woman in space, contrasted sharply with the restrained demeanours of those who surrounded her. Beside the entrance to the stairwell, a large framed poster portrayed two blue-shirted members of the Free German Youth against a backdrop of a pine forest. Casting their gaze with unbridled optimism towards the future, they declared 'Environmental protection – we play our part.'

Eventually, as Ulla was resorting to betting with herself on the colour of the next vehicle to appear in the small car park outside the Ministry building, her boss re-appeared. By lunchtime she had been shown what felt like every room in the building and had met Minister Reichelt himself plus the junior ministers for Pollution Control, Water Management, Water Supply and International Co-operation. At twelve, comrade Fischer surprisingly offered to treat his new employee to a simple lunch at the Mokka Grill, a restaurant on Karl-Marx-Allee. It was her first day, he emphasised, and it would be an opportunity to chat in a less formal setting. He would not accept her polite refusal and was unmoved by her presentation of the sandwiches that she had carefully prepared that morning. Presumably there was something he wished to share out of earshot of their fellow workers.

As the two colleagues commented on the efficiency of the Mokka Grill staff and the pleasing quality of the onion soup, the Press Secretary wondered aloud whether Ulla might like to share her impressions of Minister Reichelt. In response, Ulla diplomatically observed that he appeared to be a man fully in command of his obvious abilities.

Fischer paused and leaned in slightly. 'You may, at some point,' he said quietly, 'hear tales that the Minister was a member of the Nazi Party during the war. If so, you should regard any such reports as both mendacious and malicious. Do we understand each other, comrade Wolfram?'

'Perfectly,' said Ulla with a nod.

She was uncertain whether Fischer was attempting to protect the Minister or trying subtly to undermine him. Perhaps it was his way of saying that the past was the past and that everyone should be judged on their merits. She would, she thought, allow comrade Fischer the benefit of the doubt. Conceivably, there was a skeleton in his own political closet.

The first hour of the afternoon passed without event. At two fifteen, a group of men in tidy suits, presumably Ministry employees, entered the building and walked directly to the lift. Half an hour later a professional looking woman from the Ministry for Health presented herself for an appointment with the Junior Minister for Water Management. Little else happened that day and by five o'clock, Ulla had ascertained that the most common colour of vehicle entering the car park was pastel blue.

For the remainder of the week, Ulla's most challenging task turned out to be boredom control. By Thursday she had taken to typing letters to her friends at various universities around the GDR and usually described her work as 'manageable'. Her second week at the reception desk continued in a similar vein and the third was no better. Although Ulla was inordinately grateful not to have been assigned a job in a textiles factory or an assembly plant, she was clearly underemployed at the Ministry.

The new receptionist eventually decided that it was in her interest to look busier than she was. Having checked that there were no security cameras in the foyer, she began to pass the time by typing a rambling adventure story about a resourceful and heroic astronaut called Captain Cosmonova. The sole surviving officer following a mysterious attack on the lunar Peace Station, Cosmonova inspired a disparate international crew, now wracked by mutual distrust, to work together once more, re-establish contact with Earth and effect imaginative repairs to the station's damaged shuttle. Whilst the flame-haired Captain Cosmonova was in essence the unexplained love-child of Valentina Tereshkova and Ziggy Stardust, the cosmonaut's unflappable optimism and her unwavering faith in the leadership of the Communist Party satirised the conventions of socialist realism and therefore rendered Ulla's flight of fantasy unfit for public consumption. Once the young receptionist's irreverent pastiche was as complete as it ever would be, she walked up to the administration office on the second floor and judiciously fed it into the shredder.

17 IRONS IN THE FIRE

Madrid, Saturday 23rd November 1975

All in all, Jack Gilmore had fallen on his feet in Madrid. He was living in a compact but comfortable apartment on the fourth floor of a nineteenth-century block overlooking the noisy Glorieta Embajadores, a complex circulatory system that was nominally a straightforward roundabout. The apartment block, some twenty-five minutes' walk from the old city in one direction and the Retiro Park in another, was significantly in need of renovation but it was warm and dry and cheap. He shared the flat with its two legal tenants, Carmen and Ramón, who were both aspiring poets, and with Mirka, a fellow student from Lanchester.

Although he and Mirka had been aware since early in their second year at college that they would both be spending the first semester of their foreign study year in Madrid, they had at no point discussed the possibility of living together. Having chanced upon each other on the train from Bordeaux, they had decided there and then to join forces in the notoriously difficult search for accommodation.

Mirka Kimmich was three years older than Jack and a Swiss national. She had arrived at the British polytechnic via an expensive boarding school in Geneva, two years working as an instructor in an Alpine ski resort, and an eventful but corrosive marriage to a Zürich financier. It was Mirka who had bought the newspaper from the kiosk at Atocha station, had quickly found the advert in the classifieds and had countered Miguel's apology that both rooms had been let with the offer of a 500 Swiss franc finder's fee, payable in cash that very day. Although Mirka and Jack had previously spent little time in each other's company outside of lectures, they got on well and fell easily into shopping, cooking and cleaning as a unit.

Mirka also provided a sisterly shoulder to cry on when, two weeks after his arrival in Madrid, Jack received a deftly worded letter from his girlfriend in the UK abruptly ending their relationship. There were few senses, Hannah regretted, in which she and Jack could meaningfully be together when physically they were so far apart. Given time, she hoped, he would understand that her decision, although it would no doubt have come as a surprise, would free them both from an impossible situation.

Although the break-up with Hannah initially left Jack oscillating between hurt and indignation, Mirka took him under her wing and over the course of several evenings at a conveniently local bar, she encouraged him to accept disappointments as a fact of life and to find both the perspective and the cojones to deal with them. Under no circumstances, she repeatedly assured him, was she going to let him indulge in self-pity in the way that she had once done or become unnecessarily distracted from the opportunities that Madrid had to offer.

'You know what? We're a bit like a married couple,' said Mirka one evening in their regular corner of the bar, 'but without the arguments or the sex. Or the lawyers.'

Although Mirka and Jack flitted between languages in their day to day dealings with one another, they spoke Spanish as a matter of course with Carmen and Ramón. The couple's unabashed opinions of the recently deceased dictator,

General Franco, provided their lodgers not just with an impassioned view of contemporary Spanish history but with a whole new treasury of obscenities and disparaging idioms.

Each Saturday afternoon, Jack played five-a-side football for the Sporting Foreign Legion team at the impressive University Sports Complex. Composed predominantly of British and German nationals, the team lost more matches than they won, but it was nevertheless a regular and welcome opportunity to keep in shape and let off steam.

Returning from their defeat to Surreal Madrid, Jack was amazed to hear the bark of a dog in response to the turn of his key in the lock. Carmen and Ramón, it appeared, had acquired a pet. The six-month-old golden Labrador bounded to the door and jumped playfully at Jack's legs. She was undeniably cute, but would clearly require time to settle down.

'Do you like her?' asked Carmen with a broad smile that clearly indicated the expected response. 'We got her to celebrate the death of Franco. The next time Señora Cazorla calls me a fornicating whore and complains about the "ungodly noise" that Ramón and I make, I'll just blame it on Bonita.'

'I like the name. Where did you get her?'

'She's from the Refugio animal rescue centre in San Fermín. She's going to be a handful, I think. But every time she barks, it'll remind me of why we got her.'

Jack placed a paper bag containing four Portuguese-style pastries on the kitchen table, went to his room and slung the holdall containing his crumpled, sweaty football kit onto the bed. On his desk he spotted an envelope, presumably left there by Ramón, who acted as guardian of the mailbox.

The letter was from Professor MacKenzie. She trusted that Jack was well and was making good progress with his studies in Madrid. Turning to the question of his semester in Berlin, she alluded to the concerns she had previously expressed regarding his interest in the environmental policies of the GDR. In her time as an undergraduate at Cambridge, she reflected, she had often been impervious to advice and perhaps that had not always been a bad thing. In light of his continued determination to conduct primary research on both sides of the Wall, she had put out some feelers on his behalf and an interesting opportunity had arisen. The Professor wondered whether Jack might be interested in a part-time internship at Concordia, an environmental organisation based in the offices of the Church of Reconciliation in West Berlin. He should not, MacKenzie hastened to add, feel under any pressure and she would not explore the matter further until she had received written confirmation of his interest.

During a tutorial at Lanchester, the Professor had once referred somewhat obliquely to personal contacts who might be able to provide Jack with practical advice regarding his planned excursions to East Berlin. In subsequent meetings he had taken the careful vagueness of her references to 'avenues of enquiry' and 'irons in the fire' to indicate that tangible outcomes were uncertain. MacKenzie's letter, therefore, came as a complete and wholly welcome surprise. In the months since those initial conversations, the Professor had clearly gone to a considerable degree of effort on Jack's behalf.

The student recalled from his first-year lectures the arresting photographs of the abandoned Church of Reconciliation stranded within the East German border defences. He also knew that the Wall had ripped the entire parish in two, just as it had severed the East from the West. Jack looked again at the letter and smiled. Concordia might well have experience of dealing with the Environment Ministry in East Berlin. At the very least, he thought, they might be able to advise him on how to make an official approach.

Feeling like he'd just won the bottle of Tennessee Bourbon in a Christmas raffle, the student returned to the kitchen.

'Carmen and Ramón have taken the dog for a walk,' said Mirka. 'She was a bit too interested in the cakes. Anyway, I've made us a some tea.'

Unable to conceal his delight, Jack showed her the letter from MacKenzie.

'You know what, Jack Gilmore? You're so blinking jammy. She's definitely taken a shine to you. She really has. You're like her little project.'

'Sounds to me like someone's jealous, Ms Kimmich.'

'Well, where's *my* letter, then?'

Jack shrugged.

'I rest my case,' said Mirka. 'Guilty as charged.'

18 JUST SOUNDING OFF

East Berlin, Monday 15th December 1975

The Ministry for the Environment provided Ulla Wolfram with little respite from her frustrations at the absence of news about her grandfather. In the course of an eight-hour shift, the receptionist had welcomed perhaps four guests to the building, typed a similar number of standard letters on behalf of Press Secretary Fischer and had spent much of the remainder of the day systematically typing and shredding ever more outlandish Captain Cosmonova stories.

It was already dark when Ulla, now wrapped in her knee-length winter coat, knitted beret and multicoloured scarf, emerged from the Ministry building and set off on foot for the poorly maintained but preposterously cheap apartment that she had managed to rent through entirely unofficial channels. Although she missed her parents and the comforts of home, the flat was closer to work and, perhaps more importantly, it offered her a taste of the independence that Jenny and Rosa would be enjoying at university. The temperature had not climbed above zero all day and as Ulla walked, her breath condensed in the cold, dry air into small, wispy clouds. Already, the unmistakable smell of lignite smoke from many thousands of domestic chimneys hung heavily on the breeze. Striding purposefully, and seemingly in competition with others who were keen to escape the biting cold, Ulla turned finally into Fehrbelliner Strasse and headed in the direction of her flat. As the street itself was not well-lit, the greenish glow of the illuminated factory-chimney-and-sickle logo of the Konsum supermarket could be made out from a considerable distance. The long queue outside the shop indicated the probable arrival of goods that would normally be in short supply and suggested that Ulla would be unlikely to make it as far as the entrance before closing time.

Her enquiry to the two foot-stamping women at the back of the queue revealed that they had already waited over an hour and a half for the opportunity to buy some Christmas oranges.

'I'm going to send a petition to Honecker,' said the first of the two women, thoroughly fed up with the wait. 'It's the same every bloody year.'

'And you threaten to write to Honecker every bloody year,' replied her companion, adjusting the scarf around her neck as she spoke.

'Well, this year I really mean it. Honestly. I'm going to do it.'

'Don't listen to her,' said the woman with the scarf, now addressing Ulla. 'She's a typical Berliner. Just sounding off. She knows the General Secretary has better things to do than read petitions about fruit.'

Ulla smiled, wished the pair good luck in their quest and headed for her apartment at the far end of the street. She would buy her groceries tomorrow, she decided, once the stocks of oranges had been exhausted and the fuss had died down.

No more than three minutes later she arrived at the main door to the five-storey block, gave it a solid shove and went, as usual, straight to her mailbox. The envelope bearing Jenny's unmistakable handwriting brought an immediate smile to her face. Once in the flat, Ulla dropped the letter onto the kitchen table, flicked on the lights and, without removing her outer garments, set immediately about the task of loading lignite briquettes and dry newspaper into the wardrobe-sized, tiled oven that was her single source of heating. It would be at least an hour before she would dare to take off her coat.

Ulla sliced open the letter with a kitchen knife and was happy to read that Jenny was loving life at the University of Magdeburg. She was thoroughly enjoying her mathematics course, had also taken up fencing and in the process had met some truly wonderful people. Nevertheless, she missed Ulla and Rosa dearly and couldn't wait to see them both at Christmas. The three friends, she enthused, absolutely had to spend a celebratory evening at the Christmas market on Alexanderplatz just as soon as she and Rosa were back in Berlin. In conclusion, she hoped that Ulla's new job was going well and wondered whether she had perhaps met anyone interesting at work.

Cupping a hot mug of apple and cinnamon tea in her hands, Ulla reflected on the two shoppers outside Konsum and wondered whether they were any closer to the door or were perhaps still bickering about the advisability of submitting a petition to Erich Honecker. In one of her first Civics lessons, Ulla had been taught about, and genuinely inspired by, the Law of Petition which gave every citizen of the GDR the right to make pleas or offer advice to their Government.

'The foundation of socialism in the GDR,' her teacher had proudly declared, 'requires the extensive encouragement of criticism, in order to combat bureaucratic failings and distortions on the part of the state and prevent infringements of the legal rights of its citizens. In this regard, the Law of Petition gives individual citizens and social organisations the right, and I quote, to petition any official body or representative thereof with suggestions, advice, requests or complaints.'

The conversation outside the Konsum store, however, was the first time that Ulla had heard the slightest mention of petitions since that enlightening lesson when she was still in ninth grade. Before long, she found herself wondering how frequently her fellow citizens in reality exercised their legal right to submit proposals to those in authority. Would a skilfully worded plea to the appropriate Ministry stand a realistic chance of securing the exit visas that would allow the Wolframs to visit Opa Karl? Or would such a request simply invite yet more unwelcome attention from the representatives of the Ministry for State Security? One way or another, Ulla did not wish to end up like the recurrently disgruntled woman in the queue who seemingly did no more than salve her frustrations with idle threats to exercise her constitutional rights.

In the first instance, Ulla decided, she would talk the idea through with her parents. If they were in agreement, and she was by no means certain that they would be, she would also take the time to consult Franz Pedde, the legal adviser at the Ministry for the Environment. He would no doubt be able to offer an assessment of the advisability of the move and the likelihood of its success. He might even, if he were to give his blessing to Ulla's proposal, help her formulate the most persuasive arguments in support of her petition. Finally, Ulla wondered about the merits of sending her submission directly to a member of the Council of State, perhaps even to

Honecker himself. Whilst she could not know with absolute certainty whether such a petition would find its way onto the General Secretary's desk, she thought that it was not beyond the bounds of possibility. The law, she presumed, was there for a reason and who in their right mind would interfere with his mail?

19 PRIVATE SANCTUARIES

East Berlin, Saturday 24th January 1976

Without news from Munich or even a Christmas card from either Uncle Tommi or Opa Karl, the festive season had provided little cause for celebration and January had been uneventful and cold. Ulla thought better of petitioning Honecker to grant the family travel visas and tried to devote her considerable energies to ice hockey. With the outside temperature hovering around minus four, Ulla's parents arrived some three minutes late for the match between Dynamo Berlin and Dynamo Weisswasser. Although the official Upper League matches were always well attended, the U20 teams attracted no more than sporadic support and the Werner-Seelenbinder-Arena was far from full. In the four years that Ulla had been playing for Dynamo Berlin, her parents had not missed a single home fixture.

As they edged to their seats, their daughter was in the thick of the action. With Dynamo Berlin applying constant pressure to their rivals, the puck rimmed the boards and was deftly picked up by Ulla, who feinted past a Weisswasser defender, made space for herself and unleashed a fearsome shot at goal. The goaltender could do no more than deflect the puck into the roof of the net and the home side had an early lead.

Whilst the Wolframs were inherently vociferous supporters, neither could muster much enthusiasm for the score. This morning's letter from Munich had left the couple numb and Udo Wolfram had not the remotest inkling as to how he would break the news of his father's death to Ulla. Eva and Udo had nevertheless concluded that to make any kind of announcement immediately after the match, and particularly in the presence of Ulla's teammates, would probably be the most unkind of several undesirable options. They would, they decided, invite their daughter back to the family nest in Karlshorst before turning her world upside down. Only in the event that Ulla had already made plans for the afternoon, might they be forced to intimate that they had received some unwelcome news. That, at least, was the plan.

Almost an hour after the match, Ulla arrived in the foyer amidst a gaggle of noisy teammates, still buoyed up by their hard-fought but undoubtedly well-deserved victory.

'What's wrong?' asked Ulla, the moment she registered the ashen look on her father's face.

'Not here,' said her mother. 'We'll talk about it at home.'

'Is it Opa?' asked Ulla, more insistently this time.

A tear had already begun to slip down Udo Wolfram's cheek.

'We lost him,' said Ulla's father, his voice faltering as his emotions refused to be held in check.

'He's gone,' said Ulla's mother solemnly.

Needing both to comfort and to be comforted, Ulla dropped her kit bag and pushed herself into her father's arms. They exchanged few words beyond terse statements of disbelief, but held each other more tightly than they had done since Ulla was a child. With her head pressed into her father's chest, the visceral quality of his quiet sobs was inescapable. As the scene unfolded, Ulla's teammates, who were well aware of her grandfather's situation, put two and two together and with little more than an exchange of glances left the Wolfram family to their sorrow. When Udo finally released his daughter from the embrace, the family was alone in the foyer.

'Can I come back with you?' said Ulla. 'To Karlshorst. I really don't want to go to the flat.'

'Of course,' replied her mother. 'It's still your home.'

On the steps outside the stadium, Ulla's raw emotion suddenly provoked a blizzard of questions. When and how did they find out? Were they totally sure that Opa had died? Had there perhaps been two patients with the same name? Could they speak to someone at the hospital? Why hadn't the pacemaker done its job? Had it failed? Or had there been some other kind of problem? When would the funeral be? Would it be in Munich? If so, would they be able get a travel permit? Surely there could be no reason to refuse the family a visa now.

Udo Wolfram responded to his daughter's spiralling requests for elucidation with the well-intentioned lie that he didn't know much at this stage beyond what he had already told her. They had received a letter from Uncle Tommi that morning, he explained, and he would let Ulla read it as soon as they were back in Karlshorst. Firstly, however, they would need to go to her flat to drop off her ice hockey kit and help her pack an overnight bag.

To escape the northerly breeze, the family took the tram to Schönhauser Allee and then a bus down to Fehrbelliner Strasse. In Ulla's flat, Eva's mother could not help but lament the poor state of repair, the lack of reliable heating and Ulla's blossoming tendency towards untidiness. Yet although Eva Wolfram missed her daughter, she knew in her heart that Ulla was doing no more than embracing the kind of spirited independence that her university friends now enjoyed. She could hardly blame her daughter for that.

With clothes packed for at least a couple of days, Ulla walked with her parents to Senefelder Platz, took the U-Bahn to Alexanderplatz and waited for the S-Bahn to Karlshorst. Enveloped in the crowded warmth of a carriage and knowing that they would soon be home, the family settled into silence. Ulla became lost in memories of her Opa performing conjuring tricks, teaching her to cook or taking the sting out of her anger whenever she was upset. Her father ruminated on Ulla's likely reaction to seeing the letter from Munich and her mother allowed them both to meander about their thoughts.

Once back in the family apartment, Ulla dumped her bag in her surprisingly tidy bedroom and joined her parents in the kitchen. As her mother set about re-heating a pan of Spree Forest potato soup, Karl Wolfram fetched the letter from his uncle and without a word handed it to Ulla.

It was with deepest regret that Uncle Tommi announced himself to be the bearer of unhappy news. His dear brother Karl, he was sorry to tell them, had succumbed to sepsis following the rapid spread of an infection at the site of his pacemaker implantation. Karl's doctors had transferred their patient from the convalescent home where he had been recuperating back to the University Hospital in Munich, but sadly he had passed away in the ambulance. Uncle Thomas went on to outline the provisional arrangements for his brother's funeral. A date had been set for Friday the nineteenth of December and he hoped and prayed that the choice of date would allow sufficient time for Udo and his family to secure the necessary visas to attend.

'This doesn't make sense,' said Ulla, feeling like her brain was fit to implode. 'When did Uncle Tommi write this?'

'Look at the date,' said her father in a leaden voice. 'That's why we never got a Christmas card.'

Although the letter had apparently been written two days after Karl's death, it had taken almost seven weeks to find its way to the Wolframs' address in Karlshorst. Unless the funeral arrangements had at some point been changed, and Udo had received no communication to that effect, the family had missed Opa Karl's funeral by over a month.

'This can't be right,' said Ulla, her face a picture of confusion. 'This can't be right. It can't be. If this is right, it means that when we wrote our Christmas card to Opa, he was already...'

She could not complete the sentence. She dissolved into tears and although her mother's comforting arm was rapidly around her waist, Ulla hardly noticed.

'I know,' said her father grimly.

'You have to phone Uncle Tommi,' implored Ulla.

'I've tried,' said her father. 'As soon as I got the letter. You just get the same recorded voice saying "no connection under this number". Every bloody time.'

'It's the same from the phone box,' said her mother with a shrug.

Ulla felt like the blood was draining from her head and somehow pooling in her stomach. It was an open secret that the Stasi regularly opened mail arriving from the Federal Republic. Millions of letters arrived late, sometimes with the date stamp carefully smudged, sometimes with the expected gift of hard currency removed. Others simply did not arrive at all. No doubt Erich Mielke prided himself that he was defending the German Democratic Republic from the unholy influence of those who would seek to undermine it. No doubt Erich Honecker shared in that swollen pride. No doubt they both contended that the price of peace was constant vigilance. As far as Ulla was concerned, the price of constant vigilance was being paid by hard-working and entirely loyal families such as hers. The treatment meted out to the Wolframs rode roughshod over any pretence to humanity. This was disrespect. This was manipulation. This was the most contemptuous mistrust of the very citizens the Stasi claimed to defend.

Ulla stood up and ran to her bedroom. She sat on her bed and pulled the duvet to one side. Letting out a yowl that encapsulated every emotion she was feeling, she unleashed a torrent of blows on the undeserving pillow. When eventually she relented and stared breathlessly into space, the sickness in the pit of her stomach had eased a little but was far from gone. Attracted to their daughter's room by the angry grunts that had accompanied the belligerence, Ulla's parents stood open-mouthed at the door.

'Sorry,' said Ulla, eventually aware of their presence.

'You don't have to say sorry,' her mother replied. 'It's just... Well, I've never seen you like that.'

'Feel any better for that?' asked her father.

'Not really.'

After eating, the family took a decision to get some fresh air. Ulla's father walked to the phone booth at the S-Bahn station, where he made several more unsuccessful attempts to contact Uncle Tommi in Munich. Ulla and her mother wandered to the nearby colony of allotments and small gardens which at this time of year was almost completely deserted. As they made their way through the patchwork of private sanctuaries, they complained, speculated and listened in turn. Fearful of the consequences of kicking up a fuss, Ulla's mother rejected all suggestion of lodging an official complaint. However unjust their treatment, there was no possible course of action open to them beyond going to work on Monday and behaving as though nothing had happened.

By four, the light was fading and the wind was beginning to bite. As the pair slowly found their way back to Loreleystrasse, Ulla's thoughts of her beautiful grandfather were interspersed with images of her father quietly sobbing in her arms after the ice hockey match. Devastated at the loss of her beloved Opa Karl and incensed at the coldhearted treatment of her family, Ulla made a decision without the slightest consideration for the ramifications but certain that she should keep it from her parents. With or without the sanction of the authorities, she would find a way to travel to Munich to lay a rose on her grandfather's solitary grave.

20 WHERE TO START

East Berlin, Wednesday 28th January 1976

Given the circumstances, Ulla readily accepted her mother's invitation to retreat for a couple of weeks to the family home in Karlshorst.

For his part, Udo Wolfram sought, and was more than a little surprised to be granted, a week's compassionate leave from the Berlin Gas and Light company. During this period, the unwelcome but poignantly mundane duties that the dead bequeath to the living provided him with periods of distraction but also moments of raw distress. Udo registered his father's death, cancelled his pension and wound up the tenancy agreement to the single-bedroomed apartment in Ehrenfelsstrasse. With the rent paid only until the end of the following month, Udo would soon need to contemplate the unenviable task of sorting through his father's personal effects, disposing somehow of his furniture and donating his clothes to the Red Cross.

Eva continued to work, but returned from school at one thirty each day to offer her husband a sympathetic ear if he needed it or to be a supportive presence during his episodes of rumination.

Each morning, Ulla took the S-Bahn to Alexanderplatz, kept herself to herself at work and only mentioned the loss of Opa Karl when Press Secretary Fischer eventually commented on her unusually subdued demeanour. She spent her evenings on the sofa in the reassuring company of her parents, embracing the familiar and gaining some measure of solace from their shared experience of grief.

On the Friday evening before Ulla planned to return to her flat in Prenzlauer Berg, the Wolframs gathered around their black and white TV and watched a Bud Spencer action-comedy. Although the knockabout, low-budget movie would, under normal circumstances, have been a nailed-on guarantee of entertainment, Ulla's thoughts were palpably elsewhere. When not revisiting significant moments spent with her grandfather or considering every eventuality that might have obviated his death, she was quietly obsessing about the idea of extricating herself from the GDR.

If Ulla's decision to turn her back on the German Democratic Republic had been forged in the fire of her anger, it was by no means out of character. In her teenage years, knee-jerk reactions to stressful or unexpected events had been a regular occurrence, but she had often reversed, or at least modified, her decisions in the cold light of day. In the majority of cases, her change of perspective had followed an hour or two in the company of her grandfather, a man who had possessed the seemingly effortless knack of steering her into less stormy waters without specifically telling her what to do.

On more than one occasion during her return to Loreleystrasse, Ulla's parents had quietly alluded to the fact that they would both be retired within six years and would then be able to emigrate legally to the Federal Republic. This evening, over dinner, they once again tentatively referred to Ulla's ice hockey career as a potentially risk-free pathway to a less constricted life in the West. Their daughter's disinterested shrug suggested a reluctance even to consider such a possibility, but in reality masked both the nagging urgency of her desire to desert the GDR and the painful awareness that she lacked the wherewithal to do so. There could certainly be no question of Ulla revealing her nascent thoughts to her parents. In the first instance, the conversation would be make them complicit to a crime under East German law, were she subsequently to effect, or even attempt, an escape. More immediately, the revelation of her urge to engage in such a fundamentally risky undertaking would burden them with unnecessary anxiety and inevitably invite an ongoing barrage of dissuasion.

Although Ulla was still far from conceiving a viable plan, she knew from the outset that any bid to take on the intimidating and constantly monitored concrete and wire of the Berlin Wall would be tantamount to a death wish. In the privacy of their Karlshorst apartment, she and her parents had seen a number of West German TV shows documenting the patient construction of tunnels under the border installations or featuring dramatised reconstructions of daring and ingenious escapes. The majority, however, had been carried out in the early years of the Wall. By the 1970s, the GDR had developed both the ugly sophistication of the death strip and the rigour of its surveillance to such a degree that previously successful methods of escape were now inherently futile. In recent years, scores of aspiring escapees had lost their lives under the glare of the searchlights or had been dragged bleeding from the tangle of barbed wire to face a punitive jail term.

Successful escapes, the most recent documentaries revealed, tended to involve a small network of helpers on both sides of the border and depended on some combination of deception, disguise, counterfeit documents and knowledge of the border guards' routines. Whilst thoughts of somehow arming herself with a fake passport and breezing unchallenged through the controls still felt to Ulla like little more than a pipe-dream, others had clearly pulled it off, so why shouldn't she? As far as she could fathom, the real question that confronted her was knowing where to start. Ulla could think of only one person who might conceivably have the kind of connections that would be of use to her. His name was Mick Jaeger and he sold bootleg David Bowie cassettes.

21 EARS ONLY

East Berlin, Wednesday 4th February 1976

A peremptory summons to a meeting in Major General Konrad's office was the last thing Captain Hartling really needed. Although the head of the Main Directory for Reconnaissance had offered no hint of an agenda, his subordinate was unwilling to waste time in speculation. He had more personal matters on his mind. Chief amongst them were the almost impossible demands his British handler had made of him.

The deadline for the supply of verifiable, strategic intelligence had already boiled itself down from six months to six weeks and Hartling was no closer to his goal. Should he fail to deliver, the offer of a new identity and a generously funded life in the West would be off the table. As he approached the office occupied by Major General Konrad's secretary, the Stasi captain still had no firm idea how someone of his clearance level might access the kind of materials that MI6 had specified.

The door to room 509 was open.

'Ah, thank goodness you're here,' said Frau Schiller, clearly in a state of some agitation. 'How much do you know about typewriters?'

Hartling smiled. 'And good afternoon to you too, comrade.'

Irene Schiller's desktop lacked its usual, immaculate sense of order. Her stenographer's notebook had been pushed away in frustration, knocking her statuette of Lenin onto its side. The ripped orange and white packaging from a typewriter cartridge plus the black plastic cartridge itself lay at uncharacteristically jaunty angles on a partly opened pack of typing paper. The cover to her state-of-the-art Olympia typewriter had been pulled back to reveal a selection of hammers and a recently expired cartridge.

'I'm completely snowed under,' said Schiller. 'And a fancy new West German machine is all fine and dandy, but the long and short of it is, it's no damn good to anyone if the used-up cartridges won't come out.'

'Is there an instruction booklet?' asked Hartling.

'Yes, but for some reason, it's in Spanish.'

'Ah. Not good. Would you like me to take a look?'

'Do you speak Spanish?'

'No, I meant, would you like me to take a look at the typewriter?'

'Oh, yes. Definitely. It's a good machine, but I'd like it a whole lot better if I could work out how to change the damn ribbon. They showed me last week when they delivered it for the Major General's big pow-wow but honestly, I'm hopeless with new stuff. There's a red button next to the cartridge, but it doesn't seem to do anything and I don't want to press it too hard in case it breaks.'

Hartling joined Frau Schiller on the business side of the desk and fiddled gently with the workings of the typewriter. The red button, as his colleague had warned, resisted downward pressure, but could easily be moved backwards, immediately lifting the carbon ribbon clear of the guide mechanism and away from the hammers. With the tape also clear of the paper, Hartling was astonished to be able to make out two unbroken, parallel lines of jumbled text. Although neither row made any obvious sense, the cartridge presumably contained an encrypted record of every communication, report and protocol that Irene Schiller had typed in the past seven days. Conceivably, it might contain the minutes of meetings with high-ranking Party officials, with senior military personnel or with the Minister for State Security. Such files would be subject to the highest levels of secrecy.

'OK. That seems to have freed up the mechanism,' he said reassuringly. 'Let me try to remove it for you now. If it breaks, you can blame it on me.'

Cautiously, he eased the tape out of the guide mechanism, and popped the cartridge out of the machine.

'There we go, comrade. Job done. Shall I throw the offending item in the bin?'

'Oh, gosh no,' said Frau Schiller, a mild look of horror on her face. 'They have to be incinerated when they're finished. Hand it to me. I'll keep it in my desk and take it to the secure disposal bin in the Secretariat as soon as I have a free five minutes.'

This, Hartling recognised, was his moment.

'Relax, Irene, I can see you're under massive pressure here. I know I'm due to see Konrad in a couple of minutes, but he's clearly not ready yet. I tell you what. At the very least, allow me to carry out a favour for an overworked colleague. I'll drop this uncooperative bit of junk off at the Secretariat whilst you have a go at installing that new cartridge.'

At the door, Hartling turned, as though possessed of a sudden afterthought.

'Is there anything else you need from the Secretariat whilst I'm down there?'

Irene Schiller, however, was already too distracted by the replacement cartridge to give much thought to his question.

'No,' she said. 'No. I'm fine.'

Once in the corridor, Hartling slipped the cartridge into his jacket pocket, walked calmly to his office and exchanged the typewriter ribbon for a blank audio cassette. Less than thirty seconds later, he greeted the staff in the Secretariat and breezily enquired whether the secure disposal unit was in its usual place. Making a point of rattling the sprung steel flap at the top of the bin, he dropped the unused cassette inside. As far as appearances were concerned, he had done exactly as he had promised Frau Schiller.

Hartling returned to room 509 and smiled again at his colleague.

'All done.'

'Could you check I've put the new one in properly?' she asked.

'Sure.'

'What would I do without you?'

'Well, maybe you'd have to phone Fidel Castro for help with the instructions. But all joking aside, comrade Schiller, we stand together before a common purpose. We know only too well that the enemies of socialism never sleep and it was my duty, as well as my pleasure, to afford you whatever assistance I could.'

Major General Konrad opened the connecting door from his more spacious office, invited Hartling in and ushered him to the conference table.

The high-ranking officer glanced at the doors to ensure that both were closed. 'Much of what I am about to tell you,

Captain Hartling, is for your ears only and may not be discussed outside this room.'

'Understood.'

'Before I begin, we should remind ourselves that the primary foreign policy objective of the Soviet Union is the maintenance of peace and the preservation of the status quo in Europe. We can be proud that the GDR stands shoulder to shoulder with the USSR in its aspirations to prevent war ever again from breaking out on German soil.'

'Sir.'

'Of course, it would be unwise to assume that the Americans share the same humanitarian goals. With these realities in mind, the Main Directorate for Reconnaissance recently hosted a meeting chaired by Major General Ivanovsky, the Commander of Soviet Forces in the GDR. Around this very table we discussed the hypothetical day, codenamed Day X, on which the Soviet Union might feel so threatened by NATO that it would have no option but to launch pre-emptive strikes against targets such as West Berlin. Most of our discussion centred on the military planning for Day X and had no relevance to your particular field of expertise, but it was agreed that a key element of the operation would be the use of deep cover agents based in West Berlin.'

'As saboteurs, presumably.'

'Not exactly. The role of these agents would be to locate and neutralise certain politicians, senior police officers, journalists, academics and so on. Imperialists, bourgeois fascists, professional liars, you know the sort. In due course you will receive the exact number of agents to be recruited, trained and equipped. In the meantime, you will co-ordinate the scouting of potential assets in West Berlin. I take it, you have the capacity for this assignment.'

'Yes, sir. Absolutely.'

'Good. And one final thing, Hartling. You will refer to the assignment as "Akrobat" and, as far as your junior colleagues are concerned, it is a standalone operation. You will not, under any circumstances, refer to Day X outside these four walls. That, as I said, was for your ears only.'

'Very good, sir. Leave it with me.'

'Oh I very much intend to. Brief me on any developments. Dismissed.'

Whilst Major General Konrad had intended to tell Captain Hartling no more than he needed to know, he had told him far too much. It was now abundantly clear to the disaffected officer that the stolen typewriter cartridge in his desk drawer, if he could verify its contents, might conceal exactly the kind of high-level intelligence that MI6 had pressed him to supply.

22 KEYSTROKES

East Berlin, Thursday 12th February 1976

It was comfortably past eight o'clock in the evening and Captain Hartling, dressed in his military uniform, was still at his desk. Although a full week had elapsed since his theft of the typewriter cartridge, the hotchpotch of letters and numerals on the carbon tape had proved stubbornly resistant to decryption and a riskier approach was now required.

Confident, if by no means certain, that he was the last person on the fifth floor still at work, Hartling stood, picked up his attaché case and quietly left his office. The corridor was silent and unlit and that was exactly as he wanted it. Ghosting past each door, he listened as he passed for sounds of activity and checked that no glimmer of light betrayed the presence of a colleague.

At the Secretariat, he removed his white dress gloves from the briefcase and pulled them on. He opened the door and switched on the lights. After waiting the inevitable couple of seconds for the more reluctant fluorescent bulbs to flicker to life, the MfS officer walked calmly to an unmarked cabinet and opened it. The key to every office on the fifth floor, except for his, hung reassuringly on its hook.

Now freed of any last concern that he might have company, Hartling removed the key to the office used by Major General Konrad's secretary, extinguished the lights and left the room. Within sixty seconds he had installed himself at Irene Schiller's work station. He snapped open the cover to the typewriter, removed the cartridge and, with his gloved index finger in the teeth of the spool, advanced the ribbon slightly so that all that he could see was unadulterated tape. The cartridge re-installed, Hartling fed a sheet of blank paper into the machine and typed 'abc de f 123 45 6'. With luck, the simplicity of the input would be the key to unlocking the encryption.

When he examined the ribbon for a second time, he could have kicked himself in exasperation. So used to addressing complexity, he had been incapable of seeing a solution that was deceptive in its simplicity. The twelve letters and numerals he had typed were all present but were now distributed across two separate rows. For reasons apparent only to the developers of the typewriter, the hammers alternated between the upper and lower rows with each strike. To track the order of the keystrokes, the MfS officer needed merely to alternate between the two lines of characters and figure out where to insert the spaces. Satisfied with the outcome of his extra shift, Hartling removed the paper from the machine, placed it in his attaché case and left the room exactly as he had found it.

The fifth floor was, as far as he could ascertain, still completely deserted. The Stasi officer collected his greatcoat and returned the keys in his possession to the Secretariat. He met no-one on the stairs. Once outside the building, Hartling crossed the internal courtyard to the Ruschestrasse exit and bid a respectful goodnight to the two guards contending with the unremitting cold of a winter evening.

Perhaps forty-five minutes later, the MfS officer opened the door to his modest apartment in Klement-Gottwald-Allee. He was undoubtedly tired, but sleep was the last thing on his mind. In the kitchen, he switched on the coffee machine and dolloped two spoonfuls of Jacobs Brasiliana into the filter. As the percolator began to gurgle and spit, Hartling removed a box of GDR-produced Corn Flakes from a cupboard, pushed his fingers into the cereal and retrieved the plastic bag containing the stolen typewriter cartridge. Certain that he could read its contents, he was eager to confirm its value.

Ten painstaking minutes after initially picking out the words 'Army General Ivanovsky', Hartling knew that he had struck gold. The typewriter ribbon contained the minutes of a recent meeting in which high-ranking officers from the Soviet Union and the GDR had discussed their readiness for a military strike against West Berlin. The would-be defector allowed himself a smile. MI6, once they understood the nature of the intelligence on offer, would be only too ready to set him up with a well-funded and quietly unimpeachable life in the West.

23 CREATURES OF INSTINCT

Madrid, Saturday 21st February 1976

'Is it your birthday?' asked Carmen, as she handed Jack the mail-service card inviting the British student to collect a registered package from a local post office.

'If it's a birthday present,' he said, 'then it's either four months late or eight months early.'

Intrigued as to the likely origin of his parcel, he wandered down to the small, understaffed post office on the Ronda de Toledo. Beneath a dull sky, Madrid seemed comparatively quiet, particularly for a Saturday morning. The city had recently entered a phase of political uncertainty. Whilst the incumbent Francoist government saw little need for reform following the death of their longstanding leader, change was nevertheless in the air. From his offices in Madrid, King Juan Carlos, the new head of state, was attempting to manoeuvre the polarised nation onto a path towards pluralism, a new constitution and recognisable democracy. In a poky tobacconist's shop, Jack bought a stamp and a postcard of the King. He would in due course send the card to his father with a brief confirmation of his continued wellbeing.

Following twenty sluggish minutes in the queue for the counter and a further delay whilst the clerk sifted through a pile of deliveries in a separate room, Jack was finally rewarded for his patience with a smile, a robust A4 envelope and a small, yellow form to sign. The corporate franking indicated that the package originated from Lanchester Polytechnic. Consumed by curiosity, Jack stopped at a free counter near the entrance and, using his front door key as a knife, ripped open the end of the parcel.

Inside, he discovered two letters in crisp, unsealed envelopes. The first was from Professor MacKenzie. She acknowledged Jack's expression of interest in the possibility of an internship in West Berlin and was pleased to inform him that she had secured him a part-time, unpaid post at Concordia, the environmental initiative run by the Church of Reconciliation. In the first instance, MacKenzie wrote, the internship would undoubtedly provide Jack with useful insights into environmental policy, particularly, but not exclusively, in the West. Furthermore, Pastor Stefan Niemeyer, the priest with overarching responsibility for the fabric of the neglected church and the pastoral care of its ghost parish, had generously agreed to provide Jack with a degree of support. Not only would the pastor offer the British student guidance on dealing with official bodies in the East, he had also drafted a testimonial, an unsigned copy of which was enclosed. Pastor Niemeyer, MacKenzie added, would happily endorse the original once Jack presented himself at the Concordia offices in West Berlin.

Eagerly, Jack pulled the copy of Niemeyer's letter from the second envelope. The document, which was addressed to the Minister for the Environment in East Berlin, accredited the visiting British student as an intern at Concordia, vouched for Jack's research and confirmed the dual focus of his planned dissertation. Pastor Niemeyer concluded his letter by inviting the Minister to consider granting Jack the privilege of an interview, if not with himself, then perhaps with a suitable representative.

Demonstrating uncharacteristic care, Jack replaced the letters in their original envelopes and tucked them into his sports bag. Scarcely able to contain his delight at the extent to which Professor MacKenzie had oiled the wheels of his planned research, he walked to the Metro at a sprightly pace. In little over an hour he was sitting in a crowded changing room at the University Sports Complex, ready to put in an enthusiastic appearance for Sporting Foreign Legion.

Returning from the narrowest of victories over Simpático de Madrid, the student emerged from the Glorieta Embajadores underground station into what remained of the daylight. At the *pasteleria*, Jack invested in four custard and meringue filled pastries and hoped that his flatmates would be in.

The young Labrador scampered to greet him as he entered the apartment.

'We're in the kitchen,' shouted Mirka.

By the time Jack had hung up his coat and joined them, Ramón had produced a bottle of sparkling Cava from the fridge. On the table were four fluted glasses and two letters. The first was from Ramón's mother, a staunch supporter of the recently deceased General Franco, agreeing at last to visit her unmarried son in the flat he shared with 'that woman'. The second was from a publisher in Barcelona, expressing interest in Carmen's collection of unsettling poems.

With the Cava and the pastries finished off in a matter of minutes, the poets put a leash on the dog and dragged Jack and Mirka to a bar to continue the celebrations. After a cold beer and some indifferent tapas, Carmen and Ramón caught their second wind and announced suddenly that they were taking their eager Labrador to stretch its legs. The two Lanchester students simply ordered more beers.

Over a final glass of San Miguel, Jack told Mirka about the package he had received from Professor MacKenzie and the excitement he was consequently beginning to feel about his semester in Berlin. Mirka was, she confessed, slightly jealous of the special attention that Jack persistently received. Shortly after ten, the pair settled up at the bar and drifted back towards the flat, swapping increasingly preposterous ideas about their respective futures and trading anecdotes of loves won and lost.

As the pair made their unsteady way up the creaking stairs to the fourth floor, they linked arms for mutual support. At the door, Mirka rooted in her bag for her key, before dangling it breezily in front of Jack's face.

'Would you like to come in?'

Neither would subsequently remember who had initiated the embrace, but as they squashed together in the unlit doorway, they somehow fell into each other's arms. Although the tenderness of their kiss seemed to refute all possibility of regret, in the slow fumble to undue the buttons of each other's coats Mirka was mugged by a sudden sense of perspective. Gently grasping Jack's wrists and guiding his hands away from her body, she straightened and sighed somewhat regretfully before questioning the wisdom of taking things any further. Perhaps, she suggested, they should wind the clock back a few minutes and by-pass the risk of undermining a perfectly good friendship. Slightly confused, but guessing that Mirka had been in this kind of situation before and that it hadn't ended well, Jack deferred to her uncertainty.

Mirka proposed affectionately that they should take a moment to re-set, before attempting to restore normality with the aid of two large mugs of English breakfast tea.

'You know what?' she said, trying to catch Jack's reluctant gaze as they faced each other across the kitchen table. 'Life doesn't come with a manual. We don't need to beat ourselves up over this. Ultimately we're creatures of instinct. Desire trumps all logic at times. Put a skinful of San Miguel and a couple of sob stories into the mix and common sense doesn't stand a chance. We're not the first friends in the history of the world to almost end up into bed together and we certainly won't be the last.'

Jack knew that she was right, but had little real idea of how to respond. Although their unexpected foray into intimacy had lasted no more than sixty seconds, the pair needed the best part of two weeks before they could once more look each other in the eye.

24 CHIMNEY SMOKE

East Berlin, Saturday 1st March 1976

On each of the previous four Saturdays, ice hockey had provided Ulla with both an outlet for her considerable energies and some temporary respite from her grief. With no matches scheduled for the following two weeks, she was determined to locate her supplier of bootleg David Bowie cassettes. He might, she hoped, just possibly have connections to the kind of people who could assist her with her still shapeless plans to remove herself from the GDR. Given the illicit nature of Mick Jaeger's business, however, he was not necessarily the easiest of people to track down. On any given Saturday morning, he was careful to flit between several inconspicuous pitches in the busy shopping quarter of East Berlin. Constantly, he worked to blend in with the crowd and disappeared in an instant whenever he felt exposed.

The cagey trader had begun the second hour of his working day by stationing himself outside the Centrum department store, directly beneath the overhang of the external staircase to the walkway that ringed the first floor. The enclosed architecture coupled to the comings and goings of weekend shoppers served to afford Jaeger a reasonable sense of security from unwanted scrutiny and furthermore, the entrance to the store provided him with a bolt-hole if for any reason he suddenly felt it would be in his interest to effect a sharp exit. When footfall into Centrum was slack, the black-marketeer would invite prospective clients into the store and mooch around the ground floor as they surreptitiously discussed orders for counterfeit Rolling Stones cassettes or questionably sourced cosmetics.

Following a moderately brisk walk from her flat in Fehrbelliner Strasse and a fruitless hour visiting several of Mick Jaeger's known haunts, Ulla approached the entrance to the store and, with few shoppers yet in evidence, easily picked out the silhouette of his goatee beard against the light from behind the concrete staircase.

'What cassettes can you get me?' asked Ulla directly.

'Not here,' replied Jaeger, without engaging her gaze. 'Let's do a little shopping. I'm thinking about buying a colour TV.'

About five minutes later, Ulla located her supplier of illicit cassettes studying a bank of Colortron TVs, none of which were connected to a power supply. Without a word, she stood beside him and examined one of the sets.

'Four thousand Marks,' said Jaeger, 'and even if you want to stump up five months' salary, you can't take one away from the store. You still have to go on a freaking waiting list. Plus, and God knows why this is, they only show West-TV in black and white. I mean, what's the point? Anyway, missy. What can I do for you this time?'

'Actually, to be honest, I'm not really after cassettes. It's something a bit harder to get hold of.'

'Oh, yes?' replied Jaeger, his curiosity piqued. Had his client perhaps developed a taste for Marlboro cigarettes or did she maybe want to give her grandmother a silk scarf for her birthday?

Ulla's request caught Jaeger completely by surprise. 'I want to know if you can get hold of counterfeit passports or exit visa stamps. Or both.'

'For crying out loud, keep your bloody voice down. Listen, if I sold stuff like that, do you think I'd be telling you I can't afford a TV set?'

'But you must know,' said Ulla, trying a little harder now not to attract attention, 'the kind of people who can get things like that.'

'As I said, I don't do that sort of thing,' whispered Jaeger, now growing suspicious that Ulla might conceivably be a Stasi stooge. 'And who I know and who I don't know is none of your freaking business.'

'I'd make it worth your while,' said Ulla. 'I've just come in to some money.'

In fact, Ulla had no idea how she could finance such a transaction. Although her father had recently informed her that she was due to inherit a thousand East German marks from her grandfather, she suspected that such a sum would be nowhere near enough, particularly if the suppliers required payment in western currency. For now, she simply wanted to appraise herself of the possibilities.

'OK,' said Jaeger, clearly keen to leave the store. 'I'll meet you in Treptower Park. At three o'clock. By the *Mother Russia* statue. Make sure you're on time, because I won't wait around.'

'Thanks,' said Ulla. She turned to catch his eye, but Mick Jaeger was already heading for the staircase.

With almost four hours to kill, the prospective client found her way out of Centrum, ambled her way back to her flat and then on to a popular *Currywurst* kiosk under the Magistrate's Viaduct in Schönhauser Allee. Her hunger satisfied, Ulla slowly retraced her steps in the direction of Alexanderplatz. As she walked, she speculated as to the possible forms of assistance that Mick Jaeger's illicit contacts might offer her and she wondered how she should respond to the exorbitant fee that they would inevitably demand.

When Ulla stepped off the S-Bahn at Treptower Park shortly before twenty to three, she was nervous in the way she had sometimes been before taking her first steps onto the ice at the start of a crucial hockey match. The nerves, she had gradually learned, were old friends who turned up at inconvenient moments, but had her best interests at heart and kept her senses sharp. In the park, it was still cold and a low sun hung in a clear blue sky, slanting long shadows from the leafless maples that flanked the path towards her destination.

Within ten minutes Ulla was waiting a few metres from *Mother Russia*, the post-war Soviet statue of a woman grieving for her fallen sons. The aspiring escapee was early and there was no sign of Mick Jaeger, but he would no doubt turn up in due course. As she checked out each and every passer-by, it became clear to her that almost every visitor to the park was either heading directly to, or returning from, the Soviet War Memorial, perhaps some three hundred metres from where she was standing. The monumental statue of a Soviet soldier, carrying a child in one arm and resting his sword on a shattered swastika, both commemorated the eighty thousand Soviet troops who had lost their lives in the gruesome battle for Berlin and made an unequivocal statement about the new realities in post-war Europe. Mick Jaeger, she thought, had set up their meeting well. No-one in the vicinity of their rendezvous point seemed inclined to pay attention to anything but the towering monument at the far end of the park or the route back to the S-Bahn.

At three o'clock, there was still no sign of Ulla's contact and by twenty past, she was beginning to grow concerned. After a further twenty minutes on tenterhooks, it had become abundantly clear to her that Mick Jaeger, for whatever reason, was not going to show up and there was little point in waiting any longer. It would, in any case, soon be dark.

The most plausible explanation for Jaeger's no-show was not easy to determine. Maybe the minor criminal had suddenly found himself way out of his depth. Maybe he feared entrapment and Ulla's unexpected approach had simply spooked him. Maybe he knew that whatever the price of counterfeit visas was, a fresh-faced young woman with a penchant for David Bowie would scarcely be in a position to afford it. Whatever the case, Ulla resolved to take herself back to Centrum after work on Monday and to speak to the petty bootlegger a second time. As things stood, he was her only possible conduit to the kind of help she needed. Short, however, of presenting him with a suitcase full of American dollars, she struggled at this point to see how any subsequent approach might result in a fundamentally different outcome.

Over the following two weeks, Ulla made repeated visits to the Centrum department store plus a handful of speculative trips to Mick Jaeger's secondary haunt near the Immanuel Kant Extended Upper School. For his part, the elusive trader could no more be pinned down than chimney smoke on the Berlin air.

25 THE GARDEN PATH

West Berlin, Tuesday 16th March 1976

From a clear sky the low sunshine angled through occasional gaps between the turn-of-the century apartment blocks, contending with the chilly air and in places melting the overnight frost on the pavements or on the windscreen of a parked VW Golf. Dressed in an American overcoat and one of the sharp business suits that he customarily wore for his forays into West Berlin, Captain Hartling stood outside the Rive Gauche, the private bar in Motzstrasse where he met with his MI6 controller. In his briefcase the MfS officer carried the pencil-and-paper transcript of a high-level meeting between Major General Konrad and Army General Ivanovsky. Pending a show of good faith on the part of MI6, the typewriter cartridge which was the source of the notes would remain in a locker at Zoologischer Garten Station.

No doubt Hartling's case officer would be suspicious of the scrappy, handwritten text. Inevitably, he would question the provenance of the purported intelligence and would insist on credible evidence of its authenticity. Had the roles been reversed, Hartling would have done exactly the same thing.

The MfS officer rang the bell and waited. A few moments later, the curtain twitched and the bartender invited him in. At a table by the window, a single client was engrossed in a book. The meeting, as ever, would take place in the smoky seclusion of a side room.

Hartling knocked discretely and allowed himself in.

'Your coffee's getting cold,' said Turnbull.

Hartling shrugged. 'In time, everything gets cold.'

The Stasi officer hung his overcoat on the rack and sat down.

Turnbull looked him in the eye. 'So. What do you have for me?'

Without speaking, Hartling snapped open his attaché case and produced the handwritten transcript of the Day X meeting. Turnbull took his time to read the first and last pages before scanning the entire text. The MfS officer watched and waited.

'Very interesting,' said Turnbull, 'but how do I know this is not a complete work of fiction?'

Eminently ready for the question, Hartling calmly removed a key from his case, placed it on the table, and pinned it down with his index finger.

'This key will give you access to a locker containing a typewriter cartridge from Major General Konrad's office. On it you will find a record, not only of the document you've been reading, but of everything his secretary typed for an entire week. At first it will look as though it's been encrypted, but you just have to zig-zag your way through the letters.'

'And where, exactly, is this locker?'

'Well, before I sell you the farm,' said Hartling, pulling the key back and rotating it in his fingers, 'I'd like some evidence that you have the means to pay.'

'Evidence,' said Turnbull drily, 'is a rare commodity in this line of business.'

The MI6 officer opened his own briefcase, placed Hartling's notes inside and produced a royal blue passbook from the Bradford and Bingley Building Society made out in the name of Patrick Leckie.

'Exactly as you specified,' said Turnbull. 'Feel free to check the details. The balance currently stands at fifty thousand pounds sterling. Your British passport is, to all intents and purposes, good to go, but we obviously still require some photos. I will hang on to the bank book for the time being, but will happily present it to you along with the passport and your other documentation when we finally welcome you into the fold.'

Hartling perused the passbook. Satisfied with what he saw, he slid the locker key across the table.

'Zoologischer Garten Station.'

The Stasi officer then produced an envelope containing a strip of four passport photos.

'Wise decision not to wear your dress uniform,' said Turnbull drily.

The joke met with silence.

'Excellent,' he continued. 'I shall expedite this immediately. In the meantime, there's one more thing I'd like you to do for us. Just to be certain you're not leading us up the garden path.'

Hartling attempted a look of surprise, but it was wasted on Turnbull. They both knew how these things worked. The MI6 officer had approached their meeting with no fixed idea regarding the further demands he would inevitably make, but he saw an opportunity.

'Assuming the locker at Zoologischer Garten contains what you say it does,' said Turnbull, 'the intelligence you have supplied to us is potentially very interesting. That said, neither your handwritten notes nor this yet-to-be-seen typewriter ribbon constitute what anyone with an ounce of common sense would consider to be primary evidence. I would therefore like you to provide us now with the original documentation.'

The Stasi officer was taken aback. Whilst he had expected his MI6 handler to request further demonstrations of his veracity, the demand for the source files themselves was beyond anything he had anticipated and could expose him to massive personal risk.

Confident of his position, Turnbull waited patiently for the reply.

'It would not be easy,' said Hartling eventually.

'Indeed. But if it were easy, do you think the Service would be quite so keen to provide you with such a generous relocation package? If, however, you feel my terms are unreasonable, you are completely at liberty to withdraw from our arrangement.'

Unwilling to walk away, but reluctant to look like someone who was running out of options, Hartling allowed himself several seconds before responding.

'OK. What you are requesting is of course possible, but it would take time.'

'As I said, nothing is ever simple. Do we have an agreement?'

Hartling shifted on his haunches. 'Yes.'

'Excellent. Now that we understand each other, I will ask for the team in London to treat the finalisation of your British passport as a priority. In the meantime, you know how to get in touch. I shall look forward to an update within a month and tangible results within ninety days.'

With that, Turnbull stood and smiled. There was to be no further discussion. Hartling retrieved his overcoat, braced himself for the chill of the air on his face and left.

As the MfS officer retraced his steps towards the U-Bahn station at Nollendorfplatz, he reflected on a situation that he felt was slipping out of his control. He wondered momentarily if perhaps he should simply return to East Berlin, make no further contact with MI6 and live out his life in the GDR. The Stasi captain had, however, already committed a crime that, were it to come to light, was punishable by death. There could be no turning back and Hartling would need to use every ounce of his considerable experience to deliver exactly what MI6 had demanded.

Now ensconced at a table in the main section of the Rive Gauche, Turnbull drew hard on a cigarette and reflected on the progress he was making with the Hartling operation. Switching suddenly to English, he declared to the others in the bar that, as far as today's performance was concerned, it was time to call it a wrap and review what had been achieved. The barkeeper walked to the main door and secured the lock, before drawing up a chair next to his superior. The solitary client put down his book and joined them at the table. In due course, a dark-haired young woman with black headphones draped around her neck emerged from the room behind the bar and greeted her three Intelligence Service colleagues.

Turnbull caught her eye. 'Did you get it?'

'Every word,' said the technical officer. 'Clear as a bell.'

'Excellent. Fantastic work, everyone. Our fish, I think, is on the hook. Abbie, make two copies of the tape. Keep the master, send one copy to London and give the other to me.'

26 THE BORDER

Paris, Saturday 3rd April 1976

The Spanish leg of the overnight train journey to Paris afforded the two students ample time to celebrate their semester in Madrid, philosophise about life and generally set the world to rights. Somewhere outside Bayonne, the pair settled into silence and by the time the ambitiously named Paris Express pulled in at the Gare d'Austerlitz, Mirka was slumped on Jack's shoulder and had drooled on the sleeve of his coat.

After almost five months in each other's company they stood at the entrance to the Métro station and prepared to take their leave of one another. Cutting through the initial awkwardness of the moment, Mirka embraced her flatmate and thanked him for his unstinting friendship. She would, she promised, send him her contact details once she had found herself somewhere to live. In the meantime, she would spend a few days with an old schoolfriend who happened to be the daughter of a Swiss diplomat. Jack had not the slightest doubt that Mirka, in spite of the notorious difficulty of finding accommodation in Paris, would charm her way to a comfortable room in a well-appointed apartment in the space of a week. Having told her as much, he thanked her too for her constant companionship and for the unwavering support she had given him when his relationship with Hannah had imploded. Neither considered it useful to mention the inebriated evening when they had almost stumbled into bed together.

Mirka already had Jack's Berlin address scrawled on a piece of paper in her bag. Following a chance conversation with a German member of the Surreal Madrid five-a-side team, Jack knew exactly where he would be living. Jürgen, a stalwart footballing opponent and free-spoken drinking partner, had agreed to sub-let his unoccupied room in a shared flat in West Berlin for the duration of the summer semester. Having unwisely attempted to keep up payments for his accommodation at home whilst simultaneously studying for a year in Madrid, the German student had not paid his share of the Berlin rent for over three months. Jack's need, it turned out, had been Jürgen's salvation.

The journey from the Gare du Nord was uneventful and Jack was repeatedly lulled into sleep. It was shortly after midnight when the locomotive finally pulled in to Cologne.

The traveller had a couple of hours to kill, but resisted the temptation to doze in a waiting room. Eventually a scarcely intelligible announcement over the public address system signalled the imminent arrival of the express to Helmstedt and Berlin.

Once on board, Jack found an empty non-smoking compartment, wrestled his rucksack onto the luggage rack and, in spite of the fact that much of the world outside would be cloaked in darkness, claimed a forwards-facing window seat. He wondered if he might be lucky enough to have the compartment entirely to himself and perhaps manage to snatch a couple of hours sleep before the inevitably rigorous controls at the East German border.

Within moments of closing his eyes, the compartment door slid open and he was greeted by a casually dressed, doting couple who spoke English to each other, but sounded as though they might be Dutch. The man had nascent dreadlocks. The woman had straight, blonde hair and unusually small eyes, which a cartoonist, Jack thought, might have represented as pinpricks. The two lovers pushed their rucksacks onto the rack, installed themselves in the two seats diagonally opposite and, without the slightest intention of doing so, quietly flaunted their intimacy.

Jack's thoughts were suddenly interrupted by a wiry stick-figure of a man, perhaps somewhere in his late twenties, who bundled himself and his luggage into the compartment, slumped breathlessly onto the nearest seat and exhaled a sigh of relief. Presumably had been running to catch the train.

'Hi,' he said. 'I'm Giovanni.'

Jack reciprocated the greeting and the young lovers, who evidently spoke excellent German as well as fluent English, introduced themselves as Winston and Lotte from Amsterdam. Giovanni was wearing ripped jeans and an army-surplus combat jacket and had been hauling an olive-green kitbag which he stationed between his legs. He had straggly, shoulder length hair, a three-day beard and he wore round, wire-rimmed glasses. Having caught his breath, he rummaged a bottle of Krombacher Pils from his overstuffed bag and opened it by holding the cap firmly against the frame of the internal window and hammering it with the heel of his hand. Giovanni then fished an almost depleted packet of Marlboro and a box of matches from his jacket and promptly lit up a cigarette.

'It's a non-smoking compartment,' said Lotte, pointing to the sticker attached to the centre of the window.

'Oh thanks,' said Giovanni appreciatively. Perceiving the problem to be the sticker rather than the cigarette, he stood up, took a couple of steps to the external window and with practiced aplomb ripped the 'No smoking' sign from the glass.

'Thanks again,' he said as he sat down. 'Good call.'

The carriage door opened and a striking woman, perhaps in her mid-twenties, asked if the remaining window seat was free. She had spiky, charcoal hair, sported a shock of red lipstick and save for a washed out, purple Iggy and the Stooges tee shirt wore exclusively black clothing. She was carrying a patent leather shoulder bag, a rucksack and a guitar case that had clearly seen better days. If Dracula's daughter had fronted a glam rock band, Jack mused, this was exactly how she would have looked.

'I'm Katarina,' declared the young musician. 'And sooner or later, I'm gonna play you a song.'

'Bring it on,' said Giovanni, before filling the compartment with smoke.

'So,' said Katarina, determined not to be spending the night nodding off in the corner. 'Where are we all from and why are we going to Berlin?'

Lotte and Winston were both in their third year of studying ophthalmology at Amsterdam University Medical Center. Lotte confessed to having a wealthy uncle who lived in a villa in the well-heeled suburb of Berlin-Wannsee and she and Winston were going to spend a fortnight housesitting whilst he was in the Seychelles. The uncle's house, she enthused, backed onto Wannsee lake and had a boathouse and a small landing stage. As well as an Olympic standard sailing dinghy, her uncle owned an eight-metre motor boat which he often took to the dead centre of the lake simply to watch television in peace.

Giovanni, it turned out, was Italian and asserted that he was wanted by the authorities in Rome for a substantial number of acts of politically motivated vandalism to Government property. He also claimed that he had once tried to join the French Foreign Legion in order to escape the attentions of the Italian police. He now lived in a squat in the district of Kreuzberg and worked for an anarchist newspaper called *Krass*.

Giovanni's story, believable or otherwise, was by no means the most interesting anecdote of Jack's sleep-deprived night.

'OK,' said Katarina, rooting around in her glossy shoulder bag, 'how many of you know someone with an East German as well as a West German passport?'

As the daughter of Ingrid Kohl, a sculptor widely exhibited in the GDR, and Manfred Kohl, a prominent singer-songwriter, Katarina had grown up in East Berlin's cultural scene surrounded by art, music and revolutionary ideas. Both parents were idealists who had relocated from West to East Germany in the early fifties, keen to take part in the construction of a more equal, more humane society. In the sixties, her father had recorded a string of albums of poetic but vehemently anti-capitalist protest songs and had accrued a sizeable following in the East.

By the early seventies, however, his increasingly vociferous displeasure at the restrictions on travel and self-expression in the GDR, the all-pervading activities of the Stasi and the privileges enjoyed by high-ranking Party officials marked both parents out as unreliable dissidents. In response, the Ministry of Culture restricted Katarina's mother to the creation of purely abstract sculpture and cancelled her father's licence to record and perform. There were consequences for Katarina too. Following two successful years studying opera at the German Academy of Music, she was suddenly, and without explanation, redirected by the state to the Central School for Light Music. Her future, it had been deemed, would be to entertain the citizens of the GDR with anodyne, politically sanctioned pop songs about friendship, romance and ice cream.

Undaunted by the ban on his creative activities, Manfred Kohl, with the assistance of Ingrid, set about committing his bareknuckle songs to tape in the living room of their Prenzlauer Berg flat. Soon he had produced a suite of musical tirades that now targeted the failings of the Socialist Unity Party as much as the excesses of Wall Street. Deprived of the ability to distribute his work through official channels, Manfred simply resorted to sharing easily copiable cassettes of his home-recordings via a network of trusted friends. Almost inevitably, copies found their way across the border to the Federal Republic where a Munich record label took interest, released the songs on vinyl, and found a new audience for his iconoclasm in West Germany and beyond.

In the GDR, the Kohls were now a problem that the authorities could not solve in their habitual punitive manner. Still trying to square the circle of adorning a repressive state with a veneer of respectability, the East German government was unusually reluctant to imprison an artist with a burgeoning international profile. The Ministry for State Security was tasked with finding a more creative solution and in due course the Stasi instructed one of its assets within a trade union in the Federal Republic to book Katarina's father to perform a series of concerts in West Germany. To

Manfred's surprise, not only was he granted permission to travel, but exit visas were also provided for his wife and their daughter. Shortly before Manfred Kohl went on stage in the Hamburg Philharmonic Hall, the singer received a telegram from the GDR's Permanent Mission in Bonn informing him that he and his family had been stripped of their citizenship following 'gross neglect of their civil duties'. They would not be returning to East Berlin.

'How long ago was this?' asked Jack.

'Just over three years,' said Katarina. 'When I still had chestnut hair. Old news.'

'Not to me,' said Jack, clearly fascinated.

'Hey, wanna play Spot The Difference?' said Katarina, her eyes widening as she offered the two passports for inspection.

'I thought your name was Kohl,' said Jack, as he examined her West German passport.

'It is,' she replied. 'Or at least it was. I've legally adopted my mother's maiden name. The record company's idea.'

Jack looked up. She was signed to a record company?

'Oh yeah. Didn't I tell you. I've got a record deal. I've been kicking around the UK writing songs and I'm going to start gigging in Berlin later this year. So, my friends, watch out for the kick-ass Kate Spielmann Band coming to a venue near you. I've got no idea where we'll be playing yet, but there'll be posters everywhere. I'll tell you that for nothing.'

'Well, I'm in,' said Jack. 'One hundred per cent.'

'We still haven't heard your story,' said Winston.

Jack shrugged. 'It's hardly a story. I'm spending a semester at the Free University of Berlin. I'm writing a comparative dissertation on the emergent environmental policies on both sides of the Berlin Wall.'

'Well good luck with *that*,' said Katarina, in a tone that clearly anticipated difficulty. 'You'll do well to get anything meaningful out of the authorities in the East. If they tell you anything at all, it'll be that the Atlantic salmon are joyfully finding their way up the pristine rivers of the GDR because the capitalist Rhine is so polluted.'

'You'd better put that away,' said Giovanni, returning the East German passport to its owner. 'We'll be at the border any moment now.'

The Italian anarchist crossed the compartment, slid open the ventilation window and dispatched his exhausted beer bottle, the now-empty Marlboro packet and the crumpled 'No smoking' sticker into the night.

'You don't want to give the border guards any reason to be difficult,' he said. He'd obviously done this before. 'The best thing is just to sit there like it's your first day at school and do exactly as they say. If you stay quiet, they just stamp your passport and fuck off.'

'Quiet or not,' said Winston, 'a black man and a white woman travelling together nearly always gets a reaction. It does in the Netherlands. Even somewhere as laid-back as Amsterdam.' He turned to Lotte. 'Like that woman at the ticket office: "Don't crowd me. One at a time please. Oh I'm sorry, madam. I didn't realise you were together." That kind of thing.'

Lotte squeezed her boyfriend's hand.

Presently, the train ground to a halt at Helmstedt, the last station on West German soil. Announcements via the public-address system on the platform reminded passengers that they needed valid travel documents to cross the territory of the German Democratic Republic and that the next station at which they could alight would be Berlin Zoologischer Garten. On the platform, no-one waited to board the train.

27 SOLITARY LIGHT

East Berlin, Sunday 4th April 1976

Some two hundred kilometres to the east, Ulla Wolfram switched on the lamp next to her bed and squinted at the alarm clock. It was ten past four and she had slept for maybe three hours at best. Turning off the light once more, her mind immediately seized on the issue that was rarely far from her thoughts. Whilst Ulla's private determination to remove herself from the GDR was as pronounced as ever, viable options were in short supply. Mick Jaeger, her sole potential conduit to a counterfeit visa, was a stranger to his usual haunts and her chances of finding a means of passing unchallenged though the controls at Friedrichstrasse had, it seemed, dwindled to zero.

Ulla wondered whether, several kilometres away, her parents were also awake. In the expansive darkness of her room, she allowed her mind to alight on their repeated intimations that success at ice hockey might ultimately pave the way to a life in the West. Although Ulla had dismissed the notion as no more than wishful thinking, the linking of ice hockey to the idea of escape now triggered thoughts of a different nature. Reflecting on the 1974 Friendship Games in Bratislava, Ulla began to toy with the idea that the Czechoslovak-Austrian border might, at least in one specific location, be more porous than Honecker's Anti-Fascist Defence Wall in Berlin.

Although Devín Castle, from whose ramparts Kirsten had yelled 'Hello, gorgeous!' at an unsuspecting farmer, was perched high on a craggy promontory, it was no more than fifty metres from the foot of the cliff to the Austrian side of the river. From the team's elevated vantage point, Ulla had been able to make out the wire fences, the dog-runs and the watch-towers to either side of the cliff, but had been surprised to see that the sheer wall of rock beneath them plummeted directly into the waters of the Morava river. With her mind working overtime, she now wondered whether a fit, healthy and determined sportswoman such as herself might plan a quiet camping holiday to Bratislava, hide somewhere in the castle precincts before it closed for the day, then descend the rocky precipice under cover of darkness before swimming across the Morava under the noses of the Czechoslovak guards. Although Ulla's overwrought mind garnered a degree of solace as she imagined herself emerging from the dark waters of the Morava and walking towards the solitary light that glowed in the window of a nearby Austrian farm, she dismissed the fantasy for what it was. For all her frustrations, for all her resolve, she was not a skilled climber, she could not see in the dark and she certainly wasn't bullet-proof.

As they so often did when she awoke in the night, Ulla's thoughts drifted eventually to comforting images of her Opa smiling at her as he worked on his allotment, helped her prepare Königsberger meatballs or taught her a new conjuring technique. She recalled the times when she had so often sought solace in his company after arguing with her parents. She could so clearly recall his voice telling her to find solutions that did not just lead her to a different set of problems. She remembered his constant and gentle encouragement not to lose heart in the face of adversity. In the warm embrace of his memory, Ulla still felt his love.

Certain that she would not get back to sleep and aware that her parents were due to visit Fehrbelliner Strasse that afternoon, Ulla flicked on the lamp once more and jumped out of bed. Pulling a dressing gown over her pyjamas, she determined to divert her energies into solving a smaller but nevertheless pressing problem, namely the still noticeable funk from her ice hockey kit. As had become her habit, she had simply dumped her hockey bag in the corner of the living room following yesterday's match and had given not the slightest thought to airing out her damp and sweaty gear. Her mother, she knew, would hardly refrain from commenting on the interesting aroma which, as a result, now hung in the apartment. Concluding from the frost on the windows that it was comfortably below zero in the streets outside, Ulla unzipped the offending kit bag and emptied out her things. Opening the doors onto the balcony, she stepped barefoot into the chill morning air, hurriedly pegged her shorts, jersey and gloves to the washing line and arranged her protective pads plus the insoles from her boots on the two rickety chairs. With any luck, she thought, the bacteria inhabiting her kit would simply freeze to death. After breakfast, she would fire up the tiled heating oven in the living room, open the windows and try to banish the curious smell long before the arrival of her parents.

28 PASS AND CONTROL

Helmstedt, Sunday 4th April 1976

Following a lengthy delay, during which little seemed to happen beyond the occasional shunt or bump, the carriages of the overnight express from Cologne were coupled to an East German locomotive and Jack Gilmore's journey to Berlin resumed. At the inner German border, the British student glimpsed the floodlit death strip of concrete, fences and wire for a matter of seconds before the train rattled onwards through the darkness. Some five kilometres inside the GDR and accompanied by the screeching of metal on metal, the train drew to a standstill at Marienborn.

On the brightly illuminated platform, a troop of well-drilled border guards, some with automatic machine-pistols, waited for the signal to board. Although this working station was an integral part of the East German railway network, no access to the platforms was permitted to GDR citizens whilst the transit trains to West Berlin waited invitingly at the station.

Satisfied that no interlopers were anywhere in evidence, the commander barked his orders. Moments later, teams of Pass and Control officers boarded their designated carriages, secured the exits and entered each compartment with a smart salute and a polite but patently unrefusable request for the passengers to present their passports.

The uniformed officer who entered the compartment shared by Jack and his fellow travellers exuded an air of quiet but unimpeachable authority as he waited for the requested documents to be produced. Giovanni, the previously garrulous anarchist, now maintained a reluctant but necessary silence. Katarina shifted on her seat. The two Dutch lovers were a model of compliance.

Although Jack knew better than to pass comment, both the field grey uniform, the flashy insignia and the peremptory manner evoked immediate memories of the stiff German officers who still populated so many of the television dramas in his unforgetting homeland. Meticulously, the Pass and Control officer examined the various travel documents, ascertained that the bearers were not transporting any weapons, illicit materials or banned literature and duly stamped the passports with entry visas. The corresponding exit stamps, he informed them, would be issued at Potsdam. The formalities complete, the officer closed his attaché case, saluted the passengers once more and left. Reflecting momentarily on the work-shy appearance of so many of the young westerners he encountered, he was certain that the capitalist nations could not endure.

As soon as the uniformed officers had withdrawn to the platform and had been registered back with their units, the train continued on its journey to Berlin. This was the cue for Katarina to pull her guitar from its case and launch into a full-throated private concert of outrageously worded songs about corrupt leaders, untrustworthy boyfriends and the dualities of personal freedom. Her self-penned German-language diatribes were interspersed with hard-hitting covers such as 'Search and Destroy' by Iggy and the Stooges and Bob Marley's 'Get up, Stand up'. Over the course of a fiercely compelling performance, Katarina Spielmann revealed herself to be a phenomenal vocalist who boasted a range of over three octaves and was possessed of infallible pitch-control.

'Hell,' thought Jack, agog at what he was witnessing. 'If this woman can't make a career out of music, nobody can.'

The impromptu performance concluded, Katarina beamed at the enthusiastic response from her audience of four and placed the guitar once more in its battered case.

In due course the train pulled slowly into the station at Potsdam, the final stop before the border. A fresh squadron of armed troops and punctilious Pass and Control officers climbed on board to effect the necessary checks on the passengers and to ascertain that no GDR citizens had stowed away in the hope of ghosting themselves into West Berlin. A surprisingly genial officer furnished the occupants of Jack's compartment with their exit visas and wished them a pleasant onward trip. In the corridor, a colleague erected an aluminium stepladder, pushed his head through a ceiling hatch and, with the aid of a small torch, ensured that no unauthorised travellers lurked in the unlit void above. In the still wintry night air outside, border guards with German Shepherd Dogs on tight leashes scoured the underbelly of the carriage with powerful flashlights. After a delay of perhaps forty-five minutes, the train was finally given leave to proceed. Five minutes later, the locomotive rumbled slowly through the closely monitored, roofless duct that allowed the transit trains to pass through the Anti-Fascist Defence Wall. Jack and his companions relaxed. They were in West Berlin.

'You never forget your first time,' quipped Giovanni as he forced open another bottle of beer.

'All things considered,' said Winston, 'that wasn't too bad.'

'As long as you have the right documents,' said Katarina, clearly relieved to have crossed the border. 'I wouldn't recommend it any other way.'

'Are you OK?' asked Jack with a look of genuine sympathy.

'Yeah, I'm OK,' said Katarina. 'At least, I will be. Twenty minutes in the company of an electric guitar and I'll be fine.'

The train trundled through the sleeping suburbs of Grünewald and Halensee and stopped finally at Berlin Zoologischer Garten. As Katarina prepared to leave the compartment, she fumbled once more in her large, glossy bag, retrieved her redundant East German passport and tossed it casually to Jack.

'Souvenir,' she said with a glint in her eye. 'Free ticket to any of my shows in Berlin.'

When Jack stepped down from the train, his companions had already been subsumed into the larger cohort of passengers now hurrying for the exit. Locked on to a group of travellers who were heading for the taxi rank, Jack missed the internal staircase down to the U-Bahn lines and rapidly found himself on the street outside. It was shortly before eight. The air was cold and the sky a metallic grey. On the staircase at the external entrance to the underground station, a down-and-out put a bottle to his cracked lips and began the daily process of anaesthetising himself from his unenviable plight. A man and a woman, immaculate in their Sunday best, stopped to give him some change.

Feeling particularly cotton-brained from the sustained lack of sleep, Jack descended the stairs into Zoologischer Garten underground station and stared at the prices and ticket options on the machine in front of him. It should have been easy, but he could not immediately figure out what he needed to do.

29 LET OR HINDRANCE

East Berlin, Sunday 4th April 1976

It was not yet eight and the Main Directorate for Reconnaissance was relatively quiet. Seated behind his desk in Room 531, Captain Hartling lit a cigarette and attempted to take stock of his situation.

Whilst the MfS officer had been prepared for MI6 to require further demonstrations of his good faith, he had been upended by the ambition of their demands. The extraction of files relating to Soviet readiness for Day X was both problematic and fraught with risk. In the first place, Hartling had no way of knowing whether the relevant documents had been relocated to the safety of the Central Archive or were secured somewhere within the Main Directorate for Reconnaissance. Whichever the case, his clearance level would not grant him access. Furthermore, files of such potential value to an enemy would inevitably be protected by physical as well as administrative barriers and a hasty or ill-considered move might easily result in his exposure. Even to enquire about the files might place him in the crosshairs of suspicion. Pending the conception of a plan to locate and remove the documents without risk of detection, he would need to maintain the appearance of probity and manage his existing caseload with conspicuous zeal.

One case in particular was making a disproportionate claim on Hartling's time. Since the end of January, his lovestruck asset in the office of the Church of Reconciliation had been supplying him with bundled copies of Pastor

Niemeyer's official correspondence. Whilst the quantity of materials supplied by Petra Fichtenberg suggested a certain dedication to the task, the intelligence had thus far been poor. Not only were the photocopied documents devoid of references to the issue surrounding the abandoned church building, they offered no fresh insights into Niemeyer's psychology.

Amongst the latest batch, however, was a puzzling document addressed to the Environment Ministry in East Berlin. Prompted by earlier communications with an academic in the UK, the undated and unsigned draft appeared to be a testimonial for a British student by the name of Jack Gilmore. The undergraduate was, according to Niemeyer, working as an intern at Concordia whilst studying in West Berlin and was looking to conduct primary research into the environmental policies of the GDR.

Almost inevitably, Hartling found himself considering the possibility of an operational gambit emanating from London. Whilst it seemed unlikely that MI6 would dispatch one of their operatives to East Berlin in the guise of a research student, the MfS officer could not dismiss the notion out of hand. The Stasi had, after all, made an art form of hiding assets in plain sight. When Hartling next hooked up with Pastor Niemeyer's PA, he would ask her for evidence of Jack Gilmore's authenticity. He was not quite sure how he would dress it up, but he would think of something.

More immediately, as a servant of two masters, the Stasi officer was confronted with a dilemma. How might MI6 react if it came to light that he was running interference on one of their operations? And how might his Stasi commanders react if he wasn't?

Hartling reached for the cigarette packet and fished out another Cabinet Original. After exploring several increasingly convoluted approaches to his bind, he experienced an epiphany. The material factor in this whole conundrum, it occurred to him, was not the student, but the letter itself. Perhaps someone in the upper echelons of the Evangelical Church harboured suspicions of a mole inside Pastor Niemeyer's office. Perhaps the West German security services had become involved. The suggestion of a covert operation against the Environment Ministry might be nothing more than an attempt by the BND to smoke out the truth. A refusal to grant Jack Gilmore, whoever he might be, an entry visa to East Berlin would immediately confirm to West German intelligence that the MfS had access to the pastor's official correspondence.

Satisfied at last with his logic, Hartling drafted a memorandum for the Pass and Control units staffing the internal border checkpoints. The British citizen by the name of Jack Gilmore was to be allowed to enter and leave East Berlin without let or hindrance, but his movements through the controls were to be communicated directly to the Main Directorate for Reconnaissance.

The officer drew long and hard on his cigarette before exhaling and stubbing out the butt in the blackened bowl of a polished aluminium ashtray. In all likelihood the putative British student would do no more than pass through the security checks at Friedrichstrasse and spend a token afternoon mooching about the museums before returning quietly to West Berlin. Hartling would only need to take a closer interest in the case if Jack Gilmore were physically to present himself at the Ministry for the Environment. It was a scenario he considered to be unlikely at best.

30 THE GRAND PLAN

West Berlin, Sunday 4th April 1976

Entertained by his fellow passengers and unnerved by the rigours of the border controls, Jack had gone much of the night without sleep. As the underground train rattled through the short series of stations separating Zoologischer Garten and Nauener Platz, he succumbed to the urge to sleep, but woke with a jerk the moment his head tipped heavily forward. Realising through the fog of his exhaustion that he could easily miss his stop, Jack forced himself to his feet, breathed deeply and made a conscious effort to maintain his balance as the U-Bahn rocked continually from side to side.

Jürgen, the footballing friend who had sub-let the room to Jack, had supplied him with a single sheet of A4 containing the address, a phone number, the names of his future flatmates and some rudimentary guidance regarding the location of the apartment. The new tenant would not get anything quite so useful as a key until he showed up in person.

A reassuring female voice announced via the onboard public address system that the train had arrived at Nauener Platz. Now excited, in spite of his lack of sleep, at the prospect of meeting his new flatmates, Jack lugged his rucksack onto the platform, up the broad staircase and out of the U-Bahn station. Berlin, he decided, was a city of unfamiliar smells. The underground system was possessed of a predictably industrial aroma that was nonetheless unexpectedly distinct from that of the Madrid Metro. The

Berlin air, he immediately noted, was undoubtedly fresh but somehow smoky at the same time.

Jack dug out the now crumpled piece of paper with the instructions for locating the flat. It was no more than a ten-minute walk from the U-Bahn, Jürgen had assured him. A week before setting off for Berlin, the British student had introduced himself to his future flatmates via postcard and had informed them of the intended date of his arrival. Nevertheless, aware of the complexity of the journey and the potential for delay, he had not been remotely specific about the likely time of his appearance at their door.

Armed with a tatty, second-hand street map, Jack headed along Reinickendorfer Strasse. The length of the street, the five-storey turn-of-the-century apartment blocks with their plethora of small shops and bars fronting the pavements would not at first glance have looked out of place in Madrid.

Although there was a considerable chill in the air, Jack's rucksack and military-surplus trench coat ensured that he felt anything but cold. In spite of the weight he was carrying, Jack found himself standing outside the main door to 27 Oudenarder Strasse in less than five minutes. The facade of the apartment building had, it seemed, enjoyed little attention since the end of the Second World War. Much of the render, originally styled to mimic baroque stonework, had long since fallen away to reveal the more prosaic bricks beneath. Where the decorative layer still remained, it was grimy and riddled with bullet holes, souvenirs presumably of the desperate fighting that had occurred as the Red Army battled its way street by street and house by house to secure control of the German capital. On the fourth floor, almost directly above Jack's head, a woman of perhaps sixty rested her folded arms on a cushion, leaned on the window sill and peered downwards to observe the comings and goings in the cobbled street below. The entrance door to the building itself was securely locked and there was no intercom that would allow the newcomer to alert anyone to his arrival.

'You'll just have to wait,' Jürgen had warned him. 'People are in and out all the time.'

Presently a middle-aged man opened the dusty, wooden door and happily allowed Jack to enter.

Referring to the directions Jürgen had given him, Jack crossed the courtyard in which two headscarfed women hung washing on a line. Beyond the yard, a staircase beckoned. As he climbed nearer to the fifth floor, Jack picked up the irresistible smell of coffee and heard what sounded like a percussion-driven oratorio spliced with raucous laughter. At the top of the creaking stairs, four apartments, each with its external door wedged open, could be accessed from the small landing. Jack honed in on the smell of the coffee, the sound of the music and the continuing bursts of hilarity.

The sudden appearance of the stranger in the kitchen doorway interrupted the laughter at a stroke. Arranged around a traditional breakfast of boiled eggs, fresh rolls, jams, cheese and salami, the cheerful collective had not been expecting their new recruit simply to turn up out of the blue without phoning from Zoologischer Garten, if not from the call box at Nauener Platz. Jack could see that he had caught them by surprise.

'I've come to complain about the noise,' he declared in the manner of a disgruntled neighbour.

'You must be Jack,' said the woman closest to him. 'Jürgen warned us you might have a sense of humour. So, greetings, curious person from another country. Have you had any breakfast?'

'Nope.'

'Right. Get rid of your bag and come and sit down and I'll do the formal introductions. I'm Julia by the way. I'm studying at the Pedagogical College.'

Julia had auburn hair, brown eyes and light olive skin. She was wearing a black, hand-knitted jumper and a bluish, brownish, hippyish skirt. The trainee teacher was possessed of an effortless and engaging smile which, Jack imagined, would stand her in excellent stead in the classroom.

By the time the newcomer had taken off his trench coat and dumped his rucksack in the corridor, Julia had poured him a coffee and one of the others had placed a roll and a knife on a plate. Someone had also, it seemed, turned the music down a notch. As Jack treated himself to a welcome shock of caffeine, Julia briefly introduced the remaining breakfasters as Christa and Marco, who were both studying at the Free University of Berlin, Anna, who worked in the Running Wardrobe Team at the German Opera and Bastian, an engineering student at the Technical University. They were, Jack thought, an interesting and decidedly friendly looking bunch.

'How much did Jürgen explain to you about our set-up?' asked Julia.

'He told me the rent, the address and your names and that was pretty much it. Although, he did give me the impression that I was renting a room in a shared apartment. This looks like four separate flats.'

Julia explained that, legally speaking, the students rented the four single-bedroom apartments grouped around the top-floor landing as separate entities, but they nevertheless functioned as one household. The kitchen in which they were all currently tucking into breakfast was, for example, where they all cooked and ate; the kitchen in Jack's flat, on the other hand, was their photographic dark room.

'What you need to know,' said Marco, 'is that this is not just a practical arrangement. It's a collective and we have ideals. We work together for the good of the whole and on an individual level we try to be open and honest with each other. You'll get to know us pretty quickly. Just as we will get to know you.'

Now feeling that he might perhaps be on probation, Jack cast his eyes around the group.

The woman sitting between Julia and Marco wore a black tee shirt beneath baggy, off-white dungarees. She had dark, loosely curled hair, brown eyes and a complexion that testified both to African and European ancestry. Proud of her roots, Anna was the daughter of an American military pilot and a German music teacher. After suggesting to Jack that he must be exhausted after such a long journey, she steeled herself for the all too regular expression of surprise at her flawless grammar or the casual assumption that she had been born somewhere far from Germany. Jack simply flashed her a smile, told her that he was, as she had guessed, running on fumes and enquired about her work at the German Opera.

Bastian had brown, shoulder-length hair and wore rectangular, metal-rimmed glasses with thick lenses that made his green eyes look unusually large. He glanced frequently at Anna and hung on her every word. Jack had the distinct feeling that they might be an item.

‘So,’ said the new arrival, keen to connect the dots, ‘if my maths is correct, there are four rooms and six occupants. Who shares with who?’

Bastian said nothing. Christa put down her coffee and explained to Jack that she and Julia shared a bed in the room on the other side of the kitchen wall and that Anna and Marco lived together in the flat immediately opposite Jack’s.

‘So, if you fancy a cheeky beer, sometime,’ said Bastian. ‘I’m generally available.’

‘Done,’ said Jack with a yawn. ‘You are one hundred per cent on.’

‘You’d think he was the only one who’d ever seen the bottom of a beer glass,’ said Christa.

Julia’s partner had long, straight, black hair and green eyes. The smiling face of a blazing red sun on her fading yellow tee shirt proclaimed her polite but unequivocal opposition to nuclear power. Prompted by the sentiment, Jack described his involvement in various Friends of the Earth campaigns at Lanchester. When he revealed his intention to conduct a comparative study of East and West German environmental policy based exclusively on primary evidence, his flatmates were both surprised and impressed.

‘I’ll give you a heads-up,’ said Bastian. ‘Environmental policy’s shit on both sides of the Wall, although marginally less shit, I suppose, on this side.’

‘Thanks,’ said Jack. ‘Can I quote you on that? Although, I might have to press you for a tad more detail at some point.’

Bastian grinned. He liked the understated humour and he would definitely make a point of introducing Jack to his favourite bars.

Across the table, Marco was sawing away at the large salami he had recently shoplifted from the food hall of an upmarket department store. His keen, blue eyes peered out through wire-framed glasses. Whilst Marco's hairstyle would not have looked out of place in the nineteen-forties, his two-day beard looked altogether more modern. Over his broad frame he wore a burgundy sweatshirt sporting the words 'Summer Sale'. It looked like the name of a band.

'Anyway,' continued Jack, 'that's the grand plan for my dissertation. That's why I'm sitting here, barely awake, jacked up on coffee and trying to fit names to faces. So, what about you? What brought you all to Berlin?'

Keen to share his motivations, Marco was first in. 'I'm here essentially to avoid military service. If I'd stayed in Frankfurt, I'd have been doing my compulsory eighteen months in the army by now. But as West Berlin is a total political anomaly and not legally part of the Federal Republic, its residents are gloriously exempt from conscription. As long as I'm here, I can't be mandated to serve in the Bundeswehr, which, as far as anyone with half a brain is concerned, is no more than an instrument of American imperialism.'

'You know what, Marco,' said Anna, her nose clearly out of joint. 'Sometimes you express yourself with all the subtlety of one of those banners at an effing Trotskyist so-called Worker Party demo. If you don't want to do military service, that's fine by me. I hate the idea of war as much as you do, but let's not forget that if it hadn't been for the thousands of American soldiers who gave their lives fighting fascism and the subsequent US presence in Germany, the woman you sleep with every night would never have been born.'

'Oh my God,' retorted Marco. 'Why do you always have to personalise this? It's not about you. History is a river in which individual lives are no more than droplets.'

The ensuing silence was as uncomfortable as it was brief.

'Well,' said Anna abruptly, 'I don't know what that's supposed to mean, but don't even think about trying to explain it, because I know I'm not going to like it and you're not going to like the way I tell you.'

Without speaking another word, Marco pushed his chair back sharply, barged past Bastian and barrelled down the stairs.

There were tears in Anna's eyes.

'Sorry about that,' she said, sniffing as she looked directly at Jack. 'He's got a brain the size of a planet, but his heart goes walkabout. Anyway. Please, excuse me. It was nice to meet you.'

'Shall I come with you?' said Christa.

Anna shook her head and left them to their breakfast.

Nobody spoke. Julia poured some coffee. Bastian stared intently at his roll as he spread the jam.

'Does that happen much?' asked Jack.

'They're obviously going through a difficult phase,' said Julia. 'They've never seen eye to eye on certain political issues. Not really. But Anna can give as good as she gets and as Marco said, we try to be open and honest with each other.'

'Maybe it's better to keep some things to yourself,' mused Jack.

'Truth can be tough, but I think honesty is always the best policy,' said Julia.

'For sure, but is the naked truth always what's required? Should a doctor at a crash site tell an anxious victim that they have no chance of surviving the day?'

'Good point,' said Julia, stumped for a ready response, but appreciative of the nuance. 'Good point. I'll give that one some thought.'

After breakfast, Jack helped Bastian and Julia clear the table and do the washing up, before Julia handed him some keys and gave him an inevitably brief tour of the compact and noticeably chillier flat next door. She assured him that once he'd grabbed a few hours sleep, she would tell him a little about their domestic routines and explain how to use the tiled oven that was the only source of heat in his room. She also offered to guide Jack during the coming week through various unavoidable administrative tasks such as registering at the local police station, enrolling at university and procuring a student transport pass. And if he needed to use the phone at any time, it was located in the room that she and Christa shared. This afternoon, Julia added, Jack would also be more than welcome to accompany Bastian, Christa and herself, plus Anna and Marco if they reappeared, to a nearby park where they planned to knock a volleyball around before returning home to lay into Bastian's home-baked plum cake.

'That all sounds perfect,' said Jack. 'Please wake me if I haven't surfaced by the time you're leaving.'

As there were no sheets, pillow cases or duvet cover on Jack's bed and he confessed that he had not brought any of his own, Julia also fetched him some spare bedding from the flat that she and Christa shared. Marco, she informed him, would in all likelihood be perfectly happy to purloin whatever else he needed from one of Berlin's most exclusive department stores later in the week. Jack would simply need to draw up a list.

With the bed finally made and Julia curled up with Christa on the sofa next door, Jack kicked off his shoes, installed himself under the duvet and stared at the ceiling. After such a lengthy and convoluted journey he felt relieved to have a roof over his head and lucky to have what appeared to be a ready-made social network. Julia, he could see, possessed a natural generosity of spirit and seemed determined to help him find his feet. Although Marco clearly had the capacity to be spiky, his new acquaintances struck him collectively as fundamentally warm-hearted and he saw no reason why he could not settle into his new surroundings exactly as he had done in Madrid. As far as the weary traveller was concerned, his toast had landed jam side up.

Gradually, Jack's thoughts drifted to Mirka and, in the mistaken belief that it was already Monday, he pictured her charming the staff of a Parisian accommodation agency or leafing through the classifieds section of a newspaper as she sat with her former schoolfriend in a fancy Montmartre café.

Once the effects of Julia's robust breakfast coffee finally released Jack from its grip, sleep claimed what remained of his morning plus a chunk of the afternoon. When Bastian shook him by the shoulder shortly after two, Jack for a moment had not the faintest idea where he was.

It was perhaps a fifteen minute walk to the nearest park. Following a spirited but inevitably doomed attempt to play two-a-side volleyball in the cool afternoon air, Christa, Bastian, Julia and Jack made their way cheerfully back to the apartment to brew up yet more coffee and demolish the plum cake. Anna and Marco, they quickly established, had still not returned. With Joni Mitchell playing quietly on Christa's stereo system, Jack explained how he had got to know Jürgen through football and offered pen portraits of his travelling companions during the journey from Cologne. His fellow cake enthusiasts, it turned out, had all known each other at school in Hildesheim. Marco and Anna, on the other hand, were both from Frankfurt, but had attended different schools and had first met at a badminton club.

By the evening, Marco and Anna had reappeared and seemed to have put aside, if not exactly reconciled, their differences. After yawning his way through much of Anna's excellent pasta putanesca, Jack finished his bottle of Warsteiner beer, thanked his new flatmates for the genuine warmth of their welcome, and offered his apologies. Enveloped once more by the duvet, he slept like an overfed bear.

31 WELCOME TO BERLIN

West Berlin, Monday 5th April 1976

Following almost twelve hours of deep and beautifully oblivious sleep, Jack Gilmore's Monday arrived with a jolt. At nine thirty precisely, his peace was unceremoniously shattered by a sudden reprise of the music that had caught his attention as he came up the stairs the previous morning. Played at a robust volume through speakers that had been spirited into his room as he slept, an impassioned alto voice sang an aria depicting in eloquent Spanish the charismatic beauty of South American wildlife. Driven forward by a battery of percussion instruments and rousing choral accompaniment, the rhythms and energy of the oratorio were not to be ignored.

As Jack looked around the still unfamiliar room, he registered on the wall a sheet of file paper featuring the word 'breakfast' and an arrow pointing in the direction of the landing. Noting the movement of their flatmate's head, his tormentors turned down the volume and waited. Craning his neck towards the door, Jack recognised two smirking faces.

'They're so beautiful when they sleep,' said Julia.

'Indeed,' said Marco. 'It's a shame they have to grow up.'

'Hey, sleepyhead,' said Julia, now addressing the reluctant riser directly. 'I've prepared a *Welcome to Berlin* programme for you. It's going to take up most of your day. You can blame Marco for the wake-up call, though.'

Julia flashed her new flatmate a smile before she and Marco disappeared in the direction indicated by the arrow on the wall. When Jack at last joined them in the kitchen, his hair still wet from the shower, Julia and Marco were drinking black tea and smoking roll-ups.

'Christa and Bastian have already gone to lectures,' said Julia, 'and Anna's gone in early to complete running repairs on Madame Butterfly's gown. The last three rolls are yours.'

As Jack assembled his breakfast, Julia talked him through her beautifully designed chart delineating the household's rolling six-day rota of domestic duties ranging from cooking to cleaning to emptying the bins. Julia had been scrupulously equitable, Jack noted, in her allocation of tasks, most of which were to be completed in pairs. In Madrid, he and Mirka had simply muddled along day by day, largely inventing recipes to fit whatever was to be found in the fridge. He doubted that this ramshackle approach would continue to pass muster when catering for six, but he would no doubt be guided by the permanently upbeat Julia if he had any queries.

With the rolls, jam and cheese consumed, the smoky Lapsang Souchong tea finished and Jack's first official washing up duty duly completed, Julia presented the newcomer with a list setting out in neat columns a logical and unquestionably helpful programme of activities for his first seven days. The various tasks had been prioritised in terms of both importance and urgency and each destination was followed by the name of the nearest U-Bahn station, which in turn was neatly colour coded to indicate the relevant underground line. By the end of the first week in Berlin Jack would have completed an introductory bicycle tour with Julia of the curiously named district of Wedding, taken his passport to the local police station to register as a resident, opened an account at a bank of his choice, located the nearest doctor's practice and pharmacy, enrolled at the Free University of Berlin, acquired a subsidised student transport pass and registered, if he needed to work during his semester, with the Temporary Employment Office. Jack explained that he had managed to secure a part-time internship at Concordia, an environmental initiative based in the offices of the Church of Reconciliation and wondered if Julia knew where it was.

'Oh, I know where it is,' she reassured him. 'Add it to the list under "bicycle tour".'

As Julia was teaching Jack how to arrange the crockery in the small wooden dresser in the kitchen, Marco suddenly reappeared. Now immaculately shaven, dressed in a suit and tie and carrying an Italian leather briefcase, the architect of Jack's wake-up call surprised his new flatmate for the second time in little more than an hour.

'See you later,' he said with a cheery wave.

'He's going to KaDeWe, the so-called Department Store of the West,' said Julia, smartly anticipating Jack's question. 'He likes to dress inconspicuously.'

'I don't get it,' said Jack, none the wiser for Julia's vague pointer in the general direction of the truth. 'He looks like he's going to work in a bank.'

'That's the whole point,' said Julia. 'Well-dressed bank employees do not arouse suspicion. Marco is engaged in a campaign of punitive shoplifting against a number of businesses that once benefitted from Nazi patronage or were seized from their Jewish owners under the policy of aryanisation. Think of Marco as Robin Hood in a sharp Hugo Boss disguise. Anyway, he'll no doubt fill you in on all the details when he gets back and as I said, if there's anything that you need, just let him know. But right now, Jack, you need to shape up. You've got to help me get the bikes out of the cellar.'

The bicycles had clearly not enjoyed any recent use. Once the two flatmates had inflated the tyres, Julia set off at pace and before long they had escaped the unforgiving cobbles of Oudenarder Strasse and emerged onto the smoother asphalt of altogether busier streets. Amidst the urgency of the commercial traffic, Jack was repeatedly caught out by the need to look over his left shoulder rather than his customary right. The movement felt completely unnatural and required a conscious effort each time Julia made a sudden decision to change lanes or weave between stationary vehicles. Nevertheless, he rapidly began to enjoy his guide's wittily irreverent anecdotes about the district's amenities. Having introduced Jack to various civic buildings and local services, in addition to the nearest supermarket, a handful of bakeries, several student bars and some Turkish food outlets, Julia zigzagged her tutee along a carefully chosen route featuring quieter, leafier streets and occasional green spaces before eventually announcing their arrival at Humboldthain Park.

The sun was now high in the spring sky and as they slowly pedalled their bikes beneath the linden and hazel trees, Julia pointed out the open air pool and the public lawns where she and Christa had lazed away the warmest afternoons of the previous summer. In the branches above the walkways, Julia identified the polished, mellow tones of blackbirds advertising their presence to prospective mates.

Presently, she introduced Jack to the extensive rose garden which, she assured him, would be magical once the flowers came into bloom. A short while later, at the foot of a densely wooded hill, Julia dismounted from her bike and advised Jack to do the same. The path to the top was steep, winding and deceptively long, but at the summit, the platforms of two Second World War flak towers afforded extensive views back over Wedding. With prompts and clues from Julia, the district's newest resident eventually managed to trace out the circuitous route which the pair had followed to the park.

'Are we anywhere near the Church of Reconciliation?' asked Jack eventually.

'You can make it out through the trees from the other side of the hill. Stranded in no man's land, all empty and unused. It's in Bernauer Strasse, which is probably no more than a kilometre from here. Anyway, grab your bike. It's the final stop on our tour.'

Although Jack had seen various images of the redundant church during lectures at Lanchester and had only recently passed through the border on the train, nothing had prepared him for his first daylight encounter with the front line of an ideological standoff dating back to the end of the Second World War.

Constructed under the close direction of the ambitious Erich Honecker in August 1961, the 140-kilometre cordon of bricked-up buildings, breeze blocks and barbed wire had in one fell swoop stemmed the tide of mass emigration from the East and bolstered the authority of the Socialist Unity Party. In the intervening years the initially crude structure had been expanded, refined and reinforced to confront would-be emigrants from East Germany with a highly sophisticated system of potentially lethal obstacles. As the GDR invested ever more effort into sealing the border, successful escapes became increasingly rare.

Standing with his ever-informative guide on one of the many wooden observation platforms built by the West Berlin police, Jack peered over the Y-framed lines of barbed wire running along the three-metre high wall. Maybe fifty metres from their position, an inner wall sealed off the death strip from the quiet streets beyond. The treacherous and forbidding ribbon of land between the two blockwork barriers harboured a multi-layered system of wire fences, dog-runs, tank traps, anti-vehicle ditches, flood lamps, raked sand and a narrow concrete guard road, all of which were kept under permanent surveillance from the watchtowers. Perhaps no more than a hundred metres from the observation platform, the neo-gothic tower and steeple of the abandoned Church of Reconciliation stood incongruously amid the mass of concrete and steel and pointed constantly to the unobstructed sky.

Before long, Jack and Julia were joined by a handful of camera-wielding, English-speaking visitors, who readily snapped away at anything and everything on the far side of the border.

'Hey, check out these guys,' said one of their number suddenly. 'You really gotta see this.'

About fifty metres diagonally to their right, two East German border guards, rifles over their shoulders, stood on the concrete vehicle track and debated what they should do about the unauthorised object that had penetrated the extensive system of traps and barriers. Inadvertently or otherwise, a football had been kicked over the Wall from the western side and, after bouncing on a trip wire and triggering an alarm in two nearby watchtowers, had come to rest in the normally unblemished sand of the control strip. The border guards had dutifully investigated the apparent cause of the alert, but, uncertain whether the football was all that it seemed to be and untrained for any such eventuality, they had called for a second opinion. In less than a minute, an olive-green jeep, its exhaust intermittently belching greyish smoke, came to a halt and a captain from the Central Border Command stepped out of the vehicle and allowed the guards to point out the suspect football. The officer returned to his jeep, re-emerged with a camera and began to photograph the intrusive object from a variety of angles.

By this point, the English-speakers had begun to amuse themselves by photographing an East German soldier photographing a ball. In response, one of the border guards in the watchtower directly opposite the observation platform produced a camera with an impressive telephoto lens and assiduously documented both the actions and the facial features of the disrespectful tourists.

'I don't know where he is, but I'm not sure that kid is going to get his football back,' said Jack drily.

'You know what? Wars have started over less,' said Julia, not entirely flippantly. 'Anyway. Welcome to Berlin.'

32 NOT GETTING CAUGHT

West Berlin, Wednesday 14th April 1976

Within ten days of his arrival, Jack felt that he was settling into his new routines and was gradually managing to form a more rounded impression of his flatmates. Although eminently happy for important decisions to be discussed and agreed collectively, Julia was clearly a natural leader and a born organiser. Following the schedule laid out in her meticulous, colour coded action plan, Jack had by now registered with the local police, passed his German language exam at the Free University, enrolled officially as a student, acquired a set of passport photos, invested in a discount card for the public transport system, opened a bank account and planned the simplest route to Pastor Niemeyer's offices in Bernauer Strasse.

In the evenings, Julia and Christa often strummed their guitars and harmonised effortlessly as they rehearsed familiar songs by Neil Young or Joni Mitchell. Marco and Anna, on the other hand, seemed to be stuck on a merry-go-round of almost daily spats followed by subdued reconciliations. Bastian quietly wished that Anna would break up once and for all with Marco and seek solace in the arms of someone who would truly appreciate her. Pending that apparently unlikely scenario, he displaced his burgeoning feelings for Anna by staying late at the Technical University or working on the misfiring engine of the battered VW Beetle which he kept parked on the street outside.

For his part, Jack was also now struggling with a dilemma. Although he undoubtedly appreciated the clean, crisp feel of the Egyptian cotton bedding that Marco had, as he put it, 'liberated' from the Wertheim department store on the Kurfürstendamm, the recipient of Marco's largesse was nevertheless troubled by the idea that he was in effect an accessory to theft.

'Look, I get why you do this,' he said to Marco the morning after his first night with the luxurious bedsheets, 'but I definitely feel uneasy about accepting, you know, stuff that's not actually been paid for.'

'Well, don't,' said Marco flatly. 'The Nazis forced the original Jewish owners of Wertheim to hand over the store and its contents for an absolute pittance. Hitler's aryanisation of Jewish businesses was, whichever way you look at it, a form of legalised theft. All I'm doing is giving the long-term beneficiaries of fascism a regular kick in their swollen financial testicles.'

'But aren't you scared of getting caught?' asked Jack.

'Not at all,' said Marco. 'Given that I worked as a store detective for three months before I got into this, I've got a fairly detailed idea of the errors that shoplifters typically make. I know how to dress as though I can afford whatever I want and I know the behaviours that are characteristic of genuine shoppers. And crucially, I can spot the security staff just as easily as they can spot the most obvious thieves. The trick to not getting caught is not to be noticed in the first place.'

Marco proceeded to describe his well-practised modus operandi in such detail and with such relish that Jack wondered whether his flatmate perhaps enjoyed the thrill of the process more than the satisfaction with the outcome. In an effort to placate his own conflicted conscience, the British student resolved privately to put a twenty-mark note in the Red Cross collection box the next time he had cause to go to the Post Office.

33 FREE GERMAN YOUTH

East Berlin, Saturday 17th April 1976

Towards the end of April, Jenny and Rosa took advantage of the university holidays to return to Berlin, spend some time with their families and catch up with Ulla. The three friends had not seen each other since Christmas and had been eagerly looking forward to an opportunity to reconnect. Ulla's parents were delighted when their daughter announced that she would be spending much of the extended weekend in Karlshorst and promised her a leisurely walk in the Spree Forest on Easter Sunday. She could, if she wanted, invite her friends.

Having spent Good Friday with their families, the former classmates convened at the S-Bahn station in Karlshorst late the following morning. Significantly, it was the first time that they seen each other since the news of Karl Wolfram's death and when Jenny acknowledged that difficult fact, Ulla could do little to mask her emotion. The ensuing group hug was interrupted only by the approach of their train.

From Alexanderplatz station the friends mooched their way to a popular restaurant in Waisenstrasse. The establishment purported to be the oldest tavern in Berlin and Jenny joked as they took their seats that this claim would no doubt be reflected in the unhurried nature of the service. Set over three storeys, the restaurant looked out through leaded windows onto the narrow cobbled street outside. The traditional furniture was solid, tightly packed and allowed little room for the smartly dressed staff to negotiate a path from the kitchen to their allotted tables. By twelve, almost every seat was occupied.

Over pork knuckle, chard quiche and veal liver, the three young women relaxed into each other's company and began to open up about new experiences, new friendships and new opportunities. Although the coerced withdrawal of Ulla's application to Leipzig University remained an uncomfortable truth, she nevertheless encouraged Jenny and Rosa to spill the beans on student life. Their ice hockey playing friend, she assured them, fully intended to apply for a degree in physics in the not too distant future. Judiciously, she omitted to mention that her intention was now to attend university in Munich rather than Leipzig. Although she trusted Rosa and Jenny implicitly, she needed to avoid even the slightest allusion to her plan to extricate herself from the GDR. The last thing she wished for her two university friends was that they should be dragged into the net of suspicion that would inevitably be trawled behind any attempt, successful or otherwise, to escape to the West.

In the afternoon, Ulla introduced Jenny and Rosa to her dilapidated, poorly ventilated but undeniably cheap apartment. Whilst Ulla made apple and cinnamon tea in the kitchen, the two university students opened the windows and took it upon themselves to straighten the place up a bit.

Keen to have a celebratory Saturday night out, but afraid ever to return to the Riviera Ballroom in Grünau, Jenny announced that she had bought three tickets for the Youth and Student Disco for Peaceful Co-existence and against Colonialism, being hosted on Saturday evening in Karlshorst by the local division of the Free German Youth. Although the nomenclature accurately suggested a fundamentally political event, word had spread that the DJ for the night possessed a particularly eclectic collection of records, which everyone understood to mean that he owned a sizeable quantity of British and American music. Consequently, Jenny, Rosa and Ulla could look forward to seeing many of their old friends from the Immanuel Kant Extended Upper School at the disco. Although Ulla was the only member of the class to have remained in Berlin after graduating from school, almost all but the handful of those away on national service would be back for the Easter holidays.

The disco began punctually at seven in the Karlshorst Sports and Community Centre, a purpose-built facility with an unassuming fountain in a circular pond almost directly outside the entrance. Jenny, Rosa and Ulla arrived shortly after seven thirty and even from outside the building, the friends could pick out the English-language vocals and feel the low rumble of amplified bass. Whilst many of the attendees were already inside enjoying the music, a number sat beside by the cool water of the pond and occasionally raised a celebratory bottle of Berliner Pilsener or Schuter's Red Star to their lips.

In spite of the official GDR regulation requiring discotheques to play a minimum of sixty percent homegrown pop music, not even the hardest of hardline members of the Free German Youth could entertain the prospect of dancing for most of the night to the anodyne output of state-approved performers. As a result, the DJ had been taken quietly to one side and informed that he was at liberty to play largely whatever he liked. The powerful West German music system had been supplied for the evening by Andreas Lindemann, a serving soldier and son of the Minister for Culture. Keen to play down his father's elevated position in the Party and the privileges that such lofty status conferred, Andreas peddled the fiction that the system had been a gift from politically misguided but generous relatives in Hamburg.

Inside the sprung-floored hall, the main lights had been switched off, a rotating mirror ball filled the room with an impression of swirling stars and the banners that festooned the walls were scarcely visible. The experienced DJ knew exactly how to fill a dance floor and how to keep it full simply by playing the music that his audience wanted to hear. Throughout the evening, he interspersed floor-fillers by KC and the Sunshine Band, Stevie Wonder, and Boney M with regular doses of danceable rock classics by bands such as the Rolling Stones and Free. Unwilling to see the party as anything other than a chance to let off steam, Ulla, Jenny and Rosa, along with almost everyone else in the heaving, sweaty hall, danced like there was no tomorrow.

As the evening progressed, some of the divisions in Ulla's class that had been triggered by the Wolfram family's visa application seemed to melt away. Friends, who during the last months of school had hardly spoken to Ulla, gradually lost their inhibitions. Many of the Free German Youth members, who without exception had completely ostracised her, drank so much that they no longer cared. In a rare moment of abandon, Andreas Lindemann swallowed a Dormutil sleeping pill, washed it down with a bottle of Berliner Pilsener and was temporarily transformed from a dogmatic zealot into everyone's best friend.

Finally needing to catch her breath, Ulla pushed through the tightly-packed dancers and drifted outside into the much cooler air. Sitting on the low concrete wall surrounding the ornamental pond, she knew that the evening was drawing to a close and that thought saddened her. Still, if she suddenly heard the strains of 'Suffragette City', she would be straight back inside.

Emerging from the huddle of Free German Youth members who had come outside to smoke, Andreas Lindemann made a bee-line for Ulla and sat unexpectedly beside her.

'Great party,' he slurred. 'Like, the best ever.'

'Yeah,' she replied warily. 'Not bad at all.'

Unwilling to spend a second more in his company, Ulla decided to return to the dancing. Andreas, however, grabbed her loosely by the forearm.

'I've always liked you,' he said slowly. 'Ever since primary school. You're beautiful.'

'I think you need to be getting back to your friends over there,' said Ulla, both edgy and unimpressed. She had not the slightest desire to respond to his beery advances, but drunk as Andreas was, he remained the son of a powerful man and she knew she would have to tread carefully.

'You know,' he continued. 'It's a shame that… it's a shame we can't be together.'

'No, it's not,' she said bluntly. 'In what universe would we be together?'

Andreas was far too inebriated to cope with the subtleties of a rhetorical question.

'You're so beautiful,' he said, closing his eyes and tilting unsteadily backwards. After drifting for a few moments, he straightened himself jerkily, opened his eyes once more and tried to look directly at Ulla. She refused to meet his gaze.

'You know,' he said. 'I know the world is… it's sort of complicated. I know we can't be together. I know that. But it doesn't mean we can't make out. I mean, like right here, right now. Just one time.'

The son of a high-ranking Party member released his grip on her arm, placed his hand limply on Ulla's thigh and leaned in towards her. Ulla was having none of it. Without hesitation, she batted her suitor away and stood up sharply, causing him to slouch backwards and slump heavily into the ornamental pond.

'You can go fuck yourself,' she muttered. 'You overprivileged arsehole.'

As much as Andreas Lindemann had been a focus for her unremitting anger towards the authorities, she instantly realised she would now have to pull the drunken toad out of the water. Ulla yelled for help, stepped into the pond and, from behind, lifted Andreas by the armpits to keep his head proud of the surface. Two of the group of smokers were soon at hand and tried gamely to manhandle their well-oiled friend to his feet. As they did so, Andreas rolled his head to the left and vomited copiously down the legs of one of his rescuers. Ulla wondered, as she helped guide him over the concrete wall and out of the pond, if her rejection of his drunken advances might come back to haunt her. Given the state that he was in, it seemed highly unlikely. He would no doubt remember little, if anything at all, of her exhortation for him to spend more time in his own unwanted company.

Ulla rounded off the evening with her arms around the shoulders of Jenny and Rosa, as they collectively and passionately belted out the chorus to 'Starman'. Neither of her friends noticed that her shoes and legs were sopping wet and if Andreas was still at the party, he was presumably throwing up in the toilets. As the DJ was packing away, Ulla made a point of congratulating him on the choice of music and quietly asked him if by any chance he knew someone by the name of Mick Jaeger. Uncertain of the purpose of Ulla's enquiry and reluctant to trust a complete stranger, the DJ simply shrugged and claimed never to have heard of him.

On the slow walk back towards her parents' apartment, Ulla drew attention to the dampness of her shoes and jeans and detailed her brief encounter by, and subsequently in, the ornamental pond. She knew that she would have many joyous memories of the long overdue night out, but ninety seconds in the unsolicited company of Andreas Lindemann would not be one of them. As they walked, she wondered whether, after this weekend, she would ever see Jenny and Rosa again.

34 ONLOOKERS

West Berlin, Monday 19th April 1976

To Jack's surprise, the offices of the Church of Reconciliation were on the top floor of a modern apartment block directly overlooking the Wall. From the compact seating area where he waited for his appointment and sipped at his freshly prepared coffee, it was impossible to see the border installations some six storeys below. With the Wall obscured from sight, the tower and steeple of the church itself appeared to be no more than a short walk across the street.

At the desk in front of the young student, Pastor Niemeyer's PA typed up the slew of short letters dictated to her last thing on Friday. As she completed the first of the many tasks before her, Petra Fichtenberg granted herself a moment to examine the gold engagement ring which, for the past two days, had graced the third finger of her left hand.

On the far side of the open-plan office, two colleagues were currently engaged in a lively discussion that necessitated frequent trips to a large planning chart. Everyone who Jack had observed so far seemed pleasant enough. It would not, he imagined, be difficult to work here. To the left of the year planner, a sequence of framed posters offered guests some philosophical food for thought and perhaps presented a window into the soul of the man who Jack was waiting to meet.

'Peace without weapons,' demanded a Picasso lithograph of a dove bearing an olive branch.

'Here I stand, I can do no other,' proclaimed a mediaeval portrait, undoubtedly of Martin Luther.

'Paradise Lost,' lamented a grainy black and white image of massed and belching industrial chimneys.

In many ways, they were not unlike the posters that adorned the walls of Marco and Anna's room back in Oudenarder Strasse.

Frau Fichtenberg cast an eye over the young British intern as he stared, now lost in thought, in the general direction of the far wall. He came across as polite and inherently friendly, although he clearly had no sense of how to dress for a day in an office.

A small green light flashed on the brushed aluminium intercom that sat on her desk.

'He'll see you now,' said Frau Fichtenberg, interrupting Jack from his reverie. 'Just knock and go in.'

As soon as Jack was through the door, Pastor Niemeyer strode purposefully across the room, shook his hand warmly and offered his guest a seat. The priest was perhaps somewhere in his fifties and was noticeably shorter than Jack. Possessed of an engaging smile, his intelligent green eyes looked out from behind rimless glasses. Niemeyer's uniformly grey but neatly trimmed hair did not seem to age him, but the yellowing of the index and middle fingers of his right hand were a clue both to the longevity and the intensity of his smoking habit. Unsurprisingly for a pastor of the Lutheran church, he wore a charcoal-black, long-sleeved shirt and a white clerical collar.

'So, you're Jack Gilmore, our multilingual volunteer,' he began.

'That's me,' said Jack cheerily.

'To be honest, I wasn't entirely sure that you'd turn up. But now that you're here, I think it might be useful to have a brief, informal chat, just to ensure that you are a good fit for our set-up and, of course, that we are a good fit for you. We'll get to the nitty gritty later.'

'Of course,' said Jack, taken somewhat aback that he was about to be interviewed for a one-day-a-week, unpaid internship. Given a moment to reflect, however, the procedure made perfect sense. The pastor would no doubt be keen to ensure that his prospective intern was not a sociopath, an atheist firebrand or some kind of satanist.

Niemeyer tapped his packet of HB on the desk. 'Cigarette?'

'Thank you,' said Jack politely, 'but I don't smoke.'

'I smoke like a chimney, which is a little ironic considering the poster I put up in the office. It's not exactly a pleasant habit, but I'm too long in the tooth to give it up now. Still, we all have feet of clay.'

'I wonder,' said Jack, emboldened by the pastor's lack of affectation, 'what the impact on world hunger might be, if every tobacco field around the globe were to be reassigned to food production?'

Niemeyer drew on the cigarette and paused briefly to reflect. 'That's an interesting point. To be honest, that's not something I've ever really considered. But yes, it's definitely… well, it's definitely a good point.'

Eager to pursue their conversation against the backdrop of the stranded church whose name so obstinately mocked the military installations that enclosed it, Niemeyer invited Jack onto the balcony and allowed his guest to survey the scene for himself. Beneath them, two lines of linden trees obscured much of their view of the border and the Wall. To the left, the neo-gothic redbrick tower of the church rose high above the treetops and once again appeared eminently accessible from the West. Maybe sixty metres to their right was the wooden observation platform where Jack had stood with Julia only a fortnight before. As far as the prospective intern could make out, the itinerant football had since been removed.

'You know, Jack,' said the pastor, 'in principle, I have a house and a parish office on the other side of the Wall, no more than a hundred metres from here, just beyond those chimneys. I went there shortly after my appointment in 1970. I knew the doors and windows had been bricked up, but I just wanted to look.'

'So, is that the address that appears on your official correspondence, as well as this one.'

'Indeed. You're an observant young man. But, yes. It's still my official residence and as such it entitles me to travel back and forth largely as I please.'

'I don't expect there are many people in Berlin who can say that.'

'Very few. Most Berliners have learned to treat the other half of the city as though it were no longer there. Take these trees for example. I expect the majority of the residents in this block are thankful that they screen much of their view. And it's a welcome illusion for me too, to be honest, but the Wall is there regardless. At least, for now.'

Drawing frequently on his cigarette, Niemeyer proceeded to provide a potted history of the Church of Reconciliation, before explaining the constant pressure he was under from the authorities in the East to accede to the demolition of the isolated and unused building. In exchange, the Secretary of State for Church Affairs was offering the recalcitrant priest a purpose-built 'parish centre' on the northeastern edge of Berlin, some eight inconvenient kilometres from Bernauer Strasse.

'There's no decision to make,' said Niemeyer, breathing smoke out through his nose. 'Someone has to make a stand. For injustice to triumph, it is enough for the onlookers to do nothing. Earlier this century, the churches in Germany stood by and watched as the Jews were herded into cattle trucks. I think we have to learn from that.'

The pastor caught Jack's eye.

'Do you believe in God?' he asked, almost casually.

'Well,' said Jack, reaching for his standard response to almost any philosophical question, 'it depends what you mean by "God". If you're asking me if I believe in an old man with a flowing white beard who grants wishes and decides the outcome of every human moment, then I can give you a very easy answer. If you're asking me if I think there's more to the universe than meets the eye, then yes, that's the way it looks to me. And if you're asking me if it's right to be kind to others, then yes again, although I think it's right whether the man with the beard commands it or not. I'm sorry. This may not be the answer you were hoping I'd give, but maybe human beings don't have the brainpower to work out why anything exists and maybe we should be happy to acknowledge that.'

Niemeyer paused briefly. Most people offered no more than a single-word answer to that question. 'You know, one of the first things we learned at seminary was that it is no more possible to define God than to give a numerical value to infinity by adding one to the biggest number you can think of. I would say you have a faith, although I suspect you may not see it that way. Would you say that you believe in life after death, Jack?'

Jack pursed his lips and jigged his head momentarily from side to side. 'At the risk of sounding like a broken record, it depends on what you mean. We live on in our children, I suppose, or in the examples we set. Maybe in the music we make if you're someone like Mozart or Bob Dylan, or in the good or the evil we visit upon others.'

'Let's be more specific then,' said Niemeyer, clearly enjoying the to-and-fro of their discussion. 'Do you believe in the resurrection of the soul?'

Jack shrugged. 'I guess, death will essentially be like the time before I was born and I have no unpleasant memories of that.'

'In which case, there is no case to fear it.'

'No, although the dying part might not be so attractive.'

'Granted, but death is merely a doorway to another existence. We should fear death no more than Christ feared death. In Christ we see a maturity of love that flowers in self-sacrifice. I strongly believe, Jack, that any of us should be ready to follow his example if it absolves others of suffering or alleviates misery.'

Suddenly feeling out of his depth, Jack was unsure how to reply. 'With respect, I think that's braver than you make it sound,' he said finally. 'Don't we all instinctively fear death?'

'Perhaps. But instinct does not always serve us well. Fascism was instinct dressed up as a godless faith. Communism is solidarity in the same polished jackboots. You know, Lenin once said that capitalists are no more capable of self-sacrifice than a man is capable of lifting himself up by his own bootstraps, but I would put it to Vladimir Illich Lenin that he and his acolytes in East Berlin are really no different. Marx, it strikes me, is now as much the opium of the people as religion ever was.'

'Perhaps any form of dogma can be the opium of the people,' ventured Jack. 'Gandhi said that he liked Christ, but he didn't like an awful lot of Christians.'

'And I suspect Martin Luther might have agreed with him. Interestingly, Gandhi also saw Christ as a paragon of non-violent resistance. In the end, British imperialism was driven out of India by the most Christ-like of Hindus.'

Uncertain how the conversation had come so far in such a short space of time, Jack stared across the treetops at the dull render adorning the gable end of a building just beyond the border installations. Obscured at first by the trees, a jeep rattled along the narrow concrete pathway between the inner wall and the line of tank traps known as Czech hedgehogs.

'Anyhow,' said Niemeyer, decisively stubbing his cigarette on the parapet of the balcony, 'the internship is one day a week and will involve lending support to Frau Fichtenberg and our other administrators, particularly with English-language correspondence or communications, and some translation work too, I would imagine. Nothing too onerous. We are, after all, not paying you.'

'It all sounds fine,' said Jack. 'It will all be good experience for me.'

'Excellent. You know, Jack, it's been a pleasure to talk. Most people just agree with me, at least on this side of that monstrosity down there. There's one thing I need to say however, and please do not feel judged by this, but there is an accepted dress code for work in our office. You'll be expected to wear a tie and we don't wear jeans or sports shoes, or any kind of sports clothing for that matter. Is that likely to be a problem?'

'No,' said Jack. 'It won't be a problem.'

'Good. Excellent. So, business concluded, I think. I'm looking forward to working with you. Frau Fichtenberg will sort you out with a contract before you leave.'

The pastor ushered Jack back to his PA's desk, before initiating an enthusiastic handshake.

'By the way,' he said, 'I wish you luck with your dissertation. I'm not sure whether your desire to visit the Environment Ministry in East Berlin is impressively ambitious or just youthfully naive. Let's pray it's the former. Either way, tread carefully when you're over there, Jack. And maybe wear a tie.'

35 A MOMENT OF NEED

East Berlin, Sunday 25th April 1976

Two days after the Youth and Student Disco for Peaceful Co-existence and against Colonialism, Andreas Lindemann took a train back to his regiment on the Baltic coast and did not plan to return to Berlin until the end of the year.

Ulla was inordinately surprised, however, when her parents turned up at her apartment two weeks later bearing an official-looking letter that turned out to be from her inebriated admirer's high-ranking father. In a formal but vaguely worded statement, the Culture Minister introduced himself and took the opportunity to express his sincere gratitude for the help that Ulla had afforded his son 'in a moment of need'. He emphasised the importance of solidarity in the development of a progressive and humane society, expressed the wish that Ulla and her family were in good health and signed off with a standard valediction and a flourish of the pen.

Ulla responded to her parents' bafflement with a full and honest account of the events at the party. Keen to view an expression of gratitude from a prominent Party member as a step towards the family's rehabilitation, Udo Wolfram wondered whether there might be some benefit to framing the unexpected letter. Profoundly unimpressed, Ulla immediately rounded on the Minister's 'hypocritical bollocks about compassion and social progress'. She would not, she stated flatly, be putting his letter on the wall. To dignify a member of the regime in such a way would be an affront to her grandfather's memory. And that was that. She did not want to discuss the matter further. Anyway, they were probably all in need of something to eat. It was a point on which father and daughter were happy to agree.

After a conciliatory lunch at the Metzer Eck, Ulla walked with her parents to the U-Bahn at Senefelder Platz and hugged them both warmly. Once back in the apartment, she retrieved the Thomas Lindemann letter from her desk, took it to the kitchen and burnt it in the sink.

36 GREEN LIGHT

West Berlin, Monday 26th April 1976

Precisely a week after his initial visit to the Concordia offices, Jack got up at six thirty, showered, shaved and breakfasted alone. Having knocked up a couple of generously proportioned cheese sandwiches for his lunch, the still sleepy student turned his attention to the neat pile of clothing that Marco had so readily shoplifted from the KaDeWe department store. The black chinos and the crisp white shirt smelled of starch and the silk jacquard tie almost wilfully resisted Jack's repeated efforts to knot it correctly. Feeling decidedly uncomfortable, the new intern checked his appearance in the mirror and immediately wished he hadn't. Ultimately more at ease with his new clothing concealed beneath his familiar, navy blue trench coat, Jack left the flat, walked down the stairs and crossed the courtyard.

In the poorly lit passageway leading to the main doors of the dilapidated apartment block, he checked his mailbox. Wedged between various items of garish junk mail, he was delighted to discover a postcard from Mirka enthusiastically announcing her new address in Maison Lafitte and wondering how he was getting on. Certain that his former flatmate would be taking life in Paris at a canter and feeling the need to impress her, he resolved to write to her once he had secured an interview at the Environment Ministry in East Berlin. He would also, he thought, send a postcard of the Alexanderplatz TV tower to his father. Maybe he would even surprise him with a phone call.

Emerging into the street, Jack looked at his watch and realised that his fear of being late for work had caused him to get up far too early. He comfortably had time to make it to the Concordia offices on foot, so abandoned his plan to use the U-Bahn. Although it was noticeably less cold than of late, the now familiar smell of lignite smoke already hung in the early-morning air. Rush-hour was in full flow and both the streets and the pavements were dominated by people who clearly had somewhere to be.

Forty-five minutes after walking determinedly past the U-Bahn station at Nauener Platz, Jack climbed the six flights of stairs to Pastor Niemeyer's office and presented himself at the reception desk. He handed the signed copy of his contract to Frau Fichtenberg, who rewarded him with a freshly brewed cup of coffee and an acknowledgement of the effort he had made to dress for a professional environment. Much of Jack's morning was consumed by the challenging conversion into German of a New York Times article headlined *How to Wreck the Environment*. Although the Concordia office was busy, there appeared to be no sign of Pastor Niemeyer.

After lunch, Frau Fichtenberg looked approvingly over Jack's cogently rendered translation before inviting him to join her at her desk.

'I would like to offer you some practical advice,' she said, 'about visiting East Berlin.'

She handed the student a copy of a booklet entitled *Berlin from the Brandenburg Gate to Alexanderplatz: Guidance for West German visitors.*

'It's published here in West Berlin. By the Berlin Senate's Office of Information. Inside you'll find a beautifully set-out map of the central districts of East Berlin with just about every key location clearly identified. You'll also find detailed guidance regarding access to the checkpoints and the protocols you must adhere to and there's a useful list of tips to ensure that you don't have any unnecessary interactions with the forces of law and order.'

Although Julia had already presented Jack with a copy of the same publication two days previously, he appreciated Frau Fichtenberg's interest in him and thanked her warmly for her help. He wondered momentarily if Julia would have considered his polite acceptance of the second booklet to be an act of dishonesty. They would, no doubt, debate that question later.

'There is something else I wanted to chat to you about,' continued Frau Fichtenberg. 'We are perfectly aware, Jack, that your internship here is unremunerated. And we genuinely appreciate that. We do. But if you're interested, we might be able to offer you payment for a small freelance assignment that would sit outside the remit of your contract.'

Jack was all ears.

'Pastor Niemeyer would like to commission you to write a short report for *Green Light*, our eco-magazine, about your visit to the GDR Ministry for the Environment. Obviously you would want to mention your dissertation and the kinds of policies you were able to discuss, but he'd also be looking for a more human picture of your visit. You know the kind of thing. Who you met. How you were received, et cetera, et cetera. Standard observational stuff. Try to be positive, though. Emphasise the things we have in common rather than simply pointing out the differences. Go into as much detail as you can. It will all be of interest.'

'This sounds a little a bit like spying,' said Jack, uncertain whether he was appalled or strangely excited at the idea.

'Oh Heavens, no,' retorted Frau Fichtenberg, shaking her head. 'Perish the thought. As I said, what we'd be looking for is a simple magazine-style report on your visit. We're really not asking you to be nosy. In fact, you should as a matter of course be a model of compliance when you pay your visit to the Ministry. Do not make notes on anything that is not strictly relevant to your dissertation and readily comply with any requests to show your notes before you leave. Your article, and honestly, please don't feel under any pressure to run with the idea, would therefore need to be written directly on your return to Wedding whilst the impressions are still fresh in your mind. We'd be looking at maybe fifteen hundred words. And with regard to remuneration, Concordia would be happy to offer you a one-off fee of a hundred marks for the completed piece. But as I said, Jack, we don't want you to feel under the slightest pressure here. It's entirely up to you.'

A hundred deutschmarks was a sizeable fee, the best part of a month's rent. It was not exactly a tricky decision.

37 EYES AND EARS

East Berlin, Wednesday 28th April 1976

Captain Hartling was not a happy man. Although the clock was ticking, a formidable combination of physical and administrative security measures still precluded access to the files demanded by MI6. At the same time, he was under growing pressure from his superiors to find a way to bring the uncooperative Pastor Niemeyer to heel. Frustrated, he leaned forward and, with his elbows planted on his desk, pumped a clenched fist against his lips.

Hoping that a cigarette might clear his mind, he put a match to a Cabinet Original and turned his attention to the Niemeyer case. The most recent batch of documents supplied by Petra Fichtenberg had shed no light on the pastor's potential susceptibility to any specific line of persuasion and had revealed nothing in his affairs that might render him vulnerable to blackmail. Nevertheless, Hartling reflected, if there were no skeletons in Niemeyer's closet, it would not be impossible to have his asset place one there. She had, after all, done everything he had so far demanded of her.

When the Stasi officer phoned his putative fiancée and informed her that he had seized an opportunity to spend a long weekend in Berlin, she leapt at the chance of seeing him and promised to take a couple of days off work. They could meet, she suggested, in their customary five-star haunt on the Kurfürstendamm.

With the hotel room booked, Hartling turned his thoughts to a related case and ferreted out a file from the lower drawer of his desk. The codename Matterhorn on the cover of the folder related to the British student who purportedly harboured a desire to conduct a research interview with an official representative of the Environment Ministry. Pass and Control records, he noted, showed that a British passport holder by the name of Jack Gilmore had recently crossed the GDR by train to West Berlin, but had made no subsequent attempt to access the eastern side of the city.

Hartling leaned back on his chair, breathed out a plume of smoke and drummed the tips of his fingers on the desk. He no longer knew what to make of the case. Perhaps his suspicion of a move by MI6 had been nearer to the mark than he had initially thought. If the student were some kind of British spook, however, he would surely have been flown into West Berlin, not packed onto a train carrying a passport in his own name.

Of course, passports could be faked and there was no guarantee that the very British-sounding Jack Gilmore was not from Munich or Frankfurt am Main. The name, the nationality and the rail journey across the GDR might have been conceived by West German Intelligence as components of an elaborate cover story. With luck, Hartling might glean some useful insight into the situation from Petra Fichtenberg. In the meantime, he could no longer risk the displeasure of his commanders by appearing to have lowered his guard in some way. He needed to have eyes and ears inside the Ministry for the Environment.

From the labyrinth of ceiling-high filing units in the extensive Stasi archive, Hartling fetched the personal records of a number of potential candidates and spread them across his desk. Ninety minutes later, he had identified four members of staff who, with an absolute minimum of fuss, could be engaged to carry out close-quarters surveillance of the questionable British student, should he at any point turn up. It took no more than ten minutes to make his final selection and record the decision in the case file. As he had arranged to spend the following three nights in West Berlin with Petra Fichtenberg, he would need to leave the process of recruitment temporarily in abeyance. Not before Monday, at the earliest, would he be in a position to pay a visit to Hans-Beimler-Strasse and add the chosen collaborator to his roster of informants.

That business concluded, he would return to the increasingly pressing issue of robbing the Ministry for State Security of some of its most sensitive files.

38 WAITING FOR THE MAN

West Berlin, Thursday 29th April 1976

Although Jack Gilmore was now the somewhat embarrassed owner of two Hugo Boss ties, he opted to wear neither for his initial excursion to East Berlin. Given that his slightly off-beat attire had, the previous day, proved to be no impediment to conducting a wide-ranging interview at the Federal Environment Agency in West Berlin, he saw no reason to dress differently for his trip to the East. The FEA press secretary had been only too eager to exemplify the environmental policies of the West German government and present the Federal Republic as demonstrably the greener of the two German states. Tie or no tie, Jack saw no reason why the personnel at the Ministry for the Environment in East Berlin would not wish to respond in exactly the same way. After showering shortly before eight, he pulled on the black pants Marco had stolen for him, an old tee shirt with the words 'Bad Company' printed across the chest and the somewhat faded bottle-green sweatshirt he had worn during the long journey from Madrid. Although the chinos were a minor concession to formality, Jack still looked unquestionably like a student.

Over breakfast, Julia ensured that Jack knew exactly which checkpoint he needed to use, gave him clear expectations of the ponderous visa and entry formalities that awaited him and presented him with an up-to-date street map covering both sides of the city. Finally, having explained that day visitors to the GDR were required to exchange and spend a minimum of twenty-five deutschmarks during their brief stay, Julia asked him to visit the Centrum department store on Alexanderplatz before crossing back into the West. There, she assured him, he would be able to spend every last East German mark on the ludicrously cheap photographic paper that over time had filled the cupboards of their shared darkroom. As Anna poured herself a mug of tea, she advised Jack not to assume that he might easily locate a takeaway food outlet in East Berlin. If he wanted to eat more than a slice of dry cake during his excursion, he would do well to prepare a sandwich before he left or buy some *börek* pastries from the Turkish kiosk on Leopoldplatz Station.

Equipped with a canvas backpack containing almost everything he needed for his long-anticipated visit to the other Berlin, Jack walked brightly to the underground station at Leopoldplatz, bought some lunch and boarded a train towards Friedrichstrasse. By the time he returned to his apartment that evening, he would, he hoped, be the first student from Lanchester Polytechnic to have conducted primary research in the GDR Environment Ministry and the prospect of that success put him in a particularly buoyant mood. As the train rumbled through the final station before the border with the East, he wondered momentarily if the Bad Company tee shirt had perhaps been an ill-considered choice, but concluded that in all probability he would have no cause to remove his inoffensively plain sweatshirt.

Although Jack's map of the underground network clearly identified 'stations at which the trains do not stop' and Julia had also alluded to a sequence of ghost stations over breakfast, nothing had prepared him for the bizarre U-Bahn journey beneath the salient of East Berlin's central district.

After perhaps a minute beneath the streets of the GDR capital, the train began to decelerate noticeably, as though preparing to stop, only to trundle with tantalising slowness through a dimly lit station where the dusty, peeling posters had not changed since 1961 and only armed border guards now stood on the unswept platform. After watching two more shadowy, deserted stations drift eerily by, Jack clutched his backpack, abandoned his seat and moved in readiness to the door. Eventually, the train screeched and moaned to a halt at Friedrichstrasse, the single station in the East where westerners were permitted to alight. Once the passengers were clear of the doors, the train would rattle onwards through a second series of ghost stations before passing beneath the border once more and rejoining the western network.

On the busy Friedrichstrasse platform, a sign marked 'Border Crossing' ushered Jack up two flights of stairs and into a holding area where a gaggle of prospective visitors to East Berlin waited to be processed. Jack assumed that he was now standing at ground level, although the absence of windows made it impossible to know for sure. The walls to the wide passageway were dressed in cream tiles which reflected the light from the bare fluorescent strips above. Just below the level of the high ceiling, a number of video cameras made it clear to the hundred or so new arrivals that their presence was already being scrutinised.

Ahead of the group stood several numbered doors through which visitors were intermittently invited to pass. Having read through the selection of available provenances listed above each door, Jack opted for one of the four crowded lines specified for 'citizens of other states'. Whilst the overwhelming majority of control points were designated for 'citizens of the Federal Republic of Germany and Berlin (West)', a solitary sign welcomed returnees to the German Democratic Republic. As things stood, none were in evidence.

To pass the time in the slow-moving queue, Jack began predicting whether the next door to open would be an odd or an even number. Rapidly tiring of the exercise, he drifted into a brief internal rehearsal of his Environment Ministry interview questions before allowing his thoughts to slide towards song lyrics that might vaguely relate to his situation. Within ten minutes he was humming 'I'm Waiting for the Man' by the Velvet Underground.

Once inside the control cabin, Jack presented his passport to the uniformed officer stationed behind a high walnut-effect counter. The perfunctory mannerisms and formal tone were by now familiar and the young British student consciously responded with the unruffled patience and ready co-operation that the Italian anarchist on the transit train had recommended some four weeks previously. Behind and above Jack's head, a long, angled mirror afforded the Pass and Control officer a clear view of the visitor's back as well as the floor around his feet. It was just as well, Jack reassured himself, that he was not attempting to smuggle a mature Saint Bernard or a teak sideboard.

Without a flicker, the sergeant noted that a Jack Gilmore appeared on his watch list. Just as soon as he had processed the traveller's passport, the officer would, in accordance with the instructions on the register, alert the Main Directorate for Reconnaissance to his arrival.

Forty minutes after watching the visa being stamped unceremoniously into his passport, Jack had completed the compulsory exchange of twenty-five deutschmarks into non-returnable East German currency, had submitted a customs declaration to the effect that he had nothing to declare and emerged from the windowless security warren into the bustle and the sunshine of the street outside the station. As Jack fished Julia's city map from his backpack and set about orientating himself in his unfamiliar surroundings, a photographer was already preparing to leave the Stasi complex in Normannenstrasse.

Hoping to complete the journey to the Environment Ministry entirely on foot, Jack first headed south along Friedrichstrasse. Whilst those buildings that had been reduced to rubble during the war had since been re-built or replaced, many of the structures that had survived the onslaught still bore the scars of conflict some thirty years later. They were, it seemed, scarcely different in appearance to the bullet-riddled building in Oudenarder Strasse where Jack now lived. Presently the fascinated traveller found his way to the wide boulevard whose curious name of Unter den Linden soon revealed itself to be no more than a reference to the trees that shaded the pedestrian walkways.

East Berlin, it soon occurred to Jack, was at once familiar and strange. The pavements, though hardly deserted, appeared less crowded than their counterparts in the West and somehow presented a more subdued palette of colour to the eye. The roadways were busy without being excessively so and were dominated by perhaps no more than three or four models of automobile, produced apparently in a strictly limited range of muted tones. Yet something much less tangible than shapes and colours was in the air. In spite of the still considerable numbers of both pedestrians and vehicles, and in contrast to both Madrid and West Berlin, the city seemed to go about its business without either haste or distraction. Whilst no-one seemed particularly to be taking their time, neither did they appear to be in a rush.

In due course, Jack reached the partially restored Berlin Cathedral, a once impressive, domed church now blackened by soot and largely clad in wooden scaffolding. Across the street a long, modern building in white stone and gleaming, copper-tinted glass presented itself confidently to the visitor. Judging from the pristine appearance of the stonework, construction had perhaps only recently been completed. Although the function of the intriguing structure was not immediately obvious, above the main entrance the huge emblem of a hammer and dividers encircled by a wreath of ripening rye suggested that it was in all likelihood a government office. Closer inspection of the street map revealed it to be the Palace of the Republic.

A short distance beyond, the modernist TV tower was the one feature of the cityscape that Jack felt he already knew. Clearly visible from so many locations in Wedding, the huge tapering column of concrete supported a restaurant and observation deck within a perfect sphere of gleaming steel panels and was crowned with a massive red and white hooped spire. At 365 metres in height, the tower was by far the tallest structure on either side of the East-West border and constituted an unabashed political statement. A proud affirmation to the citizens of the GDR of the technological prowess of the their progressive motherland, it was in equal measure a permanent reminder to the inhabitants of West Berlin of both the presence and the power of the state that enclosed their half of the city.

Gradually it dawned on Jack exactly what it was that he was not seeing in East Berlin. The usual plethora of advertising hoardings competing for the attention of the western consumer were, he now realised, conspicuous by their absence. No-one was showing him how to be more attractive, imploring him to 'test the West' or seducing him to enjoy 'the taste of freedom and adventure'. Similarly, the majority of shop signs were disarmingly functional. As he walked along Karl-Liebknecht-Strasse, he passed stores designated simply as a 'savings bank', a 'household appliance service' and a 'book store'. None of these shops, it seemed, had the slightest need to distinguish itself by name, brand or sponsor.

Furthermore, Honecker's command economy did not, apparently, stretch to the provision of buskers, street comedians or kebab trolleys. On the other hand, no down-and-outs were sleeping in shop doorways, there were no beggars, no drunks and, as far as his untutored eye could tell, no hookers or drug dealers. Posters advertising chamber orchestras and theatre performances had not been ripped, defaced or covered with fly-posters for up-and-coming rock bands. No-one was insistently hawking tacky souvenirs and Jack did not feel as though he had to hang on tightly to his backpack as he had so often done in Madrid.

Now beginning to feel hungry, he was glad that he had followed Anna's advice to buy some *börek* at Leopoldplatz. At no point had he yet seen a grocery store or any obvious sort of café. Finding a bench almost directly beneath the impressively tall TV tower, he tucked into his lunch and wondered where he might possibly be able to buy something to drink. As he finished the Turkish pastries, it occurred to Jack that at no point during his admittedly short time in East Berlin had he registered anything other than white faces. He knew from his lectures back in Coventry that the GDR officially welcomed quotas of students and guest workers from countries such as Vietnam, Cuba and Angola, but none were in evidence on the streets of the East German capital. Wherever these visitors were spending their time, they certainly weren't out touring the sights.

From the bench where he had stopped for lunch, Jack needed only to cross Alexanderplatz to reach the Environment Ministry. Possessed of a self-conscious modernity, Alexanderplatz itself had something of the feel of one of those ingenuous British educational posters from the 1950s that so confidently imagined the all-problems-solved, high-rise future of the twenty-first century. As he crossed the square, Jack was pleased to spot the Centrum department store where Julia had asked him to stock up, if he could, on underpriced East German photographic paper. As soon as he had completed his visit to the Environment Ministry, he would make a trip to the store his first priority.

Passing some kind of inscrutable, rotating industrial cylinder of a clock, Jack began to feel a sense of genuine excitement as he closed in on his destination. Arriving at the intersection of Hans-Beimler-Strasse and Karl-Marx-Allee, he registered the teams of workers busily engaged in hoisting red flags along the seemingly unending lines of poles that flanked the impressively wide boulevard to his right. Without doubt, these were preparations for the highly orchestrated mass parades that would be taking place, as they did every year, on the first day of May. After a short wait, the surprisingly jovial pedestrian crossing-signal switched from red to green and invited Jack across Karl-Marx-Allee to the towering concrete and glass structure that housed the GDR Tourist Office. The Ministry for the Environment was, as far as he could make out, somewhere in the modern block on the far side of the busy Hans-Beimler-Strasse underpass. All he had to do now was cross the street.

39 DUE DILIGENCE

West Berlin, Thursday 29th April 1976

The short, staccato trill of the bell beside the door to the Rive Gauche prompted the MI6 field officer to abandon the coffee machine, walk directly to the door and squint cautiously through the net curtains. Recognising Turnbull, the spook nodded in acknowledgement and afforded his boss entry to their quiet, customer-free café. Ensconced at a table near the counter, Kate Wildegood had been killing time for several minutes.

The senior intelligence officer exhaled a plume of smoke. 'You're late.'

Turnbull glanced at his watch. 'I'm never late.'

Wildegood was having none of it. 'You arrived after me. Which means you're late. Cigarette?'

'No thanks,' said Turnbull. 'I'm trying to quit.'

'Really? That's becoming quite a fad these days. Like wholemeal bread. And streaking.'

From his post behind the noisy but gleaming coffee machine, the junior officer arrived with two large cappuccinos.

'Did you have a good flight, ma'am?' asked Turnbull, keen to move on.

'Oh, I think so. I have to say, I like flying with the RAF. Cuts out all that pointless faffing around at the airport. Anyway, let's not beat about the bush. Down to business, I think. I have an hour at best.'

She raised her eyebrows at the officer behind the counter who duly took the hint and retired to an adjacent room.

'So,' continued Wildegood, 'where are we with Hartling?'

'You listened to the tape, I presume.'

'I did indeed. That was smoothly done, might I say. And has our asset made contact since you made the recording?'

'Not as things stand. But given that someone of his rank would not have automatic access to the sort of material we're asking for, the delay is not, I think, beyond expectation.'

Wildegood nodded. 'Nevertheless, he may still be all mouth and no trousers. How sure are you that your man is the genuine article?'

'Are we ever sure? Obviously, we should tread carefully, but all things considered, I think our working assumption should be that Hartling's apparent desire to defect is not a set-up.'

'Because?'

'Because he negotiated so damn hard about his relocation package. I think he's sampled enough of the West in the course of his duties to want a slice of the pie for himself. And a substantial one at that.'

'So it's down to money. Pure and simple.'

Turnbull tilted his head slightly to one side and breathed in slowly. 'I would say so. He obviously wants the usual guarantees of his security: a new identity, a healthy bank balance, a well-appointed home somewhere in British Columbia, that kind of thing.'

Wildegood put down her coffee and pushed it to one side. 'Nevertheless, we still can't rule out the possibility that the Day X references on the typewriter ribbon might just be a load of carefully packaged tosh. What if this is no more than classic disinformation designed, say, to persuade us that Soviet forces in the GDR are much stronger and much more capable than they are in reality?'

'Is that what you think?'

'It's what certain people up the line are thinking.'

'Well, they have perfectly reasonable grounds to be cautious,' said Turnbull. 'But seeing as we're playing "What if?", what if my assessment of Hartling is accurate? I know Day X sounds like something out of Hollywood, but what if it's a fully mapped-out plan? What if we're close to opening the back door into Soviet preparations for the seizure of West Berlin? Can we honestly afford to discount that possibility?'

The senior officer drew on her cigarette as she considered her options. Knowing better than to interrupt, Turnbull took a sip of his cappuccino before wiping the froth from his upper lip.

'OK,' said Wildegood finally. 'You have my backing on this. But don't wait for Hartling to make contact. Call a meeting and ramp up the pressure. Say you expect cast-iron corroboration of the contents of the ribbon within a month or the deal is off. As soon as our friend produces tangible evidence of his value, play him your tape and see how he reacts to the prospect of being outed to his superiors. If you see anything less than genuine fear in his eyes, drop him like a stone. Otherwise, nail his feet to the floor. Keep him in place in the Ministry for State Security and maintain the flow of intelligence.'

'Understood, ma'am. Wilco.'

'And of course, if our pet Stasi officer produces files that all too conveniently match your very precise specifications, we might rapidly come to the conclusion that they're being tailor-made for the consumption of the gullible.'

'In which case?'

'In which case, we let London decide what to do next.'

'In all honesty, ma'am, I don't think it'll come to that.'

'Well let's hope so. There's far too much riding on this. The intelligence has to be rock solid before we put it in front of Supreme Allied Command.'

'That goes without saying.'

Wildegood looked her colleague in the eye. 'And yet I felt the need to say it.'

Turnbull reflected momentarily. 'Point taken, ma'am. I will take care not to get ahead of myself.'

'Simply exercise due diligence. Nothing more, nothing less. However, assuming for one moment that we satisfy ourselves of Hartling's veracity, NATO will, as you intimated, acquire a back channel into the specifics of Soviet planning for the seizure of West Berlin. And that, in as far as I am permitted to know these things, would be completely without precedent.'

'And no doubt our friends in the CIA would be green with envy that we got there first.'

'For sure. But more importantly, it might make an outbreak of hostilities between the superpowers much less likely. That is, I think, the material point.'

'Well, yes. Of course,' said Turnbull, somewhat sheepishly. 'I was rather taking that as read.'

'As a bonus, however, a successful conclusion to this operation could only be of benefit to your career. Whilst my next move will probably involve a country cottage and a bus pass, this would be a massive feather in your cap.'

Turnbull smiled appreciatively. There was no point in pretending that he hadn't thought about it.

40 HAZY COSMIC JIVE

East Berlin, Thursday 29th April 1976

The MfS photographer had little doubt of the identity of the young man in the navy blue trench coat who was hovering, map in hand, outside the entrance to the Ministry for the Environment. Although Jack was certain that he had found the correct address, the sign above the glass entrance doors unhelpfully proclaimed the building to be the House of Statistics. Asking a passer-by for clarification had elicited no more than an apologetic shrug, so the British student determined to make his way inside and present himself to the first person that he could find. At the very least, he thought, they would be able to direct him to where he wanted to go.

The young woman behind the reception desk looked up from her typing. As was often the case, no appointments had been listed for the afternoon and the visitor walking towards her did not remotely resemble someone who was on official business.

Ulla smiled. 'Good afternoon. May I help you?'

'I would like to make an appointment,' said Jack.

'I'm sorry,' said Ulla. 'What did you say?'

In the few months that she had worked on the front desk, visitors had regularly presented themselves for scheduled appointments, but none had ever breezed in off the street and asked to arrange one.

Jack offered the receptionist his National Union of Students card. 'I'm from Lanchester Polytechnic. In the UK. I'm writing a dissertation comparing the environmental policies of both the Federal Republic and the German Democratic Republic and I would like, if possible, to make an appointment to talk to someone about the work the Ministry is undertaking to protect the natural world.'

'So, Mr Gilmore,' said Ulla, reading Jack's name from the NUS card, 'just to be totally clear. You don't already have an appointment.'

'No.'

'OK. So have you received an official invitation to visit us today?'

'No. Nobody invited me as such. As I said, I'm writing a dissertation…'

'No, no, I understand you,' interrupted Ulla gently. 'Your German is fine. And, really, it sounds like you're pursuing an interesting line of study. But once again, just to be clear, you have neither an appointment nor an official invitation to visit.'

'No.'

'Well, in that case, Mr Gilmore, I am not entirely sure what to do with you. Anyone wishing to visit us would, under normal circumstances, have an appointment or an official invitation.'

'And how would I get an official invitation?'

Ulla smiled. 'That is actually a very good question. If you would perhaps be so kind as to take a seat in our waiting area, I will speak to someone who might be able to advise me. I'll try not to keep you waiting too long.'

Jack retrieved his NUS card from the desk, thanked the receptionist warmly for her help and randomly selected a seat in the otherwise deserted waiting area. After the rigid conversations he had experienced at the Friedrichstrasse checkpoint, the young woman's affable demeanour came as a breath of fresh air. For her part, the appearance of the polite British student with the unprecedented request was a hugely welcome break from the monotony of her regular day.

After phoning her boss to explain the issue, Ulla replaced the receiver, exchanged a smile with the visitor and returned to typing a Captain Cosmonova story. She could not, however, maintain any kind of focus on the latest satirical exploits of her cosmic hero. The would-be escapee could not shake off the thought that some kind of opportunity might have presented itself. Presently, Ulla's boss emerged from the echoing stairwell and approached the uninvited guest.

'Mr Gilmore?'

'Yes?'

'Press Secretary Thomas Fischer. I understand you wish to speak to someone about the environmental policies of the GDR, but you don't have an appointment.'

'Exactly. I was hoping I might be able to arrange an appointment.'

'And have you been officially invited to arrange an appointment?'

'No,' said Jack, now working hard to mask his frustration at the circular nature of the conversations. 'Not as such.'

'Well, unfortunately,' said Fischer, 'in order to be able to make an appointment, you would first need an official invitation.'

The Press Secretary tilted his head slightly and offered the visitor a restrained, regretful smile. It was without doubt the signal for Jack to apologise for the intrusion and to quietly walk away. Unwilling to give up on his vision of conducting groundbreaking academic research, Jack refused to be fobbed off so easily. 'I wonder if you might therefore be so kind as to extend me an official invitation?'

'Well,' said Fischer, now slightly irked that Jack had not absorbed his message, 'under normal circumstances the Environment Ministry extends official invitations in response to enquiries either from representatives of governmental offices or from other official bodies. You do not, I believe, fall into either category.'

Calmly, Jack slid Pastor Niemeyer's letter from its envelope and handed it to the Press Secretary. 'Would this document perhaps clarify the situation. It's a letter of introduction from an officially recognised organisation here in the GDR.'

A parish of the Lutheran Church with addresses on both sides of the city was not something Fischer had previously encountered. Now paddling in uncharted waters, the Press Secretary realised that he would need to take advice before committing himself to a decision. He excused himself and disappeared back upstairs with the curious document.

After waiting perhaps twenty minutes for anything further to happen, the British student began to amuse himself by drumming his fingers on the arm of the chair and humming 'I'm Waiting for the Man' for the second time that day. Eventually Jack's butterfly thoughts landed on a David Bowie single from his time in the Sixth Form and, pandering to his own sense of irony, he audibly vocalised two lines from the refrain.

'There's a starman waiting in the sky / He'd like to come and meet us, but he thinks he'd blow our minds.'

Ulla immediately pricked up her ears. 'Starman' was by some distance her favourite song on the *Ziggy Stardust* album. Impulsively, she replaced her unfinished Captain Cosmonova story with a fresh sheet of paper and began to hammer out Bowie's colourful lyrics to the extent that, with any degree of confidence, she felt she knew them.

'Mr Gilmore,' she said, the moment her somewhat patchy transcript was as complete as it ever could be, 'I wonder if you could come to the desk?'

More in hope than expectation, Jack wondered if he was about to be told that he had been granted an interview.

'Please fill in the missing words,' said Ulla. 'To the song you were singing.'

Jack flashed the receptionist a quizzical look.

'You were singing "Starman". I have it at home on tape but my English isn't so good that I can make out all the words. I'll make you a black tea while you fill in the missing bits. My name's Ulla by the way.'

By the time the receptionist returned with the steaming mug, Jack had plugged a number of the gaps in her knowledge and corrected some of her misunderstandings.

'What's hazy cosmic jive?' she asked as she read Jack's annotations.

'No idea. Music from another planet probably. Something like that.'

'Are you a big fan of David Bowie?'

'Some things. Not everything.'

'At least you have access to everything.'

'I like the music, but I'm not too bothered about the dressing up.'

'Ha. You sound like my mum.'

'Thanks.'

The reappearance of the Press Secretary signalled an end to their conversation.

'Mr Gilmore,' he said with an air that heralded an announcement, 'after consultation with Minister Reichelt, I am happy to invite you to make an appointment with me to discuss the important work of the Ministry. Please liaise with my secretary, comrade Wolfram, to arrange a mutually convenient date for our meeting.'

Fischer shook Jack's hand, before turning on his heels and scooting back up the stairs.

Still feeling that Jack Gilmore's unexpected appearance at the Ministry must represent some kind of opportunity, Ulla engaged in a momentary fantasy about befriending the visitor and entrusting him with a letter to her Uncle Tommi in Munich. Once back on the other side of the Wall, the British student could post it for her, confident that her communication would reach its intended recipient. Jack might, she thought, even be persuaded to accept the reply at his personal address in West Berlin. He could bring Tommi's letter across to the East and drop it off in her mailbox in Fehrbelliner Strasse. Or perhaps more wisely, he could open the mail, memorise the essential points and relay the news to her personally. Conscious that her visitor would in all likelihood baulk at such a request, she gave the idea no further thought.

Returning to the here and now, Ulla scheduled an appointment for the British student and jotted the essential details for him onto an official Ministry card.

'Finish your tea before you leave,' she said warmly. 'And the words to the song.'

'I'm not sure I know all the words.'

'Then find out the missing words before you come for your meeting. Or better still, bring a full lyric sheet from the album.'

Jack mirrored her easy smile. 'I'll see what I can do.'

The tea finished, the British student thanked Ulla for her help in securing the interview and looked forward to seeing her on his return. All in all, it had been a highly successful day.

Registering his target's departure from the Environment Ministry, the surveillance officer on the second floor of the building opposite dedicated half a roll of film to the pursuit of images that might be of assistance to Captain Hartling.

As Jack waited to cross Hans-Beimler-Strasse, the victor of the afternoon's minor bureaucratic standoff celebrated the fact that he had ignored Professor MacKenzie's initial misgivings about the risks of conducting research in East Berlin. By the end of the semester, he would be the first student from Lanchester to have written a thesis citing primary sources from both sides of the Wall. Permitting himself an almost cocky smile, he pictured the look of acknowledgement on the professor's face when he finally submitted his dissertation.

Crossing Alexanderplatz in the direction of the Centrum department store, Jack also began to wonder what kind of report he could possibly write for Frau Fichtenberg. 'It's all glass and concrete and they don't have a proper sign over the door. Neither do they know what to do with unexpected guests, but the woman on the front desk loves David Bowie and is far from the western stereotype of a communist automaton.' That would just about sum things up.

Two and a half hours later, having completed his errand to the Centrum department store and endured the dismal protocols of the Friedrichstrasse checkpoint for a second time, the British student boarded the U-Bahn back towards West Berlin.

Jack was clearly in a buoyant mood as he dished out various packs of state-subsidised East German photographic paper to his appreciative flatmates. Over the undeniable delights of Anna's chicken stew and a bottle of Warsteiner, the most recent member of the collective set about describing the events of his day in as much detail as he could. With the washing up complete and the ramshackle collection of crockery stashed carefully away, Jack excused himself, saying that he now needed some time to commit his experiences to paper whilst they were still fresh in his mind.

Revisiting the genuinely personable interactions with the young woman on reception, Jack sat at his desk and began to write. If he worked quickly, he thought, he might be able to finish it within the hour. Shortly after midnight, the first pencil-and-paper draft of his impressions was ready for review. Poring over the detail, the student paused at his use of the word 'charming' in conjunction with 'receptionist'. It might, he decided, be judicious to replace it with 'friendly'.

41 LIFESAVER

East Berlin, Monday 3rd May 1976

In Captain Hartling's in-tray lay the surveillance photographs from Hans-Beimler-Strasse and the recorded times of Jack Gilmore's passage through the border controls. A phone call to Press Secretary Fischer established that the British student had visited the Environment Ministry unannounced and had requested an appointment to conduct an academic interview. Minister Reichelt had indeed been consulted and had determined that the visitor represented an opportunity to advertise the exemplary progress of the GDR in its management of the natural world. Hartling was far from convinced. He had been right, he reassured himself, to cover his back by organising surveillance.

Although the MfS captain had closed the door to his office and had thereby signalled his reluctance to be disturbed, he was not going to be left in peace. The tentative but repeated bursts of knocking could not be ignored.

When at last he opened the door, Frau Schiller was in a lather.

'I know it's not your job, but I couldn't borrow you again, could I? I think it's jammed this time.'

Frau Schiller was right. It wasn't his job. Sensing, nevertheless, that he might be able to turn the situation to his advantage, Hartling smiled.

'I'll see what I can do,' he said. 'Just give me a minute.'

With Frau Schiller gone, the Stasi officer shuffled his files together, secured them in the upper drawer of his desk and locked the door to his office. No more than thirty seconds later, he was staring at the troublesome electric typewriter.

'You're a lifesaver,' said Frau Schiller, prising open the lid to reveal the snarled mechanism beneath. 'The Major General needs this letter typed by eleven and now the flipping ribbon is all tangled up. God, I hate these new machines.'

'I'm not exactly an expert,' said Hartling calmly, 'but I'm sure it can be fixed. So, comrade Schiller, have no fear. The Major General will have his letter.'

Following a brief examination of the problem, the MfS officer began gently to tease the twisted ribbon from the typewriter's guide mechanism. Frau Schiller looked instantly relieved.

'You really have to work under a great deal of pressure,' said Hartling sympathetically.

'You don't know the half of it,' said Frau Schiller with a subtle shake of the head.

'I'm sure I don't, although I can see that you rarely get a moment to yourself.'

'Rarely? I'd say "never" would be more like it. But our work here is important and as you so often say, Captain Hartling, the enemies of socialism never sleep.'

'Indeed they don't. But you know something, comrade, the Directorate could not function without the unstinting and, I have to say, largely unrecognised commitment of colleagues such as yourself. It's true. In fact I might even suggest to the Major General that he point it out once in a while.'

Frau Schiller looked horrified. 'Oh gosh no. Don't do that. He'll think I've been complaining. He will. So, no.

Don't say anything to him. You have to promise me you won't do that.'

Hartling smiled benignly. 'OK. I won't say a word. I promise.'

'Thank you. Honestly, you had me really worried there for a moment. It's nice to feel appreciated, though. But as I said, I'm just doing my job.'

'Well, as long as you don't end up losing sleep over your responsibilities.' Hartling waited for his moment before catching Frau Schiller's eye. 'Comrade Schiller, can I tell you something in confidence? Occasionally, just occasionally, I wake up in the night worrying about the security of the files in my office. Ridiculous, really. You know, once I even came in at two in the morning, just to check that I'd locked everything away. I had, of course. I always do.'

'Well, you don't need to worry about me on that front,' said Frau Schiller. 'Obviously I get to handle certain documents from time to time, but I'm not, thank God, entrusted with their security. In any case, that locker in the Major General's office is code-protected as well as fire-proof. And, I would hasten to add, I'm not even permitted to be in the room when he opens it or when he secures his files at the end of the day.'

As Hartling finally disentangled the troublesome typewriter ribbon, he congratulated his comrade on her forbearance with new technology and complimented her once again on her commitment to the work of the Ministry. Satisfied with the outcome of his enquiries, the Stasi captain closed the lid on the typewriter and invited his colleague to give the machine a test run. Frau Schiller's unguarded words had presented him with the first glimmer of a breakthrough.

In all probability, Major General Konrad had secured the Day X documentation in the code-protected locker in his room. And codes, Hartling knew, could be broken.

42 CONFETTI

East Berlin, Monday 3rd May 1976

Pastor Niemeyer smiled and handed his passport to the uniformed officer occupying Cabin 12 of the Friedrichstrasse checkpoint. The priest knew that he would have to be patient. Invariably, Pass and Control scrutinised each and every one of the visas evidencing Niemeyer's regular visits to the eastern half of the city.

The officer spoke without looking up. 'And the purpose of your visit today?'

'I have an appointment with the Secretary of State for Church Affairs.'

'One moment please.'

Without further ado, the officer stood up and, with Niemeyer's passport firmly in hand, promptly left the control booth. The pastor knew the drill and expected a lengthy delay. He was on the official watch list and the MfS would be alerted immediately to his arrival. By the time he had paid for his visa, had waited to complete his customs declaration and had stood in line to conduct the obligatory currency exchange, a plain-clothes officer would be standing by to tail him the moment he emerged from the checkpoint.

Pastor Niemeyer spotted the young Stasi operative instantly. He was one of a number of easily recognisable watchers whose close attentions he had enjoyed on many previous occasions. Today it was the turn of the fresh-faced one with the blue eyes and the untidy moustache. The operatives who tailed the pastor made no particular effort to disguise their presence and presumably their visibility was therefore wholly deliberate. Niemeyer had never spoken to any of his minders or communicated with them in any way, but today, as he passed, he offered the familiar attendant a modest smile of recognition. The young man did not reciprocate, but noted that Niemeyer was wearing a charcoal overcoat in spite of the fact that winter was long gone and temperatures had recently edged into the twenties. The pastor was carrying a large, dark brown dispatch case with a substantial shoulder strap and appeared to be keen to get to his destination.

Escaping the crash and the clatter of the nearby Interhotel construction site, Niemeyer soon arrived at the impressive Unter den Linden boulevard, where he surprised his dedicated follower by turning not right but left. If he had an appointment at the Interior Ministry, this was hardly the most obvious route. Along the wide avenue, the trees were now in leaf and from the street lamps, long red banners and GDR national flags, remnants from the recent May Day parades, hung in the motionless air. Taking in the blue of the sky and wondering occasionally about the lives of the individuals he passed, Pastor Niemeyer strolled along Unter den Linden, crossed the first of the bridges over the River Spree and walked diagonally across Marx-Engels-Platz in the direction of the main entrance to the recently inaugurated Palace of the Republic. On the steps outside the imposing modernist structure, groups of visitors clustered in admiration beneath the expansive wall of gleaming bronzed glass that so immediately caught the eye and boldly signalled the permanence of the GDR. At the foot of the steps, Pastor Niemeyer stopped and placed his dispatch case on the ground. After no more than a brief final reflection on his decision, he sank to his knees and began to pray.

Inevitably, the pastor rapidly claimed the attention of both the waiting tourists and the security personnel guarding the doors. Almost immediately, a uniformed police officer, convinced that the law was being broken but uncertain precisely how, disappeared inside. Moments later he reappeared with a small camera and began to document the priest's unfathomable action. From amongst the clutch of fascinated onlookers, other cameras began to appear and the unmistakable sound of their shutters soon accompanied the pastor's scarcely audible prayer. At a distance of perhaps twenty metres, the Stasi operative who had been tailing Niemeyer produced a small two-way radio transceiver from beneath his jacket, reported the unexpected turn of events and urgently requested instructions.

The prayer complete, Pastor Niemeyer opened his eyes and gathered in the scene around him. Slowly and purposefully, he unfastened his dispatch case, lifted the flap and grasped the half-ream of printed leaflets that denounced the leadership of the GDR and protested adamantly against the proposed demolition of his church. A second later, he stood up and heaved his arm skywards. The inflammatory documents scattered as they flew into the air before fluttering down like oversized confetti.

As the pastor's young Stasi watcher leapt into action and began to chase down the offending leaflets, Niemeyer bent down, reached into his shoulder bag and pulled out a bottle. Standing erect and looking directly at his photographer, he unscrewed the cap and calmly poured the contents across his torso and shoulders, soaking the upper sections of his overcoat. From his side pocket, Pastor Niemeyer produced a chrome cigarette lighter, flipped it open and flicked at the striker with his thumb. The spark ignited the petroleum vapour that now shrouded the intransigent priest and instantly engulfed him in flame.

43 PARAGON OF INTEGRITY

East Berlin, Tuesday 4th May 1976

Although news of Pastor Niemeyer's death in the intensive care unit of East Berlin's Charité hospital had been kept tightly under wraps, reports of the shocking incident on the steps of the Palace of the Republic had already appeared in the early editions of the West German press. Shortly after four thirty that morning, Major General Konrad had been unceremoniously roused from his sleep by an apoplectic call from Erich Mielke, the Minister for State Security, who was demanding both explanations and action. When Captain Hartling arrived at the Normannenstrasse complex shortly before seven, the infuriated Major General had been at his desk for almost two hours. Spread before him lay Hartling's Operation Artemis file, a set of large black and white photographs of Niemeyer's self-immolation, the detailed report from the surveillance officer who had been tailing the priest and various copies of the morning dailies from West Berlin. A phone call from one of the guards at the Ruschestrasse gate alerted the Major General to Hartling's imminent arrival.

As the MfS captain exited the stairwell and walked towards his office, Konrad was waiting impatiently at the end of the corridor. He had no desire to welcome his subordinate or even wait until it would be unnecessary to raise his voice.

'My office, Hartling. Now.'

Unaware of the incident on Marx-Engels-Platz, the lower-ranking officer had no idea why his presence was required, but he knew it could not be good. His immediate fear was that the disappearance of the typewriter ribbon had somehow come to light. However, if he were suspected of its theft, he rapidly calculated, he would have been dragged from his bed during the night or detained by the guards on his arrival. He urged himself not to panic. It was, after all, not the first time that he had seen the head of the Directorate in a foul mood.

The office door was open.

'Sit down, Hartling,' said the Major General, his face a picture of discontent. 'And do not utter a word until I invite you to speak.'

Hartling nodded and pulled up a chair. Konrad, who remained on his feet, slapped a copy of the *Frankfurter Allgemeine Zeitung* in front of him, followed by the *Berliner Morgenpost* and the *Süddeutsche Zeitung.* All three West German newspapers bore pictures of Pastor Niemeyer's self-immolation and the full text of his protest leaflet. The *Frankfurter Allgemeine* also carried an eye-witness account of the incident and bore the headline 'Death of a Martyr' with the subheading 'Reconciliation rebuffed'. Hartling scanned the article, looked dispassionately at the Major General and waited for the inevitable.

'This is on you, Hartling. This is completely on you. How could such a thing happen outside the Palace of the Republic? No more than two weeks after the inauguration, for God's sake. And how exactly could a journalist from the Federal Republic be so conveniently on hand to photograph this whole goddam mess. Did he just happen to be in the right place at the right time, in which case I shit gold coins after breakfast and eat them for lunch, or did he know in advance that something was going to happen? Which then begs the question: if some arsehole of a western journalist knew that something was about to go down, then why in God's name didn't you? This is your sodding case.'

Hartling was in a corner, but refused to flinch. His only possible recourse was to acknowledge his accountability without explicitly accepting the blame. He took Konrad's glare as an invitation to speak.

'Indeed, sir. The case is unequivocally my responsibility and I assure you, I am as disturbed by the course of events as you are. You have every right to be concerned and I will make it my absolute priority to discover who in my team is responsible for this intelligence failure and instigate immediate disciplinary procedures. I will of course report to you with my findings the moment I have any viable information.'

'You bet your lousy sodding life you will. If this is already on the front page of the *Süddeutsche Zeitung*, it'll be all over West German radio by breakfast and it'll be the lead story on the TV news. Which means that by tonight, anyone in the GDR with a radio, a TV set or a talkative friend will have picked up on the reports. I'm telling you, Mielke is seething about this. He wants someone's head on a plate and it sure as hell isn't going to be mine.'

'Nor should it be.' Hartling paused momentarily. 'Sir, if I may speak freely, scapegoats have their uses, but what we really need are material answers if we are to deal with the immediate fallout from this incident and then set about ensuring that nothing like this can ever happen again. If

Mielke wants a head on a plate, so be it, but it needs to be someone whose presence will not be missed.'

'And am I supposed to take it from that that yours would?'

'Major General Konrad, with respect, this is my case and my responsibility. I am the one person the Ministry needs right now to get the answers we require. Put someone new on this and they're starting completely from scratch. And as you made so abundantly clear, time is very much of the essence.'

As angry as Konrad was, his subordinate's logic was irrefutable. The Major General walked slowly to the window as he weighed up his options. 'You know what, Hartling, I'm going to give you the opportunity to put this right. But don't for one moment think your problem has gone away. You cannot afford to disappoint me a second time.'

'Understood.'

'So. Get on with it. Talk to your informant in Niemeyer's office. Get whatever you can out of her. She must know something about this, for crying out loud. And find out why this goddam British student has been sniffing around the Environment Ministry. That hardly strikes me as kosher. If you can find the slightest scrap of evidence to suggest he's somehow connected to this shitshow, pull him in. But make sure you have something that actually resembles evidence. Following our leadership's headlong rush to sign the Helsinki Accords, we're required to maintain a semblance of legality in our treatment of foreign nationals. The last thing we need here is the British Ambassador kicking up some kind of fuss about human so-called rights.'

'I will be a paragon of integrity, sir. You can rely on me.'

'Well?'

'Sir?'

'Why are you still sitting here? Take all this crap with you. Report to me daily. And do not for one second try to convince yourself that your career does not hang in the balance.'

As Hartling withdrew, he made a mental note that the Major General's impressive steel security cabinet was protected by a Type L surface-mounted pushbutton lock. He wondered if Konrad would be so complacent as to leave the code, perhaps disguised as a phone number, scrawled on an innocuous scrap of paper and buried somewhere in a drawer.

Having duly vented his spleen, Major General Konrad settled into his seat and pulled a half-smoked cigar and a box of matches from the uppermost drawer of his desk. Puffing out the first cloud of swirling, aromatic smoke, he reflected on Hartling's facility with words. The captain was without doubt a bullshitter of the highest order, but his arguments were fundamentally a more cogent rendition of the obfuscation and promises he had offered to Mielke no more than three hours previously. Hartling was too clever by half, he thought. With the right connections he might well have attained a more elevated rank in the Directorate. The Major General rummaged a fountain pen and a small notepad from the drawer and tried to capture his subordinate's words whilst they were fresh in his mind. He would refer carefully to his notes when he reported to the Security Minister at nine.

On Captain Hartling's desk was a handwritten message sitting atop a white cardboard box that in all probability contained a cake and was without doubt an expression of Frau Schiller's gratitude for his help with the typewriter. Needing the space for his immediate needs, he eased the box to one side and dumped the collection of newspapers, files and photographs in its place. From the cover of the *Frankfurter Allgemeine Zeitung*, the face of Pastor Niemeyer smiled warmly, almost generously. The pastor's public suicide had complicated Hartling's already precarious situation and the feelings the Stasi officer now harboured towards Niemeyer were something akin to contempt.

Competing priorities now jostled for position. Hartling's gut feeling was simply to extract himself from the entire tangled mess before Konrad's own instinct for self-preservation translated into an overwhelming need for a sacrificial offering. The MfS officer would need to do no more than draft and countersign order papers for another Romeo operation to West Berlin, cross the border and board the first available plane to London. Without the materials demanded by MI6, however, the doors to the life he desired would be slammed in his face. Isolated and unfunded, the deserter would be forever looking over his shoulder. Sooner or later, a team of his former comrades would surface with order papers of their own.

Whilst the urge to cut and run would have to be resisted, Hartling would as a matter of urgency need to placate the Major General with some demonstrable course of action involving Petra Fichtenberg or the Environment Ministry or both. He would also need to devise a safe and workable plan to dispossess the head of the Directorate of his most jealously guarded files.

The knock at Hartling's door was tentative enough to be deferential but loud enough not to be ignored. Presumably Frau Schiller was seeking approval for her gift. Having expressed his appreciation, Hartling enquired whether, at the end of an inevitably hectic day, the overworked PA might care to join him in his office to share a pot of Russian tea and help him sample the cake she had so thoughtfully made. Whilst Major General Konrad appeared to be anything but an early riser, it would be useful to confirm the impression that he was rarely at his desk before Frau Schiller's prompt arrival at seven each morning. It would also be valuable to know whether Konrad had signalled any intention to spend the forthcoming weekend at his private *dacha* on the Baltic coast.

44 BEDLAM

West Berlin, Tuesday 4th May 1976

Jack had intended to do no more than hand over his finished report to Frau Fichtenberg before returning to Oudenarder Strasse and reviewing the questions he had prepared for his official meeting at the Environment Ministry. In the course of a relaxed post-breakfast walk to the Concordia offices, he reflected on the article he had crafted and wondered whether the editor of *Green Light* would be happy with his efforts. Turning into Bernauer Strasse, the British student immediately caught sight of the green and white police vehicles and the cluster of outside broadcast vans. Perhaps inevitably, he assumed that there must have been some kind of incident at the Wall and hoped that no-one had been injured.

At the entrance to the apartment block housing the Concordia offices, a gaggle of journalists and TV crews blocked Jack's path to the door and vied for his attention. The chattering double-clicks of camera shutters and the sudden barrage of shouted questions made it abundantly clear to the intern that something highly significant had occurred.

'How well did you know Pastor Niemeyer?' was the first intelligible question.

'Did Pastor Niemeyer have cancer?'

'Are you a neighbour? Did he ever talk to you?'

'Who else knew about this?'

'What can you tell us about Niemeyer's state of mind?'

Jack claimed in convincing Spanish that he did not understand, pushed his way through the scrum and showed his Concordia ID badge to the expressionless police officer guarding both the door and the buzzers at the entrance to the block. Jack climbed the stairs, keen to understand what was going on but increasingly fearful of what he was about to hear.

At the door to the offices, a clearly perturbed Frau Fichtenberg checked that no reporters had followed her young colleague and closed the door swiftly behind him.

'Goodness, Jack, what are you doing here? You're not supposed to be in today.'

'What going on?' he asked, displaying a look of complete astonishment. 'What are all those people doing here?'

'News travels fast,' said Frau Fichtenberg, assuming that Jack had heard the reports and had come to offer his support. 'It's dreadful. It's been absolute bloody bedlam out there. And the phones haven't stopped ringing since I got here. It's quiet now, though. I've taken them all off the hook. The last thing I want to do is talk to those damned vultures down there. You didn't say anything to them, did you?'

'Not really. I didn't answer any questions, if that's what you mean.'

'Good. Don't be drawn into making a comment. You have no idea how it might be reported.'

'But why are they here in the first place? Has something happened to Pastor Niemeyer?'

It suddenly dawned on Frau Fichtenberg that she had jumped to entirely the wrong conclusion about Jack's unexpected appearance. She picked up a copy of the *Frankfurter Allgemeine* and handed it to him.

'You need to read this,' she said solemnly. 'It's all there. But sit down before you look at it.'

Jack did no more than take in the headline and stare at the shocking photograph beneath. The image made absolutely no sense to him.

'Who's that in the photo? Was Pastor Niemeyer with him? Has he been arrested or something?'

'You need to read it all.'

The first sentence, however, was enough. Jack froze in utter disbelief, but his look of stupefaction at least confirmed to Frau Fichtenberg that she would not be forced to spell out the painful truth.

'We're still waiting for Thomas Strohm from the Press Office of the Evangelical Church Council to put in an appearance,' she said. 'Presumably, he'll deal with the fuss outside and take charge of this frankly godawful state of affairs. He'll probably need to speak to all of us at some point. In the meantime, we just have to sit tight.'

'I don't get it,' said Jack eventually. 'When I was here last week, Pastor Niemeyer seemed fine. Well, more than fine, to be honest. There's no way I would have thought… well… you know.'

Frau Fichtenberg allowed herself a moment. 'Jack, I don't think this is about the fragility of his mind or whatever. He was nothing, if not a man of principle. However shocking this is, however… horrendous, I'm sure it speaks more of faith than of desperation. Pastor Niemeyer was always about making a difference. Always. As he said to me I don't know how many times: actions speak louder than words, but inaction speaks louder than both.'

45 WELCOME AND REWARD

East Berlin, Tuesday 4th May 1976

It was late afternoon when Captain Hartling, frustrated by his inability to contact Petra Fichtenberg at work, changed into his formal Stasi uniform and ordered a car and a driver to transport him to Hans-Beimler-Strasse. On arrival, he showed his MfS identity card to the young receptionist and made a point of requesting and completing a visitor permit. Ulla knew that it would be unwise to ask whether he had made an appointment.

Following a perfunctory meeting with the Minister for the Environment and a more detailed conversation with Press Secretary Fischer, Captain Hartling walked back down the stairs, the quiet clatter of his shoes echoing in the stairwell. As he crossed the polished floor of the lobby in the direction of the reception desk, Ulla Wolfram interrupted her typing. The Stasi officer and his target were the only occupants of the spacious foyer and Hartling was certain that their conversation would not be overheard. Deliberately conspicuous in his military uniform, the Captain smiled before logging his time of departure on the visitor permit and returning the document to the receptionist.

'Thank you, comrade Wolfram. I expect you will have been wondering what might possibly explain the sudden appearance of an officer from the Ministry for State Security.'

'With respect, comrade,' Ulla deftly replied, 'if I have not been informed, it is clearly not my duty to ask.'

'Excellent,' said Hartling, seemingly impressed. 'That's exactly as it should be. You do your job well.'

'I do my best.'

'I'm sure you do. Press Secretary Fischer speaks highly of you. Very highly indeed.'

Ulla was beginning to feel unsettled by the unexpected attention. Was this conversation heading somewhere?

Hartling paused and looked Ulla in the eye. 'May I speak to you in confidence?'

'Of course,' replied Ulla. What else could she say?

'I understand you recently had an unannounced visitor from Great Britain.'

'Yes, we did.'

'And how would you describe the visitor's demeanour?'

Ulla shrugged. 'Hard to say, really. Nothing out of the ordinary. I suppose I would describe him as polite. And patient. He's writing a dissertation about environmental policies in the two German states.'

'Did he ask many questions?'

'Not really. He just wanted to arrange an appointment.'

'Did he say anything that struck you as unusual?'

'I don't think so. As I said, he was very polite.'

Hartling paused and looked intently at Ulla as though trying to make a decision. Now feeling that she, rather than the foreign student, was the intended focus of Hartling's questioning, she attempted to remain calm and to mask her rising anxiety.

'The purpose of my visit,' confided Hartling eventually, 'is to review a number of security protocols here at the Environment Ministry.'

'That's excellent,' said Ulla. 'Thank you.'

'You're most welcome. But to tell you the truth, comrade Wolfram, it strikes me that someone in your position, someone who welcomes every employee and more significantly, every visitor, to the building, could, if required, play a much more active role in safeguarding the important work of the Ministry.'

'Our work is certainly important,' replied Ulla, reluctant to be drawn. Her neck began to redden and her mouth felt suddenly dry. Was the Stasi captain intending to press her into spying on her colleagues? Would he threaten her somehow, or possibly her family? Would the state be forever on her case? Although dreading what she was about to hear, she nevertheless wished that the MfS officer would get to the point.

'And of course,' continued Hartling, 'that level of commitment to national security could do no harm whatsoever to someone such as yourself, someone whose career has, shall we say, encountered a bump in the road. With support from the Ministry for State Security such a person might well find themself in a position to, for example, submit a fresh application to study physics at the University of Leipzig.'

'I don't understand,' said Ulla, completely blindsided by what seemed to be more an offer of redemption than an iron-fisted threat.

Her thoughts went into overdrive. The Stasi had clearly been taking an interest in her and that could not, under any imaginable circumstances, be a good thing. Yet these people had the power, if Hartling were to be believed, to give back as easily as they took, to reawaken long abandoned hope and to tantalise with promises of absolution. The resurrection of

Ulla's university place now dangled enticingly within her grasp, provided, it seemed, that she was prepared to sell her soul to the MfS. Ulla wished the floor would simply open up, swallow her whole and somehow let her start the day again.

Hartling smiled. 'Please do not feel alarmed, comrade Wolfram. I am simply explaining that the Ministry for State Security would both welcome and reward your input if you felt able to render certain patriotic services. Anyway, we can continue this conversation after you finish your shift tomorrow, in a less public setting.'

He placed an appointment card bearing the logo and the address of the Police Presidium on Ulla's desk.

'Thank you,' said the bewildered receptionist.

'So, comrade Wolfram, I wish you a good day. I'm sure I don't need to remind you that we spoke today in complete confidence.'

The MfS captain nodded, turned and headed directly for the exit. As the noise of the rush-hour traffic on the Hans-Beimler-Underpass assaulted his ears, he felt confident that Ulla Wolfram would snatch at the prospect of a guaranteed university place. If not, she would at the very least feel obliged to present some semblance of a desire to co-operate. Either way, she would not fail to attend the meeting he had scheduled. It would be foolhardy to do anything else.

46 ORDERS

East Berlin, Wednesday 5th May 1976

Ulla did not sleep remotely well and a characteristically uneventful Thursday offered her little in the way of distraction. As she left the Environment Ministry at the end of her shift, the prospective Stasi informant viewed her appointment at the Police Presidium with unremitting anxiety.

The massive police building in Keibelstrasse was no more than a ten-minute walk from the Environment Ministry and was impossible to miss. Constructed in the early 1930s, the seven-storey brick and stone edifice ran the length of an entire block and made an immediate and deliberate impression. The carefully understated architecture fell marginally short of outright functionalism and suggested solidity, authority and permanence.

In the huge entrance hall, a line of maybe fifty people snaked its way to the reception desk. Ulla dutifully took a numbered ticket from the dispenser and attached herself to the back of the queue. At the counter ahead of her, visitors presented their tickets and their appointment cards and were directed in turn to one of three sets of stairs. None of Ulla's fellow attendees struck her as looking particularly like a criminal, but then again, what were criminals supposed to look like?

Two floors above, Captain Hartling and Lieutenant Teresa Eckart, an MfS officer with whom he had collaborated on previous occasions, were waiting for Ulla Wolfram to appear. Although Hartling and Eckart had always worked well together, they could not at this moment see eye to eye.

'This is a wild goose chase,' said Eckart, 'an utter and complete waste of our time. It takes me a year to train Venus agents and you're asking me to set Wolfram loose with little more than a pep talk. Imagine if the air force trained its pilots like this.'

'Well, the fact of the matter is that the Major General is on the warpath, but if you feel inclined to offer him excuses rather than action, then by all means, be my guest. But don't lose sight of the fact that he has Mielke breathing down his neck too.'

Eckart shook her head. 'Classic. Mielke farts and the entire Stasi stands to attention.'

'Personally, Lieutenant, I would be more careful in my choice of words. But however you might wish to put it, you have your orders, just as I have mine.'

After shuffling forward in fits and starts, Ulla presented her card at the desk and was politely directed to the staircase for the second floor. The black and white tiled corridor that seemed to run the length of the building was empty and as Ulla sought out her allotted room, she heard only the occasional voice from behind the many doors that she passed.

Arriving at room 209, she knocked tentatively and was invited to enter. Captain Hartling and Lieutenant Eckart were sitting side by side at a narrow desk in the manner of an interview panel for some kind of job. Both officers wore military uniform. The female officer had light brown hair, tied neatly in a bun. The room itself was painted white and the walls were bare, except for the obligatory portrait of Honecker. An olive green telephone sat close to Hartling's right hand and a well-used leather briefcase lay on the desk in front of him.

'Please take a seat, Frau Wolfram. May I introduce my colleague, Lieutenant Eckart?'

Eckart nodded.

'I trust you are well,' continued Hartling. 'However, before we begin, I would like to emphasise two very important matters. Firstly, my offer to smooth your pathway to university still stands. In fact, I have the application forms here in my briefcase. Secondly, you should also understand that this is not a negotiation. Are we clear on this?'

Ulla began to feel as though the room was somehow shrinking.

'Yes,' she said, trying not to display the slightest flicker of emotion.

'Good. So, I was wondering if, on reflection, you had anything further to report about your British visitor?'

'Well, I don't think he's a spy. I'll tell you that for nothing.'

'Whether Jack Gilmore is in the employ of a foreign intelligence service will be for us to decide. Please restrict yourself to the facts and leave the analysis to the experts.'

'I'm sorry. Yes. Well, as I told you yesterday, Mr Gilmore is writing a comparative study of environmental policy in the two German states. That's pretty much all I can tell you. Except, he likes music. And he's polite. And kind of friendly, I guess.'

Lieutenant Eckart raised an eyebrow and moved her head fractionally to the left, but otherwise maintained her stony demeanour.

'Did he mention his relationship to Pastor Niemeyer or the reason for his involvement with the Church of Reconciliation?'

'No. Why?'

'Again. That is not your concern. Are you currently in a romantic relationship of any sort?'

'No.' Not that it was any of his business.

'Good. When you next see your visitor, we want you to get close to him. Find out exactly why he's sniffing around.'

'You mean spy on him?'

'I would prefer to say "conduct covert surveillance", but yes, if you like.'

'But he's only coming across for an interview with the Press Secretary. Then he'll be gone.'

'Unless, of course, you provide him with an incentive to come back. So, as I said, we want you to be friendly to him. Invite him to the theatre or to a bar. Spend some time with him. Make out that you're one of these ridiculous peace apostles who believe they can stop wars with a candle. Become intimate with him. In due course, let it slip that occasionally you are drafted in by the Minister to type up classified materials and see if that sparks his interest.'

'Hold on,' said Ulla, failing to mask the waspish look. 'What do you mean by "intimate"?'

'If you need me to spell things out, it means that you should take him back to that tatty, unregistered flat you rent and have sex with him, ideally in such a way that it leaves him gagging for more.'

'No,' said Ulla, now looking Hartling in the eye. 'No way. Absolutely not. I'm not a whore.'

'As I said, comrade Wolfram, this is not a negotiation. Having noted the obvious benefits to assisting the Ministry in its endeavours, you would be wise also to consider the consequences of disappointing us. So, keep your comments to yourself and listen carefully. There are only two possible outcomes to our conversation today. The first is that you agree to fulfil your patriotic duty and, as a consequence, you re-open the door to that coveted physics degree. The second is that you do not agree to fulfil your stated duty, in which case you will spend the next thirty years of your worthless life in a dank shit-hole of a prison with a child-killer or some unrepentant Nazi for a cell-mate. So, comrade Wolfram, have I made myself completely clear?'

Ulla paused as the hopelessness of her position sank in. She stared blankly at the table. Confronted with the simple choice of unremitting incarceration or collaboration with the MfS, there was only one response she could make and the Stasi officer knew it. Calmly, Hartling removed a typed document, a writing block and a pen from his briefcase.

'Before we discuss the practicalities any further, comrade Wolfram, you will need to copy this letter in your own handwriting and sign it.'

Without speaking, Ulla read through the statement of collaboration that Hartling required her to transcribe. Every fibre in her being told her not to sign away her soul to these people, the people who had blocked her family's visit to a dying grandfather, who had sabotaged her application to university and who now wanted her to whore herself out for their own unchallengeable purposes. Having read every last syllable of the document, Ulla tightened her lips and glared at the desk whilst she pictured herself telling Hartling to go hang himself from the nearest tree and storming defiantly out of the building. There was, however, no escaping the reality of her situation. With not the slightest room for manoeuvre, she succumbed to the inevitable, picked up the pen and slowly began to copy the declaration that she had been given.

'I, Ulla Wolfram, born on the 3rd of May 1957 in Berlin, agree to work on a voluntary basis as an informal source of intelligence for the Ministry for State Security.

I am ready to complete all tasks delegated to me conscientiously and to the best of my ability. I agree not to reveal my co-operation with the Ministry for State Security to, or discuss the nature of my duties with, my family, my friends or any other person. I agree to report any suspicion against me to the relevant officers of the Ministry for State Security. I agree to keep no records of my work for the Ministry for State Security.

I have been made fully aware of the constitutional and legal basis for my collaboration with the Ministry for State Security and understand the disciplinary and legal consequences which may arise as a result of any breach of this agreement.'

Feeling a nascent sickness in the pit of her stomach and the bizarre sense that she could scarcely move her limbs, Ulla signed the document and pushed it across the table to her MfS handler.

Given the precariousness of Hartling's own position, he felt some degree of confidence that the recruitment of the hapless receptionist would, at least in the short term, keep the disgruntled Major General Konrad off his back.

Hartling tucked the contract into his briefcase and stood up. 'So, comrade Wolfram, I think that largely concludes our business for today. I will leave you in the capable hands of Lieutenant Eckart, who will establish lines of communication and ensure that you have sufficient practical expertise for your task.'

Following Hartling's departure, Lieutenant Eckart ferreted out a small business card belonging to a hairdressing salon in Dresden. Not just the name of the establishment but also the phone number and the address, she explained, were all entirely fictitious. Concealed within the hairdresser's contact details was a telephone number that she should learn by heart and divulge to no-one. If Ulla were to substitute the threes in the seven-digit number on the card for zeros, she would have an internal Ministry for State Security contact number in Berlin. Furthermore, the house number in the phony address was a three digit extension code that would afford her direct access to the separate switchboard operated by the Main Directorate for Reconnaissance. Eckart then made Ulla practise the precise form of words that would identify her as an informal operative and enable her to be connected either to Hartling or to herself. Finally, and without explanation, the MfS lieutenant instructed Ulla to stand and to hold her arms out to the sides.

'Good,' she said, removing a tape measure from her briefcase. 'Put your shoulders back. I need to measure you.'

As Eckart set about taking precise stock of Ulla's physical attributes, the Stasi's newly acquired asset stared silently at the wall in front of her and tried to block out the surrender of her dignity. Before informing the recruit that she was free to leave, Lieutenant Eckart instructed Ulla to make a point of being at home in Fehrbelliner Strasse for the entirety of Friday evening.

Standing on the street outside the Police Presidium, Ulla felt strangely numb and struggled to process exactly what had happened. With little idea of what to do next, she turned and walked slowly in the direction of her apartment. At the Konsum supermarket, she bought a tin of goulash, a packet of Stollberger biscuits and a bottle of Polish vodka.

Captain Hartling returned directly to Normannenstrasse, where he filed the extorted statement of collaboration and drafted the order papers that would enable him to pay a visit to Petra Fichtenberg in West Berlin. With the necessary administrative tasks complete, he grabbed something decent to eat in the canteen before returning to his apartment and congratulating himself on a job well done. Tomorrow, he would be free to focus on matters of greater personal significance.

47 MANUAL LABOUR

West Berlin, Thursday 6th May 1976

It was almost eleven. Jack had eaten breakfast late and entirely alone. He knew that Anna was on dry-cleaning shift at the German Opera and would probably have been the first to leave the apartment. Marco had either gone to an early lecture, which struck the British student as unlikely, or he was out on another shoplifting spree. From the sound of things, Julia and Christa were still in bed. Bastian, according to the note on the table, was down in the street working on his unreliable VW Beetle. He would, he declared, welcome a large mug of Jacobs Gold if anybody, at any point, got round to making some. Much as Jack enjoyed the industrial-strength coffee that his flatmates regularly served up, he was still new to the concept of the filter machine and using it would involve a certain amount of guesswork.

For the moment, figuring out what to do with the conical filter papers would at least provide some temporary distraction from the nagging questions surrounding Pastor Niemeyer's death. In the West, the priest's shocking protest action still featured to some extent in every TV and radio bulletin and on the front page of every morning newspaper. One of the West German dailies, using headlines stridently underlined in red, described Niemeyer's self-immolation as 'a hammer blow for freedom'. In the East, *Neues Deutschland* denounced the pastor without hesitation as 'the shepherd who abandoned his flock'.

For his own part, Jack repeatedly returned to the thought that during his only conversation with Pastor Niemeyer, he should perhaps have spotted some clue as to his intentions. Although they had philosophised about mortality, the priest had not in any way created the impression of having given up on life. If anything, the opposite was true. The reality of the matter, Jack suspected, was either far more complicated or far more simple than anything he was hearing on the news.

Whilst the Concordia intern was still puzzling out exactly where he needed to pour the water into the coffee machine, Bastian appeared in the doorway. He was wearing a grubby, navy blue boiler suit and carrying an impressive wrench. A sympathetic smile graced his oil-smeared face.

'The lid just flips up,' he said, sensing Jack's disorientation. 'So, I've spent almost two hours draining the lubricant, disconnecting the throttle linkage and the fuel pipe and undoing all the corroded electrics. Once we've had a coffee, Jack, you can help me replace the engine. It's a two-person job. There's a spare boiler suit in my room.'

Within twenty minutes, the British student found himself at the rear end of Bastian's orange Beetle, struggling to release the defiant mounting bolts or heaving at the chrome-plated exhaust pipes whilst simultaneously contending with the kind of technical vocabulary that his lecturers had never deployed at Lanchester. Although the 1300cc engine weighed comfortably over a hundred kilograms, it proved, to Jack's surprise, to be entirely possible for two determined students to wrestle it from its mountings with little more than a professional trolley jack, a certain amount of grunting and the liberal use of expletives.

With the engine finally sitting on the cobbles behind the VW, Bastian led Jack to the cellar and pointed out the replacement that they now needed to carry up the stairs, across the courtyard and out onto the street.

'Obviously,' said Bastian, 'it's not going to be easy.'

He was right.

When, thirty minutes later and with the help of two obliging passers-by, they carefully lowered the solid hundredweight of metal onto the pavement outside the building, the sense of achievement was palpable.

'Let's take a breather,' said Bastian. 'We're not done yet.'

The pair grabbed a bottle of mineral water and some Turkish pastries from the bar that occupied the ground-floor frontage to 27 Oudenarder Strasse and enjoyed a hard-earned break before returning to their task. Distracted by Bastian's frequent anecdotes, engaged with the physicality of manoeuvring the recalcitrant engine and challenged by the barrage of technical vocabulary, Jack spared little thought for Pastor Niemeyer. Blaring out from the bar, 'Daddy Cool' by Boney M and 'Mamma Mia' by Abba at first provided an upbeat backdrop to the afternoon's exertions. Played seemingly on constant rotation, however, the two songs were gradually drained of their capacity to amuse. The moment the new engine was bolted into place, Bastian strode into the bar, pushed a coin into the juke box and selected 'Born To Run' by Bruce Springsteen.

Shortly after four in the afternoon, Bastian's beloved 1966 Beetle had a 1971 engine which, he sincerely hoped, would not share its predecessor's annoying habit of backfiring each time he put his foot on the brake. As the engineering student carefully refitted the boot lid and Jack wiped his filthy hands once more on the legs of the borrowed boiler suit, the pair were startled by the sudden, forceful crack of an object striking the roof of the car. High above them, perhaps from a fourth-storey apartment on the opposite side of the street, the two flatmates could make out uproarious and seemingly irrepressible laughter, but the authors of the unprovoked potshot refused to reveal themselves.

'Idiots,' said Bastian. 'What the hell was that?'

Jack hunted on the pavement for the offending missile and duly found, almost in the entrance to the bar, a small, transparent plastic bag that had been knotted at the neck. Collected inside were a severed household plug, a fingernail-sized, resinous lump of something and a handwritten note inviting the two downtrodden workers to free themselves from the drudgery of manual labour.

Jack looked puzzled. 'Is that what I think it is?' he asked, focussing on the mystery substance.

'I wouldn't really know,' said Bastian with an equally baffled look. 'Show it to Julia and Christa. They're the ones who smoke stuff.'

Once Jack and Bastian had lugged the redundant engine down to the cellar, the two students returned to the apartment, cleaned themselves up and put the boiler suits and the rest of their dirty clothes through the washing machine on the longest possible cycle. Over a pot of black tea, the pair discussed the likely source of their surprise package and wondered whether at some point the owners of the plug would turn up and request its return. Jack was tempted, as some kind of demonstration of solidarity, to ask Bastian about his feelings towards Anna, but it was hardly a fair question and in any case, he was sure that he knew the answer. Eventually the two friends set about polishing off the last of the most recent tray of plum cake.

While Bastian set about boiling more water for the tea, Jack fetched the initial, messy draft of the article he'd recently submitted to Concordia. The engineering student read silently through his flatmate's report, before dropping it onto the cake tray and nodding in approval.

'So how much are they paying you for this?' he asked.

'A hundred marks,' said Jack, the faintest of smiles creeping onto his face. 'Assuming they accept it. Not that I expect anyone will have the time to look at it right now.'

'Probably not. You were on TV, you know. When you all came out of the Concordia office and had to push your way past those reporters. You're famous.'

'Famous for fifteen seconds, more like.'

'If that.'

Bastian paused and tapped the table before launching into an altogether more difficult question. 'So. Why do you think he did it? Set fire to himself, I mean.'

'You know what, Bastian. I've got no more idea than you have. His PA said it was a protest. But I don't know. Will doing something like that stop the demolition of a church? Or will the government over there just rejoice that he's out of the way and then speed the whole process up?'

'The East German media are saying he was clinically insane.'

'Yeah, well. I suppose they would. They're going to condemn him one way or another. You know what, Bastian, it's been three days since I saw that photo on the front of the *Frankfurter Allgemeine* and sometimes it's a job to get it out my head. Why do they even print stuff like that?'

'I think we both know the answer to that one. They print what sells.'

'It's not like I really knew the guy. I only met him once, for heaven's sake. But I liked him. He was genuine. What's strange is that he said he was looking forward to working with me. How much sense does that make?'

'Come on,' said Bastian, getting to his feet. 'Forget the tea. The bars are open. I think it's time I dragged you to the Groninger Eck and we invited alcohol to do what alcohol does best.'

Bastian scribbled a message for Julia explaining where they'd gone and apologising that they wouldn't be back for dinner. As they left, he folded the note and dropped it onto the cake tray alongside Jack's article.

The Groninger Eck, in terms of its traditional, dark wooden fittings and furniture, was in many ways a typical street-corner bar. From its ceiling, however, hung an eclectic collection of battered motorbike exhausts and musical instruments. The atmosphere was self-consciously quirky and the establishment attracted a healthy custom from the student population as well as from its more traditional working-class clientele. Bastian insisted, as an expression of gratitude for Jack's help with the VW, on picking up the tab for the Hungarian goulash and the healthy supply of Bavarian wheat beer.

By the time they left the Groninger Eck, the sun had already set.

'The last time I drank this much,' said Jack, as they made their way along Oudenarder Strasse, 'it was in Madrid. I nearly ended up in bed with my flatmate.'

'Well, don't get your hopes up,' said Bastian. 'I'm a lousy kisser. Anyway, I think someone's got the hots for a receptionist in East Berlin. In the entire article, she was just about the only thing you really wrote about.'

'Well, I had to write about something,' said Jack, refusing to be drawn.

On their return to the apartment, the grinning pair were catapulted into apologising to Julia, who had been irked by the unattended washing in the machine. With contrition honestly demonstrated, apologies accepted and smiles of acknowledgement readily exchanged, Christa tapped her fingers on Jack's Concordia article. It was now the only thing on the table.

'I like it,' she said with a smile. 'Although, I think someone over here might have a crush on someone over there.'

'See?' said Bastian, beaming with vindication. 'What did I tell you?'

Jack took a breath. 'She was the only person I had an actual conversation with. I had to write about something.'

'Sure,' said Christa, a knowing look in her eye.

'Yeah, whatever,' said Jack, pulling a small, knotted, transparent bag from his jacket pocket. 'Anyway, Cupid, I've got a present for you. See what you make of this. You might just know what to do with it.'

48 FOREGONE CONCLUSION

East Berlin, Friday 7th May 1976

The vodka had not been a good idea. In a convoluted dream, Ulla found herself being repeatedly thwarted in her attempts to locate the entrance to the Werner-Seelenbinder-Arena. Inexplicably transported to her flat to retrieve her hockey uniform, she heard the doorbell. Ulla's visitor unlocked the door with a key and the sudden sight of her grandfather woke her with such a start that she felt as though someone has touched a live wire to her cheek.

It was shortly after five and the first reddish rays of morning light were bypassing the sloppily drawn curtains. Ulla had a throat like sandpaper and the suggestion of a headache. Drinking alone, she decided, was not a habit that she should cultivate. All too soon, the addled scenes from her dream were crowded out by crystal clear memories of the meeting at the Police Presidium and the sense of helplessness that they fostered. After visiting the bathroom, Ulla put some water on to boil and made herself two mugs of black tea. She knew that there would be little point in trying to get back to sleep.

The queasiness in the pit of her stomach had not abated. Although reason dictated that she had no real choice but to follow Hartling's instructions, Ulla nevertheless tried to wrangle some possibility of hope from her situation. Maybe the problem would simply go away. With luck, Jack Gilmore, given the evasive responses he had received from Press Secretary Fischer during his visit, would consider a second encounter to be more trouble than it was worth. If he failed to return to East Berlin, her immediate problem would be solved.

She thought back to Jack's arrival at the Ministry a week ago and racked her brains to recall whether he had written a telephone number on his visitor registration card. If so, would she have the gall simply to phone him and cancel the appointment? Ulla wondered if perhaps she should take the bottle of Wyborowa vodka into work, plonk it visibly on her desk and treat her boss to a torrent of abuse when the censure inevitably came. She would for sure be sent home and would without doubt be suspended, possibly even dismissed, in which case she would never have to cross Jack Gilmore's path again. Ulla knew, however, that she was indulging, as she often did, in fantasies. Hartling and Eckart would not be fooled by such antics and they had made the consequences of any lack of co-operation abundantly clear. For want of a better strategy, Ulla would simply have to get on with her day.

Although the water was lukewarm at best, Ulla took her time in the shower and gave little thought to the selection of clothes. Breakfast was no more than a third mug of tea. Aware that she was hardly in the most contented of moods, she set off early for work and made a conscious effort to walk slowly and to breathe deeply as she went.

Feeling that she was somehow looking at everything down a length of metal tubing about the same diameter as her head, Ulla's morning disappeared in a blur of rumination and repeated typing errors. Her lunch went untouched. Throughout the afternoon, she heard her Opa reassuring her in his inimitable way that worse things happen at sea. For the first time in her life, she was repeatedly forced to disagree.

After work, Ulla cooked herself a simple dish of boiled potatoes, liver and onions, most of which she felt able to eat. With the pots and pans washed and cleared away, she clicked *Ziggy Stardust* into the cassette player and pressed the play button.

Frustratingly, Lieutenant Eckart's insistence that she should be at home for the remainder of the day had ridden roughshod over her commitment to ice hockey training. Ulla noticed the bottle of Wyborowa on the table. Reluctant to wake up the following day feeling as rough as she had done that morning, she took the vodka and put it in the fridge. Maybe later she would pour it down the sink. It might also not be the wisest of ideas, she decided, to be playing western music when the Stasi officer eventually arrived.

The trill of the doorbell caught her by surprise. Although Lieutenant Eckart was almost unrecognisable out of uniform, the businesslike voice was unmistakeable.

'No need to offer me a coffee. I don't have long.'

She stepped into Ulla's apartment and surveyed the room. A paragon of calm, the Lieutenant placed a bulging KaDeWe shopping bag on the dining table, before removing her beige jacket and throwing it, together with her handbag, onto the sofa.

Eckart looked to Ulla as though she might have dressed for an evening at the opera. Her mustard top was close-fitting but elegant and the modestly flared, ebony trousers emphasised the length of her legs. The tan platform shoes looked positively expensive and were probably from the same

West Berlin store as the bag. It struck Ulla as completely bizarre that a Stasi officer could somehow look so stylish.

The Lieutenant sat down at the table.

'Join me, comrade Wolfram. Time is of the essence.'

Ulla did as she was instructed, but said nothing.

'Pay close attention to everything I tell you,' continued Eckart. 'Point one. From now on, in all communications with me or with Captain Hartling, you will refer to your target as "Matterhorn". Under no circumstances will you use his name. As for your assignment, you will refer to it as "Operative Personal Control Matterhorn". Are we clear? So, your objective is to get close to your target and become intimate with him. You are going to gain his trust, attract his interest and as far as sex is concerned, do whatever he wants, as often as he wants it. Your aim will be to leave the target feeling like he's been jacked up with heroin for the first time and will suffer the agonies of withdrawal if he doesn't score again soon. Report to myself or to Captain Hartling everything the target says, no matter how insignificant that information might seem.'

'Understood,' said Ulla, working hard not to betray the slightest flicker of contempt. 'Fuck his brains out. Tell you everything. Call him "Matterhorn", but not to his face.'

'In a nutshell. So, to assist the operation, I've brought you a number of things that will be of use.'

One item at a time, and with the efficiency of a quartermaster, Eckart set about revealing the contents of the orange and white KaDeWe store bag.

'One 100ml bottle of Chanel No.5 from an undeservedly famous store in the West. Wear it the first time you meet him outside work. Let him know he's special enough for you to be making an effort. Also, you might also want to straighten the place up a bit before you bring him back here.'

Ulla took the bottle of scent, sprayed her wrists and rubbed them together as she had sometimes seen her mother do before an important night out.

'Smells expensive.'

'It is. So, according to your medical records, you're not on the pill. This is a six-month supply. Read the instructions carefully. It can take up to a week before they become effective, so you also have twenty American condoms. Various flavours and configurations. Get him to wear one regardless. Don't get pregnant. It only complicates matters. But if the worst comes to the worst, you'll need to see a doctor to terminate the pregnancy. Contact me about that. And under no circumstances involve the target in any such matters.'

Eckart removed two La Voglia brand silver boxes from the KaDeWe bag and handed them to Ulla. Each package featured a photo of a slender, auburn-haired model wearing only her underwear and an alluring smile.

'Two pairs of white silk pants and two white triangle bras with ivory *frastaglio*,' said Eckart. 'Italian. Men are suckers for this kind of stuff. Unless they're gay, of course. Or dead. If anything doesn't fit, just contact me.'

Ulla had not the faintest idea what the word *frastaglio* was supposed to mean, but as far as she could tell from the image on the box, it was probably something to do with the fancy detailing.

'Presumably,' said Ulla with the disinterested tone of someone hiring a pair of skates, 'I have to return the underwear in a useable condition.'

'They're yours,' said Eckart, somewhat surprised by the query but oblivious to the veiled mockery. 'Keep them.'

'The perfume too?'

Something akin to a cautious smile appeared on Eckart's face. 'That too. Something else you can keep is this. One copy of *The Art Of Sex*. The text is in English but the pictures are impossible to misinterpret. Sign here to confirm receipt.'

Ulla used Lieutenant Eckart's biro to sign the invoice.

'Are we done?' asked Ulla, sounding almost bored.

'Indeed we are, comrade Wolfram. Perhaps I don't really need to remind you that you will need to be completely convincing from start to finish. But when you come to being intimate with your target, don't be afraid to enjoy yourself. It will pander to his ego and you've got no secrets to hide. Well, apart from one very obvious one. Any questions?'

Ulla looked away and shook her head. 'I don't think so.'

'Good. In which case, we can draw matters to a close. I'll show myself out.'

Eckart snapped the receipt into her handbag, picked up her raincoat and moments later was gone.

Ulla examined the array of operational materials that she had signed for. Although Hartling's words at the Presidium had been unequivocal, the reality of his expectations now stared her in the face.

Succumbing to curiosity, Ulla flicked idly through *The Art of Sex*. The book depicted through a series of pencil drawings, the explorations of a young heterosexual couple, who, with little apparent inclination for television, sport or housework, deployed their impressive yoga skills in the pursuit of ever more exhilarating sexual experiences.

In an act of quiet rebellion, Ulla located a pencil, ascribed roles to the adventurous lovers and began adding dialogue to the images.

'Hi, are you a spy?'

'No, are you?'

'No.'

'That's OK, then.'

'Oh, wow. You're so flexible. Do you have gold medals in yoga?'

'Oh, you know damn well I do.'

'Do you like that?'

'Oh, yes. That's good. That's so good. Yes. Yes. The secret files are in my bag. Oh, yes. Keep going. Oh my God. I think I love you.'

The flippancy granted Ulla no more than a few private moments to sneer at her oppressor. She dropped the pencil to the table, snapped the book shut and stared at the jacket for several seconds, grinding her teeth as her anger began to boil. With a start, the unwilling recruit snatched up the pencil in her fist and stabbed repeatedly and violently at the cover of the book until the nib was well and truly crushed. Consumed by the overbearing sense of injustice and the frustration at her lack of agency, Ulla grabbed *The Art Of Sex* and hurled it contemptuously at the front door, where it thudded against the lock and dropped to the floor. A moment later, she extended her right arm and swept Eckart's entire collection of offerings across the table and onto the ageing carpet.

Incapable of gathering her thoughts, Ulla drummed the ball of her right foot rapidly on the floor and stared at the empty tabletop. Eventually, she began slowly to reconnect with her surroundings. Allowing her attention to dwell on the hockey stick by the window, it occurred to her that every opponent she had faced on the ice, no matter how great their reputation, had some area of weakness, even if not immediately apparent. Whilst Ulla understood the importance of resolute defence, she had never failed to take a game to the opposition. No match, she knew from repeated experience, was ever a forgone conclusion.

49 WILL POWER

East Berlin, Monday 10th May 1976

It was shortly before two. Although it would be some weeks yet before Berliners began to swelter in the summer streets, trees throughout the city were already in leaf and it was a determinedly sunny afternoon.

Armed with an A4 block of study paper and enough pens and pencils to impress even Julia, Jack pushed open the door to the Ministry for the Environment and from across the lobby, returned the receptionist's generous smile. In spite of the suffocating context of the encounter, Ulla was genuinely pleased to see him. She welcomed the British student, asked him to sign in and issued him with a visitor permit. The formalities complete, Jack removed an envelope from his bag and dropped it onto the desk.

'More hazy cosmic jive. No gaps.'

Ulla beamed at him. 'Thank you very much, Mr Gilmore. That's perfect. So, it's room 216. There's a chair in the corridor outside comrade Fischer's room. Just wait there. And try not to sing.'

After a short and silent wait, the door to room 216 swung open. The Press Secretary welcomed Jack into his office and enquired in passing about his place of study in the UK, the course that he was following and the motivation for his research. The chitchat dispensed with, Fischer encouraged his British visitor to feel at liberty to ask whatever he wanted.

'When did the Ministry for the Environment come into being?' began Jack somewhat tamely. 'And why?'

The Press Secretary breathed in and patted his hands on his thighs. 'In the interest of the wellbeing of all citizens of the GDR, both state and society are committed to the protection of the natural environment. The Environmental Policy Act of 1952 was the first such act in German history and was most recently revised in 1970. The GDR founded the Ministry for the Environment in 1972 and was one of the first nations in the world to do so. In this regard the GDR was significantly ahead of the Federal Republic which did not have such a ministry until 1974.'

It was like interviewing a pamphlet. Jack made notes as best he could and pressed ahead with more probing questions. Carefully, he enquired about the setting of statutory limits, the monitoring of air quality and of the measurement of pollution levels in lakes and rivers. He broached the topic of enforcement and enquired about the likely response of the Ministry to breaches of policy by individual citizens, industrial units, farm collectives or any other organisations in the GDR. Each question, however, did little more than trigger a fresh monologue. Press Secretary Fischer, it seemed, had rehearsed a set of lengthy and glowing statements about GDR environmental policy which he intended to declaim without interruption. A master of dates and statistics, he repeatedly emphasised the absence of major environmental issues in the GDR, particularly when compared with the Federal Republic. With Jack assiduously scrawling notes, the conversation continued in its established vein for another forty minutes before Press Secretary Fischer looked at his watch, sucked his teeth and declared that unfortunately, he had another meeting to attend.

'Thank you for accepting our invitation to learn about the work of the Ministry,' said Fischer somewhat officiously as he stood up and offered his hand in valediction. 'If I can be of any further assistance, please do not hesitate to ask.'

Fischer's tone suggested that, in spite of his offer, he was not expecting to see the visitor again.

As Jack wandered back down to the lobby, his frustration that he had been fed a concoction of well-rehearsed statements peppered with spurious analysis was mitigated by the awareness that he had nevertheless pulled off something remarkable. He was the first student from his college, and conceivably from the UK, to have conducted primary research at the Environment Ministry in East Berlin.

In the lobby, Ulla retrieved Jack's visitor permit and recorded his time of departure.

'Thanks again for the lyrics,' she said, catching his eye. 'Do you have any other engagements in Berlin today?'

'No. Not at all. This was it.'

'Well, if you'd like to see a bit of the real Berlin and maybe talk some more about music, I'm free all evening.'

Although the invitation was the last thing Jack had been expecting, it was far from unwelcome. The receptionist was charming and unquestionably attractive. Obviously, this could not be seen as a date, but it would be a pleasant couple of hours in the company of someone he would not usually have the chance to spend time with. The only issue he could foresee was the teasing that he would inevitably have to endure upon his return to the West.

'Sure,' said Jack. 'Why not?'

'Good,' said Ulla, tilting her head slightly and returning the easy smile. 'I'll look forward to seeing you later. Do you have a map?'

'Yes.'

'Then ask me for directions to a quiet bar where you might be able to experience a decent beer and some authentic Berlin home-cooked cuisine.'

In response to his obliging enquiry, Ulla wrote the words 'Metzer Eck – Metzer Strasse' on an envelope, handed it to Jack and marked the location of the bar on his fold-out street plan.

'It's two stops on the tram,' she said. 'If you turn up at six, you might see a familiar face. I don't know if I've said this before, but my name's Ulla.'

Having whiled away a couple of hours checking out the bookstore on Karl-Marx-Allee and taking in the wide-ranging views of the city from the top of the TV Tower, Jack hopped on a tram at Alexanderplatz. The five-minute journey rapidly took him out of the city centre and past lines of modern prefabricated apartment blocks that gradually decreased in height from ten down to five storeys.

As the tram trundled its way along Prenzlauer Allee, Jack reflected on his meeting with Fischer. He would, he decided, take the Press Secretary's patently insincere offer of further assistance at face value and arrange a follow-up interview. With a degree of respectful persistence he would politely request copies of case studies that exemplified the 'historic, ground-breaking mission of the Ministry' so frequently vaunted by Fischer. How would the Press Secretary react, Jack wondered, if he were asked to comment on data produced by the Federal Environment Agency in West Berlin?

Before long, the tram rumbled to a stop and with the help of the map, Jack located Metzer Strasse almost immediately. In the cobbled, residential street, lines of juvenile linden trees sported clusters of cream flowers against a backdrop of vibrant green foliage. The Metzer Eck itself was more prosaic in its appearance. Standing at the junction with Strassburger Strasse, it had a tired facade and the flaking doors and window frames were sorely in need of attention.

A familiar voice called to him from a bench beneath the trees. After work, Ulla had made a point of going home and changing for their evening together. Whilst she had no intention whatsoever of whoring herself out for the MfS, she had been left in no doubt of the consequences of non-compliance. Hartling, Eckart or whoever they might have dispatched to keep watch on her, would therefore need to be persuaded that she was doing exactly as she had been instructed. She would at the very least need to look the part of a compliant Venus agent.

With that in mind, she had taken the time to dress as though she were out on a date. The Levi jeans that her Opa's brother had brought her from Munich were an automatic pick. Beneath a relaxed brown jacket with large buttons and wide lapels Ulla had chosen a classic blouse once worn by her mother and dating back to the late fifties. The vibrant design featured images, predominantly in purple and turquoise, of joyous, swimsuited, young women playing guitars and dancing on a beach as sailing boats tacked and gybed on a summer breeze. She had decided to go with the expensive, and surprisingly comfortable, Italian underwear that Captain

Eckart had foisted on her, although the multicoloured and implacably opaque blouse betrayed not the slightest clue as to her selection.

Jack, for his part, had thrown on that morning whatever looked clean. Over a tired, blue sweatshirt emblazoned with the words 'Will Power' and a small portrait of Shakespeare, he was wearing the loose-fitting, khaki trucker jacket recently stolen from the Hertie department store by Marco. Curiously, his straight-leg Levis were almost identical to Ulla's.

In the Metzer Eck, Ulla grabbed a corner table with an unimpeded view of the entrance. Jack hung up his jacket, placed his backpack beneath the table and ordered them each a bottle of Berliner Pilsener. Ulla requested meatballs with potato salad and recommended that Jack try the *soljanka*, a thick, spicy and sour Russian soup. Somewhat to his surprise, Ulla laid hard into the beer the moment it arrived.

'So Ulla,' said Jack, dimly recalling a list of icebreaker questions his previous girlfriend had once shared with him, 'when you're not listening to David Bowie, what do you normally do in your free time?'

'Well the short answer is ice hockey. The long answer is, I guess, pretty much the same.'

Ulla described her unshakeable love of the sport and detailed her rise to a regular spot in the GDR U20 team. When she repeated her now well-practised lie about having been forced to make a choice between ice hockey and university, the thought of Hartling's cynical offer caused a patch of skin on her neck to flush with blood. As the pair chatted, they traced the lines of similarity and contrast in their lives whilst carefully avoiding any direct reference to politics. Both Jack and Ulla lamented the absence of friends who were currently studying elsewhere. Although Ulla's regimented work life had little in common with Jack's much more fluid existence, both were having to find their feet in unfamiliar situations. As well as David Bowie, it turned out, she was a massive fan of Led Zeppelin.

'Hey,' said Jack, lifting his sweatshirt to reveal the *Physical Graffiti* tee shirt beneath. 'Snap.'

'You know what, Jack? As a representative of the enemies of the working class, you don't exactly fill me with terror. You're a kind-hearted soul, I think.'

'And I think, only a kind-hearted soul would say that. I don't know what I was expecting people in the East to be like, but not like you. You're not like the all-conquering, emotionless fanatics we see in the movies.'

'Ah, be careful,' she said, wagging a finger mischievously. 'You should see me play ice hockey.'

'Right. I'll bear that in mind. But I guess people are much the same everywhere. The same kind of hopes, probably. The same kind of fears.'

Ulla smiled. 'Don't be so sure. In the West, people exploit and abuse their fellow human beings. In the East, it's the other way round.'

The receptionist from the Environment Ministry was, Jack decided, not just witty but disarmingly so. If their increasingly easy conversation had been playing out in a café on the other side of the Wall, he would have been wondering if he dared ask her on a proper date.

In spite of the bind that she was in, Ulla felt strangely at ease in Jack's company. In another world, and given the chance to get to get to know him on her own terms, the prospect of sleeping with her supplier of David Bowie lyrics was not something that she would have rejected so categorically. With regard to this warm-hearted and slightly diffident British student, she decided, Hartling was definitely barking up the wrong tree. Jack was no more a spy than the statue of Karl Marx on Alexanderplatz was a Coca Cola machine.

As their conversation moved on, Ulla listened sympathetically to Jack's brief account of the loss of his mother when he was nine and the time warp that had engulfed his father in the intervening years. When, in response, she alluded to the more recent death of her grandfather, she stumbled on the attempt to say his name.

'Take your time,' he said to her quietly. 'I'm not going anywhere.'

Once Ulla had regained her composure, she carefully avoided all mention of the events which had followed her grandfather's illness and focussed on his generosity of spirit, his ready smile and the cornucopia of conjuring tricks he had taught her.

'Can you do one for me?' asked Jack.

'Oh, I don't know. Maybe later,' she said, patting him gently on the arm. 'To be honest, I was never that good at them and I'm way out of practice in any case.'

'Shame. But if you suddenly get the urge to saw me in half…'

Ulla smiled. 'I think that's probably illegal. Anyway, do you have any idea of the time?'

Jack glanced at his wrist, but the watch was no longer there.

‘Have you lost something?’ she asked with feigned innocence.

When finally he twigged that Ulla was wearing his watch, she flashed him another impish smile.

‘I think I’m ready to make a move,’ she said, as she returned the stolen property to its owner.

Still flush with the twenty-five East German marks that all visitors were required to spend during their day in the GDR capital, Jack offered to pay, but Ulla simply reached for her shoulder bag.

‘We’ll share the bill. But if you like, you can give me your half in deutschmarks.’

After settling up, Ulla surprised Jack by sitting noticeably much closer than before.

‘I want to talk to you about something,’ she said quietly, ‘but not here.’

Without waiting for a response, she got up and walked out of the bar. Baffled, Jack grabbed his backpack and his jacket, before following her down the steps into the street and along the tree-lined strip that ran the length of the narrow boulevard. When he caught up with his companion, she was standing by one of the benches.

‘Ulla,’ said Jack, ‘what the hell’s going on?’

‘It’s nothing to worry about,’ she lied. ‘Honestly. We’ll talk at my flat. It’s just round the corner. More or less.’

Still needing to maintain the appearance, for anyone who might be watching, of a dutiful Venus agent actively working her target. She drew him towards her and planted the softest of kisses on the lobe of his ear.

'I'm having a wonderful evening,' she said. 'I just remembered that you'll have to go back soon and I wanted to have you to myself for a bit.'

Both flattered and more than a little relieved, Jack smiled. If she had actually been intending to seduce him, Ulla thought, he would have been a pushover, fancy Italian bra or not.

50 ASSIGNATION

East Berlin, Monday 10th May 1976

In the front two seats of the grey Trabant sitting perhaps fifty metres from the Metzer Eck, the two members of the MfS surveillance team were growing increasingly impatient with their inability to contact Captain Hartling. Corporals Goretzki and Hecht had been on duty since well before Ulla Wolfram's early morning walk to work and it was now comfortably after seven in the evening. Goretzki was desperate for a smoke.

'I'll get more cigs,' he said, as he fidgeted with the vehicle's stubby keys.

'Bad idea. Unless you want to be the one to explain to Hartling that we lost our tail because you slipped out for a packet of twenty.'

'Bollocks.'

'Here, have one of mine,' said Hecht, before trying and failing once more to reach their superior over the radio.

Goretzki, drew on the cigarette and felt an immediate sense of release as the nicotine kicked into his system. 'Where's Hartling when you need him?'

'Presumably, he has more pressing matters to attend to.'

Whilst the watch team privately besmirched the integrity of their absent captain, Hartling was driving his Wartburg 353 in the direction of Woltersdorf, a small locality to the southeast of Berlin. Beside him, Irene Schiller chatted enthusiastically about the Flakensee lake and the cosy, waterside restaurant which Hartling had proposed for their assignation.

Although more than a little surprised to receive a social invitation from her colleague, the Major General's secretary had wasted no time in accepting his offer. In the six years since her divorce, she had done little on Saturday evenings beyond attending occasional get-togethers with happily married girlfriends or watching TV alone. As Irene began to open up about her background and her sorry romantic history, Hartling congratulated himself on spotting an opportunity that had been sitting right under his nose. His colleague was vulnerable, talkative and most importantly, enjoyed an enviable degree of access to Major General Konrad's office.

As ever, the Stasi captain had been meticulous in his preparations. He had studied Irene Schiller's file and had built up a detailed image of her professional history and personal interests. Seemingly casual conversations with colleagues in the Secretariat had furnished further insights into her quiet life and her shy eagerness for a soulmate.

Hartling was wearing the same suit and tie that he habitually selected for his dates with Petra Fichtenberg and he knew that he looked the part. As he drove, he took care to avoid pot-holes, refrained from accelerating or braking hard and displayed an impressive and conspicuous politeness towards other road-users. Having parked the car without fuss, the surprisingly urbane MfS captain made a point of walking around the vehicle to open the door for his passenger. He would, following his rigorous training for this line of work, be a paragon of consideration, politeness and empathy throughout the evening.

The quaint Restaurant Flakensee enjoyed views across the shallow lake and was attractively framed by the extensive treescape behind. Once seated at their table, Frau Schiller smiled somewhat nervously and expressed the hope that the pair would find enough to talk about, given that the particular nature of their professional lives made conversations about work a non-starter. Work, her comrade reassured her, was the last thing on his mind. Although the assertion was fundamentally untrue, Hartling's immediate purpose was to do no more than dangle the possibility of romance before her lonely eyes. If handled with sufficient skill, Irene Schiller might, in an unguarded moment at work, be tripped into further revelations about Major General Konrad and the files he stored in his office.

51 STANDBY

East Berlin, Monday 10th May 1976

Neither Ulla nor Jack paid much attention to the occupied grey Trabant in the line of empty vehicles. Even at a gentle pace, it took the pair no more than fifteen minutes to reach the dilapidated block in Fehrbelliner Strasse which housed Ulla's flat. A determined shove at the door was all it took to gain access to the lobby.

Along the wall immediately to Jack's right were four rows of largely redundant mail boxes which testified to the overwhelming absence of occupants in the down-at-heel building. Of the handful of boxes that were locked and in use, one was Ulla's and another belonged to the owner of the block. Two others bore the names of tenants who had also by-passed the state-run accommodation agency in favour of peppercorn rents in long neglected apartments. A good number of the redundant boxes were closed and blocked with uncollected post or old copies of *Neues Deutschland.* Some hung open on their hinges. A small number still sported keys.

The pair walked up to the first floor landing, where Ulla announced their arrival at her door and manipulated her key in the lock until it opened. The flat appeared broadly similar in its layout to Jack's own apartment, although the absence of a bed in the living room suggested that it was probably somewhat larger.

'Fifteen marks a month,' said Ulla. 'Not bad at all. How much do you pay in Wedding?'

'About seven times that.'

Ulla picked up Eckart's bottle of Chanel No.5 and gave a couple of squirts into the air. 'You'll have to excuse the kind of background aroma from my ice hockey kit. If I could make it smell like roses on a summer breeze, clearly I would. As it is, it's the price of being on the team.'

In the living room, she invited Jack to sit in the antique armchair. Ulla took a seat on the sofa directly opposite, looked into his eyes and exhaled audibly as though building up to an announcement.

'I need to tell you a bit more about my Opa,' she said.

As Ulla recounted the wanton obstruction of the Wolfram family's request to visit a dying relative, she lowered her head and allowed a tear to drip from her nose. Having arrived at the apartment believing that Ulla had conceivably been planning to make some kind of a move on him, Jack was now far from sure. He wondered if perhaps he should slip across to the sofa and put a comforting arm around her shoulder, but feared that it would only serve to complicate matters. For want of a better idea, he pulled a clean tissue from the pack in his jacket pocket and pressed it into the palm of her hand.

As Ulla sniffed her way through the crushing chain of events which followed her grandfather's illness, Jack could do no more than listen in stupefied horror. Although he had spent much of the past two and a half years engaged in the academic study of post-war Germany, Ulla's account of her family's mistreatment cut him to the quick. Perhaps, he thought, her real motivation in inviting him to the flat had not been to make out with him but simply to offload her pain to a total stranger. The notion was, Jack knew, complete conjecture, but if providing a sympathetic ear could do anything at all to mitigate her anguish, he was entirely ready to listen.

When, seemingly out of the blue, Ulla alluded to the Stasi's interest in Jack's research and confessed that she had been coerced into acting as a honeytrap, his blood ran cold. Without anything resembling a frame of reference for his situation, he did not have the faintest idea what to do.

'I'm sorry,' said Ulla, catching his eye. 'I'm really sorry. But you don't know these people. You can't say no to them. You don't know what they can do.'

Whilst Jack's desire for self-preservation told him that he should get up and leave, Ulla had clearly put herself in jeopardy by defying her Stasi controllers and revealing the truth to him. He could not simply turn his back on her.

'As far as I can see, Ulla, you *are* saying no.'

'I want to show you something,' she said.

From a walnut cabinet, she fished out her leaver's certification from the Immanuel Kant Extended Upper School and some photographs of her closest friends.

'Everyone in these photos is now at university. Jenny, Rosa, everyone. And I really wanted to go. I wanted to study physics. But I was forced to withdraw my application. What I said about choosing ice hockey is just the lie I tell everyone because the truth is just a heap of shit.'

'I'm sorry,' said Jack. 'That's awful. Just... unimaginably awful.'

'To get me to do this, you know, report on you, they dangled Leipzig in front of me. University. The chance to do what my friends are doing. The chance to do what you're doing. They show you the carrot, but they leave you in no doubt that behind their back they're holding the kind of stick that can break you in two with a single blow.'

She returned to the wooden cabinet and pulled out the battered copy of *The Art of Sex*.

'Take a look. Captain Shitface recruited me last Wednesday and Lieutenant Pimp gave me that on Friday. That was my training manual.'

In spite of the anxiety that still gripped him, Jack could not help but smirk at the derisive, pencilled-in dialogue.

'I'm guessing it was you who wrote all this.'

'Oh, yeah,' she said with a degree of pride. 'Absolutely.'

Jack allowed himself a moment. 'So. What do we do now?'

Ulla urged him not to leave immediately. If he crossed the border too soon, she suggested, the MfS might suspect that they had spent too little time in her flat for her to have fulfilled her brief. It would therefore be better if he delayed his return. Once Jack was gone, she would make contact with her handler and try to convince him that she had carried out her orders, but had been unable to glean any conclusive intelligence from her target.

In order to help Ulla preserve the illusion of acquiescence, Jack agreed not to rush back. He did, however, have to confront the possibility that his exit from the GDR might not be straightforward.

'Do you think they might pull me over at the border?'

'I don't know,' she said with a gentle shrug. 'I don't know anything about anything anymore. All I know is that I want to get out of this whole stinking mess. So Jack, if you have a way to smuggle me out of this shitstorm under your jacket, I'm all ears.'

'God, I wish it were that easy,' said Jack, unaware that he was squeezing the flesh of his right thigh whilst staring at the carpet. 'I really wish it were. But you know what we do in Britain when the shit hits the fan?'

'What?'

'We put the kettle on.'

Over a pot of tea the pair reviewed their position and determined for the second time that their immediate priorities were to get Jack safely back to West Berlin and to protect Ulla from any suspicion of duplicity.

Ulla put down her mug. 'As you said, it's possible they might ask you some awkward questions at the border, so we really have to get our story straight. As far as I can see, we need to tell the absolute minimum of lies and to construct the ones we do need to tell on a foundation of checkable truths. So, listen. It was me who persuaded you to go the Metzer Eck and it was me who invited you back to the apartment. We can both tell that part of the story exactly as it happened. And if we've been watched, Hartling will be able to verify this. More or less.'

'OK, but what about… you know, the stuff that didn't happen, but was supposed to happen?'

'Well, obviously we came back here, you already had the hots for me after the kiss in the street. One thing led to another and we ended up in bed. Then, in the afterglow of our lovemaking, I whispered softly to you that if you wanted, I might be able to get my hands on more interesting material from the Ministry than Fischer had provided you with. You, however, were completely startled at my offer and said that you would prefer to keep everything legitimate and above board. You wouldn't want to cause any problems. I will then be able to say that, as far as I could ascertain, Jack Gilmore was exactly what he said he was.'

'One question.'

'What?'

'Are you really going to use the word "afterglow"?'

It was enough of a joke to puncture the tension. Ulla shook her head and smiled.

'I'll take that as a no,' said Jack.

With a view to making their accounts of the evening as consistent as possible, the pair extemporised their way through a sequence of plausibly intimate conversations. Ulla showed Jack the colour of her bedsheets and the packet of Stasi-supplied condoms that they would claim they had used. She sat forcefully on the bed to demonstrate the creaking springs and, pulling the discarded silver packaging from the waste bin, offered him a glimpse of the expensive Italian underwear in which Lieutenant Eckart had set so much store.

'I'll give you my phone number,' said Jack. 'Obviously, you would have got that much out of me.'

'You ought to go now,' said Ulla, noticing that the light outside was beginning to fade. 'We need to get you back to Friedrichstrasse well before your visa expires. I'll walk with you to the station. That's where the big goodbyes all happen. If anyone is going to be watching, it'll be there and if I'm with you, it'll look like I'm still doing my seductive receptionist routine.'

Jack collected his things, whilst Ulla grabbed a raincoat. They looked at each other and he took her raised eyebrows and tilt of the head as the signal to leave. As they emerged from the block, Ulla checked for company. In the half-light of the evening, no-one appeared to be watching from neighbouring windows or waiting incongruously in the doorway opposite. The dark Trabant with the two occupants, however, struck Ulla as somehow familiar. Had she walked past the same vehicle when she left the Metzer Eck? She would, she decided, say nothing to Jack. He was edgy enough as it was.

Corporal Goretzki was careful not to start the engine the moment he spotted the targets.

'It's definitely them,' said Hecht. 'His visa expires at midnight. He has to be heading for Friedrichstrasse. They'll take a left at the end of the street and then left again.'

The driver of the Trabant waited for Jack and Ulla to make the expected turn out of Fehrbelliner Strasse before starting the engine. Having confirmed that the couple were heading, as anticipated, along the main highway towards Friedrichstrasse, the officers leapfrogged their targets, drove as far as the next junction and parked, with the headlamps extinguished, on the opposite side of the street. They would repeat the process as often as was necessary.

'Still no response from Hartling' said Corporal Hecht, the radio receiver to his ear.

'Is he going to want us to bring the target in, do you think?'

'Doubt it. It's not what it says on the order papers.'

'So what do we do?'

'We do what it says. Anyway. The kiosk at the station will be open and I could do with a smoke.'

Ahead of Jack and Ulla, the red lights that topped the Alexanderplatz TV tower flashed lazily in the encroaching twilight. Unable to dispel the thought that they were possibly being observed, Ulla clasped Jack's arm as they walked.

Perhaps half way along Wilhelm-Pieck-Strasse, Jack stopped suddenly.

'Listen,' he said. 'If you really want to leave the GDR, then I really want to help you.'

'No,' retorted Ulla. 'No, you don't. You wouldn't say that if you knew how stupidly dangerous it is to try to escape or if you understood the consequences for those who help. For now, let's just deal with the next twenty-four hours. You just get yourself to the checkpoint and through the controls. I'll phone you from a call box in the morning to check that you got back OK. If you don't hear from me, phone the Ministry at nine on Monday. If it's not me who answers, ask to speak to me. If they say I'm not available, you'll know what's happened.'

As the couple approached the River Spree their anxiety began to mount. Beyond the bridge, the green and white S-Bahn symbol and the illuminated capitals of the station name were already clearly visible. Determined to persuade whoever might be watching of her commitment to the honeytrap operation, Ulla squeezed Jack's arm and kissed him on the cheek. The pair turned right after the bridge, walked a short distance along the river and presently found themselves waiting outside the Palace of Tears, the departure hall for travellers returning to West Berlin. Bathed in the light which escaped its modernist glass structure and surrounded by a crowd of the soon-to-be-parted, the couple's subdued exchanges and uneasy body language looked positively ordinary.

Ulla drew her companion into a gentle embrace. 'Listen, Jack Gilmore. When we say goodbye, I'm going to kiss you, and I mean really kiss you, firstly because I sort of want to, but more importantly because you never know who might need convincing. So be ready, soldier, not to repel my advances.'

'You know what?' said Jack nervously. 'This has been the weirdest, most mind-fuckingly bizarre day of my life.'

Ulla placed her hands inside Jack's boxy jacket and gently stroked the sides of his torso. 'Come on. We can do this. But for heaven's sake, breathe. You're going to need to be calmer when you present your passport. I'll walk back and try to phone Captain Shitface. They say fortune favours the brave, so with luck you'll hear from me in the morning. If everything's OK, I'll make a point of explicitly mentioning ice hockey. Anyway, Jack Gilmore, you need to get going. Hug me like you mean it. Like you can't bear to let me go. And put your lips on standby.'

52 LIFE'S ILLUSIONS

West Berlin, Monday 10th May 1976

With an endorsement still against his name to alert the MfS of his arrival or departure but to allow him otherwise unhindered passage through the controls, Jack returned to the western side of the city with unexpected ease and no small measure of relief.

At Nauener Platz, he emerged from the U-Bahn station into lightly falling rain. Still struggling to make sense of the events of the day and fearfully uncertain of the fate that might have befallen Ulla, he made his way back to Oudenarder Strasse. Glad to close the main door securely behind him, Jack crossed the quiet and poorly lit internal courtyard and drifted up the five flights of stairs towards his flat. At the top of the stairwell, a pungent, incense-like aroma hung in the air.

Drawn to the strains of Julia and Christa singing 'Both Sides Now', Joni Mitchell's endearing meditation on perspective, he wandered into their apartment and stood in the doorway to the lounge. A large vanilla candle sitting on a plate on the floor was the only source of light in the room. The two lovers sat facing each other across a low table. A couple of half-empty bottles of Warsteiner beer stood at its centre and the unsmokable butt of a fat roll-up lay in the Bollinger-branded ashtray to the side. Christa was noticeably more proficient on the guitar than Julia, but they each matched Joni Mitchell's unwavering pitch note for note and as the pair delivered the concluding line, they harmonised with consummate ease. The wistful song wrapped up, Christa and Julia exchanged a look that conveyed not just love but devotion.

Their intimate bubble was burst by Jack's appreciative applause. They hadn't even noticed him.

'So how was your date?' asked Christa. The teasing had begun.

Although the question was laced with irony, Jack's addled brain had been robbed of all capacity for nuance.

'It was an absolute fucking disaster.'

'Well, there's a solution for that,' said Julia with a smile. 'Roll that man a joint.'

'Thanks,' replied Jack, 'but no. I don't smoke. Not even… well, not anything.'

'There's a solution for that too,' said Julia, still beaming as she levered the cap off a spare bottle of Warsteiner.

Jack flopped onto the sofa without removing his jacket. As he treated himself to a healthy swig from the bottle, Christa strummed at her guitar and reprised the refrain from the Joni Mitchell song.

'I've looked at life from both sides now / From win and lose and still somehow / It's life's illusions I recall / I really don't know life at all.'

'Yeah, that pretty much sums it up,' said Jack. 'I really don't have any effing idea about anything.'

'Wanna talk about it?' asked Julia.

'Not particularly,' said Jack. 'Although, what's the best advice you'd give to someone who's just come back from an evening that was kind of like a date for a bit and then got completely, absolutely, like, totally batshit weird?'

'It depends what you mean by "weird",' replied Julia.

'What I mean by "weird" is, well, whatever you think I might mean by "weird", my evening was definitely weirder than that.'

Jack took a slow, lengthy swig from the Warsteiner and waited for a response.

'Given the absence of specifics,' said Christa eventually, 'my advice would be to make wiser choices next time.'

'You know what,' said Jack. 'I have absolutely no idea at what point I even made a choice. It feels like it all just happened.'

'Not to choose is also a choice,' asserted Julia.

'That doesn't make sense,' said Jack, still too shellshocked to grapple with the truth of anything even remotely resembling a paradox.

'Come on, Jack,' said Julia, determined to shed light on her epiphany, 'letting things just happen by default is also a choice. If we choose to give up our right, or our responsibility, to make a choice, then we have made a choice. Not to choose is also a choice.'

'I still don't get it,' said Jack. 'All I'm hearing is the word "choice".'

As he stared at the candle, his thoughts returned to Ulla. The sense of utter relief that he had felt following his unhindered passage through the checkpoint was replaced by a nagging fear for her safety.

Jack caught Christa's eye. 'How about some more Joni Mitchell?'

'And more beer,' suggested Julia. 'Definitely more beer.'

As the two women once more applied their flawless vocals to a jaunt through the Canadian singer's best-known songs and the Warsteiner worked its magic, their audience of one began slowly to relax.

Shortly before one thirty, Jack pulled himself to his feet, wished Christa and Julia a good night and took himself to bed. Although palpably calmer now, he was nevertheless unable to settle. With his mind set to rinse and repeat, he attempted to analyse the sequence of events in East Berlin and pick out the precise moments where he might have made better choices. Hindsight, he feared, might turn out to be a punishment as much as a gift.

Although his offer to help Ulla extricate herself from East Berlin had been completely impulsive and she had rejected it out of hand, Jack inherently understood that he was far from finished with the situation that he had left behind. As eventually he drifted in the direction of sleep, he thought of his mother and petitioned her to grant Ulla the same good fortune that had accompanied his passage through the border controls. That he might already possess the tools to facilitate an escape, did not at this point enter his mind.

53 SUBDUED GLOW

East Berlin, Tuesday 11th May 1976

Whilst Jack, although rattled, had at least freed himself from the sense of lurking jeopardy, Ulla could allow herself no such luxury. The unwilling honeytrap agent lay in her bed, able to think of little else beyond the threat of footsteps on the stairs followed by insistent hammering at the door. Although her arrest was not an inevitability, Ulla could not know with any degree of certainty that the Stasi had failed to register her duplicity until she had verified Jack's safe return to West Berlin.

Beside Ulla's bed, the alarm clock marked out each indifferent second. Shortly after two forty-five, she wondered whether sufficient time had elapsed to suggest that Jack had not been detained at the border, had not been interrogated and had therefore not revealed her failure to carry out Hartling's orders.

Anxious about her erstwhile target and fearful for her own future, Ulla tried to resign herself to the idea of going an entire night without sleep. Feeling alone and strangely exposed, she listened to the stuttering of a two-stroke engine and watched the beams of light sweep across her ceiling as the occasional Trabant rattled by on the rain-soaked cobbles below. Perhaps the next vehicle, she thought each time, would be the one that stopped outside her apartment.

After an hour of unrelenting anxiety, logic slowly began to wrest control of Ulla's circling thoughts and allowed her to take more rational stock of her situation. It was entirely possible, she decided, that Hartling might not see anything amiss in the evening's events. Ulla's attempt to contact him immediately after Jack's departure would certainly have been logged at the Ministry switchboard and would tally with the Pass and Control records of the British student's exit via Friedrichstrasse. Furthermore, any video footage that the MfS might have from the pavements outside the Palace of Tears would also, she was certain, serve to shore up her verbal account of the evening. Indeed, without the kind of evidence that only her target could provide, the Stasi officer would be in no position to suspect that she had done anything but follow her instructions. It all hinged on Jack.

Incapable of switching off and determined to do something other than wait the night out, Ulla climbed out of bed, fumbled around in the dark for her clothes and groped her way to the bathroom to get dressed. Without turning on the light in her room, she moved carefully to the window and peered through a gap in the curtains. In the street below, everything appeared much as she would have expected. Emboldened, the recalcitrant Venus agent slipped on a coat, grabbed her umbrella and pocketed about half her stash of loose change. Within thirty seconds, she had left the building. It was quiet and the persistent rain, visible only in the subdued glow of the street lamps, continued to drizzle down. There was, as far as she could ascertain, not another soul to be seen.

From the call box at Senefelder Platz, Ulla dialled the number that Jack had given her and waited.

Eventually, a sleepy female voice muttered a laboured hello. It was Julia.

'Hi,' said Ulla. 'Look, I'm sorry it's so late, but I'd really like to speak to Jack.'

'What? Jesus. Jack's gone to bed. Hell, do you have any idea what time it is?'

'I know. And I'm sorry to disturb you. But, listen. Don't get up. Don't wake him. Could you just tell him later that Ulla phoned and she will try to get tickets for the ice hockey.'

'Get what now?'

'Tell him, Ulla is getting tickets for the ice hockey.'

'Yeah, whatever. Ulla. Ice hockey. Message. Got it.'

With that, Julia hung up.

Jack Gilmore, it would seem, had made it through the border controls without falling foul of the authorities. Although Ulla could not hide from the fact that she would ultimately have to confront her Stasi handlers, her sense of relief at that moment was palpable.

Back in the unlit apartment, the refusenik peeked once more through the narrow gap between the curtains. The street below was still deserted and quiet. So far, so good, she thought. So far, so good. Ulla navigated her way back to her room, threw off her damp clothing and climbed into bed. Whilst she was still not certain that sleep would claim her, neither was she convinced that it wouldn't.

54 HALF AN ANSWER

West Berlin, Tuesday 11th May 1976

It was after ten, sunlight was slanting through the bamboo blinds and Jack opened his eyes feeling not just easier but strangely invigorated. The initial, almost celebratory sense of salvation began to dissipate as inevitably his thoughts were drawn to Ulla and the uncertain fate that awaited her.

Slowly, his exploration of the previous evening's events began to coalesce around the single idea that he was, no matter how inadvertently, at least partly responsible for her plight. His first, inquisitive appearance at the Environment Ministry had attracted the attention of the MfS and had dragged the blameless receptionist into a web of exploitation from which she had little prospect of escape. Furthermore, in defying the Stasi and alerting him to the honeytrap, she had placed herself at enormous risk. He was, without question, in her debt.

As things stood, Jack had not the slightest idea whether Ulla was now having to pay the price of her insubordination. Had she been able simply to walk back to Fehrbelliner Strasse without interference or had she been intercepted, perhaps bundled into a van somewhere, and taken immediately to some anonymous location to be questioned? If that were the case, how quickly would the Stasi begin to pick holes in her story?

Through the wall to the adjoining flat, Jack could suddenly hear the raucous, pulsating strains of the opening track on Led Zeppelin's second album. He could only presume that Christa and Julia were already up and that, in combination with the drifting aroma of the coffee, the music formed part of a twin-pronged assault on his sluggishness.

As Jack pulled on exactly the same clothes that he had worn the previous day, he reflected on Julia's assertion that not to choose was also a choice. Although he had discounted her late-night observations as the product of hashish-fuelled reverie, Julia's words now resonated strongly with something that Pastor Niemeyer had said to him. The passive observers of cruelty were, through their lack of intervention, complicit in the behaviours they observed. His conscience dictated that he could not simply consign Ulla to her fate. The most shapeless of notions in his head, he located the discarded GDR passport that Katarina Kohl had given him and took it to the kitchen.

With none of his flatmates at the table and only a handful of rolls remaining, Jack filled a beer glass with tap water, slipped the passport into his back pocket and sat down to breakfast. Next to the butter was a note in Julia's immaculate handwriting.

'Dear curious and very possibly hungover friend, someone by the name of Ulla called and asked me to tell you that she would try to get you tickets for the ice hockey. (Or something along those lines.) Full explanation required when you make it as far as the kitchen.'

Jack stretched out one of his legs, tilted his head back and closed his eyes. With his arms hanging loosely by his sides, he blew a long stream of air. Ulla, he now knew, had at the very least made it back to her apartment. The feeling of deliverance that he had experienced upon waking now began to wash over him once more. He wondered if he should maybe try to phone the Environment Ministry in the hope of speaking to Ulla briefly, but it was not what they had agreed.

Julia walked barefoot into the kitchen. 'It's alive,' she said, histrionically emphasising her words in an oblique reference Dr Frankenstein.

Jack opened his eyes and smiled.

'Did you see the note?' asked Julia. 'She phoned at some ungodly hour, so I might not have got it exactly right. Either it's massively important or somebody's missing someone.'

'It's completely, massively important,' said Jack, no longer smiling. 'How good are you at solving puzzles?'

Julia shrugged. 'I dunno. Not too bad, I suppose. Depends on the puzzle. Try me.'

'So. Right. Just imagine. There is someone who wants to leave East Berlin. They have been coerced by the Stasi into doing stuff they don't want to do and they really want to get out. They know someone who lives in West Berlin, but that person has come to the attention of the Stasi because of his interest in the Environment Ministry. There is a stinking great wall between the two halves of the city and the only thing they have that might be of any use is this.'

Jack pulled the blue GDR passport from his pocket and tossed it onto the wicker table mat in front of Julia.

'Two questions,' said Julia as she picked up the passport. 'Firstly, just what in heaven's name did you get up to in East Berlin yesterday, and secondly, just how the hell did you lay your hands on *that*?'

Over the course of the next half hour Jack recounted, in as much detail as he could, both the highly unsettling events of the previous evening and his more entertaining encounter with Katarina Kohl, the expatriated rock musician whose old

GDR passport he now possessed. When finally Julia ran out of questions, she examined the passport carefully.

'When you told me you had a puzzle to solve,' she said, 'I've got to say, I was expecting some kind of lonely hearts kind of thing. You undersold the situation by several orders of magnitude.'

'Well, point taken,' said Jack. 'But the question is still the same. What the hell do I do now?'

Julia twitched her toes nervously as she reflected.

'What you definitely don't do is take yourself back to East Berlin any time soon. Maybe not ever.'

'Yeah, I've worked that much out for myself. But that's only half an answer.'

'At best. OK. I'll tell you what we need to do.'

'What?'

'We need to call a house meeting.'

55 A PATIENT MAN

West Berlin, Tuesday 11th May 1976

In the corner of the Rive Gauche café, absorbed in a substantial book, a client with a shock of platinum blonde hair alternated between spooning the froth from his cappuccino and drawing hard on his roll-up.

In a private room to the side, Hartling's MI6 handler pressed a clenched fist to his lips. Turnbull had not expected his asset to put in an appearance until he was in a position to hand over the requested intelligence. The MfS officer, however, now sat in front of him, cigarette in hand, and was coolly asking for more time. Hartling had, he claimed, identified the secure location of the documents embedded in the typewriter ribbon and was actively exploring a method of accessing them. Until he had a solution to that part of the conundrum, MI6 would have to exercise a certain degree of patience.

Turnbull looked the prospective defector in the eye and pondered the possibilities. Either Hartling was telling the truth or he was a damn good liar. Although the plea for more time, at least on the surface, seemed to indicate a desire to deliver, the British case officer had not the slightest intention of acceding to the request. He knew that he had the upper hand and he intended to keep things that way.

Hartling drew on his cigarette, exhaled slowly and waited. Finally, Turnbull tapped the table sharply with the tips of his fingers and spoke with quiet authority.

'No. Absolutely not. Either you bring us something meaningful by the end of the month or the deal is off. It's as simple as that.'

Hartling shifted on his chair, unable to mask his frustration. 'Do you want these files or not? If you want them, you have to be patient. It's not like going into a supermarket.'

'No, of course it isn't. Although, I hear some of the supermarkets over there are not exactly overstocked. I am by nature a patient man, Captain Hartling, but be in absolutely no doubt that time is not on your side.'

'This is crazy. You just have to wait. I am one step away from giving you exactly what you want.'

'Excellent. You have three weeks to work on it. In the meantime, I have something that might encourage you to achieve your objective a little quicker.' Turnbull removed a folder from his briefcase, and pulled out a series of black and white photos of their previous meetings. 'I wonder how you would explain these holiday snaps to your superiors?'

Hartling was thunderstruck. Recognising that a camera had been concealed somewhere above the door, he could not prevent himself from glancing towards its probable location.

'It's still there,' said Turnbull, with an air of unshakeable confidence, 'if you look hard enough.'

'These could be anything,' said Hartling, dismissively. 'I could just as easily be trying to recruit you to work for us.'

'That's a fair point, Captain Hartling. A very fair point. That said, the high-quality audio recordings of our conversations tell a very different story. Incontrovertible evidence, I would say. Very much our stock-in-trade.'

A brief silence ensued. The MfS officer adjusted the position of his expensive spectacles.

'Three weeks then,' said Hartling, with the paper-thin dignity of a captured general staring at a loaded rifle. The Stasi officer took his time stubbing out the cigarette before standing to leave.

'And in case there is any doubt,' said Turnbull, 'we've recorded this meeting as well. If you like, I can provide you with a copy.'

'That won't be necessary.'

As Hartling walked towards the net-curtained door which opened onto the street, he looked at the solitary client still reading in the corner and wondered whether he was also party to the whole charade. The answer would not have surprised him.

The leafy planes that flanked Motzstrasse would, in the summer months, provide an abundance of shade from the sun. For the time being, however, the canopy of leaves simply blotted out views of the spring sky. Exasperated at his blindness to his handler's duplicity, the Stasi officer headed briskly in the direction of the U-Bahn. Although MI6 now had him over a barrel, Hartling had been trained not to act precipitously when confronted with unforeseen circumstances. In the face of complication, he told himself, he needed to maintain his equilibrium, think clearly and devise a workable plan.

As Motzstrasse finally opened out onto Nollendorfplatz, Captain Hartling reminded himself that he was an MfS officer walking with complete impunity around the streets of an enemy city. In light of that fact, he should be no more intimidated by Martin than he was by the countless West

Berlin citizens who passed him by without a second look. His handler's threats, he concluded, did little more than bring timescales into sharper focus. He simply had to keep his nerve.

Given, however, that British Intelligence now had him dangling on a string, they no longer had any incentive to provide him with a cosy new life in the West. In fact, he knew exactly what he would do in their position. He would renege on the deal, keep his asset in situ and make ever-increasing demands on his services. Had he been planning to stick around, he would in due course have pulled exactly the same move on the hapless receptionist from the Environment Ministry.

As the U-Bahn to Friedrichstrasse rocked the MfS officer occasionally from side to side, he knew that his relationship with MI6 had come to the end of its useful life. Fortunately, the British were not the only show in town. Whilst Hartling had little confidence in the BND, he could at any point offer his services to the Americans. As soon as he had the Day X files in his possession, it would be a simple enough matter to secrete them in the western half of the city, present himself at the headquarter complex for the United States Army and request political asylum. As a show of good faith, he would offer his new case officer a single page from the most valuable of the stolen documents and open up negotiations on his future.

56 STILL VALID

West Berlin, Tuesday 11th May 1976

The beef stew, meticulously prepared by Julia and fortified by Marco with a healthy quantity of shoplifted Pinot Noir, had been enjoyed and appreciated by all. Anna was now flipping the caps off a small supply of bottled beers whilst in the room next door, Christa dropped the needle on a brand new Pink Floyd album. On her return, the friends clunked their bottles in a communal salute and rapidly agreed that the washing up could wait until the sun had set on their evening. Given the buoyancy of their collective mood, Julia's subsequent request for a house meeting came as something of a surprise. When she handed the floor to Jack, the others were intrigued, to say the least.

Jack took a gentle swig of Warsteiner and began the account of his tangled misadventure in East Berlin. Having responded to the inevitable requests for repetition or clarification, he dug out Katarina Kohl's discarded GDR passport, placed it in the centre of the table and reiterated his desire to help Ulla escape her unenviable plight.

Marco raised a finger. 'Look, don't get me wrong. I'm not saying that this Ulla person is not in deep shit or that she doesn't deserve to be helped, but that is clearly not her passport. If you think you can just take this over to her and then watch her wave it blithely at the border guards before skipping through the controls like a spring lamb, honestly, Jack, that's never going to happen.'

Jack shrugged. 'Well, obviously. At least, not like that.'

'In the first place,' said Julia, 'Jack's hardly in a position to go back to East Berlin, so it would have to be one of us who took it over. And secondly, as we all know, the border guards are not going to be fooled by the passport in its current state. So, what we have to ask ourselves is whether there is anything we could potentially do about that.'

'Never gonna happen,' said Marco. 'Way too risky.'

'You may well be right,' said Julia with practised diplomacy. 'Nevertheless, let's take a look at what we've got. So, what we have here is a standard, blue GDR passport with the hammer and compass watermark on every page and a printed serial number at the base of every second page. On page two we have a black and white photo of a young woman with dark, shoulder length hair. Immediately beneath the photo we have a signature in blue ink. Further details relating to the holder's appearance are listed below the signature and are clearly written, also in ink, presumably indelible. Anyway, there's nothing particularly unusual here. Height: medium. Eyes: blue. Distinguishing marks: none. On the facing page we have the holder's surname and first names, followed by date of birth, birthplace, address, profession and marital status. At the bottom of the page is the seven-digit printed serial number. And that's it. That's what we have. Any comments so far?'

'Is it still valid?' asked Christa.

'The passport has not expired, so presumably it could, in theory, still be used. The existing exit visa has been counter-stamped to indicate Katarina Kohl's date of departure from the GDR so the visa itself is no longer viable. On the other hand, it does at least provide a template to copy if we could find someone who might do that sort of thing. Any suggestions? Marco?'

'Why are you asking me? Why do you assume that I'd know someone?'

Julia raised her eyebrows. 'And do you?'

'As it happens, no. I don't. But it's immaterial because the obvious issue here is the photo. Unless Ulla Wolfram and Katarina Kohl are identical twins who were somehow separated at birth, that is the major sticking point.'

'Well, it's clearly not a photo of Ulla,' conceded Jack. 'The hair colour's wrong for a start. But if I remember correctly, she does have blue eyes. She'd certainly pass as medium height and I'd say that she has no obvious distinguishing marks. Not as far as I know, anyway.'

'Would the best option be to get a passport photo from Ulla and do a switch?' asked Christa. 'How easy would that be to do?'

Anna raised a hand. 'My bet would be that they glue the photo in so well that you'd tear the page if you tried to remove it.'

'Plus,' said Christa, as she put down her glass, 'you'd still have to counterfeit a visa stamp and create a copy of that yellow admin sticker.'

'There must be people who can do that sort of thing, though,' said Jack. 'There must be.'

'OK,' said Anna. 'How about this? There's this Canadian guy called Tony in the props department at work and he claims that he faked the Berlin residence permit in his passport. It's basically a large ink stamp, not massively unlike the exit visa in that East German passport. The thing is, although he says he did it himself, it looks completely genuine, so no-one at work is sure whether to believe him or not. Tony's a talented guy though. The props he makes are, like, really impressive. And he has a degree in fine art conservation, so, you know, he probably has that kind of skillset. I could always show him the passport and see what he says.'

'Bastian?' asked Julia, keen to ensure that everyone had contributed. 'What's your take on this? You haven't said anything so far.'

The student put down his beer. 'As far as I can see, there can't be any harm in asking. What's the worst that could happen?'

'As much as it pains me to agree,' said Marco with a reflective nod. 'You have a point. No harm in asking.'

'What if he wants paying?' said Jack. 'How much would something like that cost anyway?'

Marco smiled at Anna. 'Ask for his measurements. Maybe he'd like an off-the-peg suit from one of Berlin's more exclusive department stores.'

57 PHOTO OPPORTUNITY

East Berlin, Wednesday 12th May 1976

On waking shortly before dawn, Ulla's stomach had tightened to a squeamish knot. Unfathomably, Tuesday had passed without contact either from Hartling or from Eckart, but the hiatus had merely left the unwilling recruit convinced that she would inevitably be interviewed at some point today. Perhaps a deputation of plain-clothes officers would show up at first light and escort her to a waiting car. Perhaps she would simply find another note on her desk.

Just as she had done yesterday, Ulla went to the window and checked the street below. A solitary figure walked along the pavement, passed beneath the window and continued slowly in the direction of the U-Bahn. For perhaps thirty seconds, a dull light burned in a second-floor window across the street.

Satisfied eventually that all was quiet, Ulla was drawn to thinking about the inevitable meeting with Hartling. Even if she were to convince him of the innocence of the British student, she was certain that her MfS handler would develop a sudden case of amnesia with regard to her university application. Given that she had recently signed a commitment to do the Stasi's bidding for as long as they deemed necessary, Hartling now had little incentive to do anything but exploit his asset to the full. As soon as he had lost interest in Jack Gilmore, he would no doubt force the Environment Ministry receptionist to begin informing on her comrades at work.

Ulla was sickened to the core, not just at the cynical way that the Stasi had prostituted her out but at the entitlement Hartling clearly felt to command the lives of citizens he was in principle employed to protect. However, if she understood anything about the ugly, constricted mess in which she found herself, it was that acquiescence was undoubtedly the path to further abuse. Hartling, she decided, was no longer going to have things all his own way.

Following her habitual route to work, Ulla saw familiar faces waiting at the usual bus stops. Although the rush-hour streets were as noisy as ever and the spring air was not yet warm, the light mist in the air hinted at the possibility of a sunnier afternoon.

Waiting on the receptionist's desk lay a brown envelope, typed with her name and official position at the Ministry. Whilst Ulla was not surprised to find that it contained a summons to the Police Presidium, she was relieved to discover that she was not required until late the following day. The lack of urgency appeared to suggest that her telephoned report to Hartling had been corroborated by other, more covert sources of intelligence. Nevertheless, the Stasi officer still wanted to meet with her and she was still a signed-up collaborator. Even if the issue with Jack Gilmore could be laid to rest, Hartling would no doubt have further plans for his new acquisition.

Perhaps half an hour after Ulla had arrived at work, Press Secretary Fischer assembled a small cohort of staff in the lobby and informed them with pride that they needed to ready themselves for a visit from the General Secretary of the Central Committee of the Socialist Unity Party. Although, Fischer confessed, he had known of the planned visit for some weeks, established security protocols had precluded the release of the news until the morning of the visit.

General Secretary Honecker was currently on the crest of a political wave. The man who, before his seizure of power, had planned and overseen the construction of the Berlin Wall, was now basking in the success of his most recent appearances on the international stage. Under the General Secretary's surefooted leadership, *Neues Deutschland* regularly proclaimed, the GDR was now acknowledged throughout the world as a nation-state in its own right. Whilst Honecker's satisfaction with this achievement infused his every action, he was nevertheless careful to avoid the appearance of self-importance. In front of the TV cameras and the press, he came across as self-assured and affable, a leader with time to listen to those on whose behalf he wielded his considerable authority.

Following the predictable outbreak of murmured exchanges, the Press Secretary allowed his colleagues a moment to absorb the news before calling the meeting to order. The East German leader, he explained, was to be accompanied on the visit by his regular entourage of aides and security officers plus a number of photographers and journalists from the national press. Keen to maximise the value of the day, Fischer had convinced the General Secretary's staff that a brief conversation between Honecker and their young receptionist, who just so happened to be a star of the GDR U20 ice hockey squad, might be enlightening for both parties and provide an irresistible photo opportunity for the press pack. Although Ulla had not the slightest desire to spend a single second even in the same building as Erich Honecker, the word 'opportunity' suddenly resonated like the chime of the service bell in the lobby of a sleepy hotel.

Honecker and his extensive retinue arrived, as Fischer had indicated, precisely at ten. Noting the fuss, Ulla prepared to bite hard on her contempt. She knew that she could not muster the same obsequious demeanour that the Press Secretary would so readily display, but she would have to come up with something. Once the Minister for the Environment had formally declaimed his welcome, he proudly presented the rising star of East German ice hockey to the leader of the nation. Under a blizzard of camera flashes, Honecker smiled, shook Ulla warmly by the hand and asked her how many times she had represented the GDR.

'Probably not as many as you,' she quipped, triggering photogenic laughter all round. Ulla steeled herself and seized the moment. 'But whilst you're here, comrade General Secretary, I would like to thank you personally for everything you have done to build a better Germany.'

Honecker smiled modestly. 'It is a collective effort. We all play our part.'

The receptionist chose her words carefully. 'I wonder if, as part of that collective effort, I might at some point gather my own ideas for the advancement of the GDR and submit them to you in writing? I feel strongly that I can contribute to the creation not just of a better Germany but of a better world.'

'Well of course, comrade Wolfram. As I am sure you are aware, every citizen has the right to petition any representative of our democratic state. I look forward to reading your submission.'

With that, Honecker's aides decided that the encounter was more than complete and immediately proceeded to organise a series of more formal shots of their leader flanked by ever-changing combinations of Ministry staff. Twenty minutes later, Honecker and his team vanished upstairs.

The General Secretary spent the reminder of the day engaged in formal discussions with Minister Reichelt and his juniors or enjoying the plentiful lunch provided by the chefs of the nearby Café Moscow. Left once more to her own devices, Ulla slipped a sheet of official ministry paper into the typewriter and began to tap at the keys.

As Honecker and his party were finally leaving, the East German leader waved graciously to Ulla, who returned his gesture with a nod and a deferential smile. Unexpectedly, her encounter with the General Secretary of the Central Committee had been as useful as it had been brief.

58 IN PLAIN SIGHT

East Berlin, Wednesday 12th May 1976

Increasingly impatient for a breakthrough on the Niemeyer case, Major General Konrad summoned Hartling to his office. With little in the way of meaningful progress to report, the disaffected captain knew that it would be unwise to confine himself to the truth.

His opening statement had absolutely no basis in fact. Pastor Niemeyer, he asserted, had a safe concealed inside the fitted wardrobe in his office. The box appeared to have a standard mortice lock but his PA had so far been unable to locate the key. Hartling would therefore return to West Berlin at the weekend with a selection of specialist tools and initiate Frau Fichtenberg in the art of picking a lock. On Monday, he more accurately reported, the suspect British student had visited the Ministry for the Environment for a second time, but had categorically only been given information that was already in the public domain. One way or another, the visitor had been watched from the second he arrived in Hans-Beimler-Strasse to the moment of his return to the West. The rigorous surveillance had been effected primarily by a dedicated team of MfS officers, but in part also by the Press Secretary at the Ministry for the Environment and additionally by an informal Venus agent recruited specifically for the purpose.

Konrad shifted on his chair.

Hartling had, he assured the Major General, spent much of the morning analysing the detailed reports from his surveillance team. Nevertheless, having spent the entirety of Tuesday in West Berlin, he had not yet been able to debrief the honeytrap agent. That slight delay notwithstanding, the surveillance officers had reported that she had met Jack Gilmore soon after work and had successfully lured him back to her flat. The asset would presently be attending a debriefing at the Police Presidium and it would then become clear whether she was in possession of intelligence that would incriminate the British visitor.

The salad of lies, half-truths and verifiable facts duly served, Hartling handed his superior a typed summary of his verbal report. The Major General fished a silver pen from a drawer, leaned an elbow on his desk and scribbled frequent notes as he picked his way through the document.

With nothing to do but wait, Captain Hartling cast his eyes around the room. To his right stood the tungsten grey cabinet which was the secure repository for Konrad's most confidential documents. Silently, the surface-mounted pushbutton lock taunted its would-be hacker.

Hartling knew that Konrad was a political appointee, a Party apparatchik rather than a trained operative and suspected that his superior might well lack the necessary wherewithal and possibly the inclination for memorising lengthy codes. If the Major General were anything like Hartling's civilian targets in the West, Konrad's passcode security would be haphazard. The cypher might easily be found somewhere in the office, buried deep inside a drawer beneath a pile of dog-eared reference books or hidden in plain sight in the form of a handwritten phone number at the bottom of a neatly typed list.

The Major General placed the annotated report on his desk, exhaled slowly and looked his subordinate directly in the eye.

'The Minister will not be happy, Hartling. Not happy at all. And be in absolutely no doubt that Mielke is not a man who looks kindly on those who disappoint him. I very much hope for your sake that you can produce something of greater consequence tomorrow.'

59 NO CIGAR

West Berlin, Thursday 13th May 1976

Two hours after the curtain had fallen on *Madame Butterfly*, Anna at last completed the running repairs on a string of elaborate costumes and grabbed her shoulder bag. Although it was not yet seven thirty in the evening, the German Opera staged only matinee performances on Mondays and Thursdays and her shift was now over. Fifty-five minutes later, the young costumier walked into the bar in Groninger Strasse where her flatmates, she knew, would be waiting. It was never easy to pick out faces through the low light and evening fug of the Groninger Eck, but Anna knew exactly where the others would be and edged her way to the rectangular corner table with the dented tuba hanging directly above it.

'The Wiener schnitzel is a winner,' said Bastian, as he shuffled along the wooden bench to allow his flatmate to sit beside him.

Anna smiled, took her seat and set about catching the attention of the waiter. With a schnitzel and a glass of wheat beer duly ordered, she pulled the GDR passport from her bag, placed it carefully on the table and pushed it to the middle with her index finger.

'If you were an East German border guard,' she said almost mischievously, 'and this was put in front of you, what do you think you'd you make of it?'

Julia picked up the passport, flicked to its key pages and almost missed the skilfully executed adjustment to the handwritten surname.

'Interesting,' she said as dispassionately as she could. Curious to see what the others would say, she chose to voice no other comment at this point and handed the passport on.

'Was the name always Köhler?' queried Bastian, as he showed Jack the personal details section.

'Kohl,' said Jack. 'Or at least, it was Kohl two days ago. This clearly says Köhler.'

The British student took the passport and held it close to the light bulb that nestled inside the dangling tuba.

'You know what?' he said. 'That's impressive.'

'What about the signature?' asked Marco, as he put a match to a roll-up.

'Check it out,' said Jack.

Marco repeated Jack's trick of holding the passport directly under the light and squinted.

'Yep,' said Marco with a nod of genuine admiration. 'The signature looks perfect. I've got to admit, that's quality.'

'That's not all, though,' said Anna. 'Check out the serial number.'

'What about it?'

'He's changed one of the nines to an eight.'

'Which one?'

'Well, If you can't tell me, then I guess he's done a good job. He's done it on every page.'

The waiter duly arrived with one Wiener schnitzel and one glass of hazy wheat beer, marked the order on Anna's beermat and took a variety of follow-up requests from around the table.

'OK,' said Julia, putting her glass down. 'Your friend has done an impressive job there. No question. But what about an exit visa and that annoying little administration fee sticker? Can he do all that too?'

'He can. He said that it's all completely feasible. He could probably find a small commercial printer to produce the admin stamp, although he'd have to order several sheets of the things and we'd obviously have to cover that cost. But in terms of actual payment, he's happy to run with Marco's idea and accept a couple of high-end Hugo Boss suits. Sombre colours, though. He was adamant about that. Where it all gets a bit tricky is the creation of a replica visa stamp. He says he can make one, but it's painstaking work and could potentially take anything from three to six months. His fake residence permit took him four months before he was happy with it.'

'And what about the photo?' asked Jack, already taken aback by the timescale. 'What would he do with that?'

Anna winced apologetically. 'He said he wouldn't touch it in a month of Sundays. You'd risk damaging the page.'

'So,' said Marco. 'Let's see if we've got this straight. This guy in the props department can more or less do everything necessary and can do it to an impressively high standard, but the whole process could drag on for months and at the end of the day, we'd still have a passport with the wrong photo in it.'

'Yep,' said Anna. 'Pretty much. Close, but no cigar.'

'Shit,' said Jack, as reality trumped his initial wave of excitement.

For several seconds, no-one spoke.

Anna caught Jack's eye. 'Sorry. But it was worth a try.'

'No, absolutely,' replied Jack, keen to convey his appreciation of her efforts. 'It was definitely worth a try. Definitely. Thank you. You did your best.'

'So,' said Julia, slipping into her traditional role of consensus-builder, 'considering what we have, and what we don't have, where should we take things from here?'

60 OFFENCE

East Berlin, Thursday 13th May 1976

Her work at the Ministry done for the day, Ulla Wolfram waited quietly in a queue in the East Berlin Police Presidium. Although she felt slightly nervy, the queasiness that had plagued her earlier in the week had dissipated. As things stood, she recognised her nerves as no more than the edginess that she always experienced before a crucial ice hockey match, the edginess that always disappeared the moment the game started. It would not be long, she told herself. It would not be long. For all Hartling's hubristic threats, for all his fancy uniforms and for all his intimidating summonses, Ulla was determined that today she would take the fight to her opponent. She had an objective and she had a game plan and she was not prepared to be ground down any further. As for the risk implicit in confrontations with people like Hartling, she had exhausted her ability to care.

Having presented her card to the officer on reception, Ulla was once again directed to Room 209. Hartling responded to her knock with a curt instruction to enter. The Stasi captain was, as before, wearing his smartly pressed military uniform. He sat behind the desk, pen in hand, ready to take notes. He was alone.

Hartling rotated the orange biro smartly in his fingers and tapped it twice on his writing pad. 'So, comrade Wolfram. Take a seat. I understand you spent a substantial portion of the evening of Monday May the 12th in the company of operative target Matterhorn. Presumably you have something to report.'

Ulla removed an envelope from her bag and placed it on the table. 'What I have to report is that Jack Gilmore is exactly what he says he is. Nothing more, nothing less. But before we discuss the matter further, there is something I would like you to look at.'

Ulla pushed the unsealed envelope to Hartling, who opened it, removed two typed pages and began to read.

'Dear comrade General Secretary Honecker, it was a genuine pleasure to be presented to you in the Ministry for the Environment today. I would like to begin by reiterating my heartfelt appreciation of the unstinting work that you carry out on behalf of the people of the German Democratic Republic and I thank you also for inviting me to write to you personally. In my petition I will raise issues relating to the rights and responsibilities of individual citizens, the challenge of protecting the natural world and the promotion of women's ice hockey.

I would like to begin, if I may, by drawing your attention to the practices of what I assume to be unrepresentative elements within the Ministry for State Security. I would like to make particular reference to those officers who consider it appropriate to coerce one of the GDR's most promising sports stars into prostituting herself in the name of questionable police work.'

Hartling had read enough. Under normal circumstances he would have arrested her there and then and had her dragged to a holding cell. These were not, however, normal circumstances and he found himself suddenly in uncharted territory. The MfS officer could not rule out the possibility that a letter addressed to Honecker, and written at his personal invitation, might very well find its way onto the General Secretary's desk. Were that to happen, Hartling could not even to begin to predict what kind of reaction it would provoke. Would Honecker simply consign the letter to the waste paper bin or might he possibly invite one of his aides to look into the matter and contact the Stasi captain's superiors for clarification? Without doubt, the last thing Hartling needed right now was Major General Konrad suddenly treating him as a problem that needed to be solved.

Clenching his teeth, the suddenly unsettled officer placed the letter face down on the table, picked up his pen and tapped it nervously on the writing pad for several uncomfortable seconds. He knew that he had to respond.

'Have you already sent the letter?'

'No.'

'Then I would request, comrade Wolfram, that you do not act with unnecessary haste.'

Ulla had no idea why, but Hartling was clearly rattled. Whilst this was not the steely response that she had been expecting, she understood the value of maintaining pressure when the opponent's defence was in disarray.

'I'm sending the letter. I've had enough of being treated like some sort of subhuman non-citizen.'

'Well, if my actions have caused offence, I can only apologise,' he said in an aloof but almost conciliatory manner. 'I work tirelessly to maintain the security of the Republic in the face of enemies who would destroy our progressive way of life. It is true that sometimes the Ministry might require me to do things that seem at odds with certain ideals, but these things are always done in the best interests of every citizen.'

‘Bullshit.’

‘Again, I’m sorry if you feel I have overstepped the mark, but I would ask you once more to think before you act. I’m sure we can come to some kind of understanding. I’m sure we can find an outcome that would be agreeable to us both.’ Hartling paused. ‘What exactly is it that you want?’

‘What I want,’ said Ulla, looking him straight in the eye, ‘is to be treated with respect.’

‘Meaning?’

‘Meaning that I will no longer be pimped out by the Ministry for State Security. I want you to return the original copy of that shitty contract you made me sign.’

‘Agreed.’

‘And meaning that I will still receive an official Ministry-sponsored recommendation for university.’

‘Agreed.’

The threat of the letter to Honecker had clearly got under Hartling’s skin. Inexplicable as his acquiescence was, Ulla saw no reason to question the strength of her position and, improvising new demands, pressed home her advantage.

‘And meaning that the Ministry for State Security will provide me with an exit visa so that I can visit my grandfather’s grave in Munich.’

Hartling was focussed and silent as he weighed up his options. Simply detaining her would not necessarily eliminate the threat of the petition being sent. She would have been foolish in the extreme to have handed him the only copy. Perhaps an accomplice, in all likelihood one of her parents, would have been primed to submit the letter in the event of her arrest. The best he could do, he decided, was to play for time.

'Agreed,' he said finally. 'But this kind of thing cannot be done instantly. It would take at least a fortnight for the Travel Office to locate and process your passport, even at the request of the Ministry for State Security.'

'Somehow, Captain Hartling, I very much doubt that. But as things stand, I don't even see any reason why the state should continue to hold my passport hostage. So, you will retrieve it from wherever it is that you people keep our passports locked up and you will have it delivered to me by the end of my shift tomorrow. I'll bring the passport to our next meeting. For your part, you will have to bring everything you need to complete the visa formalities in front of me. Send me a card by the end of next week.'

Hartling tapped his fingertips uneasily on the table. Allowing Ulla Wolfram to take possession of her own passport would be a clear breach of protocol, but the travel document was of little use without the necessary stamps and visas.

'Agreed,' he said at last.

The timeframe would easily allow him to instigate searches of Ulla's apartment, her place of work and her parents' flat in Karlshorst. In fact, he would order the searches to be effected within two days.

'By the way,' said Ulla, as she made to leave, 'that's not the only copy. The original is in a safe place and will be posted if I do not check in with the holder each day and in a very specific way.'

'Understood,' said Hartling impassively. Forty-eight hours, he thought, would be the undoing of this cocky little bitch. Once he had tracked down the copies of the letter, she would suffer for her ridiculous arrogance.

Ulla had simply lied about the existence of back-up copies. Anticipating that Hartling would inevitably instigate a search for the offending material, he would discover nothing but a world of frustration and she would therefore, she hoped, maintain the upper hand. If push came to shove , Ulla would simply re-type the petition to Honecker at work and put it in the internal post. Nevertheless, she would need to keep her wits about her. Having rattled Hartling's cage in no uncertain terms, Ulla assumed that from now on she would be shadowed by one of his minions whenever she ventured outside. As for her passport, it would hardly be the wisest of moves to keep it in her own apartment. She would squirrel it away in one of the empty and unlocked flats on the upper floors of her block.

'Thank you,' said Ulla as she stood up to leave. 'I'll see myself out.'

61 NEWS

West Berlin, Monday 17th May 1976

It had been a particularly hectic day for the Running Wardrobe Team at the German Opera. Having spent the entire morning reinforcing the seams to kimonos that were repeatedly failing during the more crowded, festive scenes of *Madame Butterfly*, Anna had been on hand throughout the afternoon's performance to effect emergency repairs whenever the need arose. Following an additional hour dealing with a slew of minor issues, the overworked costumier was glad to have the evening free. On her return to Oudenarder Strasse shortly before seven thirty, Anna poked her head round the kitchen door, registered Jack's absence and made straight for his room. She had spoken during what passed for a lunch break with Tony, the Canadian props master, and there was something she urgently wanted to share. Hearing the polite knock as Anna walked through the open door, Jack looked up from the drafting of his dissertation.

'Hey, you know my Canadian colleague,' she said, 'the one who's a fine art conservationist?'

'You mean the document forger.'

'Yeah, that's the one. Well, he came to see me today with an interesting bit of news.'

'Namely?'

'Namely, it dawned on him that the only reason he spent months carving that residence permit stamp himself was that it would have been completely stupid to commission a replica from a manufacturer in West Berlin. They'd just have reported him to the police. But that said, he can't see any reason why it would be against the law on this side of the Wall to commission a counterfeit East German stamp. As long as the design was sharp, he reckons a commercial manufacturer would take it on. And if there were any raised eyebrows he could play the German Opera card and say he was creating props for a version of *La Traviata* set in East Berlin.'

'Well,' said Jack, nodding slowly as he processed the information. 'That is definitely an interesting bit of news. Absolutely. And thanks. But there is now a very specific obstacle to going any further down that particular road.'

'Which is?'

Jack paused momentarily, aware that Anna could not possibly anticipate what he was about to say.

'The passport is already in East Berlin.'

He had been right. Anna could hardly have looked less baffled, had the British student announced that he was the love-child of Marilyn Monroe and Josef Stalin. For a moment, Jack redirected his gaze towards the pages of his dissertation before looking up and offering an apologetic smile to his slack-jawed friend. He knew that he had a lot of explaining to do, and not just to Anna.

62 SURVEILLANCE

East Berlin, Monday 17th May 1976

Shortly after one thirty, a Pass and Control officer had alerted the MfS to Jack Gilmore's entry into the capital of the GDR. Although Captain Hartling had dispatched a photographer directly to Hans-Beimler-Strasse, there had been no sign of the British student at the Ministry for the Environment. By five, Border Command was able to confirm that the target, having spent almost three hours in East Berlin, had since returned to the western sectors of the city. As matters stood, it remained entirely unclear to the MfS what the visitor had done with his afternoon.

Although the highways were already congested with rush-hour traffic, Fehrbelliner Strasse was predictably much quieter. As Ulla Wolfram crossed the junction by the Konsum supermarket, she glanced over her shoulder and spotted a familiar face. The bearded twenty-something in the mushroom slacks and denim bomber jacket had, since the return of her passport, bobbed up like flotsam whenever she left her apartment or made her way home from work.

The surveillance, Ulla had rapidly realised, was not without its uses. Each evening, she made a point of visiting a phone box on Schönhauser Allee. The calls, she was confident, would be reported to Hartling and would suggest to the Stasi captain that she was checking in with a trusted contact, exactly as she had promised. If Hartling, or any of his subordinates, were able to trace the number, they would be surprised to discover that it belonged to the home phone of the Minister for Culture, Thomas Lindemann, whose semi-conscious son Ulla had rescued from the pond outside the Karlshorst District Sports and Community Centre. If the MfS were subsequently to tap the wire, they would register Ulla doing no more than asking to speak to Andreas Lindemann and being politely reminded that he was away on national service. That would be enough, she thought, to create the impression of a coded message. Furthermore, the high-ranking status of her putative contact would undoubtedly give Hartling pause for thought.

Arriving at the apartment block where she lived, Ulla resisted the temptation to turn and offer her follower a valedictory wave. There would be no benefit to overplaying her hand. With the main doors to the block shut firmly behind her, she crossed the lobby to the ramshackle bank of largely abandoned mailboxes. As she separated the relevant key from the two others on the ring, the box immediately to the right of her own caught her eye. At some point during the course of the working day, someone had sellotaped a matchbox-sized name card to the door and had inserted a key into the lock. In spite of the key, however, the door hung slightly ajar and still offered its usual glimpse of a dusty, unread fashion magazine dating back to the sixties. Ulla's immediate thought was that the owner of the block had managed to find another tenant who was keen to pay minimal rent for hopelessly substandard accommodation. Curious as to the identity of her prospective neighbour, Ulla examined the name card more closely and was puzzled by what she read. Sternenstaub was not a name she had previously encountered and it had the definite ring of a larger-than-life character in a fairy-tale or a modern morality play. Finally the scales fell from her eyes. She was looking at the German translation of the word 'stardust' and she could think of only one person who would have written that name on the card.

'Jack Gilmore,' she said to herself, still agog at the realisation, 'what the hell have you been up to?'

Ulla's mind began to race. Out of curiosity, she closed the door to the mailbox and twisted the key first clockwise, then anti-clockwise, but it steadfastly refused to rotate in either direction. Having jiggled the reluctant key from the lock, she ran her eye along the three rows of dilapidated mailboxes. Comfortably half of their number appeared to be locked, but were missing keys. One by one Ulla examined the names on the boxes until eventually, she found one with the letter Z freshly scratched into the grey paint.

'Bingo,' she thought. 'Z as in Ziggy.'

Ulla pushed the key carefully into the lock, turned it with surprising ease and pulled open the door. Concealed behind a copy of *Neues Deutschland* was a much newer manilla envelope. Only now thinking to glance over her shoulder at the main doors, Ulla put the envelope straight into her bag, re-secured Jack's improvised dead drop and put the key back where she had found it. In her regular mailbox, she discovered a postcard with a photo of the Alexanderplatz TV tower on one side and an innocuous greeting from Jack on the other. Presumably, he had left her the anodyne message for the benefit of anyone who might have followed him to Fehrbelliner Strasse and subsequently checked through her mail. Whatever the case, Jack's convoluted method of communication suggested that, although clearly aware of the need to tread extremely carefully, he had not experienced any difficulties passing through the controls at Friedrichstrasse. Her British visitor could always, Ulla cautioned herself, have been acting under duress, but given the bind in which her Stasi handler currently found himself, she felt confident enough to dismiss the idea.

As soon as Ulla was within the confines of her apartment, she pulled the envelope from her bag, opened it and was baffled by the contents. An open, all-day ticket for the West Berlin U-Bahn was accompanied by two maps of the network plus handwritten directions explaining the route from Nauener Platz to 27 Oudenarder Strasse. Most astonishingly Ulla also discovered an East German passport belonging to someone by the name of Katarina Köhler. On one of the fold-out maps, Jack had circled Nauener Platz U-Bahn station. On the other, which Ulla realised she would need to burn, he explained that the passport was authentic, but was no longer required by its previous owner. The holder's original name and signature, as well as the issue number, had all been skilfully altered. Jack expressed his hope that the passport, in spite of the expired exit visa and the obvious discrepancy in identity, might somehow prove to be of use.

Ulla could not even begin to imagine how Jack Gilmore might have laid his hands on an East German passport, let alone effected changes that, to her untutored eye, were impossible to detect. Whilst it was heartwarming to know that he had not simply washed his hands of her and that his desire to help had found some kind of practical expression, Jack's efforts had been as unnecessary as they had been risky. Given that she would soon have a valid exit visa in her own passport, he had somehow contrived to do both too much and too little. Uncertain whether she dared phone him, Ulla flicked idly through the doctored passport once more before dropping it onto the sofa. Still unable to determine the best response, she walked slowly to the kitchen, intent on concocting some kind of meal involving pasta, onions, fried sausage, a tin of peas, some tomato puree and a small tub of sour cream.

Following a substantial dinner that turned out far more successfully than she had allowed herself to hope, Ulla took a decision. To avoid storing incriminating materials in the flat, she would stash Jack Gilmore's offerings permanently in the scratched mailbox. She would also leave a note with them, in case his impetuosity drove him to a further visit. She would instruct Jack to return immediately to West Berlin and to stay there. She would reassure him that she had the situation well in hand and might appear at his door in Wedding sooner than he could possibly imagine. The weakness in the stratagem was that it would do nothing to deter him from coming through the controls in the first place.

Ulla had already succeeded in leaving a message for the British student simply by dialling his number. Would that line of communication still be open? And was her apartment being watched throughout the night? Whatever the situation, it would be unwise to risk any kind of move until well after dark.

Just before two, Ulla's alarm clock jolted her from a deep and surprisingly easy sleep. She hauled herself out of bed, but was careful not to turn on the light. At the window, she pulled back the curtain slightly and scrutinised the street below. There was no sign of life. Once dressed, she fumbled her way downstairs and, having checked a second time for obvious signs of surveillance, walked to the call box at Senefelder Platz.

It took Julia several seconds to register the ringing of the phone. In the darkness, she pushed her hand towards the bedside table and fumbled for the receiver.

'Hello,' she said, still not fully awake.

'I'm so sorry to do this to you again, but I totally need to get a message to Jack.'

'Right,' said Julia still trying to get her bearings. 'OK. This is Julia. So, yeah. Hi. Hi, Ulla. Fire away.'

'Firstly, tell him I'm OK. I'm still listening to David Bowie and still playing ice hockey. Also, can you make it crystal clear to him that I have all the ice hockey gear I need, absolutely everything, so he doesn't need to bring anything over. I'm fine with what I've got. And tell him there are no spare tickets for my next match, so he shouldn't come over on the off-chance of seeing me play. Make sure he gets that and make sure he doesn't come anyway.'

'Sure. Yeah. Got it. But listen. Don't worry on that front. Jack's let us in on the whole ice hockey thing and he honestly won't be going very far for a while. I've persuaded him to give me his passport and let me keep it somewhere safe, somewhere he's not going to find it in a hurry.'

'Good,' said Ulla. 'Sorry again about… well, all of this.'

'It's OK. No need to apologise. And good luck with the ice hockey. And if you do find you need some new hockey gloves or something, don't be afraid to call. I have a passport too.'

'That's kind. That's good to know. Sleep well.'

'Yeah. You too.'

Ulla walked back towards the apartment, unexpectedly reassured. The streets were empty and she heard nothing beyond the sound of her own footsteps. Presumably, even the Stasi had homes to go to.

In the lobby, she flicked on the lights for the staircase and glanced across at the mailboxes. Jack's 'Sternenstaub' name card now struck her as unhelpfully conspicuous. As the card had served its intended purpose, Ulla stopped and began picking away at the sellotape with her fingernail. No sooner had she removed the name from the box than the timer-controlled lights were extinguished.

Traipsing back up the stairs, it occurred to Ulla that the Katarina Köhler passport, in spite of her initially dismissive assessment of its value, might prove to be of use. Whatever the hold she had over Hartling, she could not know for sure that her name was not already sitting on some kind of arrest list at the border. An undoubtedly risky idea began to crystallise in Ulla's mind. Within two hours, she had worked the concept into a detailed plan. She now had to decide whether she had the sheer brass neck to attempt it.

63 DISTRACTED OR MISLED

East Berlin, Monday 24th May 1976

In the week following Jack's impromptu delivery of the doctored passport, Ulla had applied herself assiduously to the challenge of shaking off her denim-jacketed Stasi surveillant whenever she perceived the need. An inevitable starting point had been a reflection on her grandfather's talents for sleight of hand and his insights into the propensity of all human beings to be distracted or misled. Over several days, Ulla had established that, in spite of the careful training that her watcher had no doubt been given, his eye would habitually rove when confronted by a group of well-dressed young women. Once aware of this inclination, she quickly learned to identify the moments when she might successfully disappear into a crowded department store or down the steps of a busy U-Bahn station. Ulla's weekend purchases in the Exquisit women's outfitter's on Unter den Linden and in the Centrum department store on Alexanderplatz were, she was sure, highly unlikely to have been registered.

After an unusually busy Monday at the Ministry for the Environment, Ulla found herself waiting once again in a slow-moving queue at the Police Presidium. Although edgy, she was as confident as she dared be that she could present herself at this monumental Police building without undue fear for her safety. Whilst it seemed inevitable that Hartling would ultimately want to exact his retribution on her, the continuing surveillance suggested that the Stasi captain was still not certain of his position.

To Ulla's surprise, Hartling was already standing when she entered the now familiar office on the second floor. He greeted her curtly and in response, she smiled, asked unexpectedly after his health and offered him her hand. Although slightly unsettled by the confidence implicit in the gesture, the uniformed officer reciprocated without thinking and sat down in his chair. Privately delighted with the automatic nature of her oppressor's reaction, Ulla also took a seat and placed her shoulder bag carefully on the floor.

'I have everything you asked for,' said Hartling, betraying not the slightest emotion.

On the desk in front of the MfS officer were an A4 envelope, a small date stamp, a circular stamp with a black plastic handle and, already stationed on an ink pad, a larger rectangular rubber stamp with a lacquered, wooden handle.

'Let's start with that contract you made me sign,' said Ulla.

Hartling breathed in slowly, pulled her statement of collaboration from the A4 envelope and slid it calmly across the table. Ulla thanked him politely, picked up the handwritten document and examined it briefly before folding it in half and placing it in the bag at her feet. She then removed her GDR passport plus two sheets of blank A4 typing paper and placed them on the table. In an easily accessible pocket of her spring jacket, the Katarina Köhler passport sat flush to her hip.

'Before we get to the formalities,' said Ulla, 'I'd like you to do a dummy run with the visa stamp and the Ministry of the Interior stamp. Use one of those sheets of paper. Forgive my caution, but I'd like to see what they look like. Just to be sure.'

Hartling duly obliged and returned the stamped sheet of typing paper to Ulla for inspection. She opened her passport and, without the slightest suggestion of intent, allowed him a glimpse of her photo. A moment later, she located the exit visa dating back to her trip to Bratislava and compared it closely to the freshly inked example on the typing paper. Satisfied that the two were identical, Ulla slid the test sheet back across the table.

'Now use the date stamp. Let's see how that looks. Set it for twenty-eight days ago.'

The process lasted no more than five seconds. As Hartling focussed on making the decidedly fiddly adjustments to the date, Ulla quietly effected the switch. Opa Karl, had he been able to observe, would have been inordinately proud. The MfS officer, who had perceived nothing beyond the inconvenience of deciphering the small, inverted digits on the face of the rubber stamp, proceeded to add the requested date to the mock-up and awaited Ulla's next instruction with barely concealed displeasure.

The first step of the subterfuge behind her, Ulla demanded the ink pad, the rubber stamps and a single five-mark administration fee sticker. The Stasi officer was obliged simply to look on as she printed both the exit visa and the official Interior Ministry emblem onto a blank page of a GDR passport that he believed without question to be hers. Under his watchful eye, Ulla licked the gummed administration sticker, pressed it firmly across the edge of the visa and stamped it with her chosen date of issue. Satisfied with the quality of her work, she slid the ink pad and the rubber stamps back to Hartling.

'No need for you to fill in the expiry date or specify the border crossing to be used. I have a pen at home. I just need a valid issue number for this visa and then I'll leave you in peace.'

'As you wish.'

Ulla moved her head slightly and squinted at the clock to Hartling's left. Inevitably, his eyes followed her gaze.

'Is that even remotely accurate?' she asked disdainfully. 'I have somewhere to be.'

Hartling pulled at the cuff of his jacket with the index finger of his right hand, glanced at his Raketa timepiece and back at the clock.

'It's close enough,' he said, his nose now clearly out of joint.

The second act of misdirection complete and the Katarina Köhler passport sitting safely in her hip pocket, Ulla allowed Hartling a second glimpse of her official photo before shaking her head.

'Why do the photographers always make you look like a complete criminal?'

The Stasi captain was sorely tempted to make the obvious comment about the legitimacy of Ulla's current undertaking, but thought better of it. Biting hard on his contempt, he tore a sheet of paper from his notepad and handed her the issue number for the exit visa.

'Thank you,' said Ulla impassively. 'I expect you're wondering whether you can trust me not to submit my petition to Honecker now that I've got what I wanted. I guess what I'm wondering is whether you'll give me a reason to.'

‘Are we done?’ said Hartling, now betraying his eagerness to be rid of her.

The uneasy balance of power that now prevailed between the MfS officer and his former asset was, inevitably, precarious. Neither could afford to relax.

Hartling was only too aware that allowing Ulla Wolfram to leave the GDR would not automatically remove the threat posed by her potentially incendiary petition. The searches and the surveillance would therefore continue and her name would be on a Border Command watchlist within minutes of her departure.

For her part, Ulla could not assume that Hartling would simply let matters rest. Whilst her Stasi watchers might allow her to go about her daily business unchallenged, attempting to approach the border controls at Friedrichstrasse might provoke an entirely different response. She would take nothing for granted.

As the refusenik walked out of the Police Presidium, she looked for her Stasi minder and picked him out from the handful of pedestrians in the street. Ulla planned to make a brief stop at the Konsum supermarket on the way back to the apartment. There was something that she still needed to buy, an item that she had been surprised to discover was out of stock at Centrum and was unlikely to be available for several months. If supplies in Konsum were no better, Ulla would make another early-hours call to West Berlin and avail herself of Julia’s offer to do some shopping for her on the other side of the Wall.

64 NUMBERS

East Berlin, Wednesday 26th May 1976

The sun had not yet risen. With his mind set to overdrive and scant prospect of further sleep, Captain Hartling showered, pulled on his uniform and took the decision to walk the five kilometres to work. As he presented his ID to the guards on the Ruschestrasse gate, the MfS officer drew hard on his cigarette. It was going to be a long day.

Sitting in his office, a mug of Russian tea on the desk, Hartling reviewed the reports on Ulla Wolfram. Unwilling to detail the occasions when they had lost sight of their target, her watchers noted that they had maintained almost total surveillance of her movements. When not at home, she did little more than walk to and from work, attend ice hockey training or occasionally conduct a little shopping at Centrum or in the Konsum store in Fehrbelliner Strasse. Furthermore, searches of her flat, the family apartment in Karlshorst and locations within the Environment Ministry had failed to unearth anything out of the ordinary. Remarkably, the surveillance team had established that the private residential number phoned by their target each evening belonged to none other than Culture Minister Thomas Lindemann.

Whilst it bordered on inconceivable that a high-ranking Party official could somehow be involved in Ulla Wolfram's protection, alternative explanations were equally preposterous. As matters stood, Hartling was not a millimetre closer to understanding where his former informant had concealed the master copy of her petition.

Still under pressure from Major General Konrad to demonstrate progress on the Niemeyer case, the MfS officer inserted a sheet of A4 into his typewriter and began to concoct the kind of report that he hoped would mollify his superior. The honeytrap agent, Hartling immediately lied, had established that Jack Gilmore harboured an interest in the monitoring of radiation levels across the GDR. It was reasonable to infer at this juncture that the suspect was fishing for clues regarding the location of nuclear facilities on East German soil. In the first instance, Hartling would use his contact in the Concordia office to provide him with information regarding the British student's provenance, his schedule of visits to East Berlin and the precise nature of his links to Pastor Niemeyer. He would also install full audio surveillance in Ulla Wolfram's apartment. Once incontrovertible evidence of Jack Gilmore's status and intentions had been acquired, the British passport-holder would, immediately upon his return to the GDR, be arrested.

The first draft of his fiction almost complete, Hartling walked down to the canteen to buy himself breakfast and another mug of tea. On his return to the fifth floor, he could hear the quietly determined tapping of Frau Schiller's electric typewriter in room 509. Perhaps an hour later, his colleague poked her head around the door and greeted him in a way that transcended office formality without exactly bordering on flirtation.

'Sorry to be such a pain,' she said, 'but it's jammed again.'

The latest typewriter issue was patently something that by now she could have addressed without his help, but it provided her with the opportunity to make contact.

‘OK,’ said Hartling, trying not to sigh. ‘Give me ten minutes.’

‘Busy?’ said Frau Schiller, clearly aware that she was interrupting him, but angling for a less formal interaction. The pair had ended their assignation in Woltersdorf on the understanding that it would be pleasant, once Hartling’s irregular duties permitted, to spend another evening in each other’s company. Judiciously, they had also agreed not to draw attention to their nascent relationship and to behave with the utmost professionalism whilst at work.

‘I have a report to finish,’ he said, ‘for the Major General. And he won’t be pleased if it’s late.’

‘Relax,’ said Frau Schiller. ‘You’ve got no chance of seeing him any day this week. He’s not even in the country.’

‘I see. Where is he?’

‘Captain Hartling, you should know better than to ask me things like that. That information is confidential. But don’t be surprised if there’s a small bottle of Polish vodka on my desk next week.’

Hartling smiled. ‘On the contrary. I’ll be very surprised.’

It took a moment for her to process the logic.

‘Ah, yes. No. Yes, that’s better. Be very surprised.’

‘Anyway, Frau Schiller, I still need at the very least to finish this section of my report. I’ll come along as soon as I can.’

A short time later, the Stasi captain once more impressed his colleague with his technical skills before returning to his desk in room 531. The news of Konrad’s extended absence was as close as he would come to a guarantee that, for a short period, the Major General’s office would be both unoccupied and easily accessible outside Frau Schiller’s normal working hours. Regardless of the early start to his day, Hartling would, he decided, work particularly late that night.

In the corner of Captain Hartling's office, by the door, stood both the strapped leather case and the attaché case which he used for his operations in West Berlin. Whilst he was unsure exactly how many files he might find in Major General Konrad's security locker, he was confident that the well-used travel bag would be more than enough for his needs. As soon as he had the documents he wanted, he would create order papers for an operation in West Berlin and forge Konrad's signature.

Before leaving at five, Frau Schiller looked in on him once more and thanked him for his help with her ongoing typewriter troubles. As she hovered in the doorway, Hartling found himself suggesting out of the blue that she might like to celebrate his forty-first birthday with him the following month. His delighted comrade made a mental note of the date and promised to keep the evening free. Despite the warmth of his assertion that he was already looking forward to their rendezvous, the MfS captain had not the slightest intention of making another booking at the Restaurant Flakensee. He would be living in an entirely different country by then.

By seven in the evening, only Hartling was still at work on the fifth floor. After an hour without registering any suggestion of movement in the corridor, he pulled on his white dress gloves and picked up the travel bag which now contained his report on the Niemeyer case. From the small, unmarked cabinet in the Secretariat, he pocketed the key to Major General Konrad's office, walked quietly to room 510 and let himself in. The intruder was careful not to close the door. Should he hear footsteps, he would re-secure the locker, remove his gloves and, if it came to it, explain his presence by pointing to the urgent report he had left on Konrad's desk. The officer looked at his watch and set himself an absolute maximum of ten minutes to get the job done.

Although Hartling was not privy to the code that would unlock the imposing security cabinet, he was as confident as he could be that his commander, like every human being who had ever forgotten something important, would have squirrelled away some form of back-up. The prospective thief's first objective, therefore, was to find it.

But for the freshly delivered Niemeyer report, Konrad's desktop was completely bare. The drawers, however, were unlocked. Within sixty seconds, Hartling had rummaged out a list of what purported to be the birth dates of family members, but to his eager eye looked like nothing of the sort. Selecting the first entry on the crumpled sheet, he pressed the six digits into the keypad of the security locker and slowly twisted the handle. It refused to give. Reversing the sequence proved ineffective and a series of basic substitution techniques failed equally to yield a result. The MfS officer glanced at his watch. Almost three minutes had elapsed.

Growing steadily more conscious of the passage of time, Hartling worked his way through each of the eleven dates on the list, but to absolutely no avail. The interloper checked his watch once more. He had subjected himself to a nine-minute exercise in frustration and, for all that he had achieved, might just as well have been punching in numbers at random. Running low on strategies and unwilling to linger, he returned the contact list to the drawer, retrieved his report from Konrad's desk and locked the door as he left.

It was already dark when Hartling saluted the duty guards and marched along Ruschestrasse in the direction of the S-Bahn. Although it would be another four days before the Major General returned from Poland, his subordinate now questioned the prospects of lifting the all-important security code from a dog-eared list in a drawer. Perhaps a more direct approach was required.

65 ALLIES

East Berlin, Thursday 27th May 1976

It was a warm, cloudless afternoon. As Anna and Julia emerged from the border controls into Friedrichstrasse, the costumier from the German Opera foresaw the inevitable, removed her jacket and draped it over her shoulders. Before the pair had reached Unter den Linden, Julia followed suit. Both women had been to East Berlin before, but neither had ventured beyond the confines of the heavily redeveloped central district. Having cleared the controls more quickly than they had anticipated, the two friends passed the best part of the next hour meandering their way to the seventeen-storey state-run Tourist Office. On the ground floor, beneath lines of fluorescent strip lights, half a dozen slow-moving queues led the eye to the discrete sections of a long, wooden service counter.

'Strange kind of travel agency,' said Anna quietly to her companion. 'More like an understaffed post office on pension day.'

The two friends joined the line for Theatrical and Cultural Events and within half an hour had acquired surprisingly inexpensive tickets to an evening performance of Bertolt Brecht's *The Caucasian Chalk Circle*, a play they had both studied at school.

In a quiet green space not far from Rosa-Luxemburg-Platz, the two West Berliners located a metal bench where they could sit and enjoy Anna's beautifully prepared cheese and salami sandwiches. Their hunger satisfied, they dug out the theatre tickets and ripped away the stubs. Screwing the tickets into tight balls, Julia strolled across the lawn and dropped them into a litter bin. They would retain the stubs as evidence, in the unlikely event that evidence might be needed, of an evening spent at the theatre. Before leaving the park, they opened up a street map and confirmed that they were heading in the right direction to make it to Fehrbelliner Strasse before Ulla returned from work.

During the most recent, and most fleeting, of the ice hockey player's late-night calls to West Berlin, her solitary request had been for hair colourant. Her insistence that she needed nothing else had left Julia to infer that Ulla had somehow managed to acquire an exit visa for the Katarina Köhler passport. Without doubt, it could not have been obtained by legal means.

It would take, the two flatmates figured, no more than twenty minutes to reach their destination. Whilst Anna and Julia were hardly dressed flamboyantly, most East Berliners could pick them out as coming from the other side of the Wall. Anna, however, was painfully aware that it was not just her clothing that attracted attention. By the time they reached Lottumstrasse, she had had enough.

'For crying out loud,' she muttered to Julia. 'Is this some kind of freak show? Haven't they seen anyone with black skin before?'

'On TV probably, but not walking along the street where they live. Anna, I'm sorry this is happening. It's not right. It really isn't. I guess the best you can say is that they don't get out much.'

'Is that an excuse?'

'No. No, it's not. Not at all.'

‘Maybe you should have brought Christa.’

‘You mean the woman who’s never used makeup in her life? Anyway, they’re staring at me too.’

‘Only because you’re with me. You know what, Julia? You can’t even begin to know what it’s like having people gawp at you like this. Like you don’t belong. Like you can’t possibly belong. Just wait. Any minute now, someone will ask us if we’re lost.’

The women walked on, quietly spoiling to challenge the next person who looked askance at Anna but aware of the need to avoid the slightest fuss. They reached Ulla’s block a good fifteen minutes before the agreed time of six thirty. The main door, as Jack had warned them, required something of a shove to force it open. When Ulla appeared, she had little doubt as to the identity of the two women sitting at the foot of the stairs, but was wary of taking the situation for granted.

She closed the door firmly behind her. ‘Are you here about the ice hockey gloves?’

‘We’re here,’ said Julia, ‘to add a bit of colour to your day.’

That was good enough.

‘Excellent,’ said Ulla. ‘Let’s go upstairs. But stay away from the windows until I’ve drawn the curtains. There’s someone outside the building who follows me home every night and who hangs around till dark.’

Since walking out of the station at Friedrichstrasse, neither Julia nor Anna had experienced any tangible sense of threat. Ulla’s mention of surveillance and the implicit potential for complication suddenly brought the gravity of their undertaking into sharp relief. They would have to be careful.

Once inside the apartment, the three women introduced themselves properly and Ulla apologised, as ever, for the lingering smell of her hockey kit. Although Julia and Ulla recognised each other's voices and it was more than interesting to meet each other in the flesh, they both understood that this was hardly a social call and fought shy of engaging in anything approaching chit-chat. Julia rooted around in her bag and handed over a box of chestnut brown hair dye.

Ulla flashed her the warmest of smiles.

'Brilliant. Perfect. Just what I need. But now, and don't take this personally, you shouldn't hang around any longer than is totally necessary. So, listen. I'm going to go for a short walk in the direction of the Konsum supermarket and I'm going to be gone for at least twenty minutes. Give me maybe five minutes' start, then leave the apartment and get back to Friedrichstrasse as quickly as you can. Turn left out of this building and then right when you get to Kastanienallee. A couple of hundred metres towards the city centre there's a tram stop. The number seventy will take you directly to the checkpoint. With a fair wind behind me, I'll see you again on Saturday.'

'No, no, no. Just hold your horses,' said Julia. 'We're not going anywhere just yet.'

Ulla looked puzzled.

'That hair dye,' said Anna, 'is only part of the story. If you're going to walk through the controls with that passport, we need to make your eyebrows, nose and lips look convincing too. Fortunately for you, you're looking at an expert.'

Julia's eyes widened as she smiled. 'Like I said, you don't get rid of us that easy. Anyway, while I make us some tea or coffee or something, give Anna the Katarina Köhler passport to study, then find a mirror so you can watch what she does.'

There was no questioning Julia's logic. Ulla duly fetched the passport from Jack's dead drop in the lobby and brought a small, oval mirror from her bedroom. She allowed Julia and Anna a few seconds to marvel at the recently acquired exit visa, before responding to the inevitable question.

'The short answer,' said Ulla, 'is that someone decided it would be wiser to do me a favour than not to do me a favour. The long answer is... well, it's a really long answer. Probably too long for the time we have here. I'll tell you the whole story when I'm sitting safely on the other side of the border. I promise.'

'So. Down to business then,' said Julia, still consumed by curiosity. 'I presume I'll find tea in the kitchen.'

'OK,' said Anna, as she scrutinised the black and white passport photo. 'The thing is, you can change your hair colour easily enough, but your nose is slightly more triangular than this, your lips are not as full and your eyebrows are, to be honest, completely different. But don't worry. It's not a situation we can't do something about. That said, it's going to involve tweezers, so I can't promise it won't be painful.'

'Do it,' said Ulla, buoyed up by the presence of allies. 'Just do it.'

For the best part of an hour, and with unstinting determination demonstrated by both parties, Anna tweezed Ulla's indistinct but slightly bushy eyebrows to the clearly defined, softly angled shape so clearly apparent in the

Katarina Köhler passport photo. Her warning that the procedure might not be pain-free had been entirely accurate.

'Here,' said Anna, handing Ulla an eyebrow stick once she was finally done with the tweezers. 'Use this to darken the tone. Build it up gradually. And stick to the shape I've created.'

Ulla had never before paid the slightest attention to the shape of her eyebrows or applied any form of makeup to them, but she had a steady hand and the task proved to be relatively straightforward.

'Right,' said Anna. 'That's good. Onto the lips.'

With Julia trying her best to document the process on a small notepad, Anna talked Ulla through the use of a natural-tone pencil to capture the necessary outline and the application of gloss lipstick to emphasise the final shape.

'That's incredible,' said Ulla, checking her lips in the mirror once Anna had finished. 'That's definitely starting to look like someone else.'

'Well, by the time I'm done,' said Anna confidently, 'your own mother won't recognise you.'

Delving into her small bag of Leichner professional makeup, Anna set about adjusting the appearance of Ulla's nose by contouring the tip and applying highlighter beneath the inner corners of her eyebrows.

'It's looking good,' said Julia, comparing Ulla's makeover to the face in the photo. 'You know what, Anna? You're an effing miracle worker.'

Anna looked at Ulla. 'What do you think?'

'Hell, that's weird,' she said. 'It genuinely doesn't look like me. I'll tell you that for nothing. The question is, I guess, does it look like her?'

‘Once the hair is the right colour,’ said Julia, ‘I think that’ll be pretty convincing.’

‘I won’t do my hair until Friday evening,’ said Ulla. ‘No point in inviting comments at work. The eyebrows are brilliant, though. Perfect. Like Julia said, Anna, you’re a magician.’

‘Thanks. It’s astounding what you can do with some small implements of torture and a bit of slap. And don’t forget that this passport photo is six years old now. You’re going to need to look like you’re twenty-four, so the flashy lipstick won’t be an issue.’

‘Well, it looks pretty damn good to me,’ said Julia, ‘but in the end, Ulla, it’s your decision. Here. I’ve made some half-decent notes for you to keep. It should all make some sort of sense.’

‘It might take a bit of practice,’ said Anna. ‘And come Saturday, if you’re not happy, clean it off and start again. And if you’re still not happy, don’t do anything stupid. Don’t take unnecessary risks.’

‘To be honest, I’ve only got this far by taking unnecessary risks. I don’t think now’s really the time to stop.’

‘Well, on the bright side, every couple of months there’s a report on TV about an escape using false papers, so the controls can’t be a hundred percent perfect. They’re still staffed by human beings.’

‘My Opa used to say that every human being can be misled. And if you nudge them in the right direction, you can make most people believe what they know to be impossible.’

‘What will you say if they ask you any awkward questions?’

'Oh, don't worry about that. I know exactly what I'm going to say. But listen, I can't even begin to tell you how much I appreciate this and I'd love to sit and get to know you both, but now is not the time. You really need to go.'

'Saturday, then?'

'Saturday. And give my regards to Mr Hazy Cosmic Jive.'

66 MATTERHORN

East Berlin, Saturday 30th May 1976

When, shortly after six, Ulla put on her dressing gown and drifted into the bathroom, the sight of her chestnut hair provoked something of a double take. In an attempt to wake herself up after a predictably uneasy night, she took the decision to begin the day with a cold shower, but lasted no more than five seconds before shutting off the tap. She still had some Mokkafix coffee in a tin in the kitchen. That would have to do.

Although Anna and Julia had discouraged her from taking risks, she knew that there could be no turning back. In a matter of hours, she would present herself at the border controls as Katarina Köhler and she would have to make certain that she applied the makeup exactly as Anna had shown her.

After a breakfast of Mokkafix, rye bread, butter and black cherry jam, Ulla caught herself washing her knife and plate as though it were a regular Saturday morning. Suddenly, it struck her as completely nonsensical that she was bothering with domestics. She could leave the apartment in a total mess if she liked. However the day panned out, she wouldn't be coming back.

The coffee jug abandoned unwashed, Ulla attempted a second shower before selecting the comfortable Italian underwear that Lieutenant Eckart had given her and concealing it beneath a beige A-line skirt and a plain, pale blue blouse. From her wardrobe she pulled out the yellow jacket that she planned to wear on the short journey to Alexanderplatz Station. That ought, she decided, be bright enough for her constant companion from the MfS to pick her out in a crowd.

Taking the trouble to breathe deeply whenever she began to feel the slightest bit on edge, Ulla gathered together the remaining items she needed for the execution of her plan. She unzipped the red, collapsible travel bag that she had bought the previous weekend from Centrum and began by folding a similar black bag into the large side pocket. Having packed several changes of clothing, she checked that her wash bag contained the Eckart-supplied perfume and contraceptives which, she hoped, would reinforce the impression of a trusted Stasi collaborator embarking on a Venus operation to West Berlin.

In the bathroom, Ulla turned her attention to the all-important task of applying her makeup. The eyebrows proved straightforward and after two attempts at the nose and lips, she was eventually satisfied that she looked more or less exactly as Anna had intended.

From the wardrobe in the unoccupied flat above, she fetched the blonde wig that she had recently purchased from the Exquisit women's outfitters and gave it a loose shake. With her freshly coloured hair tied in a flat bun and grips holding the hairpiece firmly in place, Ulla became once more the easily identifiable target that her regular watchers would be expecting to see.

Finally, from the dead drop in the lobby, she collected the counterfeit passport, Jack's map of West Berlin, the all-day U-Bahn ticket and the fold-out guide to the western network. She was ready.

Shortly after eight, Ulla pulled at the door to her apartment block and emerged into the sunshine of a May morning. The plain-clothes MfS corporal sitting in the white Trabant noted immediately that she was dressed particularly smartly. Although this was unusual, Corporal Feldmann was far more interested in the travel bag. Ulla Wolfram had the distinct look of someone who might be going further than the city centre. Feldmann's orders required him to monitor his target's movements closely and to detain her only if she presented herself at the border controls. Confident that his morning would end with another successful arrest to his name, the Stasi corporal determined not to let her out of his sight.

From the apartment block in Fehrbelliner Strasse, Ulla made her way to the U-Bahn station at Senefelder Platz and, with her bag pressed between her knees and Feldmann at the other end of the carriage, rode the two stops to Alexanderplatz.

Even though it was still not yet eight thirty, the station was busy. Ulla made her way calmly to the ticket hall, queued briefly for the nearest hatch and bought a single ticket to Gera, a town in the south of the GDR, close to the border crossing into Bavaria. As she made a point of poring over the timetables posted at the back of the hall, her young Stasi watcher bypassed the queue, flashed his badge at the ticketing clerk and demanded to know the destination of the blonde woman in the yellow jacket. His hunch that Ulla Wolfram intended to leave Berlin, he congratulated himself, had been right on the money, but he was now confronted with a dilemma. He could not simply follow her all the way to Gera, but if he reported his discovery to the Main Directorate, he might well lose sight of his quarry in the process. Ulla did not immediately leave the ticket hall and seemed intent simply to hang around as though waiting perhaps for a travelling companion to appear. The junior MfS officer made a calculated decision, located the office of the Transport Police and relayed the intelligence regarding Ulla Wolfram's travel plans to the switchboard of the Main Directorate for Reconnaissance. Captain Hartling, they assured him, would be informed as soon as he could be contacted. When Corporal Feldmann returned to the ticket hall, he was relieved to find his target still waiting beneath the clock, her luggage at her feet.

Seemingly bored with marking the passage of time, Ulla picked up her bag, left the station and crossed the wide, paved square towards the Centrum department store. In the Ladies' Fashion department, she mooched about the racks of clothing until eventually a pair of GDR-produced jeans caught her eye. Having identified a size that might conceivably fit, the young shopper took them to the changing rooms where, as was usual on a Saturday, she was forced to wait in line for a spare cabin.

Once safely behind the floral curtain, Ulla unzipped her scarlet travel bag and removed a pair of black slacks, some matching summer socks, a pair of black plimsolls, her wash bag and a blue Free German Youth shirt, complete with military shoulder lapels and the official sunrise logo on the arm. She retrieved the collapsible, black holdall from the side pocket and eased the original red travel bag into its less conspicuous counterpart. Her change of outfit folded neatly on the cubicle bench, Ulla turned her attention to her hair. Studying her reflection in the wall mirror, she teased the hair grips from the blonde wig, dropped them one by one into her wash bag and carefully pulled the hairpiece from her head. Having released her own hair from the bun, Ulla stuffed the wig into the black holdall, gave her head a shake and ran her fingers through her freshly tinted locks. With the first part of the transformation complete, she slipped off her shoes, removed the yellow jacket, the skirt and her blouse and changed into the socks, the black slacks and the blue Free German Youth shirt. With her shoes and the redundant clothing stowed neatly in her holdall, she pulled on the black plimsolls and checked her appearance in the mirror. It was exactly as she wanted.

In the narrow corridor outside the changing booths, Ulla waited for another client to leave one of the cabins and, as the woman edged past, commented to her on the paucity of the stock in the 'so-called Fashion department'.

'What can you do?' said the woman with a shrug. 'This is just about the only thing I could find that was even worth trying on.'

Ulla looked at the shopper's prospective purchase, expressed her approval and asked her fellow browser if she would be so kind as to show her where she had found it. Moments later, the two women emerged from the changing area, chatting to all intents and purposes as though they were sisters on a long-awaited shopping trip.

Having noted with satisfaction Corporal Feldmann's continued focus on the changing rooms as she walked out of the store, Ulla carried her black holdall along Karl-Liebknecht-Strasse, confident that she would not be followed. At some point, she was sure, her Stasi watcher would realise that he had lost sight of his target. Whether he would appreciate the irony in her use of the changing rooms for an unexpected but entirely literal purpose was, she thought, another matter entirely. Either way, her surveillant could have no possible way of predicting her immediate destination and would in all likelihood return to Alexanderplatz station.

As Ulla had anticipated, Corporal Feldmann eventually began to grow uneasy at his target's failure to emerge from the changing rooms and commissioned a female assistant to check the cabins for a woman matching Ulla's description. Some three minutes later, the assistant reappeared and shrugged apologetically. Wrestling with the uncomfortable realisation that his quarry had somehow contrived to give him the slip, Feldmann hurried back to the station but found no sign of Ulla Wolfram either in the ticket hall or on any of the platforms. Making use once more of the Transport Police office, he left a second message for the still unavailable Captain Hartling. In the absence of guidance from above, the corporal took it upon himself to alert both the Stasi office in Gera and the Central Border Command at the crossing into Bavaria to Ulla Wolfram's likely arrival, to request her immediate detention and to report any interventions directly to the Main Directorate for Reconnaissance in Berlin.

At nine forty, some twenty-five minutes after slipping out of the department store, Ulla walked into the German State Library on Unter den Linden and made her way to the toilets. In a locked cubicle, she waited until the facilities were quiet before opening up her bag once more. She took off the Free German Youth shirt, replaced it with the brightly coloured blouse that she had worn on her evening with Jack and draped a thin blue cardigan over her shoulders. The blonde wig found its way into the cistern and the paramilitary blue shirt and the yellow spring jacket would go no further than the coat peg on the inside of the door. Once out of the cubicle, Ulla checked her appearance in a mirror and sprayed her wrists and neck with the Chanel No.5 supplied by Lieutenant Eckart. From the State Library, it would be no more than a ten-minute walk to Friedrichstrasse Station.

When Ulla arrived at the Palace of Tears, it was shortly after ten. She quickly located the sign marked 'Exit to Berlin (West) – GDR Citizens' and attached herself to a line of overdressed pensioners who chatted quietly as they waited to be processed. With time to kill, Ulla alternated between silent rehearsal of the personal data contained within her adopted passport and excursions through the now complete lyrics to David Bowie's 'Starman'.

An hour after attaching herself to the queue, Ulla was ushered into a control cabin, where she removed her passport from her holdall and presented it politely to the uniformed officer. The border official recorded the holder's name and the serial number of the passport before scrutinising the exit visa. Returning to the personal details page, he flipped his attention repeatedly from the black and white photo to the traveller and back again. Ulla simply waited. Having satisfied himself that the visa was in order and that the passport holder was indeed Katarina Köhler, the guard checked the watch lists but found no mention of her name. Still, something struck him as odd. Although it was not yet midday, the woman before him had adorned herself with what he imagined to be expensive perfume and was dressed as though for a big night out.

He caught Ulla's eye once more.

'And what is the purpose of your visit to the West?'

As a result of the rigorous briefing on the part of Lieutenant Eckart, Ulla knew exactly what she was going to say. Possessed of a quiet resolve, she maintained the eye contact.

'Operative Personal Control Matterhorn.'

The specific use of MfS terminology caught the Pass and Control officer by surprise. Whilst Katarina Köhler was conceivably old enough to be an operational Stasi officer, he would have expected any comrade to be using their discrete conduit to the U-Bahn platform.

'Why are you using this exit?'

'Those are the instructions I was given. If there's an issue, you should phone 590 59 00. The code 161 will connect you directly to the internal switchboard for the Main Directorate for Reconnaissance. Ask for Captain Hartling.'

'Give me that extension number again,' said the border official, picking up a pen.

With the number duly noted, the officer checked that the electronic exit gate to the control booth was locked, picked up the receiver of the internal phone and dialled the code for an outside line.

67 HARDWARE

East Berlin, Saturday 30th May 1976

As Ulla Wolfram stood and waited impassively for the Pass and Control officer to make the call, Captain Hartling was nowhere near his office. Dressed in a plain shirt, factory dungarees and walking boots and carrying a metal toolbox that clearly had some weight to it, he emerged from the Schuster hardware store in the peripheral locality of Erkner. Satisfied with his purchase, the MfS officer drove to the nearby Dämeritzsee lake, parked close to the public bathing area and laid claim to an unoccupied bench.

Here and there, families had collected in small groups and were chatting eagerly or relaxing in the May sunshine. To his left a girl and a boy in blue bathing costumes caught their breath and exchanged high-pitched shrieks as they edged ever further into the water.

Determined to clear his thoughts before reviewing his decisions, the Stasi officer removed a flask from his knapsack, poured some black Russian tea and contemplated the gently lapping waves or the occasional wispy cloud.

The tea eventually finished, the owner of a brand-new toolbox reflected calmly on his plan of action. Undeterred by his failure to figure out the code to the Major General's security cabinet, Hartling had decided on a more muscular strategy. In the final analysis, the technique did not need to be subtle. It simply had to work.

Furthermore, it had dawned on him that his initial deal with MI6 was not necessarily dead in the water. Martin could only compel him to function as a mole for as long as his cover remained intact. To liberate himself, Hartling would need only to compromise his viability as an embedded asset and to do so in such a way that he would be across the border before evidence of his duplicity had emerged. As soon as he had secreted the Day X files in West Berlin, he would simply offer his MI6 handler the choice of honouring their original agreement or losing the stolen intelligence to the Americans.

With regard to Ulla Wolfram, there was no indication that she had attempted to leave the territory of the GDR or that she had submitted her potentially inflammatory accusations to Honecker. Whilst her petition would be of no consequence to Hartling once he had relocated to the West, he nevertheless wanted the obnoxious toe rag to reap the rewards of her impudence. Wolfram's name would therefore remain indefinitely on the Border Command watchlist. The moment she dared to present her passport at any of the controls, she would be detained, dragged to a cell and interrogated until she could take no more. Convicted of criminal deception as well as conspiracy to flee the Republic, she would receive an absolute minimum of thirty years in Hoheneck prison. Time enough, Hartling thought, for her to repent of her insufferable audacity.

68 THE HALF-CITY

East Berlin, Saturday 30th May 1976

The ease with which Ulla had trotted out a Stasi phone number and deployed MfS terminology had lent her an immediate air of authenticity, but she knew that it had been a massive gamble. What were the chances that Hartling would be at his desk when the call came through? As the Pass and Control officer waited for a response from the switchboard at the Main Directorate for Reconnaissance, he found himself trying to assemble the pieces of this unprecedented puzzle into a coherent whole. It was conceivable, given the woman's demeanour, the attractive clothing and the rich perfume, that Operative Personal Control Matterhorn might be some kind of honeytrap operation. Furthermore, if the young woman were not a regular MfS officer but an informal or conscripted collaborator, she would certainly not have been made privy to the existence of the Stasi's covert exit channels.

When, after some delay, the switchboard operator reported that Captain Hartling was unavailable, the control officer took the confirmation of his comrade's name as evidence enough of the young woman's integrity. Calmly, he replaced the receiver, stamped the exit date across the visa and wished Katarina Köhler a successful day. When the electronically controlled gate clunked open, Ulla nodded, picked up her holdall and followed the signs to the U-Bahn platform, all the while expecting to feel a tug on her arm or a barked order not to go any further. From the map supplied by Jack, she knew that she would need to take the U6 towards Tegel and change at Leopoldplatz. Only when the U-Bahn arrived at the first stop on the western side of the border would she permit herself any sense of celebration.

As the underground train rattled and squealed its way into the station, Ulla was so focussed on identifying the word 'Tegel' above the front windscreen that she failed to notice that Julia and Anna were now standing either side of her.

'This is the one,' said Anna as the doors to the carriage disgorged the clutch of passengers heading for the East.

Ulla looked suddenly to her right and offered Anna a look of astonishment.

'Stay calm,' said a familiar voice to her left. 'We're right beside you from this point. Just get on, sit down and try to not to worry. You've done the hard part.'

In the carriage, Anna and Julia positioned themselves once more to either side of her. Julia, squeezed her forearm reassuringly, but said nothing.

Anna caught Ulla's eye and smiled. 'You did it.'

'Tell me that once we're off the train,' said Ulla. 'Right now, we're still in East Berlin.'

'More under it than in it, I guess, but it won't be long.'

Ulla looked at the purple U6 line map above the window opposite. As the U-Bahn maps in the East did not feature the western lines, the majority of station names had a thoroughly unfamiliar ring to them. Above some of the windows, jaunty adverts for employment agencies, French cigarettes, a BMW dealership and an exciting new brand of yoghurt jostled for the passengers' attention. After barely a minute, the U-Bahn decelerated before trundling slowly through the first of three dimly lit ghost stations. The two armed border guards positioned in the permanent twilight were an unnerving reminder that, at least for the next few minutes, Ulla inhabited a strange, subterranean limbo, no longer in the East, but certainly not yet in the West.

'It's OK,' said Julia sensing her unease and patting her on the forearm. 'It feels like the trains are going to stop, but they don't.'

With the desolate and disused stations behind them, the U-Bahn came to a halt at Reinickendorfer Strasse and the doors slid open.

Anna beamed at Ulla. 'Now I can say you've done it.'

For all the morning's machinations, the GDR's most recent deserter was little more than two kilometres from her apartment. The anticipated feeling of celebration was suddenly hijacked by an overwhelming sense of relief which expressed itself as a flood of tears.

On the far side of the carriage, a woman with two young children stared.

'Are you enjoying this?' asked Julia pointedly.

The woman looked away, but not for long.

With the sobs showing no sign of abating, Anna dug a clean paper tissue from her jacket pocket and pressed it into Ulla's hand. The escapee tried to wipe the wetness from beneath her eyes and her nose, but succeeded, as she did so, in smudging the carefully applied lipstick and smearing it onto her face. Julia could not help but smile at the undeniably comic effect, before digging out a fresh tissue, licking it and dabbing at the reddish smears like a mother wiping food from a toddler's cheek.

'Sorry about that,' said Ulla, finally surfacing from the sea of conflicting emotions.

'Hey, no,' said Julia. 'Don't worry. Better to let it out. You're with friends. Anyway, that's about as tidy a makeover as I can manage with a spitty tissue. I'll make a better job of it when we get to the flat.'

Two stops later they needed to change from the U6 onto the U9 line, but once the three women were on the platform, Anna decided it might be better to steer Ulla out into the fresh air. Catching Julia's eye, she glanced upwards as a signal that they should leave the station. They could walk the final kilometre to Oudenarder Strasse. Almost as soon as they had emerged into the brightness of the afternoon, Ulla spotted a phone box.

'I need to make a call,' she said, now processing the enormity of her achievement. 'I need to call my parents and let them know where I am. Do you have any change I could borrow?'

Julia pinched her lips momentarily. 'You know what? I know making that call's a big deal, but they swallow up coins like nobody's business. You'll be welcome to use our phone. You know, the one that rings in the middle of the night. Honestly, it's not far to the flat. We'll be there soon. Fifteen minutes at most.'

Ulla reflected for a moment, looked at Julia and smiled.

'OK. It's a deal. I can wait fifteen minutes.'

As the three women crossed the square, Ulla began to take note of this other Berlin, the half-city that had been hidden behind barbed wire and concrete for almost fifteen years. Although the air smelled exactly the same, an almost unfathomable variety of vehicles populated the streets. Many were noticeably larger, appeared to have been sprayed in bolder colours and emitted significantly more noise than their GDR counterparts.

As on the eastern side of the city, stores closed at lunchtime on Saturdays and the pavements were less crowded than they had been earlier in the day. Many of the West Berliners who were still out and about carried plastic shopping bags in vibrant colours. A number sported fashions that looked somehow brighter or more expensive than the clothes on offer in the East. Other West Berliners, by way of contrast, looked positively down at heel.

Along the street bordering the square were a modern-looking savings bank, a tobacconist with an impossibly cluttered window display and a triple-fronted franchise for a prominent American sewing machine company. Taking turns to carry the holdall, the three women walked at the leisurely pace determined by Ulla's curiosity, her frequent questions about the locality and Julia's typically authoritative answers. At the quirkily named Belle-Et-Triste bookshop, Ulla stopped to admire the profusion of unfamiliar writers and titles in the imaginative window displays. Moving onwards, the companions passed a crèche painted in bright primary colours, a tatty driving school and finally the Groninger Eck, where the six flatmates had so earnestly debated what to do with the redundant Katarina Kohl passport. When Anna finally announced their arrival at 27 Oudenarder Strasse, the insistent strains of Boney M were, as happened several times a day, blaring out from the ground floor bar. Nearby, Bastian squatted in his overalls and tinkered with the carburettor on his temperamental VW Beetle.

Hearing Anna's voice, he turned, stood up and wiped his hands on his overalls.

'Hi, I'm Bastian,' he said cheerily. 'You must be Ulla. Or possibly even Katarina Köhler.'

'Ulla is fine,' she said, reciprocating his smile.

'I have to say, I've been worrying about you. You've just done something amazing, you know.'

'I think that's starting to sink in.'

'Look, I don't mean to be rude, but for the moment, I won't shake your hand, not while I'm covered in all this grease. Anyway, the others are all upstairs. Shit, Jack's going to be so pleased to see you. He's been like a cat on hot bricks all day. I had to put him onto some seriously time-consuming vegetable preparation to put a stop to the jabbering. Anyway. Go on up. I've made a half-decent Dutch apple cake to be going on with and if Jack's followed my instructions properly, there'll be a ragout in the slow cooker that should be edible by early this evening. Give me a few minutes and I'll be up. But shit, Ulla, you made it. You got out.'

The tears began to dribble down Ulla's cheek once more.

'Can we go inside?' she said to Julia. 'Make that phone call?'

69 THE PRIZE

West Berlin, Saturday 30th May 1976

The taxi from Spandau pulled up a short distance from the entrance to RAF Gatow, the British military airstrip sandwiched between the Havel lake to the east and the GDR border installations to the west. Turnbull thanked the driver, handed him a five-mark note and climbed out of the cream Mercedes without waiting for the change. He bypassed the red and white boom that blocked vehicular access, walked directly to the guards' cabin and presented his Secret Intelligence Service identity card. The RAF sergeant disappeared inside for maybe thirty seconds before returning the ID and directing Turnbull to Meeting Room A in the Education Centre. There was no need for directions, the visitor assured the guard. He had been there many times before.

Turnbull knocked at the plain door and recognised Wildegood's voice inviting him to enter, but was surprised to discover that she was not alone. Sitting to her immediate left was Richard Spedding, Deputy Director of Operations for Europe.

'David,' said Spedding affably, 'so very good to see you. I understand you've been doing some fine work here at Berlin Station.'

'Thank you, sir,' said Turnbull, trying to sound as though the whole thing had been close to effortless.

The Deputy Director was, as ever, smartly turned out in a navy business suit and a green and navy plaid tie. He had blue eyes and a diminutive nose. Although Spedding's residual hair, swept back from his temples, was almost as white as his shirt, the black, bushy eyebrows betrayed the darker colouring of his youth. A pair of heavy framed glasses intensified the somewhat owlish look and served only to reinforce his natural gravitas.

'Sit down, would you? I don't have long.'

Turnbull took a seat and politely nodded at Wildegood.

'What can I do for you, sir?'

'Well, not to beat about the bush, we've had a team of analysts working intensively on the typewriter ribbon you acquired from your asset. We've looked closely at the dynamics implicit in the protocols of the meetings between Major General Konrad and Army General Ivanovsky and we've compared particular turns of phrase attributed to the Soviet commander with peculiarities of his speech patterns documented in authenticated sources. As far as we can be certain, both pass muster. As well as the minutes of a separate meeting with Mielke also present, the ribbon contains a variety of fairly routine letters and memoranda, some of which appear to have been redrafted and retyped a number of times.'

'So the intel is solid?'

'I would be inclined, without throwing caution to the wind here, to proceed on the working assumption that the ribbon and its contents are genuine. It follows, therefore, that under no circumstances should you allow your Stasi captain to quit his post in the MfS. Leave him as a sleeper and direct him to work his way incrementally into further involvement with Konrad, Ivanovsky or anything relating to the invasion planning. The minutes of the meeting on the ribbon are all well and good, a glimpse through the keyhole, but they indicate little more than the Stasi's unquestionable enthusiasm and apparently high level of readiness for the planned military operation without shedding too much light on the specifics. So. Keep your man in place, at least for the foreseeable future. Promise him an eventual way out, and a more handsome pay off if you like, but only if he can supply us with detailed tactical plans for Day X.'

'Understood, sir. Very good.' Turnbull was quietly delighted with the implicit vindication of his position.

'And as previously agreed,' said Wildegood, predominantly for the benefit of the Deputy Director, 'if the little arse refuses to play ball, threaten him with exposure. And if he still fails to co-operate, be ready to send our friends in the MfS a copy of the recordings from the Rive Gauche.'

'Indeed,' said Spedding. 'But we won't scuttle the ship unless we have no other option. Check with me personally before doing anything precipitous. The final decision will rest with me and with me alone. Let's keep our eyes on the prize.'

70 OVER THE WALL

West Berlin, Saturday 30th May 1976

Reluctant to wait in the street like an overanxious parent, Jack had made it no further than the courtyard of 27 Oudenarder Strasse. Locked in an occasionally faltering conversation with the ever-friendly Mrs Aydem, he engaged her young sons, Deniz and Kaan, in a lively backyard kickabout. Stationed between two of the tall metal dustbins, the impromptu goalkeeper fended off their increasingly vigorous and close-range shots as often and as well as he could. As the game wore on, it seemed to Jack that the two boys had somehow conspired not to score but to take potshots at the goalkeeper as though he were a target in a fairground shy. When eventually Kaan booted the ball so hard that it flew above Jack's head, over the wall and into the neighbouring yard, Mrs Aydem unleashed a short, waspish admonition in the language of her heart. With her son looking suitably chastised, she looked at Jack and shrugged, perhaps in frustration that the loss of the ball was far from unprecedented.

It took the student no more than a few seconds to clamber onto one of the bins, call to an elderly resident in the yard beyond and bring about the return of the football. When he turned to climb down, a familiar face with untidy makeup and a markedly different hair colour was positively beaming at him. Impulsively, Jack jumped from the dustbin, but lost his footing as he landed and fell to the paving in a manner that defied any attempt to preserve his dignity. The moment he straightened himself up, Ulla was in his arms and held him as though, at least for that moment, she had no other purpose in life.

'You did it,' he said, incapable in his relief of doing no more than stating the obvious.

Before releasing Jack from the embrace, Ulla kissed him softly on the ear.

'Is that his girlfriend?' asked Kaan.

Anna smiled at him. 'Something like that.'

Disappointed, the young boy could see that his goalkeeping friend would probably not be returning to their game.

Julia spotted Ulla wiping fresh tears from her cheek.

'Come on, Katarina Köhler,' she said. 'Let's get you upstairs. I'm bang out of tissues down here.'

As the four arrived on the fifth floor landing, the drifting, homely smell of the ragout in the slow cooker reminded Ulla vaguely of the Metzer Eck. In the kitchen, Marco and Christa greeted them with an excited cheer.

'Never in doubt,' said Marco with all the bluster of hindsight. 'Never in doubt.'

'Welcome,' said Christa. 'Come and sit down. We have cake and I'll make coffee. Later there'll be dinner.'

'That's great,' said Ulla, 'but if it's still OK, I'd really like to make that call.'

Julia took Ulla to the phone, told her to take as long as she liked and pointed out the box of tissues on the bookshelf.

Confronted with the reality of telling her parents that she and they would probably not see each other for the next six years, Ulla reminded herself that she had done no more than they had encouraged her to do. Nevertheless, her news would come as a bolt from the blue and there would be pain as well as joy. She breathed deeply and dialled. It was not by any stretch of the imagination the hardest thing she had done that day, but somehow it was starting to feel like it. Listening to the ringtone, Ulla had no idea what she was going to say, but at the sound of her mother's voice, she was embraced by an unexpected sense of calm.

'Hi, Mum,' she said almost breezily. 'You'll never guess where I'm calling from.'

Presently, Bastian appeared in the kitchen, savoured the smell of fresh coffee and announced that as soon as he had changed out of his filthy overalls, it would be open season on the cake. In response to his comment on the manifest absence of their guest, Christa explained that Ulla was in the bedroom next door, probably giving her parents the shock of their lives.

Once a less oily Bastian had joined the others at the table, Julia and Anna began to recount in detail their part in the day's events. By dint of the insubstantial adjoining wall, their report was punctuated ever more frequently by the indistinct but clearly celebratory exclamations from the room next door. After the best part of an hour, Ulla reappeared in the kitchen doorway and looked at Anna.

'You don't have any makeup remover do you?'

'I don't know,' said Anna, with a glint in her eye. 'Is the Pope a Catholic?'

'How did it go?' asked Julia. 'The call to your parents?'

'Flabbergasted. No. Flabbergasted doesn't even come close. Astonished, dumbfounded, amazed. All of that at once. Anyway. You get the picture. Once it had sunk in though, they were both kind of happy and unhappy at the same time. But it was their idea in the first place for me to leave the

GDR. I just hadn't let them in on the secret. And my God, were they full of questions. But I just completely refused to tell them anything about how I'd made it out. The less they know, the better, to be honest. Then they won't have to lie when one of the comrades from the Stasi decides to come asking questions.'

With the makeup gone, Ulla took a seat at the table and was presented with a generous slice of apple cake. As she reached for a fork, Bastian smiled and invited her to complete his still patchy understanding of how an East German ice hockey player came to be sitting in their kitchen. The ragout, he promised, would be ready in an hour.

Ulla breathed in and began her account with the shock of her Opa's cardiac arrest and the blocking of the Wolframs' visa applications. As she spoke, Christa and Julia quietly fashioned themselves roll-ups and Marco prised the tops from seven bottles of Warsteiner. Although questions inevitably arose, the flatmates hung on their visitor's every word.

With hardly a pause for thought, Ulla talked of her friends in the East, of her frustrated desire to study physics and of the stultifying nature of her work at the Ministry. She detailed the subversion of her family's communications with Munich and, with her voice beginning to falter, identified the callously delayed news of her Opa's death as the trigger for her decision to leave.

When the young refusenik eventually described as 'oddly persistent' the British student who had turned up unannounced at her place of work, Marco stated drily that everyone else in the kitchen perceived Jack Gilmore as persistently odd.

The mirth was merely transient. A silence descended once more as Ulla recounted how she had been coerced into working as a honeytrap. That ultimately she had bamboozled the MfS with skills acquired from her grandfather now provided her with an enormous sense of satisfaction.

Engaging everyone around the table, Ulla thanked them for their invaluable help in supplying her with the doctored passport and in transforming her into a plausible rendition of Katarina Köhler. Never again, she vowed, would she allow anyone to pluck her eyebrows.

Eventually, the smell of the ragout in the slow cooker could be resisted no longer and Bastian set about serving up plates of the thick, warming stew. As they ate, Ulla related the events of that morning, impressing them in equal measure with her meticulous acts of misdirection and her brassy responses to the Pass and Control officer's queries.

'So, here I am,' she said with a smile. 'That's why I'm sitting here in Oudenarder Strasse, finishing off this plate of your wonderful stew and trying to pretend that I have the faintest idea about what to do next.'

'Well,' said Julia, stubbing out a roll-up, 'funny you should say that. I made a few enquiries at the local police station yesterday regarding visitors from East Berlin who might not wish to return. Their advice was categorically that for your own wellbeing you should present yourself to them as soon as you arrive in the West. They would provide you with somewhere safe to stay whilst they met your immediate needs. Nobody said it out loud, but I'm sure that means a bunk in the reception centre in Marienfelde. They did say that the whole legal business of furnishing you with a West Berlin ID card and processing an application for a West

German passport would begin fairly promptly. That said, they would need to authenticate your identity before the whole process could begin. Did you bring any kind of documentation apart from that dodgy passport?'

'I did. I spent an hour last night stitching the key pages from my real passport into the lining of my wash bag. But you know what? I'm not doing anything about it tonight. I've seen enough uniforms for one day.'

'Sure. There's no rush. It can all wait until tomorrow. If you want, I can phone the police station for you in the morning.'

'That would be good, but maybe not first thing in the morning.'

'Oh, definitely not first thing,' said Julia. 'I think you're entitled to a lie-in.'

'Anyway,' said Christa, 'enough talk of tomorrow. Why don't we move next door, light a few candles and tune up the guitars?'

'Good call,' said Marco. 'I'll bring a few bottles of liquid dessert.'

Ulla lent across to Jack and whispered in his ear. 'I seem to be the only one here who has no idea of where I'm sleeping tonight.'

'Ah, sorry,' he said awkwardly. 'That's my fault. We should have done that when you arrived. OK. Better late than never. Come on. I'll show you the set-up.'

At no point had the question of sleeping arrangements featured in any of the flatmates' conversations regarding Ulla's potential arrival. The others, it seemed, had simply taken it for granted that Jack and Ulla would share his room, regardless of whether they intended to sleep together or not.

For his part, Jack had given little thought to how he would handle this moment once it came. Ideally, things would somehow fall into place of their own accord. If not, he would rely on his capacity for improvisation. Turning down a beer, he made his excuses to the others, grabbed Ulla's bag and showed her to the neighbouring apartment.

In his room, beneath the window, was a single bed with a brand-new Egyptian cotton sheet and matching duvet cover, shoplifted the previous morning by Marco. On one of the pillows lay a pair of blue cotton pyjamas, also acquired from KaDeWe. To the other side of the room was a maroon sofa sporting a sleeping bag and a cushion.

'You take the bed,' said Jack. 'You're probably exhausted. I hope the bedding and the pyjamas are OK. Marco got them all. Long story. Plus, he's left you that fancy-looking travel bag he carried everything home in. I think the girls have put a few items of clothing in it for you and some, you know, toiletries and stuff. Anyway, I don't know if you're wanting to go to bed right this minute, but if you are, I can wait next door while you sort yourself out.'

Ulla turned to face Jack, stepped close and slipped her arms around his waist, just as she had done before they had separated at Friedrichstrasse.

'You know what, Jack Gilmore,' she said, gently stroking his side, 'you're not going to spend the night on the sofa and for that matter, neither am I.'

Ulla leaned in and kissed him.

'Are you sure about this?' said Jack. 'I mean, it's not like things aren't already massively complicated.'

'Well, I'm not really sure about a whole lot of things, but no-one's instructing me, no-one's controlling me, no-one's deciding for me. This is all me. And yes, I know we can't exactly make each other promises. For all I know, I won't even be in Berlin tomorrow night. But right here, right now, we both like each other, don't we?'

'We do.'

'OK. Then for now, let's just make the most of that. Deal?'

'Deal.'

Ulla steered Jack's hands to her midriff, kissed him softly on the lips and stroked the nape of his neck with her fingers. Jack reciprocated the kiss and fumbled with the buttons of her blouse. The first button undone, he paused.

'One problem, though,' said Jack. 'I haven't got any, you know, contraception.'

'Well, by a happy coincidence, Mr Gilmore, you don't need to worry on that score. I packed a few essentials as part of my whole Stasi honeytrap act. So, lucky you. Problem solved, I would say. At least for tonight.'

71 HAMMER AND CHISEL

East Berlin, Sunday 31st May 1976

In southwest Africa, Cuban troops were successfully supporting the People's Movement for the Liberation of Angola in their fight against counter-revolutionary forces. In the wake of Franco's death, trade unions across Spain were challenging the power of the bourgeoisie. At home, the Evangelical priest who had distributed mendacious leaflets outside the Palace of the Republic was denounced as a traitor to his Christian principles. It was six in the morning and the two guards on the gate to the MfS complex in Normannenstrasse had, in turns, read every front-page article in the copy of *Neues Deutschland* that had, for some reason, been abandoned on their desk. Although Captain Hartling was not the first of their MfS comrades to have come in to work so early, he was one of the few. Pleased to have something to do, if only for a few moments, the first of the guards checked Hartling's identity card, saluted and waved him through.

As was usual before a covert trip to the western sectors of the city, the Stasi captain was immaculately shaven, had picked out his designer glasses, a silk tie and a sharp business suit. He was carrying his calfskin briefcase in one hand and had draped the strapped leather travel bag over his shoulder. He climbed the stairs to the fifth floor of the Main Directorate for Reconnaissance, walked directly to the Secretariat and removed the key to Major General Konrad's office. Once inside, Hartling placed his briefcase on the floor and unzipped the bag. In addition to a small wash bag, changes of underwear and the usual cash and documents that he needed for an operation in the West, the MfS captain was carrying a loaded Walther PPK service pistol and a silencer plus the lump hammer and the wide-bladed bolster chisel from the recently purchased toolbox. There would be no concealing what he had done, no way of explaining and no going back. He planned to be in West Berlin within ninety minutes at the most.

Hartling suspected that a direct assault on the lock itself might only serve to jam the mechanism. Whilst the locking system was impressive, the hinges appeared to be more rudimentary in their design. Placing the bolster chisel beneath the upper hinge on the right hand door, Hartling swung the hammer with every ounce of force that he could muster. A second hefty blow caused the blade to wedge itself between the hinge and the door and a third completely severed the heads from two of the holding pins. A fourth and final blow detached the hinge from the door completely. Within twenty seconds Hartling had repeated the process with the lower hinge and had managed to ease the door from the frame. From amongst the rack of manilla folders on the central shelf, he rapidly identified ten marked for Konrad's eyes only, leafed through the first three and found references to Day X in each. He would take them all.

With his briefcase in one hand and the travel bag in the other, the Stasi officer walked out of the office leaving the hammer and chisel on the floor and his fingerprints over everything he had touched. It was a masterstroke. Under no circumstances would MI6 now be able to return him to East Berlin for exploitation as an embedded asset.

In spite of the considerable noise that Hartling had made, the corridor outside the office was still quiet and there was no sound of footsteps on the stairs. Although the Stasi captain's heart rate was climbing, it was completely conceivable, he told himself, that the burglary had escaped the notice of the few people already in the building. Equally, it was possible that the sequence of loud, metallic bangs had been heard, but would be dismissed as the sound of an out-of-hours maintenance team conducting long-overdue repairs on the famously unreliable plumbing. Every MfS officer knew that Normannenstrasse was one of the most secure locations in the GDR. Why would their immediate assumption be that the complex was being burgled?

As Hartling walked across the internal courtyard and drew ever closer to the Ruschestrasse exit, his calm appearance belied a nascent sense of triumph coupled to the unshakeable awareness that he was not yet out of jeopardy.

Happy again to have something to do, the guard on the gate checked his watch, logged Captain Hartling's departure and saluted him for the second time that morning.

The Stasi officer had parked his car no more than fifty metres along Ruschestrasse. Although it was still early and the traffic was light, the drive to Friedrichstrasse was at once annoyingly slow but reassuringly uneventful. At the discrete MfS checkpoint deep within the station complex, the uniformed officer controlling the conduit into West Berlin recognised his comrade and treated Hartling's departure as a matter of routine.

By eight fifteen, the smartly dressed defector was sitting in an almost empty S-Bahn carriage trundling its way across West Berlin to the Zoologischer Garten interchange. He was in possession of documents of such enormous value that he could readily offer them to the Americans if the British no longer agreed to his terms. For a few moments at least, he could not have been happier.

It was, however, merely a matter of time before the theft of the files was discovered and the prints he had purposefully left at the scene were identified. At that moment the MfS machine would do everything within its power to retrieve the stolen materials and treat its wayward comrade to the payback he deserved. Although Hartling had given himself a head start, it was far from an indefinite guarantee of his safety. He would not feel secure until the British had green-lit his extraction and he was sitting on an RAF transport bound for the UK. In the meantime he would go to ground, contact the woman who believed herself to be his fiancée and inveigle her to dead drop a sample of his wares to MI6.

72 RIGHT TO REMAIN

West Berlin, Sunday 31st May 1976

When Jack finally awoke, he had a dry mouth and it was a warm day. Ulla lay on her side in the narrow bed and was gently stroking his hair.

'Hey. You're awake at last. Did you sleep OK?'

'I think so. What time is it?'

'No idea. Don't really care.'

Ulla lay partly across him and kissed him affectionately. In spite of the fact that the future seemed to offer them few immediate possibilities, she was glad that this had happened. Jack, for his part, liked the smoothness and the warmth of Ulla's body next to his and the feel of her hair as it occasionally drifted onto his shoulder.

'What do you think of the colour?' she asked. 'I think chestnut kind of suits me.'

'Well,' he said, clearly unsure. 'It's definitely different. But I could get used to it.'

The seemingly throwaway remark triggered an uncomfortable pause. Who knew when, or even if, they might see each other again?

'Come, on, Jack,' said Ulla, giving him a friendly push on the nose. 'We talked about this. Let's not get ahead of ourselves.'

Before their conversation had a chance to resume, they heard Julia's soulful singing from the other side of the bedroom door.

The refrain from a Steven Stills song was as much warning as Ulla and Jack were going to get. Without knocking, Julia pushed at the bedroom door with her hip, greeting them as she entered. She had a smile of approval on her face and a steaming mug in each hand.

'I assume you two are both naked.'

'Pretty much,' said Ulla. 'Jack definitely is. I'm still wearing a bracelet.'

'See. I told Marco that stealing those pyjamas was a complete waste of time. Anyway, I brought you both tea. Breakfast is next door.'

At about ten thirty, Ulla appeared in the kitchen, wearing her black slacks and a faded *Physical Graffiti* tee shirt.

'Jack's still in the shower,' she said.

Anna and Marco were yet to appear, Christa was in the bedroom, selecting the musical accompaniment to Ulla's first breakfast on this side of the Wall and Bastian was sawing at a fresh roll.

'Help yourself,' said Julia. 'It's going to be a busy day.'

'If it's OK, after breakfast I'd like to phone Uncle Tommi in Munich and let him know he might be having a guest. His head will literally explode.'

'Sure. Whatever you need. I'm not sure you'll make it that far by tonight, but you never know. And if you need money for the train or a flight–'

'Oh, no. No. That's really kind, but no. You've done enough already. And my dad said that Uncle Tommi would definitely be able to sort all of that out. So, thanks, but no thanks. Anyway, have you phoned the police?'

'Not yet. I was waiting for you to give me the go-ahead.'

'Well, consider the go-ahead given.'

Having dropped the needle on a Vivaldi lute concerto, Christa appeared, greeted Ulla and Bastian and grabbed a seat.

'OK,' said Julia, getting to her feet. 'Time for the big phone call to the guardians of law and order.'

Bastian asked Ulla how she had slept. Christa decided to make fresh coffee and Julia disappeared into the bedroom to turn down the music before making the call. With his hair still dripping, Jack finally slouched in.

'Ah, I was wondering where that was,' he said looking at the tee shirt. 'Also, who did the washing up last night? I think it should've been me.'

'You owe me one,' said Bastian.

By the time Julia reappeared, Anna and Marco had arrived. They were clearly in one of their more harmonious phases.

'So Ulla,' said Julia, 'they were really very helpful and I have to say, surprisingly friendly. They seemed keen to make sure that you're OK and to help you sort out your right to remain in the Federal Republic. They said that the pages from your original passport would probably be perfectly fine, as long as they're still legible. It's a good job you're already showered, though. They're going to send a car about twelve. So if you want to phone your uncle in Munich, you'd probably best do it right away.'

Ulla looked directly at Jack and raised her eyebrows. Keen to speak to her uncle, she stood up and edged round the table. Jack grabbed himself a roll, smeared it with butter and tried to behave as though it were a regular Sunday morning.

'Will Ulla need some sandwiches to take with her?' he asked. 'Maybe I should make some.'

‘Let me do it,’ said Anna. ‘I’ve seen the kind of logic-free lunches you just sling together.’

Twenty minutes later, Ulla returned to the kitchen and Anna presented her with an immaculately wrapped lunch pack ‘just in case’. Jack, she reported, was in his room.

He smiled as she entered.

‘I’d like to keep this,’ she said, referring to his washed out tee shirt.

‘Sure. Be my guest.’

Ulla collected together the few items she had brought from Fehrbelliner Strasse and stuffed them into her fancy new holdall.

‘So,’ said Jack. ‘Is this the end? Or just the end of the beginning?’

Ulla was fairly subdued. ‘Who knows? Time will tell, I guess.’

‘We should stay in touch.’

‘We should. I’d like that. But don’t forget, Jack. We can’t get ahead of ourselves. Nothing about this is certain.’

‘I know.’

Ulla smiled. Jack pulled her towards him and they hugged it out.

‘Don’t come down to the street, though,’ she said. ‘When it’s time, I don’t want the police as an audience. We’ll say our goodbyes here.’

73 OPEN DOORS

West Berlin, Sunday 31st May 1976

Frau Auerbach, the first point of contact at the Marienfelde Emergency Reception Centre, thanked the police officer who had guided Ulla to the door of the central office. Throughout the extensive site, lawns, flower beds and well-established birch trees mitigated the rather austere look of the cheaply constructed buildings. Although the office itself was sorely in need of renovation, Frau Auerbach was welcoming and exuded generosity. Gently and without fuss, she noted the new arrival's personal details and recorded the time, date and context of her departure from the GDR. Once she had finished listing the addresses and telephone numbers of Ulla's contacts in the West, Frau Auerbach sat back and smiled at her charge.

'Any questions?'

At that precise moment, Ulla could think of only one thing.

'How long will I be here?'

'Well the first thing I need to make clear, Frau Wolfram, is that this is not a prison or any form of detention camp. You're free to leave at any time. That said, there will be a number of examinations and interviews to establish that you are who you say you are and that you are not a person of interest either to the Police over here or to the Allied Powers in the western zones. After that, it's just a case of providing you with an official ID card, processing your passport application and ensuring that you have somewhere to go and the wherewithal to get there.'

'Meaning how long exactly?'

'Well, assuming you attend your appointments on time and there are no issues, maybe by next Saturday. Who knows? Maybe sooner than that. We're not, if I'm being honest, actually that busy.'

Frau Auerbach handed Ulla the official welcome gift of thirty deutschmarks and asked her to sign a receipt.

'So, Frau Wolfram, that's everything for now. Grab your things. I'll show you the washrooms, the refectory, the library and of course your room. And I'll get you a towel. There's no charge either for the accommodation or the meals. Any problems, any questions, just ask. Otherwise, come to my office first thing in the morning and I'll give you the full programme of meetings and medical appointments that you'll need to attend. As soon as they're all done and dusted, you can return those keys to me and step into a world of open doors.'

The tour lasted no more than twenty minutes. Once alone in her room, Ulla kicked off her shoes and lay on the bed. For all the newness and the change, she was at ease. Her body felt lighter, her mind somehow less congested. The gnawing sense of tension which she had experienced to one degree or another since the first unsettling news of her grandfather's hospitalisation was now conspicuously absent.

With time to herself, the enormity of what Ulla had done began slowly to sink in. Beneath the supposedly unblinking eye of the Stasi, she had extricated herself from its coercive control, from a bind which had laid permanent claim both to her freedom and her self-respect. Yet, for all the open doors that Frau Auerbach had alluded to, those facing east were now shut. There could be no return to the other Germany, the Germany she knew, the Germany where her parents and her friends were now living their lives without her.

The reception centre's latest resident stared at the slats of the bunk above and tried to figure out at which point she had boarded the runaway train of impossible choices. Although Ulla knew that she and her parents would eventually be reunited, six years was six years and the separation would be anything but easy.

During the astonishing phone call from Oudenarder Strasse, her parents had realised that they would not need to lie when inevitably the MfS enquired into her disappearance. The Wolframs could inform the investigators in all honesty that their daughter had revealed nothing of her plans and that her call from West Berlin had come as a complete shock. In her heart of hearts, Ulla knew that there was not a scrap of evidence that could link either her mother or her father to her desertion from the GDR. Nevertheless, the interactions with the MfS would, by their very nature, be prolonged and massively stressful.

Had there been a time, Ulla wondered, when she might perhaps have abandoned her chosen course of action and spared them all this fate? She could undoubtedly have held back from slapping a copy of her petition to Honecker right under Hartling's nose. She could have remained in East Berlin, trying to make the best of things and following the instructions of her Stasi handlers for the remainder of her days. Had she taken the decision to stay, she reflected, Udo and Eva Wolfram would have lost their daughter anyway. She would have been used and abused by the MfS for their own unchallengeable ends. Her Stasi controller would have hollowed the life out of her until all that remained was an empty shell, devoid of love, dreams or ambition. In the end, the decision whether to fight or to submit had been no decision at all.

Feeling suddenly tired, Ulla deferred her plan to take a stroll in the streets outside. She would wait until after dinner, she decided, before asking Frau Auerbach for directions to the nearest phone booth. Gradually, it dawned on Ulla that during her stay in Marienfelde she would have few decisions to make beyond deciding whether she was hungry. For the time being, she thought, she could definitely live with that.

Within a week perhaps, she would be in Munich and would fulfil her mission to lay flowers on her grandfather's grave. After that, the future was in many ways unclear, but she would no doubt begin to fathom things out. Relieved beyond measure to have thrown off the shackles of her allotted future in the GDR, Ulla saw the uncertainties that lay before her as a blessing. Not quite a world of open doors, but close.

74 DEAD DROP

West Berlin, Sunday 31st May 1976

The Savigny was not a hotel that Hartling had ever used whilst on operations in the West, but it suited his purposes perfectly. The suite he had selected was eminently comfortable, enjoyed prompt room service and benefitted from a phone with an outside line. Having read through the stolen files and satisfied himself of their value, the defector considered his options. Logically, only one course of action lay open to him. He would remain within the confines of the hotel until the arrangements for his extraction by MI6 had been agreed.

On receiving her fiancé's call, Petra Fichtenberg expressed her joy at his return from what he described as 'a spot of BND business in Frankfurt'. She would, she promised, grab some things together and make her way to his hotel just as soon as she possibly could. His devoted lover duly summoned, Hartling turned his attention to the errand he would need her to run.

The Stasi officer selected one of the files and removed a page that referenced both Day X and the Commander of Soviet Forces in the GDR. Using the system prescribed by his British case officer, Hartling encrypted his contact details and jotted them neatly beside the text. Finally, he folded the page, sealed it in one of the unmarked envelopes from the writing desk and wrapped the sample of his haul in a small polythene bag. The delivery would be a signal to MI6 that he had, without any shadow of a doubt, come up with the goods.

Petra Fichtenberg found her way to the Hotel Savigny in little more than an hour. Following the inevitable tenderness of their reunion, Hartling confessed that he had a favour to ask of his beautiful fiancée, a favour that related to his work for the BND. It was not the first time he had asked for her help and he knew that she was so deeply invested in their love that her acquiescence could be taken for granted. There was no threat to her safety, he stressed, but she would have to ensure that her actions were not observed.

Over the course of an impressive room-service rigatoni bolognese, Hartling coached his attentive assistant through the process of making the drop. She was, it transpired, a remarkably quick learner. Having twice repeated her fiancé's instructions both precisely and in their entirety, Petra declared herself ready to make the delivery. She placed the package in her bag, swore solemnly not to look at its contents and left. It would be fine, Hartling reassured himself. She would do anything to please him, to be a part of his shadowy but quietly heroic life. He had trained this asset well.

With the suite to himself, he mulled over the security of the sensitive files. Unwilling to consign anything to the safekeeping of the reception staff, he decided to stow both the travel bag and the briefcase in the wardrobe and to keep the Walther PPK close to him at all times.

Some three hours elapsed before Petra returned. Her beaming face and the headlong rush into his arms told him everything he needed to know.

'Rainer, I can't believe what I've just done. I can't believe it. I mean, it took a long time before I was certain that no-one would see me, but hell, Rainer, I did it. I left it in the rusty coffee tin, just like you said. And I scratched a mark on the back of the notice board and everything. Amazing. I mean, completely amazing.'

Her bloodstream probably still pumped with adrenalin, Petra was acting as though this were some kind of a game. It wasn't. And he needed to impress that fact upon her. Hartling pushed her away slightly and took her hands.

'Slow down, Petra. Slow down. Listen to me. You've done a brilliant job today. Really brilliant. But listen. I know that I said that there was no threat to your safety and that was true, completely true, but I need to warn you that I'm carrying a weapon, a service pistol. I'll be keeping it under my pillow during the night. But don't let that alarm you. I'm not going to need it and the safety catch will be on.'

'Shit, Rainer, a gun? What in heaven's name do you need a gun for?'

'I know it's a bit of a surprise, but honestly, it's really no big deal. Try not to read too much into it. We just have to carry them sometimes. You know, like pilots carry parachutes. In the entire course of my career, I've never discharged a weapon outside the firing range. I've never even come close.'

'Are you sure?'

'Totally.'

'You swear?'

'On my mother's life.'

Petra looked him in the eye and for a few seconds said nothing.

'Can I see it?'

Carefully, Hartling removed the Walther PPK from the desk drawer, ensured that the safety catch was on and showed the pistol to Petra. Once she had calmed down and had promised him not to go anywhere near it, he placed the weapon for the time being on the writing desk and covered it with a glossy magazine. If his fiancée had ever entertained the slightest doubt that he exposed himself to personal risk in pursuit of the nation's security, the evidence was there for her to see. He knew that she would be concerned, but also impressed. She might possibly even be proud.

Petra kissed him.

'I've been missing you so much,' she said, walking her fingers slowly up his arm. Whether it had been the result of their whirlwind engagement, the revelation that he was a BND officer or some heady cocktail of the two, Petra was increasingly the one to initiate their lovemaking and he knew how the evening would unfold. He didn't even have to try any more.

When, in the early hours of the morning, Hartling was dredged from his slumbers by the insistence of a passing siren, Petra was no longer beside him and the bedroom door was slightly ajar.

'Everything OK?' he called wearily.

'I'm just going to the loo,' she shouted. 'I keep having to pee. I think I've got a urine infection.'

Reassured that it was nothing that needed concern him, he checked that the weapon was still under the pillow, rolled over and went back to sleep.

As soon as she heard the snores, Petra slipped on the clothes she had brought from the bedroom, picked up the phone and dialled a familiar number. At her feet lay Hartling's travel bag.

'Extension one-seven,' she said calmly, before waiting a few seconds for a colleague to pick up. 'Hi, it's Schneider. I have the paperwork. Hostile extraction team to Hotel Savigny, room five-zero-seven. Immediate.'

When, perhaps twenty minutes later, Hartling stirred for a second time, Petra was sitting on a chair in the doorway, silhouetted by the light from the lounge. Oddly, it appeared as though she might already be dressed. Perhaps the urine infection had kept her up. Although the Stasi captain could not make it out in the half-light, she was holding the Walther PPK in her hand.

'What are you doing?' he asked, as he reached for his glasses.

'Waiting.'

'What? What for?'

'Back-up.'

Initially incapable of processing the concise response, Hartling was momentarily speechless. A second later, the truth struck him like a wrecking ball. He had been played. Petra Fichtenberg, his infinitely acquiescent fiancée had taken him hook, line and sinker. Squinting towards the doorway, Hartling shuffled himself into a more upright position, surreptitiously feeling for the gun as he did so.

'Yeah, it's not there,' said Petra coolly. 'Nice weapon though. Well balanced. Even with the silencer fitted.'

'What do you want?' he said dispassionately.

'Well, Captain Hartling, the good news is that I don't have a urine infection. I am, on the other hand, massively intrigued by the documents in your luggage and what you are intending to do with them. My name is not Fichtenberg, by the way, just in case you were wondering. Anyhow, it turns out you're not the only one here with a BND identity card, the only difference being that mine wasn't knocked up in a back room at the Main Directorate for Reconnaissance.'

'I would have thought that any BND officer with a quantum of common sense would see from those files that I'm here to defect. That holdall contains the kind of intelligence your bosses have wet dreams about.'

'Possibly. Or it could just be a shed load of well-dressed disinformation, a bit like the worthless chaff I've been feeding you for the past couple of months. That said, Captain Hartling, exactly what you're up to is ultimately for my superiors to decide. In the meantime, we're just going to wait here quietly until my colleagues arrive.'

'If you say so.'

Whilst it was in essence true that Hartling was seeking to defect, he had no intention whatsoever of offering his services to the BND. There were more than enough MfS operatives embedded within the West German intelligence service for the Stasi to acquire precise knowledge of his whereabouts and to arrange for his elimination. He weighed up his options. The woman he knew as Petra Fichtenberg was blocking his exit and holding a loaded weapon. It made sense to assume that she knew how to use it. He was sitting in bed, stark naked, with no more than a duvet at his disposal, but he had not the slightest intention of being taken captive by the BND. If he could distract her momentarily, he could be at the door in less than a second, slam her wrist against the corner of the wardrobe and overpower her. He just had to be decisive. If she was foolish enough to put up a fight, she would suffer the consequences.

'You know the clip's empty,' he said.

Before she could reply, he flung the duvet aside and made his move. Instantly, she had aimed the gun at his legs and fired off two rounds in rapid succession. The first took out a perfectly serviceable electric heater, but the second ripped through his right quadricep. Hartling fell to the floor like a bag of sand.

'You bitch,' he cursed, clutching at his thigh. 'You fucking whore.'

'So, as I said, Captain Hartling, it's very much in your interest to stay exactly where you are. Obviously, if you bleed to death, it will be difficult to debrief you, so I'm going to throw you a towelling robe. Press it hard wherever you think necessary. Breathe steadily and try to stay calm. My team will have a first aid kit.'

'Fuck you.'

'Copy that. Also, whilst you're applying pressure to the wound, you might want to consider whether I still really qualify as marriage material.'

75 REMEMBRANCE

Munich, Monday 8th June, 1976

The Federal Government in Bonn classified the flight from West Berlin to Munich-Riem as internal and consequently Ulla was required to show no more than her ticket at the check-in desk in order to board the aircraft. Although the Pan Am Boeing 727 would in part overfly the territory of the GDR, it would use one of the three air corridors agreed in 1945 between the western powers and the Soviet Union. Unlike those travellers using the road or rail transit routes, Ulla would not encounter a single East German uniform on her journey to the West.

It was shortly before eleven in the morning. The former GDR citizen had never flown before and had little idea of what to expect. Although Ulla had seen aircraft interiors on TV, the unbridled power of the triple turbofan engines pushing her into her seat as it accelerated along the runway was not something she could have anticipated. Immediately after take-off, the window-seat view of the sprawling city intersected by Honecker's extensive Anti-Fascist Defence Wall was at once fascinating and deeply unsettling. Within minutes, however, the human world below was obscured by a blanket of cloud. The well-dressed, grey-haired lady in the neighbouring seat sought to assuage her own fear of flying by repeatedly clenching her fists as she expressed her delight at the imminent prospect of seeing her two grandchildren. Before long, she was mining an apparently inexhaustible seam of anecdotes from her family's long and complicated history.

Ulla sat back, made the most of the free coffee and the slice of cellophane-wrapped ginger cake and listened. Within an hour, the aircraft was beginning its approach into Munich.

Although Ulla had been completely unprepared for the build-up of pressure in her ears as the plane descended, she enjoyed the expansive views of farmland, forest and roads once the aircraft emerged from the clouds. In the opinion of her anxious companion, the landing at Munich-Riem airport was unnecessarily bumpy. Ulla, for her part, was mildly entertained by the bounce and, with the exception of the aerial view of the Berlin Wall, she had loved every second of her experience. In the absence of border controls, the holder of a new West German passport needed to do no more than follow the exit signs to locate the arrivals hall.

The years had been kind to Uncle Tommi. The infectious smile, the smart clothing and the confident demeanour created the impression of a man who was younger than his seventy-six years. Whilst the two Wolfram brothers had never been so similar in their looks as to merit confusion, Ulla had met him before and recognised him immediately. Although she had warned her great-uncle that her hair would be much darker than he would remember, he was nevertheless bemused by her appearance.

Tommi offered, exactly as Ulla's grandfather would have done, to relieve his visitor of her luggage. The young ice hockey player's refusal to have a significantly older man carry her bag was, however, as polite as it was implacable. As they followed the signs towards the car park, Ulla drew a measure of comfort from her great-uncle's oddly familiar gait and from some of his mannerisms of speech.

'Are you hungry?' he asked.

'Kind of,' said Ulla, 'but before we go anywhere else, Uncle Tommi, I'd really like to go to the cemetery.'

He was far from surprised. Ulla had expressed this wish at some point during each of their four telephone conversations since her escape from the GDR. The most recent had been from a call box at Berlin-Tegel airport only three hours previously.

'I know how important this is to you, Ulla, but I'm just wondering about flowers. There's a stall here at the entrance to the airport and another florist just around the corner, but not far from the cemetery there's a restaurant with an excellent flower shop right next door. We'd probably have a much greater choice if we bought them there. Two birds with one stone, I would say.'

Ulla smiled. Uncle Tommi was too similar to his brother to refuse.

At one thirty, her great-uncle parked his Mercedes outside the quiet Casa Nostra restaurant. As they ate, Ulla recapped the chain of events that had triggered her decision to leave and said little more about her escape at this stage beyond alluding to the use of a counterfeit visa. It was a long story and she would, she promised, give him a more detailed picture after they had paid their respects to Opa. Uncle Tommi assured Ulla that he would do everything in his power to help her find her feet in Munich and that he would be honouring his brother's memory in doing so.

Thomas Wolfram, it transpired, was a wealthy man. Not only had he enjoyed a successful career as a TV producer for Bayerischer Rundfunk but he also owned a fifty-percent stake in a successful carpet factory in Augsburg. With a homely smile, he informed Ulla that, if she wished, she was more than welcome to pick out one of the guest rooms in his spacious apartment and use it for as long as she liked without payment or precondition. When Ulla insisted that he should keep a record of any out-of-pocket expenditure so that one day she might repay him, he fully understood her desire not to been seen as a freeloader. Although Tommi readily feigned agreement to Ulla's wishes, he had not the slightest intention of keeping any kind of account or of pressing her for restitution.

In the florist's shop bedside the restaurant, Ulla commissioned a bunch of nineteen white roses before walking with Uncle Tommi the short distance to Bogenhausen cemetery. Of the two hundred plots, some were shaded by birch, linden or beech trees. Many featured distinctly modest memorials and had been lovingly tended as compact gardens. Karl Wolfram's headstone bore only his name and two dates.

'I wanted your mum and dad to write the inscription,' said Tommi, 'but getting through on the phone was impossible and I have no idea whether they got any of my letters. I certainly didn't get any replies.'

'They got some,' said Ulla quietly.

'I know your grandmother is buried in East Berlin, but it wasn't really an option.'

'I never knew her, but I'm sure Opa would have wanted to be with her.'

'For sure. And we'll do something about that. One day.'

As Ulla snuffled, Tommi produced a small pair of black secateurs from the inside pocket of his suit and carefully trimmed the odd stray growth of flowering thyme. He got slowly to his feet, recited a short prayer and invited his great-niece to place her bunch of roses in the stone vase at the centre of the plot. Ulla arranged the flowers as neatly as she could, stood up and looked intently at her grandfather's name carved into the pale stone. Standing before his grave in the partial shade of the trees, she experienced no reassuring sense of communion. Whilst the memorial in one sense brought her closer to her Opa, it also laid bare the finality of his death.

Furthermore, if the decision to leave the GDR and conduct this simple act of remembrance had served to provide Ulla with a sense of purpose in a world of shrinking choices, she knew that it had come at a cost. It would be six long years before her parents retired and would be permitted by the authorities to emigrate. How the young escapee would cope with the enforced separation was a question she could not yet hope to answer.

76 INTERNATIONAL PEDIGREE

Munich, Tuesday 9th June, 1976

Ulla had slept surprisingly well. After breakfast, Uncle Tommi presented his guest with an envelope containing five one-hundred-mark notes. This, he insisted, was a gift and not subject to the agreement they had made the previous day. He had an incontestable duty to help his great-niece and the money would, he hoped, enable her to buy a selection of clothes plus any personal items that she might immediately require. Tommi reminded Ulla that life had been enormously kind to him and that he in turn could afford to be generous. She should buy exactly what she wanted and if it transpired that five hundred marks was insufficient for her needs, the fault would be entirely his.

Shortly after ten, Uncle Tommi dropped his great-niece off outside the Ludwig Beck department store on Marienplatz and told her to call him when she needed to be picked up. Once inside the impressive building, Ulla prised open the crisp, white envelope and looked at the bank notes. Five hundred deutschmarks seemed like an awful lot of money and she had little real appreciation of what she could buy with such a sum. Nevertheless, she was curious to find out.

Compared to the Centrum store on Alexanderplatz, Ludwig Beck was remarkably well-stocked, beautifully laid out and unashamedly self-confident in its pricing. In the space of little more than two hours, Ulla bought two pairs of Levis, a supply of underwear, a selection of tee shirts, two blouses, a loose-fitting jacket and a plain black, hooded sweatshirt. After paying for the clothing, she took her bags to the ground floor and bought some toiletries, a block of writing paper, a pack of envelopes and a stylish, American ballpoint pen. Finally installed in the café on the fourth floor, Ulla ordered some lunch and penned letters to her parents, to Rosa and Jenny, to Kirsten and to Jack. Her personal supplier of illicit passports, she knew, would now be working hard to complete his dissertation before returning to Britain at the end of the academic year. She assured him that she was well and explained that she was living in her great-uncle's comfortable and astonishingly large apartment in a quiet suburb of Munich. She thanked Jack again for playing such an instrumental role in her escape from the GDR, wished him a safe return to England and, without dwelling on exactly what she meant by it, hoped that perhaps one day they might have the chance to see each other again.

With her shopping complete and little else to do, Ulla wandered out of the store and decided to explore the city centre. Munich contrasted sharply with East Berlin. Sympathetically restored and rebuilt over three decades, the historic centre belied to a considerable degree the devastation visited upon the central districts as the Second World War ground to its conclusion. As in so many West German cities, the careful reconstruction was testament to the economic boom of the 1960s and both the shops and the shoppers created the impression that life was good and that money, in most cases, was not in short supply.

In the former market square of Marienplatz, the blue-and-white, diamond-chequered flags of Bavaria swayed lazily in the wind as municipal workers watered the displays of summer flowers. On Karlsplatz, low-arching fountains played in the square and children dodged excitedly between the jets of water. Nearby, a young couple in matching jeans and identical hooped tee shirts strolled aimlessly in the sunshine.

Eventually Ulla found her way to the Viktualienmarkt, Munich's central outdoor food market. From somewhere nearby, the strains of a saxophone drifted above the chatter of the shoppers and the occasional shouts of stall holders. Although the majority of East Germans were well aware that supplies of particular foodstuffs were more plentiful in the West, the sheer quantities of oranges on display were beyond anything that Ulla could have anticipated. As for bananas, she could not remember ever having seen any on the shelves either at Konsum or in any other store. At the first stall, she bought a large pineapple, put it to her nose and lingered over its satisfying smell.

Tucking the purchase into her bag, Ulla drifted on. As fascinating as the goods on offer were, they could never begin to compensate for what she had left behind, the things she couldn't buy at a market stall. In an effort not to be ambushed by regret, Ulla reminded herself of the impossible life she would have faced, had she remained in East Berlin.

'You can't dance at two weddings,' her grandfather had often said of mutually exclusive choices. The aphorism made sense to her now.

Apart from Uncle Tommi, Ulla knew absolutely no-one in Munich and until she could find an ice hockey team to join, she would have to apply herself to the challenge of finding something to do. Ambling back towards Marienplatz once more, her eye was drawn to a colourful poster in a travel agent's window. Designed in the vibrant style of a comic strip, the InterRail advert depicted a group of happy, guitar-wielding backpackers about to board a train to some distant destination. For little more than two hundred marks, the poster proclaimed, young Europeans could enjoy a month of unlimited, visa-free rail travel throughout twenty-one countries ranging from Finland to Greece. For the former citizen of the GDR, the notion bordered on the unthinkable.

In the evening, having treated Ulla to a classic Bavarian dish of roast pork and potato dumplings, Uncle Tommi sat his great-niece down on the sofa, poured them each a glass of Pinot Blanc and invited her to recount the events of the past year in their entirety. Two hours later, having exhausted himself of questions, Ulla's great-uncle eventually broached the subject of her immediate plans. In the first instance, Ulla confirmed, she would need to register with the local police and, as she was hoping to find a temporary job during the summer, with the nearest employment office. She would need to set up a bank account, find an ice hockey club with a women's section and make contact with the admissions office at the University of Munich. She would also need to find herself a doctor and a dentist.

Pouring himself a second glass of wine, Tommi reiterated how happy he was to welcome Ulla to his apartment, but wondered whether she realised that Munich, for all its charms, was by no means her only option and neither, for that matter, was Germany. Far from certain that the established ice hockey clubs in Bavaria even had women's teams, Tommi suggested that she might possibly wish to consider applying for a sports scholarship at a university in the USA or Canada. They would, he felt sure, jump at the chance of recruiting a player with a proven international pedigree.

77 DRIFT

West Berlin, Friday 12th June 1976

As Jack's semester in Berlin edged towards its conclusion, the British student felt under increasing pressure to bring some kind of order to his still somewhat meandering dissertation on environmental policy in the two Germanies. Ideally he would have requested a second meeting at the Ministry for the Environment and attempted to put more probing questions to Press Secretary Fischer. In the light of his involvement with a recent escapee, however, a return to the East was hardly the most rational of ideas. To circumvent any possibility of complication, Jack had sent a letter to comrade Fischer inviting him to respond in writing to a list of supplementary questions and requesting copies of relevant case studies. To date he had not yet received a reply. Neither was he really expecting one.

With regard to the young receptionist whose life had briefly been so closely intertwined with his own, Jack had nothing remotely resembling a frame of reference to help him understand what kind of relationship they had embarked upon. The medley of anxiety, relief and celebration which had accompanied his fleeting but charged involvement with Ulla had been supplanted in her absence by a pronounced sense of drift. They had, he accepted, probably been wise not to make each other promises. No matter how forcefully circumstance had pushed the pair together, they were already some six hundred kilometres and two imposing frontiers apart. By the end of the month, Jack would be back in the

UK, reconnecting with friends, hunting for accommodation and gearing up for the final year of his degree. As things stood, explorations of his feelings towards Ulla were entirely academic. Certainly he could not respond with any degree of consistency to Julia's regular but honest enquiries regarding the state of his heart or the likelihood that he might visit Ulla before returning to Britain. What he wanted, and what he felt it was realistic to want, varied from day to day and sometimes from hour to hour.

Although Jack would have preferred to spend the entire day at his desk, a number of pressing matters competed for his time, not least of which was the need to present himself at Concordia to collect the hundred-mark cheque for his article on the Environment Ministry. It was to be his final visit to the office in Bernauer Strasse and his only duties for the day would be to hand in his ID card to Frau Fichtenberg's successor, thank his colleagues for their support and leave an appreciative card and an outsized box of pralines on the counter by the sink.

An airless and muggy day had descended on Berlin. Squinting into the sunlight as he emerged from the relative cool of Voltastrasse U-Bahn station, Jack turned into Bernauer Strasse and immediately caught sight of the abandoned Church of Reconciliation. Inevitably his thoughts turned to Pastor Niemeyer. He wondered whether the priest's still shocking act of self-sacrifice had secured the future of the isolated building or had simply hastened its demise. He wondered how the leadership of the Lutheran Church would judge the pastor's actions. Did suicide still count as a sin? He wondered whether there would eventually be some kind of physical memorial to the priest and whether Jack would one day be able to pay his respects to a man who had looked at life through a very different lens, but had nevertheless made a lasting impression on him.

In the Concordia office, Frau Kerber expressed her appreciation of Jack's commitment to their campaigns and regretted the troubled events that had enveloped the organisation. Although his internship had been overwhelmingly enjoyable, in the light of Pastor Niemeyer's death Jack hardly knew what to say. Once the necessary administrative formalities had been wrapped up, the intern exchanged a respectful wave with his colleagues and was gone.

A little over an hour later, the British student was installed once more at his desk and was analysing the handwritten notes from his single interview with Press Secretary Fischer. Aware that Jack was working on his dissertation, Julia slipped quietly into his room armed with a knowing smile and a glass of mineral water laced with ice cubes.

'Sorry to disturb you, Professor Gilmore, but you've got a phone call. From your friend in Munich. She phones during the hours of daylight now, so at least we know she's not a vampire.'

Jack had not been expecting the call and wondered if Ulla had some kind of news. Perhaps she had found a job already or had discovered an ice hockey club in the city. Maybe she just wanted to talk. He followed Julia to her room, picked up the receiver and warmly greeted the object of his ill-defined expectations.

'Hey Jack,' said Ulla, brightly, 'I've got a question for you. Have you ever heard of something called InterRail?'

78 PUZZLE

La Rochelle, Saturday 21st July 1976

Almost six weeks later and at some godforsaken hour of the night, a pair of French police officers shook the two beach-sleepers awake, shone torches into their faces and demanded their identity papers. Sluggishly, both Jack and Ulla stirred from their fragmented dreams and retrieved their passports from their sleeping bags. Satisfied that the young couple were neither wanted criminals nor deserters from the army, the police officers informed them that they would have to vacate the beach by sunrise and bid them a curt but nevertheless respectful goodnight. La Rochelle was not the first French beach the two InterRailers had slept on and they were no longer surprised by the attention. Once the police officers were gone, the travellers exchanged a kiss and went immediately back to sleep. Whether they would be off the beach before daylight was doubtful at best.

Just before seven, with the sun comfortably above the horizon, Jack and Ulla shook the sand from their sleeping bags, rolled them into their rucksacks and wandered back in the direction of La Rochelle station. The sky was cloudless, there was little wind off the Atlantic and the morning seemed already to presage another glorious day. Unable to find a nearby café where they could order a coffee and make use of the sanitary facilities, the couple headed in the general direction of the station, hugging the ancient defensive wall that once protected the historic harbour. With the morning sun directly in their eyes, they passed the five-hundred-year-old lighthouse known as the Lantern Tower and wound their way through ancient cobbled streets where the shutters to the first-floor apartments were largely still closed and the shops and cafés below were not yet ready to greet their clients. The marina was quiet, save for the occasional cries of the gulls and the regular, gentle clanking of radar reflectors against aluminium masts. Meandering south from the end of the Quai Maubec along comparatively anonymous streets, the two backpackers eventually discovered a mid-sized chain hotel not far from the station. It looked perfect. Jack took Ulla's rucksack and sat beneath the trees in the small parking area opposite. Ulla dusted herself down a little, retrieved her body wash, toothbrush and toothpaste from her pack and concealed them in a cotton shoulder bag. Greeting the receptionist in the manner of a guest returning from a gentle morning stroll, she breezed in, took the elevator to the first floor and eventually found a bathroom where she could take a shower. When she emerged from the hotel, smiling and refreshed, she had considerably more gel than when she had entered. Jack and Ulla chatted for maybe fifteen minutes and once they judged that enough time had elapsed for suspicions not to be aroused, he simply repeated their well-practised routine.

Two hours later the pair had eaten an overpriced croissant and drunk a milky coffee at the station, bought a supply of long, crusty sandwiches and a bottle of water at the kiosk and were ensconced in a second-class carriage on the train to Bordeaux. Their original itinerary long since abandoned, the couple were confronted each day with decisions about where to travel next or whether to sleep on the train or under the stars. In the three weeks they had spent in each other's company, the overwhelming majority of these decisions had been been taken without much debate and often on the spur of the moment following a brief investigation of a timetable.

Ulla was still utterly enthralled with their freedom to travel from country to country largely as the fancy took them. Not once during their trip had a border guard demanded that they explain the purpose of their visit, produce visas that had been processed several weeks in advance or demonstrate that they had booked accommodation from a list of state-approved hotels. For the former citizen of the German Democratic Republic, crossing a frontier so effortlessly became an unbridled pleasure in itself. The hurriedly scrawled messages on garish postcards that Jack and Ulla regularly sent to family and friends testified to the obvious fun that they were having without offering too much in the way of detail. Although they had rarely been more than twenty metres apart since the start of the trip, the couple were at ease in their inseparability. They were warm, attentive and tactile without embarrassing others in their presence. From the moment they left Germany, Ulla had insisted on speaking English. The practice, she said, would do her good, especially as she was planning to apply for an ice hockey scholarship at a Canadian university.

As the train laboured south along the Atlantic coast, Ulla and Jack soaked up the views, swigged from their water bottle and wondered whether it was too soon to start on their ham and tomato baguettes. After Bordeaux, they would ride the train to Biarritz, find somewhere half-decent to eat, then take a decision on what to do next.

Ulla kissed Jack softly.

'I can't tell you how brilliant this has been. I'm starting to feel like, I don't know, like I've come back a bit, like I've woken up. I don't know how to really say it in English, but I feel like I'm maybe not so connected, not so stuck to some of the really shitty stuff that happened. Like some of it doesn't have its claws in me so much.'

Since leaving Munich, Jack had left it to Ulla to choose the moments when she wanted to revisit, explore or analyse her experiences in the GDR. Whilst it was impossible to predict precisely when these occasions would arise, empty railway compartments seemed to offer the perfect setting for her to put her tangled feelings into words or externalise her resurfacing thoughts.

'I can't imagine,' said Jack, 'how you got through any of it, though. Day to day.'

Ulla shrugged. 'In the end, I just did. You know how you felt that day when you came to Fehrbelliner Strasse. All of a sudden, you were scared and you had no idea what to do or even if you could trust me. Imagine feeling like that almost every day of your life for almost a year. In some ways, it wasn't really me any more. It was like this broken, empty version of me. It was like angry Ulla or caged Ulla or frightened Ulla. It was like the real Ulla was hiding and I didn't know where. You know what. When I phoned you in Oudenarder Strasse, I really wasn't sure that you'd want to do this whole InterRail thing. At the same time, though, I wasn't sure that you wouldn't.'

Jack reflected for a moment.

'I think, in Berlin I'd seen something of the smiley Ulla and the brave Ulla. And I was happy to go on holiday with either of them.'

The carriage door opened and they were joined by a woman with two young children and a large suitcase. Jack helped the traveller wrestle the heavy leather case onto the luggage rack and was rewarded with a simple 'thank you' spoken in French. As the two children gazed out of the window at the constantly shifting views, their mother smiled diffidently at the two backpackers before removing a magazine from her shoulder bag. As happened with increasing frequency, encounters with young families triggered memories of Ulla's own childhood, of holidays with her parents in the Carpathian Mountains or by the side of a Hungarian lake. On occasions during the trip, Ulla had been momentarily convinced that she had spotted her parents entering a shop or disappearing into the crowd on a busy market square.

As Ulla allowed her attention to linger on the largely inconsequential interactions of the young French family, an unexpected thought began to take root in her mind. At that moment, it was little more than the vaguest of notions, but she knew that it was the kind of idea that would patently refuse to be silent. It would grow louder and ever more insistent, like a baby crying in the night. Sooner or later, she knew, she would have to speak to Jack.

Having changed at Bordeaux, and sharing an empty compartment once more, Ulla could no longer contain her thoughts. She caught Jack's eye and gave his hand a gentle squeeze.

'So, Mr Hazy Cosmic Jive, would you agree that we make a pretty good team?'

'Yep. Absolutely. Not gonna argue with that.'

'OK. Listen carefully. I have a puzzle for you. But it's not a puzzle with an easy solution.'

'OK, Cosmonova. Fire away.'

'So. Imagine you knew someone who had recently used fake documents to get herself out of East Berlin. She was really happy to be out of the whole shitty mess she was in, but everything came at a price. This person wasn't going to see her parents for six years and although she was trying to make the best of the whole situation, six years was beginning to feel like forever. She was applying to university in Canada and might not even be in Germany by October of next year. And in lots of ways, a sports scholarship in Calgary was the ideal way forward for this person. It would enable her to study for a physics degree and still play ice hockey and the prospect of doing all of that was truly, truly amazing. But. Although she'd definitely done the right thing in coming over to the West, it was not enough. She also wanted to figure out a way to help her parents leave the GDR before they retired.'

'And?'

'Well, imagine she had a friend somewhere who, once he'd finished his studies next June, might be persuaded to help her somehow get her parents out of East Berlin. How would this person and this person's friend go about making that happen? Hypothetically.'

ACKNOWLEDGEMENTS

For help, encouragement and advice: To my wife, Suzanne. Also to Celia Almeida, David Coombes, Sue Colclough, Tony Cox, Chris Freudenthal, Heather Morgan, Glyn Jones, Maria Labedzka, Ashley Nixon, Lynne Preece, David Ripley, Jo Ripley, Dawn Sayers, Dave Twine, Vidar Utne, Tima Iyer-Utne. And to James Essinger and Zoe Verner at the Conrad Press and Gregory Motton at Levellers, without whose skills and professionalism this book would not have found its way into your hands.